P9-DFP-609

small town

ALSO BY LAWRENCE BLOCK

The Matthew Scudder Novels

The Sins of the Fathers • Time to Murder and Create • In the Midst of Death • A Stab in the Dark • Eight Million Ways to Die • When the Sacred Ginmill Closes • Out on the Cutting Edge • A Ticket to the Boneyard • A Dance at the Slaughterhouse • A Walk Among the Tombstones • The Devil Knows You're Dead • A Long Line of Dead Men • Even the Wicked • Everybody Dies • Hope to Die

The Bernie Rhodenbarr Mysteries

Burglars Can't Be Choosers • The Burglar in the Closet • The Burglar Who Liked to Quote Kipling • The Burglar Who Studied Spinoza • The Burglar Who Painted Like Mondrian • The Burglar Who Traded Ted Williams • The Burglar Who Thought He Was Bogart • The Burglar in the Library • The Burglar in the Rye

The Adventures of Evan Tanner

The Thief Who Couldn't Sleep • The Canceled Czech • Tanner's Twelve Swingers • Two for Tanner • Tanner's Tiger • Here Comes a Hero • Me Tanner, You Jane • Tanner on Ice

The Affairs of Chip Harrison

No Score • Chip Harrison Scores Again • Make Out with Murder • The Topless Tulip Caper

Keller's Greatest Hits

Hit Man • Hit List

Other Novels

After the First Death • Ariel • Coward's Kiss • Deadly Honeymoon • The Girl with the Long Green Heart • Mona • Not Comin' Home to You • Random Walk • Ronald Rabbit Is a Dirty Old Man • The Specialists • Such Men Are Dangerous • The Triumph of Evil • You Could Call It Murder

Collected Short Stories

Sometimes They Bite • Like a Lamb to Slaughter • Some Days You Get the Bear • Ehrengraf for the Defense • One Night Stands • The Lost Cases of Ed London • Enough Rope

Books for Writers

Writing the Novel: From Plot to Print • Telling Lies for Fun & Profit • Write for Your Life • Spider, Spin Me a Web

Anthologies Edited

Death Cruise • Master's Choice • Opening Shots • Master's Choice 2 • Speaking of Lust • Opening Shots 2 • Speaking of Greed

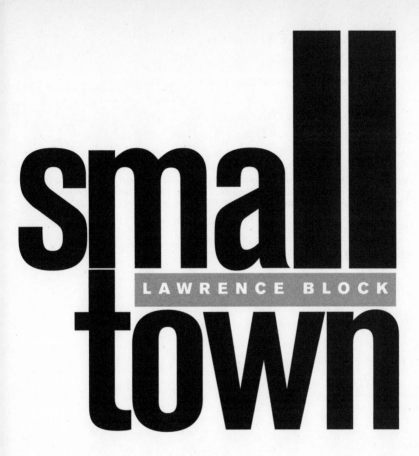

small town

LAWRENCE BLOCK

town

WM

WILLIAM MORROW
An Imprint of HarperCollinsPublishers

SMALL TOWN. Copyright © 2003 by Lawrence Block. All rights reserved. Printed in the
United States of America. No part of this book may be used or reproduced in any manner
whatsoever without written permission except in the case of brief quotations embodied in
critical articles and reviews. For information address HarperCollins Publishers Inc.,
10 East 53rd Street, New York, NY 10022.

Designed by Debbie Glasserman

ISBN 0-06-001190-4

THIS ONE'S FOR THE RABBIT

New York City, the incomparable, the brilliant star city of cities, the forty-ninth state, a law unto itself, the Cyclopean paradox, the inferno with no out-of-bounds, the supreme expression of both the miseries and the splendors of contemporary civilization, the Macedonia of the United States. It meets the most severe test that may be applied to definition of a metropolis—it stays up all night. But it also becomes a small town when it rains.

—John Gunther

The city exulted, all in flowers.
Soon it will end: a fashion, a phase, the epoch, life.
The mirror and sweetness of a final dissolution.
Let the first bombs fall without delay.

—Czeslaw Milosz,
"The City"

author's note

Once again, it's my great pleasure to thank the Ragdale Foundation, of Lake Forest, Illinois, where this book was written.

Between the time my last book was published and this one completed, I lost three dear old friends, and list them now in the order of their passing: Dave Van Ronk, Jimmy Armstrong, and John B. Keane, to whom *Hope to Die* was dedicated. One of my early books was dedicated to Dave. I never got around to dedicating one to Jimmy. I miss them all.

Earlier, I lost my mother, who came to the end of a good long life two weeks and two days after the twin towers fell. Like my wife and daughters, she read each of my books in manuscript. Thus she had a chance to read *Hope to Die,* although she died before it was published. This book, then, is the first she won't get to read.

small town

before . . .

On September 11, 2001, sunrise came at 6:33 A.M. The forecast called for clear skies and a beautiful day.

At 8:45 A.M., American Airlines Flight 11, bound from Boston to Los Angeles, struck the North Tower of the World Trade Center.

At 9:05 A.M., United Airlines Flight 175, also bound from Boston to Los Angeles, struck the South Tower.

At 9:50 A.M., forty-five minutes after it had been hit, the South Tower fell.

At 10:30 A.M., an hour and forty-five minutes after it had been hit, the North Tower fell.

At 10:29 A.M., on May 30, 2002, cleanup efforts at Ground Zero were completed.

There was widespread agreement throughout the city that nothing would ever be the same again.

BY THE TIME Jerry Pankow was ready for breakfast, he'd already been to three bars and a whorehouse.

It was, he'd discovered, a great opening line. "By the time I had my eggs and hash browns this morning . . ." Wherever he delivered it, in backroom bars or church basements, it got attention. Made him sound interesting, and wasn't that one of the reasons he'd come to New York? To lead an interesting life, certainly, and to make himself interesting to others.

And, one had to admit, to plumb the depths of depravity, which resonated well enough with the notion of three bars and a whorehouse before breakfast.

Today he was having his breakfast in Joe Jr.'s, a Greek coffee shop at the corner of Sixth Avenue and West Twelfth Street. He wasn't exactly a regular here. The whorehouse was on Twenty-eighth, two doors east of Lexington, right around the corner from the Indian delis and restaurants that had people calling the area Curry Hill. Samosa and aloo gobi wasn't his idea of breakfast, and anyway those places wouldn't open until lunchtime, but he liked the Sunflower coffee shop on Third Avenue, and stopped there more often than not after he finished up at the whorehouse.

This morning, though, he was several degrees short of ravenous, and his next scheduled stop was in the Village, at Charles and Waverly. So he'd walked across Twenty-third and down Sixth. That stretch of Sixth Avenue had once afforded a good view of the twin towers, and now it showed you where they'd been, showed you the gap in the downtown skyline. A view of omission, he'd thought more than once.

And now here he was in a booth at Joe's with orange juice and a western omelet and a cup of coffee, light, no sugar, and how depraved was that? It was ten o'clock, and he'd get to Marilyn's by eleven and be out of there by one, with the rest of the day free and clear. Maybe he'd catch the two-thirty meeting at Perry Street. He could stop by after he left Marilyn's and put his keys on a chair so he'd have a seat when he came back at meeting time. You had to do that there, it was always standing-room-only by the time the meeting started.

Recovery, he thought. The hottest ticket in town.

He let the waiter refill his coffee cup, smiled his thanks, then automatically checked the fellow out as he walked away, only to roll his eyes at his own behavior. Cute butt, he thought, but so what?

If he were to show up at a meeting of Sex Addicts Anonymous, he thought, nobody would tell him to get the hell out. But did it make his life unmanageable? Not really. And, more to the point, could he handle another program? He was in AA, sober a little over three years, and, because drugs played a part in his story, he managed to fit a couple of NA meetings into his weekly schedule. And, because his parents were both drunks—his father died of it, his mother lived with it—he was an Adult Child of Alcoholics, and went to their meetings now and then. (But not too often, because all the whining and bitching and getting-in-touch-with-my-completely-appropriate-anger made his teeth ache.)

And, because John-Michael was an alcoholic (and also sober, and anyway they weren't lovers anymore), he went to Al-Anon a couple of times a month. He hated the meetings, and he wanted to slap most of the people he saw there—the Al-Anon-Entities, his sponsor called them. But that just showed how much he needed the program, didn't it? Or maybe it didn't. It was hard to tell.

Three years sober, and he started each day by visiting three bars and a whorehouse, inhaling the reek of stale beer and rancid semen. The bars were in Chelsea, all within a few blocks of his top-floor walkup on Seventeenth west of Ninth, and of course they were closed when he arrived for the morning cleanup. He had keys, and he would let himself in, trying not to dwell on the way the place stank, the odor of booze and bodies and various kinds of smoke, the dirty-socks smell of amyl nitrite, and something else, some indefinable morning-after stench that was somehow more than the sum of its parts. He'd note that and dismiss it, and he'd sweep and mop the floor and clean the lavatories—God, human beings were disgusting—and finally he'd take down the chairs from the tables and the stools from the bar top and set them up where they belonged. Then he'd lock up, and off to the next.

He hit the bars in what he thought of as working his way up from the depths, starting with Death Row, a leather bar west of Tenth Avenue with a back room where safe sex required not just condoms but full body ar-

mor. Then one called Cheek, on Eighth and Twentieth, with a neighborhood crowd that ran to preppy types and the aging queens who loved
them. And, finally, a straight bar on Twenty-third Street—well, a mixed
crowd, really, typical for the neighborhood, straight and gay, male and female, young and old, the common denominator being an abiding thirst.
The place was called Harrigan's—Harridan's, some called it—and it
didn't reek of pot and poppers and nocturnal emissions, but that didn't
mean a blind man might mistake it for the Brooklyn Botanical Gardens.

In his drinking days, Jerry might have started the evening at Harrigan's. He could tell himself he was just stopping for a quick social drink
before he settled in for the night. He wasn't cruising, certainly, because
nobody went to a place like that trolling for a sexual partner. He supposed
people who got drunk there sometimes went home with each other, but
that was essentially beside the point.

But after a few drinks there, and maybe a line or two in the men's
room, a gay bar would seem like a good idea, and he'd be on his way to a
place like Cheek. And there he might meet someone he'd take home or go
home with, but he might not, and before the night was over he could well
wind up at Death Row or some equivalent thereof, barely knowing what
he was doing or with whom he was doing it, and, when he woke up hours
later, sickened by what he remembered or terrified of what he didn't remember, depending on just when the blackout curtain had dropped.

Now he frequented the bars only in the morning, to sweep and mop
and straighten up, and on his way out he'd pick up the twenty dollars left
for him. The management of Death Row, perhaps overcompensating for
the relentless squalor of the premises, tucked his payment into an envelope with his name on it; at Harrigan's and Cheek, they just left a $20 bill
on the back bar, next to the register.

Then the whorehouse, which took longer, but he was still in and out
of the place in not much more than an hour, and his envelope, with *Jerry*
in purple Pentel in a precise feminine hand, held a hundred dollars. Always a single bill, and always a crisp new one, and, when you thought
about it, an outrageous payment for the time it took.

Then again, he sometimes thought, look what *they* got for a simple
blow job.

MARILYN FAIRCHILD'S APARTMENT WAS on the third floor of a
four-story brownstone on Charles Street off Waverly Place, not a five-
minute walk from Joe Jr.'s. The sky, overcast at daybreak, was clear now.
It was the second week in June, and the weather had been glorious for the
past several days, and on the way to Marilyn's he realized he'd had a
melody running through his head, just at the outer edge of consciousness,

and sometimes that was how he sent himself a message, found out what he was really feeling. Now he registered the song, and it was the one about loving potato chips and motor trips, and especially New York in June.

Well, he thought, who wouldn't? He'd lived briefly in San Francisco, where every day was spring, and in L.A., where every day was summer, and had decided the trouble with Paradise was you got tired of it. If the weather wasn't lousy a fair proportion of the time, how much of a charge could you get from a beautiful day? Here the weather could be genuinely shitty in a rich variety of ways—rainy, drizzly, bleak, freezing, raw, windy, hot, muggy, stifling. Every season had its own characteristic un-pleasantness, and every season sported the occasional perfect days, and how you treasured each when it came along! How your heart sang!

> *I love New York*
> *More than ever . . .*

The new slogan, the post-9/11 slogan, with the Milton Glaser logo adapted to show the heart scarred, like a human heart after a heart attack. First time he saw the new version, on a T-shirt in a shop window, the damn thing moved him to tears. But then for a while there almost every-thing did. The capsule biographies of the dead that ran every day in the *Times,* for instance. He couldn't read them, and he couldn't keep from reading them.

It wore off, though. You were scarred, like the heart, you took a lick-ing and kept on ticking, and you healed.

More or less.

The entrance to Marilyn's brownstone was a half flight up from the street. He mounted the steps and rang her bell, gave her plenty of time to respond, then used his key. He took the steps two at a time—three years ago, bottoming out on drugs and alcohol, it was all he could do to drag himself up a flight of stairs, and baby, look at me now—and poked the buzzer alongside her door. He got the key ready—he carried more keys than a super these days, and rather liked the butch effect of it all—and when there was no response to his buzz he let himself in.

Place was a pigsty.

Well, that was an exaggeration. It wasn't filthy. He cleaned for her once a week, and the apartment was never seriously dirty, but sometimes it was a mess, and it was certainly a godawful disaster area this morning.

Ashtrays overflowing with cigarette butts, some of them lipsticked, some of them not. A pair of rocks glasses, one holding a half inch of pale amber liquid, the other dry. The dry one showed lipstick, the other didn't.

Yesterday's *Times,* in all its many sections, was scattered all over the living room. An oblong pocket mirror, and he'd bet anything there was cocaine residue on it, lay on the mahogany coffee table, next to an uncapped bottle half full of Wild Turkey and a plastic ice bucket half full of water. A bra was on the other side of the ice bucket, half on and half off the coffee table, and yes, there was her blouse, lime green raw silk, he'd seen her wearing it once, and now it was tossed on the Queen Anne wing chair. Could her skirt be far off? No skirt, he determined, but there was a pair of black slacks on the floor next to the club chair, and were those black panties wedged into the corner of the club chair?

Egad, Holmes, I do believe they are.

One of the cushions from the sofa was halfway across the room, and he wondered how that had happened. A pair of mahogany tables flanked the couch—like the coffee table, they were from The Bombay Company, cheaply made but attractively styled. One held three hardcover novels between a pair of bronze bookends—Susan Isaacs, Nelson DeMille, and Judith Rossner's *Looking for Mister Goodbar*, which he'd always assumed had some sort of totemic value for Marilyn. The other table, to the right of the sofa, held three little figurines of animals, Zuni fetishes from the Southwest. There was a bison carved from Picasso marble, a rose quartz bear with a bundle of arrows on his back, and a turquoise rabbit, all of them grouped around the white saucer from a child's tea set. The saucer held cornmeal—except it didn't, its contents had been spilled onto the table and floor, and the bison and bear were lying on their sides, and where was the little rabbit?

With the cornmeal spilled, he thought, maybe the bear had gotten hungry enough to eat the rabbit. Failing that, he supposed he'd find it somewhere in the chaos of the apartment.

Not for the first time, he contrasted Marilyn's place with the last premises he'd tidied, the whorehouse on East Twenty-eighth Street. In all the months he'd been cleaning for them, they'd never once left a real mess. As a matter of fact, the parlor and the individual bedrooms were always surprisingly tidy. There might be some dirty dishes and glassware on the kitchen counter, waiting for him to load them into the dishwasher, and there were wastebaskets that had to be emptied of their unmentionable contents, trash to be bagged and taken downstairs. But the place was always sanitary and usually neat.

Well, wasn't that the difference between your professionals and your amateurs?

He rolled his eyes, ashamed of himself. Marilyn was a sweetie, and where did he get off calling her a whore? Still, he could imagine her coming up with some version of the line on her own, a half-smile on her full mouth and an ironic edge to the bourbon-and-cigarette voice. Her self-deprecating sense of humor was one of the things he liked most about her, and—

Jesus, was she home?

Because her bedroom door was shut, and that was unusual. That might explain the extent of the mess, too. Her apartment was usually messy, she wasn't the sort to preclean out of concern for the good opinion of her cleaning person, but he'd never before found undergarments in the living room, and she'd have at least capped the bourbon bottle and put away the little mirror.

Sleeping late, wasn't she? Well, she'd very likely been up late. He'd let her sleep, hold off running the vacuum until he was done with everything else. If that woke her he could do the bedroom after she emerged from it; otherwise he'd skip it this week.

She didn't have company, did she?

He decided that wasn't too likely. The clothes in the living room were all hers, and the guy, whoever he might be, wouldn't have kept all his clothes on while she took everything off. Somewhere along the way he'd returned from the bedroom, thoughtfully closing the door, and dressed and left the apartment, pulling the door shut. It hadn't been double-locked when he arrived, he recalled, but that didn't mean anything; Marilyn forgot to double-lock the door as often as not, whether she was at home or gone for the day.

He started to whistle—the same song, New York in June, he couldn't get it out of his head—and went into the kitchen to get started.

HE'D MET HER AT an ACOA meeting, had heard her sharing wryly about her parents, and had assumed she was in show business. An actress, a nightclub chanteuse, at the very least a waitress who went to all the cattle calls, got roles in off-off-Broadway showcases, and had a card in the Screen Extras Guild. And maybe did voice-overs, because God knows she had the voice for it, pitched low, seasoned with booze and tobacco, coming across like honey-dipped sandpaper.

She looked the part. It wasn't that she was beautiful. Her features were a little too strong for beauty, her facial planes too angular. It was more that she was totally Out There, her energy expanding to fill whatever room she was in. You noticed her, you paid attention to her. You couldn't buy that, or learn it at Actors Studio. You had it or you didn't, and she did.

"It's all my Leo stuff," she explained. "I got my sun and three or four planets in Leo, and maybe I should have been an actress, as much as I like being the center of attention, but I always had zero desire in that direction, and thank God, because what kind of a life is that?"

She'd been born in Brooklyn, grew up on Long Island, went to college in Pennsylvania, married young and divorced young, and had been living in the Village for a dozen years, first in a small studio in an ugly postwar white brick building on Greenwich Avenue, and, for the past seven years, in this brownstone floor-through on Charles Street.

"I had the usual array of jobs, and the only one I might have kept was assisting this photographer, a really sweet boy, but he got too sick to work. And then I took a class at the Learning Annex, if you can believe it, and it was like I found my purpose in life. No time at all I had my Realtor's license and a job to go with it, and this place was maybe the fourth rental I ever showed. I showed no end of co-ops, and I handled subletting some of them, but as far as straight rentals, this was the fourth, and I took one look at it and saw it was rent-stabilized and what the price was, and no way was I gonna let it go to some fucking client. So of course my first job was convincing this darling young couple that it was all wrong for them, and once I got rid of them I put in an application and rented it myself. I got fired for that, it's a major no-no, but who gave a shit? I had my dream apartment, and how long was it going to take me to get another job? Five minutes?"

They'd stopped at a Starbucks after the meeting, and otherwise he might never have gotten to know her, because she never went back to ACOA. It was too humorless for her, she told him, and he could understand that, but suspected she also wanted to keep her distance from any program that might make her face up to her own relationship with alcohol, which he had to figure was at least somewhat problematical. She reined it in when she was with him—people often did in the presence of sober alcoholics—but one time she'd been a toke over the line, as it were, and he got to see the change in her eyes and in the cast of her features.

Well, it was his job to clean her apartment, not to take her inventory. Someday he might see her at an AA meeting, and maybe she'd get sober and maybe she wouldn't, but for now her life seemed to work okay, or at least she thought it did.

Though you wouldn't have guessed it from the state of her living room. Not this morning, anyway.

And that was where he came in, wasn't it? He cleaned and straightened, washed glasses, emptied ashtrays, stuffed her dirty clothes in the bathroom hamper, put things where they belonged. He couldn't seem to find the turquoise rabbit—maybe she'd taken it to bed with her, though animals carved from stone weren't really ideal for cuddling—but he put fresh cornmeal in the little saucer and positioned the bear and the bison on either side of it. He bagged the garbage, carried it downstairs and stowed it in one of the trash cans in the rear courtyard. He cleaned the bathroom, scouring the sink and toilet and clawfooted old tub, getting the curious satisfaction this chore always brought him. The first time he cleaned someone's toilet he wanted to retch, but you got over that, and nowadays he felt this great sense of accomplishment. Odd how it worked. Was it that way for everybody, or was it a gay thing?

When he'd finished in the living room and kitchen and bathroom, and the small second bedroom she used for an office, he got out the vacuum cleaner and hesitated. He went to the bedroom door, put an ear to it, then turned the knob and eased it open.

It was dark within, but enough light came through around the black-out shades for him to make out her form in the bed at the far end of the room. He said her name—"Marilyn?"—to get her attention if she was just lying there half-awake, but not loud enough to rouse her from a sound sleep. And she was evidently sleeping soundly, because she didn't stir.

Should he vacuum? It was that or quit for the day, leaving her bedroom untouched and the whole apartment unvacuumed. The noise might wake her, but she'd probably want to be up by now anyway, might even have appointments scheduled. If she could leave her underwear in the living room and her Wild Turkey uncapped, wasting its fragrance on the desert air, she might well have neglected to set her clock. Even now some Wall Street hotshot could be cooling his heels in a lobby somewhere, waiting for Marilyn to show him the condo of his dreams.

He plugged in the old Hoover and had at it. If she slept through it, fine, it proved she really needed the sleep. If she woke up, even better.

He remembered how delighted she'd been to learn what he did for a living. "It's a get-well job," he'd explained. "Although it could be a career, if I want. All I have to do is let it grow itself into an agency, a cleaning service. But that's too complicated for now. I like to keep it real simple. I make okay money and my rent's low and I get paid in cash and I'm done for the day in plenty of time to make an afternoon meeting."

"But a whorehouse," she said. "How did that happen?"

"The way it always does. You clean for one person and he recommends you to somebody else."

"So one of the bar owners was a customer at the whorehouse—"

"Actually, I think it was the other way around."

"What are they like? The girls?"

"I think it's more PC to call them women. No, seriously, I never see

anybody. I did go up there one time to pick up the key and arrange everything, and I caught glimpses of one or two women, and they just looked
like, I don't know, like women."

"What were they wearing?"

"Oh, please. I didn't notice. The woman I spoke to, and I gather she
was the manager—"

"The madam."

"I suppose. She was forty or forty-five, and if I'd met her on the street
I'd have guessed she was a beautician."

"Really."

"Or possibly, you know, an executive secretary, or maybe a show-
room manager. Not exactly brassy, but that kind of self-assurance."

She'd had more questions, and at the end she asked if he cleaned for
any ordinary people. "Like me," she said.

He said, "Ordinary?" and raised an eyebrow. And went on to say that
he did indeed have a couple of private clients, no more than one a day,
whose apartments he cleaned once a week. By the time they left the coffee shop they'd arranged that she would be one of them.

Most of the time she was out when he cleaned, but not always, and
sometimes she'd be at her desk, working, and they'd chat between phone
calls. A couple of times they ran into each other on the street. She talked
wryly about her love life, asked his advice about her hair (a rich auburn,
shoulder-length when he'd met her, short and pixyish as of two months
ago), and generally used him as her Gay Male Confidante, a sort of girlfriend with a Y chromosome, or perhaps a younger brother but without all
that family baggage.

"I wonder," she'd said. "Do you think I could ever take a turn at your
whorehouse?"

"You mean like *Belle du Jour*?"

"Sort of, except I have a hunch it works better if you look like
Catherine Deneuve. Anyway, I'm probably too old."

"You're what, thirty-eight?"

" 'You're only thirty-eight, and could pass for twenty-nine' is what
you meant to say, isn't it?"

"Word for word. Thirty-eight's not old."

"How old are the girls in your whorehouse?"

"It's not my whorehouse, and I don't have any idea how old they are.
There's nobody home when I do my thing."

"Men want young girls, don't they? In a place like that?"

"I have no idea what men want," he said, archly. "In a place like that
or anywhere else. What's this all about? You wouldn't really want to do it,
would you?"

"Probably not, but it's an awfully nice fantasy."

"Well, enjoy yourself," he said. "There's no age limit in fantasies."

THE VACUUMING DIDN'T WAKE her. Neither did the phone, which he couldn't hear over the noise of the vacuum cleaner; he only realized it was ringing when the blinking light on the dial of the office extension caught his eye. He switched off the vacuum and listened, waiting for her to answer it, but she didn't, and after two more rings her voice mail picked up.

He stood still for a moment, frowning. Then he went back to work. Using one of the long skinny attachments to slurp the dust off the top of a window molding, he visualized a giraffe doing a line of coke. That reminded him of the little mirror he'd found in the living room. It was in the strainer on the kitchen sinkboard now, any cocaine residue washed off and down the drain, and . . .

Maybe you should just go home.

The thought was just *there*, all at once. He stood still and looked at his own anxiety and wondered where the hell it had come from. Yes, there had almost certainly been cocaine on that mirror, but Marilyn and her friend had long since Hoovered it away. And yes, there had been an open bottle of bourbon in the living room, and he'd caught a whiff of it, and smelled it again in the glasses he'd washed. And yes, he was an alcoholic, sober now by the grace of whatever God you wanted to credit, and could be rendered anxious by anything that might pose a threat, real or imaginary, to his sobriety.

But the coke was gone and the bottle capped and put away, and didn't he start every day in rooms that smelled of beer and hard booze, with dozens of bottles just standing there, waiting to be sampled? He was like a fox with the keys to the henhouse, all alone in Death Row and Cheek and Harrigan's, just him and all that booze. And, while his mind could conjure up no end of harrowing scenarios—a mind, his sponsor had told him, was a terrible thing to have—in point of fact it never really bothered him at all.

He'd run across drugs in the bars he cleaned, too, because people who were drunk and stoned tended to be careless, and the odd Baggie would turn up on the floor, or in the john, or, more than once, right out there in plain sight on top of the bar. And the apartments he cleaned had their stashes, legal and otherwise—the few ounces of pot in the model's undies drawer, the huge jar of Dexamil on the dot-com exec's bedside table, and with all that speed wouldn't you think the guy would do his own cleaning? Like four or five times a day?

And every medicine cabinet held pills. Valium and all its cousins, and no end of ups and downs, many of which he recognized of old—a few years in the trenches were a veritable college of pharmacological knowledge—and some of which were new to him, because the drug trade didn't go into freeze-frame the day he stopped using. It evolved, everything evolved, and he might spot something new on the shelf next to the shaving cream and wonder where it would take him if the lid happened to pop off the little vial and if two (oh might as well make it three) pills leapt up and out and into his open-in-astonishment mouth and down his throat before he quite knew what was happening. I mean, it wasn't a real slip, was it, if it just sort of took you by surprise like that?

Thoughts like that just helped him remember who he was. They didn't really upset him, and weren't cause for alarm. And if they kept him going to meetings, well, then they served a purpose, didn't they?

So he wasn't afraid of what was in Marilyn's liquor bottle or medicine cabinet. Or, God help us, her undies drawer.

But really, now, couldn't he just pack up and go? He'd cleaned everything but the bedroom, cleaned really quite thoroughly, and he couldn't do any more without disturbing her sleep, and for all he knew she really needed her sleep, for all he knew she'd been up past dawn. Why, she could have been partying while he cleaned the bars and the whorehouse, and he might have been tucking into his omelet right around the time her companion thoughtfully closed the bedroom door and let himself out of her apartment, leaving her sleeping . . .

Sleeping?

If she was asleep, he told himself, then he would indeed just slip out and allow her to awaken on her own, and in her own good time. He'd leave a note—"*I was fresh out of kisses and couldn't figure out how to wake Sleeping Beauty. I'll stop by tomorrow and do the bedroom. Love, Jerry.*"

If she was asleep . . .

He paused at her bedroom door, took a deep breath, let it out, took another. He opened the door, let his eyes accustom themselves to the dimness.

There she was, just as he'd seen her earlier. Sprawled out on her bed, obviously in deep slumber. It looked as though she hadn't stirred since he'd first looked in on her.

Room had an odor. Nothing too rank, but even if he was going to let her sleep he ought to open a window. Hard to sort out the smells. Sex, booze, cigarette smoke . . .

He walked over to the side of the bed, looked down at her. She was on her back, her head to one side. The sheet covered her just past her waist.

He looked at her full breasts, willing them to rise and fall with her breathing, but they didn't move, and he knew he hadn't expected them to move,
hadn't expected her to be breathing, had known what he'd find before he
opened the door.

He took another breath—yes, there were other elements in the
room's odor besides sex and booze and smoke, there was a bathroom
smell and a meat-market smell—and he reached out a hand and touched
the tips of two fingers to her forehead.

Like a priest, he thought, anointing the dead.

And of course her flesh was cool to the touch. He couldn't will it into
warmth, any more than he could make her chest rise and fall.

"Oh, Mairsie," he said aloud. "Oh, baby, what the hell did you do to
yourself?"

He reached for the bedside lamp, then drew his hand back. You
weren't supposed to touch anything, he knew that much, but wasn't it per-
missible to turn on a light? Otherwise how could you know for sure what
you were looking at?

He touched only the switch, turned it, blinked at the brightness. He
looked at her and saw the marks on her throat and said, "Oh, God, somebody did this to you." And covered you to the waist, he thought, and
closed the door on his way out.

He reached for her wrist, felt for a pulse, but that was ridiculous, he
wasn't going to find one, she was dead, his friend Marilyn was dead. He
didn't want to touch her, hadn't wanted to put his fingers to her forehead,
but he did anyway, perhaps to make sure of what he already knew, perhaps to demonstrate to himself that he could do this if he had to. And her
wrist was cold, lifeless, and there was no pulse, and he let go of her and
took a step back from the bed.

Before he opened the door, he'd considered leaving. Now, though,
it was no longer an option. He had a moral obligation, and a legal one
as well, and he knew what he had to do, however little he looked forward to it.

There was a phone on the bedside table, but he stopped himself and
used the one in her office instead. He dialed 911 and gave his own name
and her address. Yes, he was certain she was dead. Yes, he would stay
where he was until the officers arrived. No, he wouldn't touch anything.

He hung up the phone and started to laugh. It was wildly inappropri-
ate, his friend and client was dead in the next room, his buddy Marilyn,
and he supposed it was shock that propelled the laughter.

But it was funny, wasn't it? You had to admit it was funny.

Oh, no, he wouldn't touch anything. God forbid he do anything to compromise the integrity of the crime scene. He'd used his thumb and forefinger to switch on the lamp, he'd nudged the door open with his foot. He'd been ever so careful.

Locking the barn door, he thought, after all the horses had bolted. Because, God help him, he'd already cleaned the apartment to the best of his professional ability. You could eat off the fucking floor, if you were so inclined, and what do you suppose that did to the integrity of the crime scene?

SHE WAS AT her desk by ten. She turned on the radio—it was preset to WQXR—and raised the volume a notch. She'd lower it in the afternoon, when people who were so inclined made the rounds of art galleries, but for now she could play it as loud as she liked. Not rock-concert loud, not even Carnegie Hall loud, but with sufficient volume so that it was real music, not just background noise.

Though it might as well have been background noise for all the attention she paid to it. She busied herself in correspondence, real mail and e-mail, made phone calls, and sprang up from her chair from time to time to walk around the gallery, straightening a painting that had gotten itself tilted, dusting a piece of sculpture, and just claiming the place as her own, like a cowboy riding his fences.

Mornings were her favorite time. No one came to the door, and the phone hardly ever rang. She had the place to herself, and the work to herself, and she liked it that way. Chloe would come at one o'clock and station herself at the reception desk, and potential customers would drift in, stare thoughtfully at the work, and wander off again. She enjoyed it when one of them wanted to talk about the art, enjoyed it even more when someone actually bought something. (And it did happen sometimes. You knocked yourself out making phone calls and working your mailing list, you eighty-sixed the jug wine and cheese cubes and got Fabulous Food to cater the opening, and then someone walked in off the street, someone you never heard of who never heard of you, either, and he fell in love with something and wanted to know if you took American Express. Damn right she did.)

She enjoyed all that, and couldn't have stayed open without it, but the sheer contentment of her morning routine, all by herself in her ever-changing private museum—that was the real payoff. That was close to heaven.

But there was something she was supposed to do, and she couldn't remember what it was.

At eleven o'clock they interrupted the music for a five-minute news summary, and she wasn't paying any attention to it until she heard a name she recognized. "Marilyn Fairchild," the announcer said, and said something else about the police pursuing several leads, and then the item was past, and he was saying something no doubt important about India and Pakistan.

Marilyn Fairchild, murdered the other night in her West Village apartment. She'd been aware of the murder, she was always aware of it when a woman was murdered in Manhattan, but either the name hadn't registered or, more likely, they hadn't announced it. Pending notification of kin—wasn't that what they always said? And now she could understand the policy, because she could imagine how a person would feel, getting the news of a loved one's death over the radio. She was a little bit shocked and stunned herself, and she barely knew Marilyn Fairchild.

She'd been found in her bed, strangled. She hoped they'd find the bastard, hoped some slick son of a bitch didn't get him off, hoped—

That's what she couldn't remember!

Maury Winters's number was on her speed dial, and she pushed the button and drummed her fingers waiting for the receptionist to pick up. She said, "Susan Pomerance for Mr. Winters," and looked up when a buzzer sounded. There was a young man at her door.

Was it safe to let him in? He was black, and that automatically triggered a mental alarm, she couldn't help it, she was white and that was how she reacted. She sized him up at a glance and noted his short hair, his regular features, his skin tone that suggested a Caucasian grandparent or great-grandparent. He was clean-shaven, his jeans had been ironed, his sneakers were tied.

None of this meant anything—you could be neatly dressed and nice-looking and white in the bargain, with your fucking arm in a cast yet, and turn out to be Ted Bundy—but he looked all right, he really did, and he was carrying an envelope, just an ordinary six-by-nine manila clasp envelope, and she didn't see how he could tuck a knife or a gun into it.

Marilyn Fairchild, who'd found her the perfect co-op at London Towers, high ceilings and casement windows and an attended lobby and she could even walk to work, Marilyn Fairchild had let someone into her apartment, someone who hadn't needed a knife or a gun, and now she was dead and—

He was probably a messenger, she thought, but he didn't look like a messenger. He seemed too purposeful, somehow.

She buzzed him in, and when the attorney came on the line she said, "Hold on a sec, Maury. Someone at the door." To the young man she said, "How may I help you?"

"Are you Miss Pomerance?" When she nodded he said, "I have these pictures, and Mr. Andriani said you might look at them."

"David Andriani?"

"That has the gallery on Fifty-seventh Street?" He smiled, showing perfect teeth. "He said you might be interested."

"You're an artist?"

He shook his head. "My uncle."

"Have a seat," she said. "Or have a look around, if you like. I'll be with you in a moment."

She picked up the phone. "Sorry," she said. "Maury, I got something in the mail the other day. They want me to report Monday morning for jury duty."

"So?"

"So how do I get out of it?"

"You don't," he said. "You've already postponed it twice, if I remember correctly."

"Can't I postpone it again?"

"No."

"Why the hell not? And why can't I get out of it altogether? I have my own business to run, for God's sake. What happens to this place if I get stuck in a courtroom?"

"You're right," he said. "Three days in the Criminal Courts Building and the Susan Pomerance Gallery would go right down the tubes, triggering a stock-market crash that would make Black Tuesday look like—"

"Very funny. I don't see why I have to do this."

"Everybody has to."

"I thought if you were the sole proprietor of a business—"

"They changed the rules, sweetie. It used to be very different. Loopholes all over the place. There was even a joke going around for years, like how would you like your fate to be in the hands of twelve people who weren't bright enough to get out of jury duty?"

"That's my point. I ought to be bright enough to—"

"But they changed the rules," he went on, "and now everybody has to serve. Lawyers, ex-cops, everybody. Rudy got called a couple of years ago, if you'll recall, and he was the mayor, and he served just like everybody else."

"I bet he could have gotten out of it if he'd wanted to."

"I think you're probably right, and that'll be an option for you when you're elected mayor, but for the time being—"

"I'm supposed to go to the Hamptons next week."

"Now that's different," he said.

She grinned in spite of herself. "I'm serious," she said. "Can't you do something? Tell him I'm blind or I've got agoraphobia?"

"I like that last," he said. "You've got a fear of empty spaces, all right. On other people's walls. Do you have the letter they sent you?"

"Well, I wouldn't throw it out, would I?"

"You might, but I meant do you have it handy."

"It's somewhere," she said. "Hold on a minute. Here it is. You want me to fax it to you?"

"That's exactly what I want."

"Coming at you," she said, and rang off, then found his card in her Rolodex and carried it and the offending letter to the fax machine. She sent the fax, and while it made its magical way across town she looked over at the young man, who was standing in front of a painting by Aleesha MacReady, an elderly woman who lived in rural West Virginia and painted formal oil portraits of biblical figures, all of them somehow looking as though they were undergoing torture, but didn't really mind.

"That's Moses," she said. "That's the golden calf in the bulrushes. She puts in a batch of props that don't necessarily go together, but all relate to the person portrayed. She's self-taught, of course. I suppose that's true of your uncle?"

"My mom's uncle," he said. "My great-uncle. Emory Allgood, that's his name. And he never had lessons."

She nodded at the envelope. "You have slides?"

He opened the envelope, handed her a color print that looked to have been run off a computer. It showed an assemblage, an abstract sculpture fashioned from bits of junk. You couldn't tell the scale of the thing, and the printing was bad, and you were seeing it from only one angle, but she felt the power of the piece all the same, the raw kinetic energy of it.

And something else, something that gave her a little frisson, a pinging sensation, almost, in the center of her chest.

"Is this the only—"

He shook his head, drew out a disk. "A friend of mine has this digital camera. He only printed out the one picture, but he said if you has, if you have a computer . . ."

She did, at the desk in her office, and she popped in the disk and went through the images, almost two dozen of them, and before she was halfway through the pinging had become a bell pealing in her chest, resonating throughout her whole being.

She said, "Tell me his name again."

"Emory Allgood."

"And you are . . ."

"His great-nephew. My mom's mom, my gran, was his sister."

"I meant your name."

"Oh, didn't I say? I'm sorry. It's Reginald Barron."

"Do they call you Reginald or Reggie?"

"Mostly Reginald."

If you has, if you have *a computer.* Just the slightest stress on *have.* He was careful to speak correctly, but care was required. She found it charming.

"Reginald," she said, and looked at him. He was several inches taller than she was, say an inch or so over six feet. Slender but well muscled, with broad shoulders, and muscles in his arms that stretched the sleeves of his red polo shirt. She kept her eyes away from his crotch, but couldn't stop her mind from going there.

She said, "Tell me about your uncle. When did he start making art?"

"About five years ago. No, that's not exactly right. Five years ago he stopped paying much mind to people, and then a year or so after that he started making these things."

"First he withdrew."

"He stopped answering," he said. "Took less and less notice of people. He'd be staring, and there wouldn't be anything there for him to stare at."

"I understand."

"What I think, he was going inside."

"Yes."

"And he'd go in the street like a junk picker and come home with all this trash, and my mom was worried, like he'd have to, you know, go away or something, but it turned out he was bringing all this shit—"

He winced, and she was touched. Gently she said, "I've heard the word before, Reginald."

"Well."

"I may even have said it once or twice."

"Well, what I was saying. He was bringing these things home for a reason, to use them in what he was making. But we didn't know that until one day he showed my mom what he was working on, and that made it better. The junk-picking and all."

"Because he had a reason."

"Right, and so it wasn't so crazy."

"Did he talk about his work?"

"He, uh, pretty much stopped talking. I don't know what you'd call him, if he's crazy or what. He's not scary, except the way any old man's scary who keeps to himself and doesn't say nothing, anything, and just stares off into space. But he never makes trouble or disturbs anybody, and there's people who know what he does and bring him things, empty spools of thread and bottle caps and pieces of wire and, well, you seen, *saw*, the kind of things he uses."

"Yes."

"So this man on the next block said there's people who pay attention to this type of art, and I got some pictures taken, and I went around different people until somebody sent me to Mr. Andriani, and he said you were the person to come see."

"And here you are."

He nodded.

She said, "They call it outsider art, Reginald, because it's produced by artists who are outside the mainstream, generally self-taught, and often entirely unaware of the art world. But it seems to me you could just as easily call it insider art. You were just looking at Aleesha MacReady's painting of Moses. Could any work of art be more internal than hers? She's communicating a wholly private vision. It's outside as far as the New York art scene is concerned, but it comes from deep inside of Aleesha MacReady."

"And my uncle's work's like that?"

"Very much so." She walked around him, careful not to touch him, but passing close enough so that she fancied she could feel his body heat. "I don't know much about Aleesha," she went on. "I've never met her, she's never come to New York. I'd be surprised if she's ever been out of West Virginia. But I gather she's quite normal in her day-to-day life. When she picks up a paintbrush, though, she accesses whatever it is we see in her paintings."

She moved to stand in front of another work, painted in Day-Glo colors on a Masonite panel that had been primed in black. Like all the artist's work, it showed a monster—this one was rather dragonlike—devouring a child.

"Jeffcoate Walker," she said. "Nice, huh? How'd you like this hanging on your living room wall?"

"Uh . . ."

"Of course you wouldn't. His work's impossible to live with, and my guess is that he creates it so he won't have to live with it inside him. But it's only a guess, because Mr. Walker's been institutionalized for the past thirty-some years. I believe the diagnosis is some form of schizophrenia, and it's severe enough to keep him permanently locked up."

"My uncle's nowhere near that bad."

"What he has in common with both of these artists, and with just about everyone whose work I show, is an internal vision, a very personal vision, along with the ability to communicate that vision. I find that very exciting."

"I see."

She had, suddenly and entirely unbidden, a personal vision of her own. Reginald Barron, stripped naked, all done up in a complicated leather harness suspended from a nasty-looking meat hook mounted in the ceiling. His muscles strained against the leather straps that cut into his glistening teak-colored skin, and more leather girded his loins, painfully tight on his balls and the base of his engorged penis, and—

Turning from him, she said, "I had a background in art history and went to work for a traditional gallery on upper Madison Avenue. I worked for several galleries, and I got married and divorced, and I lived with an artist for a while, which is something no one should have to do, and when that ended I went to Switzerland for two weeks. I'd been to Europe several times, of course, and I'd spent a few days each in Zurich and Geneva, so I went to a few other cities this time, I got a rail pass and just bounced around, and I read in one of the guidebooks about a museum in Lausanne devoted to art produced by the insane. After six months with Marc Oberbauer I inclined toward the belief that *all* art was produced by the insane, but this was different. This was the most exciting work I'd ever seen in my life."

"And that got you started?"

She nodded. She was able to look at him now without seeing him as she had a few moments ago. He was a nice polite young man now, that's all. Undoubtedly attractive, she had to admit she was more than a little attracted, but that didn't mean she was going to act out, or let her imagination run wild.

"I came home," she said, "and learned everything I could. I'd always been drawn to folk art, I did my thesis on Colonial weather vanes, but now I was seeing it all differently. Now some of it looked cute and amusing, while the work that really moved me came from somewhere deep within the person who made it. And it didn't have to be folk art. When I went to the Prado in Madrid, the work that most affected me was Goya's series of Black Paintings, all created late at night during a period when the artist was profoundly disturbed and quite possibly ill. Goya was hardly self-taught, he was arguably Spain's greatest painter, but the Black Paintings would have been right at home in La Musée de l'Art Brut in

Lausanne. Or in this gallery—his *Cronos Devouring His Children* might have been painted by Jeffcoate Walker, if Mr. Walker had had the advantage of formal training and a classical education."

She was telling him too much. What did he know about Goya or the Prado? But he seemed interested.

"My artists rarely know how to talk about their work," she said, "if they talk at all. But how many artists can speak intelligently about what they do? If you've ever read the silly statements they prepare for their show openings—"

But he wouldn't know what she was talking about, he wouldn't have been to an opening, might never have been to a gallery. She shifted gears and said, "I went all over the country looking at things, including an outdoor shrine in Iowa that a priest spent his life creating, with shells and crystals and semiprecious gemstones. And the Watts towers, of course, and a house made entirely of Coke bottles, and, oh, all sorts of things. And I came home and sold everything I owned and opened this place."

Enough life history, she thought. Cut to the chase.

"I'd like to show your uncle's work, Reginald. I'd like to give him a one-man show sometime in the fall. I'd love it if he could supervise the installation and come to the opening, but that's not a requirement. The work speaks for itself, and I'll be here to speak for it."

He nodded, taking it in. After a moment he said, "I don't know what he'll want to do. I don't guess he'll mind parting with the work, on account of he'll give a piece away if anyone tells him they really like it."

"Don't let him give anything else away, okay?"

"No, he hasn't been doing that lately. On account of not talking to people, you know, and keeping to himself." He pointed at the wall, where Jeffcoate Walker's dragon loomed a few yards from Aleesha MacReady's Moses. "I didn't see anything there about the prices."

"It's considered a little crass to post them. This"—she crossed to the front desk, brought back a price list in an acetate sleeve—"is considered more discreet."

"These the kind of prices you'd put on Uncle Emory's things?"

"I'm not sure. Pricing's tricky, there are a lot of factors to consider. Artists command higher prices as they gain a reputation, and your uncle's unknown." She gave him a smile. "But that won't be true for long."

"He gonna be famous?"

"Well, is Aleesha MacReady famous? Or Jeffcoate Walker? Perhaps, but to a relatively small circle of collectors. Howard Finster's fairly famous, you may have heard of him. And you probably know Grandma Moses."

"Yes."

"I can't be specific about prices," she went on, "but I can explain the way we work." And she told him the gallery took fifty percent of sales proceeds, noticing as she spoke that he looked tense. Well, why shouldn't he? Fifty percent was high, but it was standard, and it was hard enough to come out ahead in this business, and—

But that wasn't it. "I got to ask this," he said, "so there won't be any misunderstanding. We won't have to come up with any money in front, will we?"

"Money in front?"

"'Cause this one dealer was talking about what we'd have to front him to cover expenses, and we can't afford to do anything like that."

"That's not how we work," she assured him. "Expenses are my problem. In fact, there'll be a token good-faith advance for you when we get the paperwork signed."

"Paperwork?"

"We'll want exclusive rights to represent the artist's work. In return, you'll get an advance from us against future earnings. It won't be much, maybe a thousand dollars, but that's better than having to pay money to some vanity gallery, isn't it?"

He nodded, still taking it all in. "When you say *we* . . ."

"I mean me," she said. "The editorial *we*, or perhaps it's more the entrepreneurial *we*. The Pomerance Gallery is a one-person show in itself, and—"

The phone rang, and caller ID showed it was Maury Winters. "I have to take this," she told Reginald, and picked up and said, "Well? Did you work a miracle?"

"I hope you have good weather in the Hamptons."

"You got me out of it."

"I got you a postponement," he said, "to which you're not entitled, but it'd be a hard life if we never got more than we deserved. You're committed to show up the second week in October, and—"

"October? That's—"

"—a busy time for you," he supplied, "and that's too bad. Susan, sweetheart, we're talking about a probable three days, starting on a Monday, and you're closed Mondays, right?"

"Yes, but—"

"And how busy are you on Tuesdays and Wednesdays? Don't answer that, because I don't care how busy you are then or any other time. You'll go and do your duty as a citizen, and you won't get picked because this is criminal court and nobody's going to want you on a jury."

"Why's that?"

"Because you're smart and chic and in the arts."

"So?"

"So either the prosecution or the defense is going to want you out of there. And even if they don't, you can keep from being selected. The judge'll ask if any of the prospective jurors feel incapable of being fair and open-minded about the case at hand, and that's when you raise your hand and say you couldn't possibly be fair to Joe Blow because he looks just like the uncle who tried to get in your pants when you were eleven."

"And he'll believe me?"

"No, he'll probably figure you just don't want to be on a jury, but what do you care about his good opinion? He'll excuse you, because after you've said that he'll have to. Three days, Susan, and they'll be over before you know it, and you won't have to serve again for four more years."

"If I'd known it was just three days . . ."

"What?"

"Well, as far as next week is concerned—"

"Forget next week. You're off the hook for next week and you can't get back on."

"I'd rather wait until October anyway," she said. "You're a love, Maury. I appreciate it, I really do."

"You should. You know, you shouldn't call me for something like this. You should ignore the summons and wait until you're arrested, and then you call me. I'm a criminal defense attorney, and—"

"One of the best in the country."

"What are you buttering me up for? I already did you the favor. But every time you have a legal question you call me, and most of it's stuff I'm rusty on. You must know other lawyers."

"Not as well as I know you, Maury." She nibbled her lower lip. "You're the only one on my speed dial. If there's anything I can do in return . . ."

"Well, now that you mention it, one of your famous blow jobs would be more than welcome."

She let the silence stretch as long as she could. Then, her voice strained, she said, "Maury, you're on speakerphone. I thought you knew that."

He didn't say anything, and the silence was delicious.

"Gotcha," she said.

"Yeah, I guess you did. I get you out of jury duty and you give me a heart attack. Nice."

"Just wanted to keep you on your toes," she said, and blew him a kiss, and rang off.

CHLOE WAS A FEW minutes late, but no more than you'd expect from a twenty-three-year-old blonde with a crew cut and a nose ring. She took up her post at the front desk and Susan, who generally had lunch delivered, decided it was too nice a day to stay indoors. She walked over to Empire Diner and had a large orange juice and a salmon salad, then browsed a couple of Ninth Avenue antique shops and was back at the gallery a little after two.

She'd sent Reginald Barron off earlier with papers for his uncle to sign and a $500 check as a good-faith advance, and now she had another look at the photos of Emory Allgood's extraordinary work. She'd kept the disk—Reginald hadn't thought to ask for its return, and she would have talked him out of it if he had. She didn't need it, she'd already downloaded the images, but she didn't want it floating around, not until she had the artist firmly committed to the Susan Pomerance Gallery.

Not that anyone else was likely to respond as strongly as she had, but you never knew, and why take chances? She knew how good the man was, she'd learned to trust that bell in her chest, that tingling in her fingertips, and now, looking again at the pictures, taking more time with them, she found herself running through her client list, picking out those who'd be particularly likely to respond to what she saw.

Before the show she'd invite a few of her best prospects to preview the work. (The show would probably be in late October or early November, and if jury duty cost her a few days in early October, well, she could work around that.) Ideally, there'd be red dots on a third of the pieces by the time the show opened, even if she had to give some of the early birds an unannounced break on the price.

Of course a lot depended on the artist, on the likelihood of his continuing to produce work in quantity. Most of them kept at it, but sometimes an artist would stop making art as abruptly and incomprehensibly as he'd started. If Emory Allgood was likely to pull the plug, she'd do best for his sake and hers to get the highest possible prices for the work at hand.

But if there was more work to come, she could afford for both their sakes to take a different tack. Her goal would be to get those red dots up as quickly as possible, and to sell out the whole show in the first week. Then, when she showed his new work a year later, the buyers who'd been shut out the first time would be primed for a feeding frenzy. And she'd boost the prices and make everybody happy.

She returned to one image, frustrated by the limitation of a two-dimensional representation of a three-dimensional object. She wanted to be right there in the room with the piece, wanted it life-size and smack in front of her, wanted to be able to walk around it and see it from every angle, to reach out and touch it, to feel the up-close-and-personal energy of it.

Eventually, of course, she'd go out and look at the work. She'd assumed they lived in Harlem, but the address Reginald Barron had given her was in Brooklyn, and she had no idea where Quincy Street might be. Bedford-Stuyvesant, she supposed, or Brownsville, or, well, some neighborhood unknown to her. She'd spent a little time in Brooklyn Heights and Cobble Hill, and she'd been a few times to Carroll Gardens, and of course she'd been to galleries and loft parties in Williamsburg, but that left most of Brooklyn as foreign to her as the dark side of the moon.

The hourly news summary came on. A suicide bomber had taken eleven lives (including, thank God, his own) in a café in Jerusalem. A mining disaster in the Ukraine had left forty-some miners trapped and presumed dead. The mine, she noted, was a mere eighty miles from Chernobyl.

She turned up the volume when they got to the Marilyn Fairchild murder. That was the name, she hadn't misheard it, and they identified her as a real estate agent and gave her age as thirty-eight.

The announcer moved on to something else and she lowered the volume, and Chloe buzzed her—would she take a call from a Mr. Winters?

She picked up and said, "I was just thinking of you."

"You got a traffic ticket and you want me to fix it."

"Silly. I don't have a car."

"Jaywalking, then."

"I was thinking about Marilyn Fairchild. I knew her, Maury."

"The actress? No, that's something else."

"Morgan."

"That's it, Morgan Fairchild. There's something automatically sexy about a woman with two last names. Ashleigh Banfield, I watch her on MSNBC and I get a hard-on. She's good-looking, but I think it's the name as much as anything else. Who's Marilyn Fairchild?"

"She was murdered the day before yesterday."

"Oh, of course. The name didn't register. Lived in the Village, strangled in bed. You say you knew her?"

"Not terribly well. She showed me five or six apartments, including the one I bought."

"You still at London Towers?"

"Until I leave feet first. I love it there."

"And you've been there what, three years?"

"Almost five."

"That long? You stay in touch with her after the closing?"

"No." She frowned. "I thought at the time we might get to be friends. They just said she was thirty-eight, so we were a year apart, and—"

"You're thirty-nine?"

"Fuck you."

He laughed, delighted. "So you're thirty-seven. Two years is worth *fuck you?*"

"We were a year apart," she went on, "and she was a successful professional woman living alone in the Village, and I'm a successful professional woman living alone in Chelsea, and, oh, I don't know . . ."

"You identified."

"I'm taller by an inch or two. Her figure was fuller. Her hair had a lot of red in it, but I have a hunch it would have been the same dark brown as mine without professional intervention. I don't smoke, but she did, and that may have given her the throaty voice. She liked a drink."

"Who doesn't?"

"Did I identify? I suppose."

" 'If it could happen to her . . .' "

"It could happen to me." She frowned. "Maury, you called me, and probably not because I was thinking of you."

"I don't know. Your thoughts are pretty powerful."

"What did you want?"

"I was thinking it's been a while, and I was thinking we should have dinner."

"You still married, Maury?"

"Like you and your apartment," he said. "Till the day I die."

"That's good, and I'd love to have dinner with you. Not tonight, I hope, because—"

"Tonight's no good for me either. I was thinking the day after tomorrow."

"Let me check. . . . That's Friday night? I accept with pleasure."

"I'll call you when I know where and when. It'll be someplace nice."

"I'm sure it will. And I'll look forward to it, unless someone strangles me in my bed between now and then. I hope they catch the son of a bitch."

"They probably will."

"I hope they put him away."

"Again, they probably will," he said. "Unless he gets a good lawyer."

three

LATER ON, HE could never get over the fact that he'd actually welcomed the interruption. The doorbell rang and he heard it over the music and rose eagerly from his chair, came out from behind his desk, and hurried to let them in.

And his life would never be the same again.

There were two of them, two clean-shaven short-haired white guys wearing suits and ties and polished shoes, and his first thought was that they were Mormons or Jehovah's Witnesses, because who else dressed like that outside of bankers and corporate lawyers, and when did those guys start going door to door? And if they had been religious fanatics, well, hell, he probably would have invited them in and listened respectfully to what they had to say, even poured them cups of coffee if their religion allowed them to have it. Not out of fear of hell or hope of heaven, but because it had to be better than staring at a PC monitor on which words stubbornly refused to appear.

An hour ago he had written *He walked over and opened the window.* He'd stared at it for a while, then deleted *and*, replacing it with a comma. He played a hand of solitaire before highlighting the last four words of the sentence and replacing them with *to the window and opened it*. He looked at that, shook his head, highlighted *opened it*, and changed it to *flung it open*.

Nothing happened, except that Coltrane gave way to Joshua Redman and cigarette butts began to fill the ashtray. Then, a few minutes before the doorbell sounded, he'd deleted the entire sentence. And now he'd pushed the button to open the downstairs door, and then he'd walked over and opened the door to his apartment, and you could play with *that* sentence all you wanted, but here he was, standing in the doorway, and there they were, coming up the stairs, and . . .

"Mr. Creighton? I'm Detective Kevin Slaughter and this is Detective Alan Reade. Could we talk with you?"

"Uh, sure," he said.

"May we come in?"

"Oh, right," he said, and stepped back. "Sure. Come right in, guys."

They did, and sent their eyes around the room, not at all shy about looking at things. He'd noticed that about cops, had watched uniformed officers in the subway and on the street, staring right at people without the least embarrassment.

He stood six two, a bear of a man, big in the chest and shoulders, with a mane of brown hair and a full beard that he trimmed himself. His waist was a little thicker than he'd have liked, but not too bad. He stood a good two inches taller than Slaughter, who in turn was an inch or two taller than Reade.

Slaughter was lean, wiry—reedy, Creighton thought, while Reade was anything but, and had a gut on him that the suit jacket couldn't hide. They were younger than he was, but that was true of more people every year, wasn't it? Midthirties, at a guess, and he was forty-seven, which was still pretty young, especially when you kept yourself in decent shape, but it was closer to fifty than forty, closer to sixty than thirty, closer to the grave than to the cradle, and—

And they were standing in his studio apartment, looking at his things, looking at him.

"What's this about?"

"Music's a little loud," Slaughter said. "Any chance you could turn it down a notch?"

"Somebody complained about the music? Jesus, at this hour? I remember years ago we had a saxophone player across the courtyard, he used to practice at all hours, thought he was Sonny Rollins and this was the Williamsburg Bridge, but—"

"It's just a little hard to talk over," Slaughter said smoothly. "Nobody complained."

"Oh, sure," he said, and lowered the volume. "So if it's not the music . . ."

"Just a few questions," Reade said. His voice was reedy, even if he wasn't. And Slaughter asked if this was a bad time, and he said that it wasn't, that he welcomed the interruption, that he'd been writing the same stupid sentence over and over.

"After a while," he said, "the words stop making sense. They don't even look right, you find yourself staring at the word *cat* and wondering if it's supposed to have two *t*s."

"You're a writer, Mr. Creighton?"

"Sometimes I wonder. But yes"—he indicated the big oak desk at the side of the room, the computer, the big dictionary on its stand, the rack of briar pipes—"I'm a writer."

"Have you had anything published?" It was Slaughter who asked, and he must have rolled his eyes in response, because the man said, "I'm sorry, was that a stupid question?"

"Well, maybe a little," he said, and softened the remark with a grin. "I suppose there are people who'd call themselves writers without having published anything, and who's to say they don't have the right? I mean, look at Emily Dickinson."

Reade said, "Friend of yours?" and Creighton looked at him and couldn't say for sure if the guy was playing him.

"Nineteenth-century poet," he said. "She never published anything during her lifetime."

"But you have."

"Six novels," he said. "Working on number seven, and the only thing that sustains me on days like this is reminding myself they were *all* like this."

"Tough going, you mean."

"Not every day, some days it's like turning on a faucet. It just flows. But every book had days like this, and a couple of them had whole months like this."

"But you make a living at it."

"I'm forty-seven years old and I live in one room," he said. "You do the math."

"Just the one room," Reade said, "but it's got some size to it. Plenty of landlords'd throw up a couple of walls, call it a three-room apartment."

You could stick a plank out the window, he thought, and call it a terrace.

"Good neighborhood, too. Bank and Waverly, heart of the West Village. Gotta be rent stabilized, huh?"

Meaning *You couldn't afford it otherwise*, he thought, and he couldn't argue the point. Free market rent on his apartment would be well over two thousand a month, and probably closer to three. Could he afford that? Maybe once, before the divorce, before the sales leveled off and the advances dipped, but now?

Not unless he gave up eating and drinking and—he patted his shirt pocket, found it empty—and smoking.

"Rent controlled," he said.

"Even better. You've been here a long time, then."

"Off and on. I was married for a few years and we moved across the river."

"Jersey?"

He nodded. "Jersey City, walking distance of the PATH train. I kept this place as an office. Then we bought a house in Montclair, and I didn't get in as much, but I hung on to it anyway."

"Be crazy to give it up."

"And then the marriage fell apart," he said, "and she kept the house, and I moved back in here."

"They always get the house," Slaughter said. He sounded as if he spoke from experience. He shook his head and walked over to a book-case, leaned in for a closer look at the spines. " 'Blair Creighton,' " he read. "That's you, but on the bell it said John Creighton."

"Blair's my middle name, my mother's maiden name."

"And your first name's John?"

"That's right. Some of my early stories, I used J. Blair Creighton. An editor convinced me to drop the initial, said I was running the risk that people would mistake me for F. Scott Fitzgerald. I, uh, took his point."

"I don't know, it sounds good with the initial. What's this, French? You write books in French?"

"I have enough trouble in English," he said. "Those are translations, foreign editions."

"Here's one in English. *Edged Weapons*. That's like what, knives and swords?"

"And daggers, I suppose. Or words, metaphorically." It was interest-ing, observing them at it. Did Slaughter really think he wrote in French, or was he playing a role, lacking only the ratty raincoat to qualify as a road-company Columbo? "It's a collection of short stories," he explained. "Presumably, they have an edge to them."

"Like a knife."

"Well, sure."

"But you have an interest in knives, right? And swords and daggers?"

He was puzzled until he followed Slaughter's gaze to the far wall be-tween the two windows. There was a cased Samurai sword, a Malayan kris with the traditional wavy blade, and a dagger of indeterminate origin with a blade of Damascus steel.

"Gifts," he said. "When the book came out. Edged weapons to go with *Edged Weapons,* so to speak."

"They look nice," Reade said, "displayed like that."

"The book's working title was *Masks,*" he recalled, "but we changed it when we heard that was going to be T. C. Boyle's collection, or maybe

it was Ethan Canin. Whoever it was, he wound up calling his book something else, too. But one way or another I was a sure bet to wind up with
something to hang on the wall."

"You see masks all the time," Reade said. "These here are a little
more unique."

Something was either unique or it wasn't, there weren't gradations of
it. It was an error his students made all the time, a particularly annoying
one, and he must have winced now because Slaughter immediately asked
him if something was wrong."

"No, why?"

"Expression on your face."

He touched the back of his neck. "I've been getting twinges off and
on all day," he said. "I must have slept in an awkward position, because I
woke up with a stiff neck."

"I hate when that happens," Reade said.

"I imagine most people do. You know, this is pleasant enough, but do
you want to give me a hint what this is all about?"

"Just a few questions, John. Or do people call you Blair?"

"It depends how long they've known me." And you've barely known
me long enough to call me Mr. Creighton, he thought. "Say, do you mind
if I smoke?"

"It's your house, John."

"It bothers some people."

"Even if it did," Slaughter said, "it's your house. You do what you
want."

He patted his breast pocket again, and of course it was still empty,
cigarettes hadn't mysteriously appeared in it since he last checked. He
walked over to the desk and shook a cigarette out of the pack and lit it, relaxing as the nicotine soothed the anxiety it had largely created. That was
all smoking did for you, it poured oil on waters it had troubled in the first
place, and what earthly good did it do him to know that? He'd known that
for years, and he went on smoking the fucking things all the same.

"A couple of questions," he said.

"Right, we're taking up enough of your time as it is, John. So why
don't you tell us about the last time you saw Marilyn Fairchild."

"Marilyn Fairchild."

"Right."

"I don't know anybody by that name."

"You sure of that, John?"

"It has a familiar ring to it, though, doesn't it? Isn't there an actress
by that name?"

"You're thinking of Morgan Fairchild, John."

"Of course," he said. "Well, I don't know either of them, Morgan or Marilyn. I wouldn't mind knowing Morgan, though. Or Marilyn, if she looks anything like her sister."

"They're sisters?"

"That was sort of a joke. I never heard of Marilyn Fairchild until you mentioned her."

"Never heard of her."

"No."

Reade took a step toward him, moved right into his space, and said, "Are you sure of that, John? Because we understand you went home with her the other night."

He shook his head. "If that's what this is about," he said, "I think you have the wrong guy."

"You do, huh?"

"There used to be a John Creighton in the phone book," he said. "Lived somewhere in the West Seventies, and I'd get phone calls for him all the time."

"So maybe it's him we should be looking for."

"Well, maybe he's the one who got lucky with Marilyn Fairchild."

"Because you didn't."

"Never even met the lady."

Slaughter said, "You mind telling us what you were doing the night before last?"

"The night before last?"

"That's right."

"That would be Monday night? Well, that's easy. I was teaching a class."

"You're a teacher, John?"

"I conduct a workshop once a week at the New School," he said. "Wannabe writers. They critique one another's work and I lead the discussion."

"You enjoy it, John?"

"I need the money," he said. "Not that it amounts to much, but it keeps me in beer and cigarettes."

"That's something."

"I guess it is. Anyway, that's what I was doing Monday night."

"From when to when, John?"

"Seven-thirty to ten. You can check with the school and they'll confirm that I was there, but don't make me prove it by telling you what the stories were about. I forget all that crap the minute I leave the classroom. I'd go nuts if I didn't."

"They're pretty bad, huh?"

"I don't like being read to," he said, "even if it's Dylan Thomas reading *A Child's Christmas in Wales*. But they're not all that bad, actually, and some of them are pretty good. I don't know that I'm doing them any good, but I can't be doing them much harm. And it gives them a structure, keeps them writing."

"Must be a good place to meet women," Reade said.

"You know what's funny? I've been doing this for three years now, and when I started I had the same thought. I mean, a majority of students are women, a majority of everything is women, and these are women with an interest in literature and I'm up there, the designated authority, and how can you miss, right?"

"And?"

"Somebody, I think it was Samuel Johnson, read another writer's book. And he said, 'Your work is both original and excellent. However, the parts that are original are not excellent, and the parts that are excellent are not original.' "

They looked puzzled.

"In the classroom," he explained, "the women are both attractive and available. However, the ones who are available are not attractive, and—"

"And the ones who are attractive aren't available," Slaughter said. "Was Marilyn Fairchild one of your students?"

"You know," he said, "I don't recognize the name, but I don't know all their names. It's not impossible. I have a list of them someplace, hang on and let me see if I can find it."

It was where it was supposed to be, in the New School file folder, and he checked it and handed the list to Slaughter. "No Marilyn Fairchild," he said. "There's a woman named Mary Franklin, but I can't believe anybody went home with her Monday night. She's writing her memoirs, she was a WAF in the Second World War. The last person who got lucky with her was Jimmy Doolittle."

"So I guess it's not the same woman."

"Evidently not."

"And you're covered from seven-thirty to ten, but that leaves the whole rest of the night, doesn't it? And the thing is, John, you fit the description we're working with, right down to the cigarettes you smoke. Unfiltered Camels, there's not that many people smoking them anymore."

"We're an endangered species, but . . ."

"But what, John?"

He took the cigarette out of his mouth, looked at it, put it out in an ashtray. " 'The description you're working with.' Who gave you a description?"

"Sort of a group effort," Slaughter said. "And it included the fact that you were a writer, and your name was Blair Creighton."

"So we wouldn't likely mix you up with the other John," Reade offered.

"And I'm supposed to have gone home with Marilyn Fairchild. Home from where?"

"A bar called the Kettle of Fish, John. You wouldn't happen to know it, would you? It's a few blocks from here on Sheridan Square."

"On Christopher Street," he said. "Of course I know it. I probably go there three, four times a week. I went there when it was the Lion's Head, and I stopped going there when it reopened as the Monkey's Paw, and then the old Kettle of Fish, which was on Macdougal Street just about forever and then moved around the corner to West Third, well, *they* moved into the old Lion's Head space, or at least the *name* moved there . . ."

"And you started drinking there again."

"It's one of the places I tend to go to. In the late afternoon, mostly, when the writing's done for the day."

"And sometimes at night, John? Like the night before last?"

"The night before last . . ."

"Take your time, give it some thought. You just think of something, John? You have the look of a man who just now thought of something."

"Oh, for Chrissake," he said. "That dizzy bitch."

"You remember now, huh, John?"

"If it's the same woman," he said. "Short hair, sort of reddish brown? Lives on Waverly?"

"I believe it's Charles Street," Reade said.

"But you're right about the hair," Slaughter said. "The length and the color. You're doing great, John."

Patronizing son of a bitch. "Charles Street," he said. "We walked up Waverly from the Kettle, but I guess she was around the corner on Charles. Must have been Charles. What's her name supposed to be? Marilyn Fairchild? Because that's not the name she gave me."

"And what name did she give you, John?"

"I might recognize it if I heard it again. I don't think we got as far as last names, but the first name she gave me certainly wasn't Marilyn."

"You met her in the Kettle of Fish, John."

"I was having a drink at the bar. She walked in and picked me up."

"*She* picked *you* up."

"Why, isn't that how she remembers it? If I'd have been looking to pick somebody up, I wouldn't have gone to the Kettle."

"Why not?"

"People go there to drink," he said. "And to talk and hang out. Sometimes you might go home with somebody, but it'll most likely be somebody you've known forever from a whole lot of boozy conversations, and one night you're both drunk enough to think you ought to go home together, and it generally turns out to be a mistake, but the next time you run into each other you both either pretend it never happened or that you had a good time."

"And that's how it was with Marilyn Fairchild?"

He shook his head. "That's the point. She wasn't a regular, or at least I never saw her there before. And she walked in and scanned the bar like she was shopping, and I guess I was close enough to what she was looking for, because she came right over to me and put a cigarette between her lips."

"So you could light it for her."

"Except she took it out," he remembered, "and saw my cigarettes on the bar."

"Camels."

"And she said how she hadn't had one of those in ages, and I gave her one and lit it for her, and I said if she was going to smoke she'd better drink, too, and I bought her whatever she was having."

"Wild Turkey."

"Is that what it was? Yes, by God, it was, because the next thing I knew she was saying she had a whole bottle of the stuff just around the corner, and she whisked me out of there and up to her apartment, and I might like to flatter myself that I picked her up, but it was very much the other way around. She picked me up."

"And took you home."

"That's right. What does she say happened? I picked her up?"

"Why do you figure she would say that, John?"

"Who the hell knows what she'd say? She was a dizzy bitch. I'll tell you one thing, I'm too fucking old for barroom pickups, I really am. I'm forty-seven, I'll be forty-eight next month, I'm too old to go around sleeping with people I don't know."

"Sometimes, though, a couple of drinks . . ."

"It clouds your judgment," he agreed.

"And you had more drinks at her apartment?"

"A drink. Then I went home."

"One drink and you went home?"

"That's what I just said. What's her story?"

"Right now we just want to get your story, John."

"Why? Did she make a complaint? If she did, I think I have a right to hear it before I respond to it. What does she say I did?"

They looked at each other, and he took a step backward, as if someone had struck him a blow in the chest. He said, "She's dead, isn't she?"

"What makes you say that, John?"

"That's why you're here. What happened to her? What did she do, go out looking for somebody else?"

"Why would she do that, John?"

"Because she was still horny, I guess."

"What did you do, John? Turn the lady down? Had a glass of her Wild Turkey and decided you didn't want to get naked with her after all?"

"The chemistry wasn't right."

"So you kept your clothes on?"

"I didn't say that."

"You took them off?"

He stood still for a long moment. They were asking more questions but he had stopped listening. He turned from them, walked to his desk.

"John?"

"I want to make a phone call," he said. "I have a right to make a phone call, don't I?"

"You're not under arrest, John," Slaughter said, and Reade told him it was his phone, and of course he had the right to use it. But if he could answer a few questions first maybe they could get this all cleared up and then he could make all the calls he wanted.

Yeah, right. He dialed, and Nancy put him through to Roz. "I need a lawyer," he said. "I've got a couple of cops here, and I think I'm a suspect in the murder of a woman I met the other night." He looked across the desk at them. "Is that right? Am I a suspect?"

They didn't respond, but that was as good as if they had.

He talked for a minute or two, then replaced the receiver. "No more questions," he said. "I'm done talking until my lawyer gets here."

"Was that your lawyer just now, John?"

He didn't have a lawyer. The last lawyer he'd used was the moron who represented him in the divorce, and he'd since heard the guy was ill with something, and could only hope he'd died of it. He needed a criminal lawyer, and he didn't know any, had never had need of one. And Roz wasn't a lawyer, she was a literary agent, but she'd know what to do and whom to call.

He didn't say any of this, however. He sat at his desk, and they continued to ask questions, but he'd answered as many questions as he was going to.

And, now that he'd stopped saying anything, one of them, Slaughter or Reade, took a card from his wallet and read him his Miranda rights. Now that he'd finally elected to remain silent, now that he'd finally called for an attorney, they told him it was his right to do so.

He had the feeling he'd already said a lot more than he should have.

four

L'**AIGLON D'OR WAS** on Fifty-fifth between Park and Madison, and had been there for decades. A classic French restaurant, it had long since ceased to be trendy, and the right side of the menu guaranteed that it would never be a bargain. The great majority of its patrons had been coming for years, cherishing the superb cuisine, the restrained yet elegant decor, and the unobtrusively impeccable service. The tables, set luxuriously far apart, were hardly ever all taken, nor were there often more than two or three of them vacant. This, in fact, was very much as the proprietor preferred it. A Belgian from Bruges, who most people assumed was French, he wanted to make a good profit, but hated to turn anyone away. "The man who cannot get a table one week," he had said more than once, "will not come back the next week."

In response, one customer quoted Yogi Berra—*Nobody goes there anymore, it's too crowded.* The proprietor nodded in agreement. "*Précisément*," he said. "If it is too crowded, no one comes."

Francis Buckram saw he was a few minutes early and had the cab drop him at the corner. He found things to look at in a couple of Madison Avenue shop windows, and contrived to make his entrance at 8:05.

They were waiting for him at the table, three middle-aged men in dark suits and ties. Buckram, wearing a blazer and tan slacks, wondered if he should have chosen a suit himself. His clothes had nothing to apologize for, the blazer was by Turnbull & Asser, the slacks were Armani, the brown wing tips were Allen Edmonds, and he knew he wore the clothes well, but did they lack the gravitas the meeting required?

No, he decided, that was the point. The meeting was their idea, and he wasn't coming hat in hand. Insouciance was the ticket, not gravitas.

Fancy words for a cop.

Well, he was a fancy kind of a cop, always had been. Always had the expensive clothes and the extensive vocabulary, and knew when to trot them out and when to leave them in the closet. Growing up in Park Slope, he'd been as well liked as Willy Loman ever hoped to be, and he was good enough in sports and enough of a cutup in class to mask an ambition that got him a full scholarship to Colgate. That was the next thing to Ivy League and a healthy cut above Brooklyn College, which was where most of his classmates went, if they went anywhere at all. He'd surprised them by going away to a fancy school, and he surprised his classmates at Colgate by going straight from the campus to the NYPD. He'd scored well on the LSAT and got accepted at four of the five law schools he'd applied to, told them all thanks but no thanks and went on the cops.

He stopped at the bar to say hello to Claudia Gerndorf, who'd profiled him for *New York* magazine shortly after he was appointed commissioner. She introduced him to her companion, a labor leader he'd met in passing, and he gave the man a nod and a smile but didn't offer to shake hands. The guy had never been arrested, not so far as Buckram knew, but that didn't mean his hands were clean enough to shake.

"I've got a column now in the *New York Observer*," she said. "You know, we really ought to sit down one of these days and catch up."

"We'll do that," he said. "Meanwhile, there's a table of fellows I've got to sit down with right now."

And you can put that in your column, he thought. Former Police Commissioner Francis J. Buckram—and don't make it Francis X., assuming that every Francis gets stuck with Xavier for a middle name, and for God's sake don't make the last name Bushman—that Francis J. Buckram was spotted at a fashionable East Side eatery, sharing vichyssoise and frogs' legs with three real estate heavies. He might not get anything out of the evening but heartburn and a headache, but a little ink linking his name with some serious New York money couldn't do him any harm.

They were on their feet when he reached their table. He knew Avery Davis, who said, "Fran, it's good to see you. You know these fellows, don't you? Irv Boasberg and Hartley Saft."

He shook hands all around, apologizing for keeping them waiting, and was assured they'd just gotten there themselves. They had drinks in front of them, and when the waiter came over he ordered a Bombay martini, straight up and extra dry, with a twist. Hartley Saft, who had a drinker's complexion, took a refill on the Scotch. Davis and Boasberg said they were fine.

The conversation throughout the meal steered clear of Topic A. Ongoing terrorism got some of their attention, along with speculation about the eventual development of the Ground Zero site. Someone brought up a current scandal involving the health inspector's office. "I remember when the papers used to print a weekly list of restaurants that got cited for violations," Irv Boasberg said. "You'd look at the list, terrified you'd find your favorite Chinese restaurant on it, and what did it mean if you did?"

"That somebody forgot to slip the inspector a couple of bucks," Hartley Saft said. "But it killed your appetite, didn't it? You know what? Let's not talk about restaurant violations."

So they ate French food and drank California wine, and he made everybody happy by telling cop stories. That was always safe because everybody liked cop stories, and Fran Buckram had a batch of them that had stood the test of time.

Not every former police commissioner could say the same. Buckram was atypical in that he had come up through the ranks. New York's top cop more often than not lacked any real police experience. The position was largely administrative, and the present holder of the office had previously served as fire commissioner in Detroit; he'd never been a policeman, or a fireman either, as far as that went.

It made a certain amount of sense. The president of the United States, after all, was commander in chief of the armed forces, but that didn't mean he had to have been an army general in order to do the job.

As far as most cops were concerned, anyone fairly high up in the NYPD was light-years away from the street, and chiefly concerned with covering asses, his own and the department's. The man at the top, the commissioner, was first and foremost a politician, then an administrator, and not a real cop at all.

Still, the street cops liked it when the top slot was filled by someone who'd been on the job himself. Buckram, who started out walking a beat in the Gravesend section of Brooklyn and put in his time as a detective with Major Cases, eventually parlayed a saloon-born friendship into a stint as police commissioner of Portland, Oregon. He spent three years there, and got a ton of good press; the crime rate dropped, and the Portland cops went up a few notches in everybody's esteem, not least of all their own.

He'd liked the job, but he missed New York every single day he was out there. Portland was a good place, it had a lot to offer, but it wasn't New York, and that was the thing about New York—if you loved it, if it worked for you, it ruined you for anyplace else in the world.

Out of lust and boredom, he had an affair with a TV reporter, and that only made things worse. He'd had affairs before, he neither chased women nor ran away from them, but affairs seemed to mean more in Portland, somehow, and by the time this one had run its course, so had his marriage. His wife, who'd never wanted to go to Oregon in the first place, moved back to New York and took the kids with her. He stayed where he was, hating it now, and when the New York offer came he had to hold himself in check to keep from appearing too eager. If he didn't get the job, he decided, he was moving back anyway. He'd go into private security, he'd open a restaurant, he'd sell shoes, but whatever it was he'd damn well do it in New York.

He got the job. The mayor who gave it to him wanted someone who would jump right in and make waves, and Buckram gave him what he wanted and then some. He'd tried out some theories in Portland, his own and some other people's, and he'd learned how to make a police force proactive, not just responding to crime but targeting career criminals and getting them off the street. Crime dropped when there were fewer criminals out there to commit it, and there were perfectly legitimate ways to take them out of the game without trampling all over their civil rights. It had worked in Portland, and it damn well worked in New York.

He did so well it cost him the job.

There's no limit to what a man can accomplish if he doesn't care who gets the credit.

He'd heard the line somewhere, and he didn't know the source and wasn't sure of the precise wording, but a few weeks ago he'd been fooling around on his home computer and he dummied it up, printed it out, and kept forgetting to pick up a frame for it. It belonged on the wall over his desk, but what was the point? He'd learned the lesson, though not in time to save his job.

Because the commissioner's job wasn't just about covering asses. It was also about kissing one—specifically, the mayor's. And this particular mayor had wanted the credit for every positive thing that happened on his watch, and couldn't stand it when any of it went to somebody else.

Buckram had known that (though no one had known the full megalomaniacal extent of it) but the media loved him and he was great on camera, the expensive clothes showing to good advantage on his lean frame, the natural wave in his styled hair, the easy smile on his lips, the glint in his Irish blue eyes. The mayor was pudgy, with a narrow chest and a potbelly, and a comb-over that might have been endearing on a humbler man. Buckram spoke in bracing sound bites; the mayor's on-camera remarks seemed harsh and mean-spirited at best, and out of context they often came across as heartless.

Three and a half years on the job, and the crime rate dropped and the streets got safer and people felt great about the city, and hotel room occupancy soared with an increase in convention bookings, because suddenly New York was everybody's favorite city. Foreign tourists flocked to it, and midwesterners, who for years wouldn't even change planes at JFK, were pouring in, rushing to see lousy musicals and stand in line outside cookie-cutter theme restaurants on Fifty-seventh Street.

The mayor got plenty of credit, and deservedly so, but he wanted it all, and Buckram was too cocky to get out of the way whenever somebody showed up with a camera and a notepad. So one day he was out of work, and the city was up in arms about it for a few minutes, but the crime rate kept on dropping and the tourists kept on coming, and that was that. The mayor got re-elected and Fran Buckram signed up with a lecture bureau, giving after-dinner speeches for $3,500 a pop.

He was forty-three when he got the job, and had just turned forty-seven when he had to give it back. Now he was fifty-three, and the mayor had finished his second term a hero, elevated to that status by his performance during 9/11 and its aftermath. The voters would have given him a third term—they'd have made him dictator for life if they'd had the chance, and awarded him both ears and the tail in the bargain—but constitutional term limits forced him to step down, and his replacement was halfway through his first year in office and seemed to be doing just fine.

The new man had three and a half years to go, plus four more if he ran again and won. So it was far too early for anyone to enter the lists to succeed him, but people had a pretty good idea who was in the running.

Buckram's name was at the top of the *Maybe* column.

And that was what this dinner was about. He knew that, and his three dinner partners knew it, and so did Claudia Gerndorf and that demi-hoodlum from Local 802 of the Amalgamated Federation of Widget Makers. Anyone who recognized the four of them could figure out why they were sitting there together, washing down sole meunière with pinot grigio.

Meanwhile, he told his cop stories. The three men seemed to enjoy them.

"NOW THAT'S INTERESTING," MAURY Winters said. "To your left, four men sitting together, the waiter's just now pouring their wine."

She looked, saw three men in suits and one in a blazer, and asked what was interesting about them.

"That they're here together," the lawyer said. "Recognize anybody?"

"No," she said, and considered. "The one in the blazer looks familiar. Who is he?"

"Nobody at the moment, but a few years ago he was police commissioner."

"Of course, Buckley, but no, that's not right. Buckman?"

"Buckram, sweetheart. Like a fine binding. First name Francis, but don't call him Frank. He prefers Fran. The other men, well, I recognize two of them, and they're both real estate *machers,* and so's the third, I'd be willing to bet you. Do you suppose they've banded together to help our former top cop find an apartment?"

"I have a feeling the answer is no."

"But to find a job, that's another possibility altogether. How's your tornado?"

Her dish was tournedos Rossini, filet mignon capped with foie gras, tender as butter and wonderfully savory, and his mispronunciation was an affectation, a part of the diamond-in-the-rough image he'd perfected. His gray hair was shaggy, his suit imperfectly tailored for his fleshy physique, and his tie showed the odd food stain. She wasn't sure of his age but knew he was well into his sixties, and the years showed in his face and carriage. And yet he remained an extremely attractive man, and how fair was that? If a woman let herself go like that, no one would look at her twice. With a man, well, if he had the right sort of energy emanating from him, you overlooked some of the flaws, called the rest *character,* and wound up with wet panties.

"My tornado is gale force," she told him. "If there's a trailer park in the neighborhood, its days are numbered. How's your veal?"

"It would make a PETA activist rethink his whole program. I'll tell you, it's a pleasure to watch a woman with an appetite."

"Oh?"

"People say they hate to eat alone. What's so terrible? You go to a nice restaurant, you take a book, you eat a meal at your own pace. Listen to me, but do I listen to myself? I'm out five nights a week with someone adorable, and they're all either trying to lose weight or trying to keep from gaining it, and either way, as far as their value as company, you'd be better off going to a whorehouse with Ed Koch. See, you laugh. They don't get my jokes, or maybe they just don't think they're funny. You eat, you laugh, Susan, you can call me for free legal advice for the rest of your life."

"As long as I keep on eating and laughing."

"Why would you want to stop? You never gain an ounce, you got a better figure than the models."

"Why do you go out with them, Maury?"

"Besides the obvious?"

"You don't have to take them to L'Aiglon for that."

"Them I don't take to L'Aiglon. Them I take to someplace flashier, so they can say they've been there. But what they are is arm candy, darling. *Look at that* alte kacher, *out with that sweet young thing. He must have something, the old bastard.*" He shrugged. "Anyway, they're cute, they're cuddly, they're adorable, they're like a kitten or a rabbit. You don't expect to have a conversation with a bunny rabbit, do you?"

"It would be one-sided."

"But you'd still want to pet it," he said, "and stroke it behind the ears."

"So why did you call me? Old times' sake?"

They'd had an affair, if you wanted to call it that, a dozen years ago, not long after her marriage came apart. They'd already known each other—her ex was an assistant district attorney whom Maury had befriended after excoriating him in court, and who had since crossed the aisle and set up as a defense attorney, and you could bet she'd never call *him* for free legal advice, the asshole.

He hadn't taken her to L'Aiglon, but it had been something comparable, Le Cirque or La Côte Basque, something French and fancy, and over Drambuie he told her he kept an apartment in town, for when he had to stay over, and he'd like nothing better than to show it to her.

She'd said, "You're married, right?"

"Absolutely!"

"Good," she'd said. "Because you're a very attractive man, Maury, and I'd love to spend a little quality time in your apartment, but I don't want to get involved any more than you do."

"What I figured," he said. "The fellow who introduced me to Drambuie told me you had to sip it and savor it and make it last, but you know what?" He tossed off his drink. "Turns out he was full of crap. Drink up, Susan. I've had a yen for you for the past hour. Well, longer than that, but you were married. C'mon, how long are you gonna keep an old man waiting?"

Now, twelve years later, he said, "Why did I call you? For the pleasure of your company. And because it doesn't hurt for the world to see me now and then with a woman of substance instead of an adorable airhead. *A woman like that, she could be with anybody, and she's with him? What's he got?*"

"What's he got? He's got an awfully good line."

"My stock-in-trade. This silver tongue has kept a lot of worthy young men out of prison. Of course"—he showed her the tip of it—"that's not all it's done."

She felt herself blushing. "Dirty old man."

"C'est moi, chérie."

"Speaking of prison . . ."

"Oh, is that what we were speaking of?"

"I see they made an arrest in my friend's murder."

"She showed you an apartment. It's not like you were sorority sisters in Chi Zeta Chi."

"My acquaintance, if you like that better, but—"

"Now that was one joke you didn't get. Chi Zeta Chi? In Yiddish that means Chew, Grandpa, chew."

"They arrested a writer. The name's familiar, but I've never read anything of his. Blair Creighton?"

"John Blair Creighton, but he drops the John on his books. And that's as much as we're going to talk about him, or your late lamented real estate person." And, when she looked blank, he added, "Because I'm representing him, sweetie, and I can't talk about the case."

"You're representing him? But he . . ."

"Killed somebody, except we don't know that, do we? And that's what I do, darling. People kill each other, and I represent the survivors."

WHEN THE COFFEE WAS poured, Irv Boasberg wondered aloud if anyone had dessert anymore. "My granddaughter turned down a piece of Shirley's chocolate cake last week," he said, "announcing that she had to watch her weight. A, she's not fat to begin with, and B, she's all of eleven years old."

"I don't know what it is, society or the parents," Avery Davis said. "If they're not obese you find yourself worrying that they're anorexic. Life doesn't cut a person much slack nowadays, does it? Fran, you could have dessert. I'll bet you haven't put on an ounce since you walked a beat."

"If he hasn't," Hartley Saft said, "maybe that's *why* he hasn't. How'd you escape the cops-and-doughnuts syndrome, Fran?"

"Just dumb luck," he said. "I never had a sweet tooth."

"That's luck, all right," Davis said. "I don't have dessert because if I did I'd want six of them. Now there's a man who's not skipping dessert, and he looks as though sometimes he has the whole pie. And, unless we're supposed to believe that's his niece, the pleasures of the table aren't the only sort he enjoys. Do I know him? Because he looks familiar."

"All fat men look alike," Saft said, "but I know what you mean. I don't know him, but I've seen him before."

"Probably in restaurants," Boasberg said.

"I think you're right, Irving, and if it's the man I'm thinking of he's always got something young and fluffy across the table from him. As a matter of fact, they're usually younger and fluffier than the current example. She looks as though she actually has a thought in her head from time to time."

"Less of a tootsie and more of a trophy wife," Avery Davis suggested.

"His name's Maury Winters," Buckram told them. He'd spotted the lawyer when he first sat down, and would have said hello if he'd caught his eye. "He's a criminal lawyer, a good one, and like most of them he's something of a character."

"Of course," Davis said. "I've seen him on television. He was on *Larry King,* along with three or four other experts, talking about that little girl in Colorado. You never had anything to do with the Boulder Police Department, did you, Fran?"

"I taught them everything they know."

They laughed. "He had one great line, Winters did. I think he must have used it before, because he sort of shoehorned it in. It didn't particularly fit, but he wasn't going to let that stop him. He prefers murder trials, and do you know why?"

"I know the line," Buckram said, "and you're right, he's used it before."

"One less witness," Davis said.

"That's it." He took a sip of coffee. The others had ordered decaf, but his was the real deal. He told himself decaf never tasted right to him, but maybe that was only true if he knew it was decaf. Maybe he just plain wanted the caffeine.

Either way, L'Aiglon d'Or's coffee was delicious, a richly aromatic French roast you could sip like a tawny port. He put his cup down and said, "Maury must be feeling good. Great food and attractive company, and he's got a murderer to defend."

"Oh?"

"That writer, I forget his name. The one who strangled that woman in the Village."

"Crichton," Boasberg said.

"That's a different writer, but now I remember, and you're close. It's Creighton."

"And you figure he did it?"

"I don't know enough to have an opinion," he said, "but they've evidently got enough to charge him. That doesn't necessarily mean they've got enough to convict him, far from it, but it shows you they believe he did it, and they're usually right."

"Anybody read anything he's written?"

Nobody had.

"Well, now he's got something new to write about," Avery Davis said. "You ever think about writing a book yourself, Fran?"

"I've thought about it."

"And?"

"I've been approached a few times."

"I should think so. It'd sell a few copies."

"I don't know, Avery. In this town, maybe, but would anybody out in Idaho give a rat's ass? And what do I know about writing a book?"

"Would you have to write it yourself?"

"Oh, everybody was quick to tell me I'd never have to touch a keyboard or look at a computer screen. I'd work with a writer." He rolled his eyes. "God knows there's enough of them in this town. Of course most of them are loaded down with work. That's why it's standing room only every night in Stelli's."

"There's one I can think of who's going to have some time on his hands," Saft offered. "Unless our fat friend over there gets him off the hook in a hurry."

"There you go. I'll collaborate with the Charles Street Strangler. Maybe that'll get their attention in Pocatello."

They laughed, and Boasberg said, "You could just tell some stories like the ones you told tonight."

"War stories? No, they'd expect more than that. Some personal history, the story behind the story, and how much of that does a man want to get into? Plus what what's-his-name would call 'the vision thing.'"

He'd intended that as an opening, and they seized it as such; he caught Avery Davis shooting a glance at each of his companions before leaning forward and narrowing his eyes. "The vision thing," he echoed. "You know, Fran, a lot of people are looking at you with more than the bestseller list in mind. I'm sure you're happy living where you are, but I'd be surprised if you haven't thought now and then of moving a few blocks uptown and closer to the river."

In other words, Gracie Mansion.

"And you've probably thought about some of the changes you'd like to implement if you found yourself living there."

He considered this. "Be hard not to," he acknowledged.

"Impossible, I should think."

"You pick up a paper or turn on New York One, you hear speculation. Not so much now, but a year or two ago, say."

"A lot of people thought you might take a shot at it last fall."

"The timing was wrong," he said. "I'd have been running against Rudy, and he wouldn't have been running, and you just look like you're kicking a guy when he's down, between the prostate cancer and the divorce. Of course that was before anyone knew he'd turn out to be a national hero, which made running against him completely impossible." He grinned. "So now they're talking about 2005, and it's way too early for that, but even so you have to think about it. Whether it's what you want, and what you'd do if you got it."

"And?"

"And what do I see myself doing? Or at least championing?"

He let the moment stretch, then looked off into the middle distance. "Landmark areas," he said. "Every time an older building gets pulled down, a piece of the city's history is lost forever. It's vital that we protect what we've got by designating more landmark areas, and that doesn't mean only the remote past, the obviously historical. What about the white-brick apartment buildings that went up in the sixties? They're not building any more of them, and once they're gone they're gone forever. Fortunately there's still time to save them."

"Landmark areas," Hartley Saft said.

"Hand in hand with that," he went on, "is rent control. A noble experiment, as I'm sure you'll agree . . ."

They were nodding, a little more sanguine now. Brace yourselves, he thought.

". . . but time has made serious inroads on rent control, and both working-class and middle-class tenants are being priced out of the market. All new housing, including conversions of factory and warehouse space to residential use, has to come under rent control, and the process of decontrol has to be stopped in its tracks and reversed. Otherwise where are we?"

God, the looks on their faces! He kept his own straight for as long as he could, then let his merriment show.

"Jesus Christ," Irv Boasberg said.

"Guys, I'm sorry. I couldn't resist. Look, I'm not about to make a policy statement, on or off the record. At this stage you probably know as much as I do about what I'd be likely to do as mayor of New York."

"If nothing else," Davis said, "you just demonstrated a subtler sense of humor than the last man to hold the office."

Or a stronger suicidal streak, he thought, talking up rent control and preservationism to three titans of New York real estate.

"SWEETHEART, YOU'LL EXCUSE ME," Maurice Winters said, and pushed back from the table. "I'll be right back."

He didn't wait for a response, but headed straight for the men's room. When his bladder prompted him, social graces were a luxury he couldn't afford. He had to respond in a hurry.

And then, of course, he would wind up standing in front of the urinal trying to trick his prostate into getting out of the way long enough to allow the stream to flow. Magically, peeing became the only thing more difficult than resisting the urge to pee. It was a hell of a thing, getting old, and the only thing that made it remotely attractive was when you considered the alternative.

Which was something he'd been forced to consider more and more lately, ever since he'd been diagnosed with prostate cancer.

Eight months now. Back in August his internist did a PSA and made an appointment for him with a urologist, and then the fucking Arabs killed three thousand people for no reason whatsoever, and he canceled the appointment and forgot to make another until his internist called him, all concerned, and got him into the urologist's office for an ultrasound and a biopsy in early November. Both procedures were literally a pain in the ass, and they only confirmed what everyone had pretty much known from the PSA, which was that he had prostate cancer, and that it had very likely metastasized.

There were choices, the urologist assured him. You could have surgery or you could have radiation, and if you took the latter course you could have radioactive seeds implanted that avoided some of the worst effects of radiation therapy. What he'd recommend, himself, was surgery first, to remove the prostate and if nothing else make urination less problematic, followed by a course of radiation to zap whatever adventurous cancer cells might have migrated outside the walls of the prostate gland.

And then, should the cancer return, then they could knock it back with hormonal treatments. What that amounted to, he learned, was chemical castration, although nobody liked to call it that because it sounded as though they were going to cut off your balls. Which they sometimes did as an alternative, as it saved you from having to go in for the shots, and it was guaranteed one hundred percent effective. Not at curing the cancer, but at shutting down your production of testosterone, which propelled the cancer.

It also shut down your sex life. Coincidentally, Winters had run into an old friend, a law school professor in his eighties who'd still been sexually active until he'd had the shots as a last-ditch effort to delay the cancer long enough to—what, die from something else? "I dreaded this," the fellow told him. "I thought this means the end, you're not a man anymore, you've got nothing to live for. But the shots took away everything, including the desire, the interest. I couldn't do anything, but I didn't want to do anything. I didn't care!"

Wonderful.

If not caring was such a blessing, he could take a fistful of sleeping pills and not care about anything.

He did some research, and the surgery the urologist wanted to do wasn't like having a hangnail trimmed. Assuming you didn't die on the table, you could look forward to a minimum of several months of incontinence and impotence, either or both of which could turn out to be permanent. So you walked around leaking pee into an adult diaper, and you still had the desire for sex but couldn't do anything about it, and, the best part of all, the cancer came back and you died anyway.

He talked to two men who'd had radiation, and they both said the same thing: *If I'd known it was going to be anywhere near that bad, I would never have put myself through it.*

Wonderful.

"Finally," the doctor said, reluctantly, "there's watchful waiting. You come in every three months for a PSA, and we keep a close eye on it, and see how it goes." Why, he wondered, did he have to come in for those PSAs? "So we'll know how you're doing." But if he'd already decided that he wasn't going to have any treatment, regardless of his PSA score? "Well, we want to keep tabs on this thing. We want to keep our options open."

"I'll tell you," he said, "looking back, I've got just one regret. If I had it all to do over again, I'd never have gone into criminal law." He'd waited, and the poor schmuck had to ask what he'd have chosen instead, and he said, "Malpractice litigation. It barely existed as a specialty when I got out of law school, but if I'd seen the handwriting on the wall I could have cashed in. And even if I didn't make so much money, think of the emotional satisfaction!"

And he got the hell out of there and never went back.

He was taking herbs now, which maybe did him some good and maybe didn't, he'd have had to take another PSA to tell. It was only a needle stick, any doctor could do it, but for what?

He hadn't said a word to anybody. Except his old law professor, but he wasn't going to tell anybody, and, hormone shots or no hormone shots, it didn't look as though the guy was going to be around too long. Except for Ruthie, there wasn't really anybody he had to tell.

Sooner or later he'd have to tell her. They'd been married forever, they went down to City Hall two days after he found out he'd passed the bar exam, and if he lived seven more years they'd celebrate their fiftieth. He'd be seventy-four, and it would be nice to live longer than that, it would be nice to last until ninety if you could walk and talk and think straight, but he'd settle for seventy-four. If somebody offered him a deal, seventy-four, no more no less, he'd sign on the dotted line.

The urologist couldn't offer him that deal. He stood as good a chance on his own, thank you very much.

And, in the meantime, he'd just enjoyed every minute of a wonderful dinner with a beautiful woman, and he wasn't done enjoying the evening, not by a long shot.

And, miracle of miracles, he'd managed to empty his bladder.

Washing his hands, he looked at himself in the mirror. Everybody

said he looked terrific, which was a neat trick because he was a fat old
man who hadn't looked so great when he was a thin young man, so how
terrific could he possibly look, cancer or no cancer? But he didn't look
so bad.

He went back to the table, and evidently he'd been gone long enough
for the waiter to bring dessert and for Susan to answer her own call of nature, because she was absent and his cheesecake and her fresh strawber-
ries were on the table, along with a pot of coffee and two cups.

He sat down and regarded his cheesecake, and his mouth watered. He
picked up his fork, then decided he could wait. It wouldn't take her that
long, she didn't even have a prostate gland.

He reached for the coffee, stopped himself when he felt a hand on his
thigh.

Jesus Christ, she was under the table! What did she think she was going to do down there?

And wasn't *that* a stupid question?

If there was any doubt, it was erased quickly enough. Her hand
moved to his groin, her fingers worked his zipper, and in seconds he felt
her breath on him, and then she had him in her mouth.

He sat there, thrilled beyond description, and wondered if anyone in
the room had a clue what was going on. Someone must have seen her get
under the table. Did anyone know? And did it matter?

Oh, hell, nothing mattered but the sheer pleasure of it. It wasn't just
that he was getting a secret blow job in a public place from a beautiful
woman, but that it was a remarkably artful blow job in the bargain. And
she was in no hurry, either, she was taking her time, the little angel, she
was making it last.

Well, she was already having her dessert, wasn't she? Feeling devilish himself, he took a bite of the cheesecake.

"I'VE HAD MY PROBLEMS with Rudy," Fran Buckram said, "but most
of them were with him personally, not with the directions he took. Most
of my policies probably wouldn't differ all that greatly with what you saw
for the past eight years."

"We're in better shape than we were eight years ago, Fran. Of course
we've got a financial crunch we didn't have this time last year, thanks to
9/11."

"And that'll be a lot better or a lot worse by the time 2005 rolls
around, so there's not much point in telling you how I'd respond to it. I
can't contrast my style with Michael's because he doesn't have one yet."

"Rudy Lite," Hartley Saft suggested.

"As a manager, well, I'd do what I did at One Police Plaza, and in

Portland before that. Pick good people, make them accountable, and then let them do their jobs. Keep my eyes on them and my hands off."

They were nodding. Good.

"I'd try to run the city more for the benefit of the people who live in it and less for the convenience of those who drive in to do business and then go home. That might mean pedestrianizing parts of Midtown Manhattan, it might mean limiting truck deliveries to off-peak hours. I'd need to run feasibility studies first, but those are both attractive options."

More nods. They were less certain about this, but open to it.

He elaborated, giving them an informal version of the speech that brought him $3,500 when he delivered it to civic groups and fraternal organizations. He'd increase the budgets for the Parks Department and the library. He'd keep support for the arts a priority, but he'd hold off telling a museum curator what to hang on his walls. All in all, he'd be guided by the principle that a city had to serve its citizenry, guaranteeing their personal security and well-being while providing the most supportive framework possible for their growth and self-realization.

He broke off when the waiter brought Hartley Saft a brandy and refilled the coffee cups, and when the man was out of range he said, "Without being obvious about it, you might want to glance over at Maury Winters's table."

"He's all by himself," Boasberg said. "What did she do, walk out on him?"

"If she did, it didn't break his heart. She left him the cheesecake, and I have to say he looks happy with it."

"More than happy," Buckram said. "Try ecstatic."

"I grant you he's enjoying himself."

"And she didn't walk out," he told them, "and she didn't go to the can, either."

"What did he do, devour her? Little black dress and all?"

"You're closer than you realize," he said. "I think she's under the table."

"How the hell—"

"I'm a trained observer," he said. "Once a cop, always a cop. Look at the expression on his face, will you? That's more than cheesecake."

GOD, IT WAS EXQUISITE.

The feeling of utter submission, kneeling unseen before him, servicing him invisibly, almost anonymously. And, one with it, the sense of being wholly in control.

His penis in her mouth was an iron rod in a velvet glove, so sweetly soft on the surface, so iron-hard within. She cupped his balls in her hand, ringed the base of his cock with her thumb and forefinger. He gasped when she tucked the tip of one finger into him, and she thrilled at that, and at the way the sphincter tightened and relaxed, tightened and relaxed . . .

She was in charge, and she at once played him like a flute and conducted him like an orchestra, raising the pitch, building toward a climax, then easing off, tightening her grip on the base of his penis to choke off his orgasm before it could start. Then building again, moving toward the finish, and backing off, and resuming, and . . .

There were women who hated to do this. There were women who point-blank refused to do it. Fewer with each generation, from what she heard, and girls Chloe's age seemed to regard a quick BJ as an easy way to satisfy a man, less intimate than intercourse and not much more than a step up from a goodnight kiss. Her own generation saw it as more intimate, and her mother's generation saw it as unacceptably intimate.

Did her mother give her father blow jobs? Well, not now, obviously, but when he was alive? That was something she didn't want to think about, so she forced herself, pushing against the resistance, and for a moment she became her mother and she was on her knees sucking her father's cock.

God, if people could read her mind they'd lock her up . . .

Maury played his own part so perfectly. Not a sound, except for that one sharp intake of breath when she'd worked her finger into him. He'd been silent since then, and utterly passive, and he kept his hands above the table, not reaching down to stroke her hair, or, God forbid, holding her head in place. He didn't need to be in control, he could let her be in control, and this was delicious, just delicious, and she could let it go on forever, but she couldn't, not really, and it was time, wasn't it? Wasn't it time?

This time she let the crescendo reach all the way to the coda, and his semen spurted and she drank it down and fancied that she could feel the energy of it radiating outward through her whole body all the way to her fingers and toes. She kept him in her mouth and sucked him, but gently now, gently, and felt him soften and shrink, and she sipped the last drop from him and wiped him dry with her napkin and tucked him back into his pants. And zipped him up.

She couldn't have enjoyed the orgasm more if it had been her own.

After a long moment she said, softly, "Is anyone looking our way?"

"I can't tell."

"It doesn't matter," she murmured, and reached to remove an earring. She got out from under the table, holding up the earring in triumph, and refastened it to her ear before sitting down again.

He looked transformed, radiant. "You amaze me," he said.

"If anyone was watching," she said, "they saw a woman who dropped an earring and managed to find it again."

"Unless they've been glancing over here off and on for the last ten minutes."

"Is that how long I was down there?"

"I wasn't checking my watch, you'll be surprised to learn. You don't care if anybody knows what just happened, do you?"

"No."

"You even get a kick out of the idea."

"A little bit," she admitted. "I'm a naughty girl."

"I was planning to take you home and punish you," he said, "but I don't know if I've got the strength. And I've got a bail hearing first thing in the morning."

"For the case we're not allowed to talk about?"

"I'm allowed, I'm just not inclined. And yes, for my newest client."

"I should keep you up all night and let the bastard rot in jail. But I don't mind an early night myself, Maury. Get the check and you can put me in a cab."

"You won't feel . . ."

"Unfulfilled? What we just did, I think I got as much out of it as you did."

On the street she said, "I didn't even tell you about my new artist. A black kid, he walked in while I was talking to you the other day with pictures of the sculptures his crazy uncle has been making out of junk he finds on the street."

"Good?"

"Better than that, I think. Important. You're going to buy a piece."

"All right."

"I'm giving him a show in the fall, and you'll get to see it ahead of time, and we'll pick out the best piece together. Unless you don't like the work, but I think you will."

"You generally know what I like."

She squeezed his hand. "It'll be late October or early November. And don't worry, I know I've got jury duty the beginning of October. Maybe I'll be on your jury."

"My jury?"

"Your new client."

He shook his head. "We won't go to trial until the spring," he said. "Maybe later than that. And you couldn't be on the jury anyway."

"Because I'm smart and chic and in the arts?"

"Because you knew the deceased, because you've already formed an opinion about the guilt or innocence of the defendant, and because you've enjoyed an intimate relationship with defense counsel."

"*Enjoyed* is the word, all right. Also *intimate*. Maury? Do you think a blow job is more intimate or less intimate than fucking?"

"I think that's your cab," he said, and stepped to the curb and hailed it.

"IF HE COULD RUN for reelection tomorrow," Avery Davis said of the current mayor, "he'd win in a walk. But a lot can happen in three and a half years. Everybody's been waiting for him to step on his dick."

"He hasn't so far," Saft pointed out.

"No, he's handled himself well, which doesn't surprise me, I must say. He's the mayor now, not the head of a private corporation, and he's bright enough to know the difference and behave accordingly."

Boasberg said, " 'Yes, I tried marijuana. And I enjoyed it.' "

"So? That makes a refreshing change from *I never inhaled*. But it's all moot, because he's not going to run again in 2005. Either he'll decide he's had enough fun in politics, or he'll try for Albany in oh-six. Pataki's going to win this year, everybody knows that, and four years later his second term'll be up and why wouldn't Mike want to trade up?"

But wouldn't he first run for reelection and use that as a springboard for Albany?

"He'll have to pledge that he's going to serve a full term. If he waffles it'll hurt him during the campaign, and if he reneges on his promise that'll hurt him, too. But, as we've been saying all evening, it's all a long ways off."

Everyone agreed that it was.

"Now the big question," Irv Boasberg said. "Mets or Yankees?"

Buckram laughed, and they joined him. "Naturally, I support all the local teams. It's my private opinion that anyone over the age of sixteen who still cares deeply about the outcome of a sports event more than half an hour after it's over is a pretty clear case of arrested development. Unless he's on the team, of course. Or owns it."

"You read my mind," Boasberg said. "I was just thinking of a particular club owner, and you can probably guess which one. But he *is* a case of arrested development, so the hell with him."

"I agree all across the board," Saft said, "except when it comes to the Knicks. That's different."

Someone told a sports story, and that led to another. A few minutes later Avery Davis looked up from signing the check and said, "Well, I think this was a good meeting, Fran. We'll walk away from it with a better sense of who you are, and hopefully you'll know us a little better as well."

Outside, Davis held up a hand, and half a block away a limousine blinked its lights in acknowledgment. "I'm going to run these bozos home," he said. "How about you, Fran? Can we drop you anywhere?" He said thanks, but he thought he'd like to walk off some of his dinner. "Which is one more reason why you haven't put on weight," Davis said.

The two other men got into the limo, and Davis drew Buckram aside. "You made a good impression," he said. "It's early days, but, just so you know, if the time comes that you decide to take your shot, I think you'll find the support you need."

"That's very good to know," he said.

"It's always a consideration."

It was, he thought. But first he'd have to figure out if he really wanted the job.

five

JOHN BLAIR CREIGHTON looked at his attorney, standing there with his thumbs hooked under his suspenders and his stomach pushing forcefully against his shirtfront, and decided the man looked like Clarence Darrow—or, more accurately, like the actor playing Darrow in *Inherit the Wind*. Well, he thought, if the man had to imitate someone, he could do worse. Darrow, as he recalled, generally won.

"Your Honor," Winters was saying. "Your Honor, you can see how little regard Ms. Fabrizzio has for her own case. Her office is trying to imprison my client before trial because they realize it's the only chance they'll get."

"Ah, Mr. Winters," the judge said. "I suppose you feel the best way to demonstrate confidence in the prosecution's case would be to release your client on his own recognizance."

"That's exactly what they should do," Winters said, "if only out of good sportsmanship and a love of the arts. Mr. Creighton is a writer, Your Honor, and a respected one with a good critical reputation and an international readership. Unfortunately, our society doesn't always reward an artist commensurate with his talent, and—"

The assistant DA, a deceptively soft-faced blonde, sighed theatrically. "Mr. Winters's client is charged with strangling a woman, not splitting an infinitive. His talent or lack thereof—"

"His talent is unquestioned, Your Honor."

"He's charged with a capital offense," the judge pointed out. "High bail is hardly unusual in such circumstances."

"Excessive bail is punishment in advance, Your Honor. Mr. Creighton has no criminal record whatsoever, and his roots in the community make it clear he's no flight risk."

Fabrizzio said, "Roots in the community? The man doesn't have a job, he doesn't own property, he's unmarried, he lives alone . . ."

"He has children whom he sees regularly," Winters countered. "He's on the faculty of an important local university. Furthermore, Ms. Fabrizzio might want to note the distinction between unemployment and self-employment, should she one day leave the comforting embrace of the district attorney's office. Your Honor, jobs come and go, as do relationships, but my client has something more, something nobody would walk away from. The man is the statutory tenant of a rent-controlled apartment on one of the best blocks in the West Village. Does Ms. Fabrizzio honestly think . . ."

Laughter drowned out the rest of the sentence, and the judge let it build for a moment before he used his gavel. "A rent-controlled apartment," he said. "All right, Mr. Winters. Your point is taken. If your client can come up with fifty thousand dollars, he can go back and stare at his bargain-priced walls."

AND HE WAS STARING at them now. He didn't know what else to do.

It beat staring at the walls of a cell. That's where they'd put him when they arrested him, and that's where they stowed him again after the arraignment, after Winters had done such a skillful job of getting his bail reduced to a tenth of what the prosecution had been demanding. The lawyer had been beaming in triumph, but bail might as well have been five million dollars as far as he was concerned, or five hundred million, because $50,000 was four times what he'd had in the bank, checking and savings accounts combined, the day his callers turned out to be cops instead of Jehovah's Witnesses.

Of course you didn't have to come up with the whole amount, you could make use of a bail bondsman, but you had to have *some* cash, and he'd already written out a check for ten grand to Maury Winters as a retainer, and had rushed to move money from savings to checking to cover it. Because it wouldn't do to bounce a check to your attorney, would it?

Winters had wanted to know whom he could call to post bond, and he'd been unable to come up with a name. His publishers? Jesus, it had been hard enough to get the cheap bastards to spring for airfare and pocket money for that book-and-author luncheon in Kansas City. Posting bail for a writer with dwindling sales seemed out of the question.

His agent? Roz was a pit bull in negotiations, a mother hen when the words wouldn't come, but she wasn't rolling in cash herself. She'd set up shop three years ago, when they'd cut her loose after a merger. Until then she'd been his editor—they let him go, too—and it had seemed sensible enough to go with her, and his former agents didn't break down and weep when he told them he was leaving. Roz had made some sales for him since then, and she always returned his calls, but he didn't know that her fifteen percent commission bought him a *Get Out of Jail Free* card.

His friends? You made a list, Winters had told him, and you worked your way down it and made the calls, and you got a few dollars here and a few dollars there, and yes, it was marginally humiliating, but so was Rikers Island, and, you should pardon the expression, making a few phone calls wouldn't get you fucked in the ass.

Except it might, he thought. Metaphorically, anyway.

He'd begun making the list, but before he could finish it or start calling any of the names on it, he was out of jail. His ex-wife, the once and once again Karin Frechette (Karin Frechette-Creighton-Frechette, he'd called her, when she'd informed him she had decided to return to her maiden name), had put up her equity in the Montclair house as surety for his bond.

"Well, of course," she'd said, when he called to thank her. "How could I leave you in a jail cell?"

The conversation was a difficult one. He'd asked about the kids, whom he didn't see as often as his lawyer had suggested, and she said she didn't think they really knew what was going on. "But I suppose they will," she said, "before this is over. I just wish it would get cleared up in a hurry."

"You're not the only one."

"Listen," she said toward the end, "you're not going to catch a plane to Brazil or anything, are you?"

"Brazil?"

"I mean, you won't skip bail, will you? Because I'd hate it if they took the house away from me."

"I'm not going anywhere," he told her.

He went to the refrigerator, found a stray bottle of Beck's hiding behind a carton of orange juice. The juice was clearly past it and he poured it down the sink, then uncapped the beer and drank deeply from the bottle.

Brazil, for the love of God.

What she hadn't asked—what no one had asked, aside from the two cops, Slaughter and Reade—was whether or not he had done it.

THE PHONE RANG, AND he had to stop himself from reaching for it, waited dutifully while the machine picked up. "Blair? Hey, guy, been trying to reach you. Could you pick up?"

The manner was that of a close friend, a buddy, but the voice was not one he recognized, and the people he was that close to mostly called him

John. He waited, and the fellow left a number and an extension. And, not too surprisingly, no name.

On a hunch he rang the number but didn't punch in the three-digit extension, waiting until an operator came on the line and said, "*New York Post,* will you hold please?" He replaced the receiver and drank the rest of his beer.

All in all, he preferred the straightforward approach. "Mr. Creighton, my name's Alison Mowbray, with the *Daily News*. I'd love to give you a chance to get your side of the story in front of the public."

His side of the story.

"They'll try to persuade you that it's dangerous to get all the pretrial publicity flowing in the prosecution's direction," Maury Winters had told him, "and there's some truth in that, but we have to pick the time and the place, and most important the person we talk to. It's way too early, you haven't even been indicted yet."

He'd be indicted?

"You think you're less than a ham sandwich?" And, when he'd just stared in response, the lawyer had explained that one judge had said famously that any good DA could get a ham sandwich indicted. "A grand jury does pretty much what a prosecutor asks it to do, John. You ever been on a grand jury? You're stuck there every day for a month. After a week or so you're mean enough to indict a blind man for peeping in windows. You'll be indicted, and the sooner the better."

"Why's that?"

"Because, my friend, I'm happy to say I don't think much of their case. Usual procedure, I'm out there asking for postponements, looking to delay the start of the trial as long as possible. You know why? Because time's a great fixer. Witnesses disappear, they change their testimony, sometimes they're even considerate enough to drop dead. Evidence gets tainted and can't be introduced, or, even better, it gets lost. They lock it away somewhere and forget where they put it. Don't laugh, sonny boy, it happens more often than you'd think possible. I stall, and I'm a hell of a staller when I want to be, and some innocent little ADA like Fabrizzio, who's got a cute little ass on her, I don't know if you happened to notice, stands there with her mouth open and watches her whole case fall apart. My client's guilty and everybody knows it including his own mother and they have to give him a walk."

"But because I'm innocent . . ."

"Guilt, innocence, who ever said that's got anything to do with it? A case is strong or it's weak, and that's what we're dealing with here, not does she or doesn't she. Their case is weak as midwestern coffee, my friend. You ever been to the Midwest? You ever had coffee there? Then you know what I'm talking about. They got a roomful of drunks who saw you leave a bar with the dead girl. Not that she was dead at the time, but she got that way before too long, though exactly how long's a matter of opinion. They got evidence'll place you in her apartment, though how strong and solid it is remains to be seen."

"I already admitted I was in the apartment."

"Who says the jury's gonna get to hear that? Never mind, beside the point. You got a whole apartment full of evidence, all of which gets cleaned and scrubbed by this darling little faygeleh who couldn't have done better by us if we were the ones paying him. He sweeps, he dusts, he wipes, he mops, he vacuums—I tell my wife, all she wants to know is has he got two afternoons a week open. He's a jewel, this kid. Time he trips over the dead girl, he's got half the evidence stuffed in the garbage cans along with everybody else's in the building, so how can you tell whose is whose, and the rest of it's down the drain, and so's their case. You sure he's not your cousin?"

Winters hadn't waited for an answer. "Constitution says you're entitled to a speedy trial," he said, "and for a change that's what we want. Their mistake was arresting you as early as they did. Granted, there's pressure, a professional woman murdered in her own bed in a decent neighborhood. High-profile case, so you got all these newspaper readers thinking that could be me, that could be my daughter, that could be my sister, so why don't the cops get off their asses and do something? Case like that you want to be able to announce an arrest, and, my opinion, they jumped the gun. Now they got to indict you, and once they indict you they got to give you your speedy trial, and once that's over, my friend, you can forget the whole thing ever happened."

"Just like that?"

"Better yet, write about it. Don't forget, I want an autographed copy."

And if they were to drop the charges?

"They got that option, drop 'em and reinstate 'em later on. But they hate to do that because it makes them look like morons, tells the world they can't make a case. And later on that's what everybody remembers. *Hey, didn't they drop this case once already? What's the matter, they can't find the guy who did it so they're picking on this poor zhlub again?*"

MEANWHILE, HE WAS THE poor zhlub. And what was he supposed to do with himself?

His apartment—his legendary rent-controlled apartment, that even the judge had to agree he'd be crazy to jeopardize—was a good deal larger and more comfortable than a jail cell. Quieter, too. It was funny, but none of the books he'd read over the years, none of the TV shows, none of the prison movies, had suggested how fiercely noisy the place could be. But his apartment, on a lazy weekday afternoon, was as quiet as a grave.

THEY'D BURIED HER, OF course. Or did whatever they did, whoever they were. She must have had family, and they'd buried her or had her cremated, whatever they decided, whoever they were.

Or did they hold the body of a murder victim for a certain amount of time? He'd watched countless episodes of *Law & Order*, you'd think he'd have learned something about forensic procedures by now.

Then again, what did it matter?

Marilyn Fairchild.

He tried to remember what she looked like, but his own memory had been supplanted by the picture they'd run over and over in the papers and on television, a photo that must have been taken four or five years earlier. She'd had long hair then, and when he pictured her now that's what he saw, long hair, and he had to remind himself that the woman he'd gone home with had had short hair.

He remembered her voice, pitched low, with an edge to it. The voice had been part of the initial attraction, it had seemed to promise something, though he was unsure just what. A low voice was supposed to be sexy, and he had to wonder why. Was it some kind of latent gay thing? But her voice was neither mannish nor boyish. There was just something about it that managed to suggest he'd find the owner engaging.

Yeah, right.

His other images of her were more fragmentary, rendered so by the drinks he'd had before and after their time together. He remembered the look on her face when she paused on her way to the kitchen and glanced over her shoulder at him. He'd been turning the pages of a magazine, more a brochure, her office's portfolio of co-ops and condos for sale, and something made him look up, and she was looking at him. There'd been something enigmatic in her expression, something that even now kept the image in his memory, but before he could work it out she'd turned again, and when she came back with the bottle and glasses whatever it had been was gone.

He raised the beer bottle to his lips, remembered he'd finished it. There was booze in the house, unless the cops had gotten into it while they went through his things. They'd had a warrant, and they'd come back and searched the place after they took him to Central Booking, and predictably enough they'd left the place a mess. He wasn't what you'd call compulsively neat, and Karin had once accused him of being the third Collyer brother, but the clutter he lived with was his own, and it had taken him a while to restore some semblance of order (or manageable disorder) to the scene.

He checked, and the liquor was apparently untouched, and he left it that way and lit another cigarette instead. Drinking alone, he decided, was probably not the best idea in the world.

So what was he supposed to do? Drop by the Kettle?

He was free, he could go anywhere and do anything, but how free was he? Where could he go, when you came right down to it? What could he do?

Yesterday he'd forced himself to go out for a walk. Picked up a carton of Camels, bought coffee at Starbucks. They gave you a free cup of coffee when you bought a pound, and he'd sat at a window table and watched the people pass. He felt throughout as though he was being watched in turn, but the tables near his were unoccupied, the baristas too busy or too self-involved to notice him.

He'd finished the coffee and left, unable to shake the feeling that people were staring at him, recognizing him. Later, when he was hungry enough for dinner, he'd been unable to bring himself to leave the apartment. He wound up ordering Chinese food, and the kid from Sung Chu Mei was concerned only with getting paid and stuffing menus under the doors of the building's other tenants. He clearly had no idea he had just brought an order of beef with orange flavor to a man who'd been charged with murder.

And now it was a gorgeous day, New York at its best, and the thought of leaving his apartment was entirely without appeal. No, wrong, it was hugely appealing, but the appeal was more than offset by a reluctance to subject himself to the real or imagined stares of his fellow citizens.

Maybe he'd just stay put. For today, or maybe not just for today. That was one thing about New York—barring eviction, you never had to leave your apartment. You could stay inside 24/7, and, as long as the phone and the doorbell worked, you could arrange to provide yourself with everything you needed. Because everybody delivered—the deli, the liquor store, and all the restaurants, even the fancy ones.

He had plenty to read, a whole wall full of books. He wouldn't run out, not with two dozen Russian novels sitting there, the complete works of Tolstoy and Dostoyevsky and Turgenev, all bought during a spell of manic optimism and untouched since the day he'd put them on the shelves. And there were other books, ones he might actually want to read. (Although who was to say that now wasn't the time to get through *Crime and Punishment*?)

And every week the mailman would bring him fresh copies of *New York* and *The New Yorker*. Of course he'd have to go downstairs for the mail, the guy wouldn't bring it to his door, but he could wait until four in the morning, say, and slip silently out his door and down the stairs, returning with the mail before a neighbor could catch a glimpse of him.

The crazy part was that he could imagine himself sinking into that sort of existence. He didn't really believe it was likely, but his imagination was more than equal to the task of conjuring up a life of deliberate agoraphobia. A recluse, eyes darting around suspiciously at the slightest sound, hair uncut and beard unshaven, wearing the same clothes until they fell apart. (But was that necessary? Gap and Lands' End would clothe him if he called their 800 numbers, and damn near everything was available online. Dry cleaners would pick up and deliver. And no doubt there were barbers who'd make house calls, if the money was right.)

He shook his head, trying to shake off the life he was envisioning for himself. He decided the silence wasn't helping, and looked for a record to play. But no, the last thing he needed was to be forced to make choices. He put on the radio, found the jazz station, and listened to something he didn't recognize. There was a trumpet player, and he was trying to decide if it was Clifford Brown.

His mind wandered, and he was thinking of something else when the announcer ran down the personnel on the cut she'd just played. He realized as much after the fact, and thought of calling the station. He could do that, and she would never realize she was talking to an accused murderer. Unless she had caller ID, but even then—

Oh, really, did he honestly give a rat's ass who'd been playing the trumpet?

He was in jail, he realized. He was home, but he was in jail, and nobody could come along and bail him out of it.

six

J

ERRY PANKOW CAUGHT the two-thirty meeting at Perry Street. During the sharing he raised his hand early on, but when he didn't get called on right away he stopped trying. When the meeting ended he was angry with himself, so he left his keys on his chair and went around the corner to the Arab deli for a cup of coffee, then came back for the four o'clock meeting. This time he raised his hand and got called on, but he talked about something else, not what was most on his mind, because he'd decided that was something he should talk about with his sponsor.

He called her, and relaxed when he heard her voice. Funny how it worked. You relaxed in anticipation of the relief. He remembered times, fiercely hungover, shaking, when he'd stand at the bar and watch the bartender pour the drink. And then, before he even had the glass in his hand, he'd feel as if the drink were already in him, smoothing the rough edges, quieting the storm.

He said, "Oh, I'm glad you're in. There's something that's driving me crazy, and I really need to talk to you about it."

"So talk."

"Could I come over? Or meet you someplace?"

"Well . . ."

"I'm probably being paranoid, but I'd rather not do this over the phone."

"I've got somebody coming at six-thirty," she said, "but if you come over now we'll have time. I'll even fix you a sandwich, because I'm planning to have one myself."

The conventional wisdom in AA was that one ought to choose a sponsor of one's own sex, to keep sexual tension from undermining the relationship. That was fine for straights, but it wasn't that simple in gay

AA, where the term *pigeon-fucker* had been coined to label sponsors who took sexual advantage of sponsees. (He'd heard the term at his first meeting, and thought it was some kinky practice he'd somehow missed out on.) Most gay men did in fact have gay male sponsors, and it worked out most of the time, but, when his first sponsor had looked him dead in the eye and said, "Jer, I think I'm going to have to resign as your sponsor, because I'm starting to have feelings that get in the way," he'd decided his next sponsor wouldn't ever have to face that problem.

Lois Appling was a forty-something lesbian, a professional photographer and a serious amateur bodybuilder, who shared a loft on Greenwich Street with a woman named Jacqui. They'd both been sober a dozen years, and had been together for ten of those years, and sometimes he found himself wondering whether they'd reached that stage of Sapphic intimacy called Lesbian Bed Death, where you feel closer together than ever but, for some unfathomable reason, never have sex anymore. It was, he'd decided, none of his business, but he couldn't keep from wondering.

He'd called from a pay phone at Fourth and Charles, and Lois and Jacqui's loft was on Greenwich Street between Tenth and Christopher, so he would ordinarily have walked west on either Charles or Tenth. But that would have meant walking past either the front or the rear of the Sixth Precinct station house, which would ordinarily not have been something to think twice about, or even once, but not today, thanks all the same. And he didn't want to walk over to Christopher, which was a little bit out of his way, because at this hour on this nice a day it would be a little bit cruisier than he could stand. So he walked a block back to Perry Street, which added a full two blocks to the trip. He asked himself if he was being neurotic, and decided that he was, and so what?

"**I WENT TO TWO** meetings today," he said, "and I wound up deciding I didn't want to share this at a meeting. But I have to talk about it, and I need advice, or at the very least a sounding board, because I don't know what I should do."

"If you're thinking of selling your story to the *National Enquirer,*" she said, "I'd advise against it."

"My story?"

" 'I Cleaned Up after the Charles Street Strangler.' "

"Oh, please. You're going to think I'm an idiot."

"What I think of you," she said, "is none of your business."

"I feel better already. Oh, this is stupid. What it is, there's something I forgot to tell the police."

" 'I love you, Officer.' "

"Ha! No, I don't think so. Lois, there was something I saw that maybe was a clue, and I didn't say anything."

"Why?"

"Because I forgot. Because I was flustered, and I already felt like such an idiot, and they clearly thought I was hopeless, and it slipped my mind."

"If it was a clue," she said, "maybe they stumbled on it themselves, without Lord Peter's invaluable assistance."

"Lord Peter?"

"Lord Peter Wimsey, the talented amateur, without whom Scotland Yard would be powerless in the fight against crime. Don't you read books? Never mind, sweetie. Maybe they worked it out on their own."

"They couldn't have," he said, "because it wasn't something that was there. It was something that wasn't there."

"Huh?"

"A little turquoise rabbit," he said, "about so big, and it was one of three fetishes she had, and they were always together, grouped around the little dish of cornmeal, and when I got there the place was a mess, the bison and the bear were lying on their sides and the cornmeal was spilled, and—"

"Whoa," she said. "Cornmeal?"

"Yellow cornmeal, like you'd make cornbread with, in a little china saucer. Oh, why the cornmeal? That was for them to eat."

"For . . ."

"The three of them, the bison and the bear and the rabbit."

"Was she some kind of a flake?"

"It's traditional," he explained. "You're supposed to put out food for them."

"Like milk and cookies for Santa?"

"I suppose so. Anyway, the rabbit was missing, and since they never would have known it was there in the first place—"

"I get it. Maybe the killer took it."

"That's what I was thinking."

"As a souvenir. Instead of cutting off an ear or a clitoris, like any halfway normal person would do—"

"Jesus!"

"When you thought of it," she said, "how come you didn't call them?"

"Because I'm a cowardly custard."

"Bullshit. Nobody ever stayed sober on cowardice. We're all heroes."

"I was afraid to call."

"That's something else. What's the fear?"

"That they'll think I'm an idiot."

"You said they already think that."

"Yes, but—"

"What they think of is none of your business, anyway. Is that all?"

He thought for a moment. "Well, see, I'm out of it now. I had a horrible couple of hours, first finding the body and then being asked the same questions over and over and finally giving a formal statement. I mean, they were perfectly nice, they were almost too polite, but underneath all that respectful politeness it was obvious they despised me. And it's none of my business, right, but it's not much fun to be around."

"Of course it isn't."

"So why don't I just leave well enough alone? I mean, for all I know she dropped the rabbit days ago and its ear broke off and she threw it out. Or it got lost, or, I don't know . . ."

"The bear ate it."

"Actually, I thought of that myself. Early on, before I knew what I'd find behind Door Number One. It was just a nice little whimsical thought. I have to call them, don't I?"

"Yep."

"Because it's my civic duty?"

She shook her head. "Because it's driving you nuts," she said, "and you can't get it out of your head, so for God's sake tell them and be done with it."

He stood up. "Thank God you're my sponsor," he said.

ALAN READE SAID, "HE called *you*? Why the hell did he call you and not me?"

"I guess I'm cuter," Slaughter said.

"I was nicer to him than you were, man. I was the perfect Sensitive New Age Guy, treating him like a human being instead of a dizzy little flit."

"Maybe your sincerity came shining through," Slaughter suggested. "Did you even give him your card?"

"Of course I gave him my card. Call anytime, I told him. You think of anything, I don't care if it's the middle of the night, just pick up the phone."

"Maybe he tried you first and your line was busy."

"Musta been," Reade said. "Now what's this shit about a rabbit?"

"He called it a fetish, which to me is a sex thing, fur or high heels or leather, shit like that."

"Black rubber."

"Hey, whatever works for you, Alan. These are little figurines, the Indians carve 'em out in Arizona and New Mexico. You keep 'em around and feed 'em cornmeal."

"Cornmeal?"

"Don't worry about it. She had three of them, according to Pankow, and one was missing."

"The rabbit."

"Right. The others were a bear and a bison. You remember seeing them, because I have to say I don't."

"No."

"Well, he says they were there, and—"

"Wait a minute, it's coming back to me. On a little table, two little animals, and one was a buffalo. The other was pink—"

"Rose quartz, he said."

"—and I couldn't tell what it was, but I suppose it coulda been a bear. I don't remember any rabbit."

"That's the point. The rabbit was missing."

"Same size as the others?"

"A little smaller, he said. Maybe two and a half inches long."

"Does that include the ears? Never mind. What did you say, turquoise?"

"That's a kind of blue stone."

"Jesus," Reade said, "I know what fucking turquoise is. My wife's got this silver necklace, her brother gave it to her, and he's as light in his loafers as Pankow, incidentally. A turquoise rabbit, and he says it was there the week before?"

"Swears to it."

"I didn't see any kind of a rabbit in Creighton's apartment," he said, "unless you count the bunny on the cover of *Playboy*. But would you even notice something like that if you weren't looking for it?"

"This time we'll be looking for it."

"If we can find a judge who'll write out a warrant."

Slaughter, beaming, pulled a folded piece of paper from his jacket pocket. "All taken care of," he said. "Courtesy of Judge Garamond, the policeman's best friend."

Reade finished his coffee, pushed back his chair. "You want to go over there? It's a little early, he might be sleeping in."

"So we'll wake him up."

On the way Reade said, "Creighton seem to you like the type to take a souvenir?"

"No."

"Me neither. That's a serial killer thing, isn't it? I didn't see a whole lot of ritual in Fairchild's apartment."

"There wasn't all that much to see, thanks to Mr. Clean. But I agree with you, Alan. Looks of it, two drunks went to bed, and one of them strangled the other either in the act or afterward."

"I wonder how drunk he was."

"Pretty far gone, would be my guess. Say he's in and out of blackout, he could kill her and not know it. On his way out he's in the living room getting dressed, because we know from Pankow that she left her clothes in the living room so he probably did, too . . ."

"And he picks up the rabbit and puts it in his pocket, and the next day he doesn't remember killing her, and he doesn't know where the rabbit came from, either. In fact . . ."

"What?"

"Well, if he puts it away when he gets home, and when he wakes up he doesn't remember taking it *or* putting it away—"

"It could still be there," Slaughter said. "Even if he came across it in a drawer or a jacket pocket, he wouldn't see any reason why he had to get rid of it. By the way, I didn't call it a fetish in my application for a warrant. I called it a figurine."

"Good thinking."

"Why would he pick it up in the first place, you got any theories about that?"

"We already said he was drunk, right? And who knows what's gonna seem like a good idea to a drunk?" He shrugged. "Maybe he just likes rabbits."

THE DOWNSTAIRS DOORBELL SOUNDED, one long buzz. He was drinking a cup of coffee and set it down on his desk and looked at his watch. It wasn't quite nine yet, and who would be leaning on his bell at this hour? Some pest from the media? Or the Jehovah's Witnesses he'd been expecting last week?

Before he'd finished wondering, the buzzer sounded again, two bursts this time. And he knew who it was, because who else would so effectively distill impatience and lack of consideration into noise?

He pressed the intercom and said, "Yes?"

"Detectives Slaughter and Reade, Mr. Creighton. Okay if we come up?"

"No," he said.

"If you'd buzz us in, Mr. Creighton, it'd save making a scene in front of the neighbors."

It was *Mr. Creighton* now, he noticed, because they weren't in his space or his face, and the excessive familiarity could evidently wait until they were. "You're not supposed to ask me any more questions," he said, "and I don't have to talk to you, and I don't intend to."

"Mr. Creighton—"

"Go away," he said, and let go of the intercom button. He got all the way back to his desk before the next buzz. He ignored it, but when it was repeated he went and pressed the button again, told them again to go away.

"Mr. Creighton, we don't have any questions and you don't have to talk to us, but you have to let us in. We have a warrant."

"For what? You're going to arrest me again? You already arrested me, I'm on bail, remember?"

"A warrant to search your apartment."

"You already searched it!"

"It's a new warrant, Mr. Creighton, and—"

"Give me a moment," he said, and went to the phone and found the slip of paper with his lawyer's number. Would Winters be at his desk this early?

He was, and the first thing he did was assure Creighton he'd been right to call him. "You don't have to answer a question, you don't have to say a word," he said. "What you do have to do, though, is let 'em in if they got a warrant. Where are they now?"

"Downstairs in the vestibule," he said, and before he'd finished he heard them knocking on his door. "At least they were a minute ago. Somebody must have let them in, because they're upstairs pounding on my door and calling for me to open it."

"Don't open it yet."

"All right."

"Tell them you want to see the warrant before you'll open the door."

He delivered that message through the closed door to Slaughter and Reade. One of them—Reade, with the reedy voice—said they'd be happy to show him the warrant, but first he should open the door. He relayed messages back and forth between Winters and the cops. They wouldn't stick it under the door, but they compromised that he'd open the door a few inches with the chain latch on and he could read the warrant before letting them in.

He had the phone to his ear and Winters was telling him that the warrant had to be specific, that they couldn't search the place again for general evidence, that they had to be looking for something they hadn't known to look for earlier. And it would say what it was in the warrant.

His reading glasses were on the desk, so he had to squint, but the warrant was short and the part that was typed in was in larger print than the boilerplate. " 'A blue rabbit figurine,' " he read aloud.

"A blue what? Did you say rabbi or rabbit?"

"Rabbit."

"What the hell does that mean?"

"I have no idea."

"Last time you looked, were there any blue rabbits in your apartment?"

"No," he said. "No purple cows, either. What do I do now, Maury?"

"Let 'em in, and let me talk to one of them, and then stay on the phone with me until they're out of there. And not a word to them, not even agreeing it's a nice day out, which it isn't anyway, it looks like it's gonna rain. You got that?"

"All of it," he said, "including the weather report." And he opened the door and handed the phone to Slaughter. "My lawyer wants to talk to you," he said. "But I don't."

THEY WERE THERE FOR close to two hours, but it wasn't that bad. His lawyer chatted with him for a while, then put him on speakerphone with instructions to speak up if the cops pulled anything out of line. He picked up the magazine he'd been reading and poured himself a fresh cup of coffee and kept an eye on Slaughter and Reade, which wasn't difficult because the apartment consisted of a single room.

They took as long as they did because they were being thorough, not wanting to miss the mysterious blue rabbit if it was there to be found, and also because they were less cavalier in their search, probably because he was there watching them. Whatever the cause, the difference was palpable; first time around they'd made a mess, and now they were as neat as cadets preparing for inspection.

A blue rabbit. Had he ever in his life even seen a blue rabbit?

The critters came in all shapes and sizes, he thought, and in a wide variety of colors, but blue? Maybe some Luther Burbank of the rabbit world was working on it now, but so far he figured blue rabbits were pretty thin on the ground. Of course it wasn't a living breathing hopping rabbit they were looking for, it was a figurine, and they could be any color. You didn't have to manipulate the DNA of some little stone carving, did you?

Wait a minute . . .

Three little animals on the table alongside the couch. In her apartment, Marilyn Fairchild's apartment. He'd picked them up and set them down again, and was one of them a rabbit? And was it blue?

Maybe.

He seemed to remember it now, but he didn't know to what extent he could trust his memory. His imagination got in the way. That was a blessing for a writer, an imagination like his, but it could be a curse, because it was possible to imagine something vividly enough to convince yourself it was a memory.

And that was especially true when your memory was patchy anyway after a night of fairly serious drinking. He wasn't sure just how drunk he'd been, but going home with Marilyn Fairchild had not been the act of a sober man. De mortuis and all that, but you'd need a few drinks in you before a flop in the feathers with that husky-voiced predator seemed like a good idea.

And he'd done some drinking at her apartment. Just one drink, he'd for some reason insisted to the cops, but was that true? If so, it was a technicality, because he seemed to recall a rocks glass, devoid of rocks but brimful of Wild Turkey. And then, of course, he'd come home from her place and drunk himself to sleep, desperate to wash the memory of the encounter from his system.

So who knew what happened and what didn't? Maybe he'd had more than one drink at her place on Charles Street. Maybe she'd told him her name, her real name, and it hadn't registered. And maybe he'd seen the blue rabbit, and picked it up, and played with it.

If they were looking for it . . .

If they were looking for it, duh, that meant it wasn't on Charles Street anymore. Which meant what exactly?

That the killer had taken it away with him?

Maybe it was another Maltese falcon, the stuff that dreams were made of. And someone had traced the legendary Cypriot Rabbit to an apartment on Charles near Waverly, and killed its owner in order to gain possession of it.

Alternatively, maybe someone had killed the lady for reasons of his own—it probably wouldn't be too hard to come up with a couple—and had been unable to resist taking the rabbit home with him, as a memento of the occasion.

Jesus, suppose they found it in his apartment?

But they couldn't, not unless they planted it, because he hadn't taken it with him.

Or had he?

He didn't remember taking the rabbit with him, wasn't even sure he remembered seeing it there in the first place. But he didn't remember *not* taking it, either, because how could you recall a negative? And he could imagine taking it, out of resentment or petulance or just drunken absent-mindedness. Pick it up, look at it, and the next thing you know you're out the door and the damn thing's in your pocket.

If they found it . . .

All it would prove was he'd been there, and they already knew that, he'd blurted out an admission the first time around, before he knew better. Maury had said his admission might not be admissible in court, and the blue rabbit would be, but there was sure to be physical evidence putting him at the scene, no matter how good a cleanup job had been done by the fellow who discovered the body.

But it would prove he'd taken the rabbit and lied about it. And it was direct physical evidence, something she owned that was now in his apartment, and it was small and personal, and it would look like a murderer's souvenir, it would look like that and nothing else.

Jesus Christ, a little blue rabbit could put a rope around his neck.

Not literally. Not a rope, because New York State used lethal injection, or would if they ever got around to slipping the needle to the guys on death row in Dannemora. *(How are things in Dannemora? Is that lethal brook still babbling there?)* And not a needle, either, because they wouldn't make this a death penalty case, it didn't meet the standards, and would you even call it premeditated? A man goes home with a woman, they argue, whatever, and she winds up dead. That wasn't premeditated, you could certainly call it manslaughter without stretching a point, and—

Except he hadn't done it!

Could he have taken that fucking rabbit? Could he have brought it home and stashed it someplace? And would they find it?

THEY DIDN'T.

They left around eleven, perfectly polite, saying only that they were sorry to have disturbed him.

It had begun raining while they were searching the apartment, and when Slaughter switched on the wipers they smeared the windshield. He used the thing that was supposed to squirt Windex onto the glass, and it was empty. He found a paper napkin, used it to clean the windshield, and pulled away from the curb.

Reade said, "No rabbit."

"Did you really expect to find it? If it was even there in the first place. Maybe it's Harvey, maybe Pankow's the only person who can see it."

"What's funny, though, is how he acted just now."

"Creighton?"

"He didn't want us in there, but not because he was afraid we'd find anything. He just didn't want us around."

"And we're such likable guys."

"But once the lawyer told him to let us in he was okay about it. He still didn't want to deal with us, and he didn't, but he wasn't anxious. Like, you want to toss the place, be my fucking guests. Like he knew what we were looking for—"

"Which he had to know, it was spelled out on the warrant."

"—and he knew we weren't going to find it."

"Which we didn't."

"But here's the thing, Kevin. He wasn't nervous, but we went on searching, and we weren't getting anyplace, and then he started to *get* nervous. Like the longer we were there, the more chance we had to come up with a little blue rabbit."

"You're saying it wasn't there when we walked in, but it sneaked in while we were there?"

"Hop hop hop. It's just interesting, is all."

"He did it."

"Oh, hell, I know he did it. And I don't think he remembers it. But you know what? I think he's starting to. I think it's beginning to come back to him."

seven

HE WOKE TO the sound of bells, probably from the Franciscan church on Thirty-first Street. His hotel—the hotel where he was staying, it was by no means *his* hotel—was on Eighth Avenue at Thirty-second. It was thus convenient to Penn Station, but it would have had to be a much better hotel than it was for this to be anything more than coincidental. It was an SRO (for Single Room Occupancy, not Standing Room Only), which was essentially a euphemism for *flophouse*—small rooms for $30 a night, $200 a week, a sink in the room, a toilet down the hall, a tub and shower on the floors above and below. Cash in advance, no credit cards. No cooking, no pets, no guests in rooms.

He liked it well enough.

When the bells ceased to ring he dressed, used the hall toilet, and returned to his room. The room had a single chair, which looked to have had an earlier life as part of a dinette set. He posted it next to the window and sat in it with his current book, a volume of George Templeton Strong's diary, an exhaustive record of life in nineteenth-century New York.

His name for now, the name he'd used registering at the hotel, was G. T. Strong. No one had asked what the *G* stood for, and no one knew the name but the clerk who had signed him in, and who had very likely long since forgotten it. For six weeks now he'd paid each week's rent in advance, and he never had calls or callers, never spoke to anyone, never made any trouble, asked any favors, or registered any complaints.

He read thirty pages of his book, the third volume of his edition of Strong's diary, then marked his place and tucked it under his mattress. This was almost certainly an unnecessary precaution, the sort of person who'd break into this sort of room would be unlikely to consider a book worth stealing, but it would inconvenience him greatly to lose the book, and it was little trouble to tuck it out of sight.

He'd finish the book in a few days or a week, and then he would exchange it for the next volume at the warehouse on Seventeenth Street west of Eleventh Avenue, where he rented a storage cubicle. He had hardly anything there, three cartons full of books and a fourth holding the few other articles he still owned, but it was well worth the monthly charge to keep the books where they'd be safe yet readily accessible. They were all historical works about New York City. That had always been a chief interest of his, and, when he walked away from everything else he owned, those were the volumes he kept.

He'd even enlarged his collection, browsing at the Strand, picking up, oh, ten or a dozen books over the months.

He made the bed, and when he put his tweed cap on his head and left the room it looked unoccupied. His clothes were in the cigarette-scarred mahogany dresser—a few changes of socks and underwear, a couple of plaid shirts like the one he wore, an extra pair of dark trousers. But, unless you pulled open a drawer, you wouldn't know anyone lived there.

He bought a sandwich and a can of V8 juice at a nearby deli. He walked a mile downtown, stopping along the way to salvage that morning's *Times* from a trash can, and a block below Fourteenth Street he came to Jackson Square, a little pocket park with benches and ornamental plantings. There was a fountain, turned off on account of the drought.

Fountains don't use water, they recirculate the same water over and over, and the loss from evaporation doesn't amount to much. But they look as though they use water, so the law requires that they be turned off during water shortages.

He found this fascinating.

He ate his sandwich, drank his V-8, and read his newspaper. When he'd finished he put the paper and the sandwich wrapper in a mesh trash can and set the empty juice can on top of it, where it could be easily retrieved by one of the men and women who made a living redeeming cans and bottles.

Then he left the park and walked south and east on West Fourth Street.

IT WAS ON AN afternoon like this one, a lazy overcast afternoon in the middle of the week, that Eddie Ragan had first realized material success was not likely to come his way.

He'd been behind the stick at the Kettle, with a pair of beer drinkers at one end and a regular, Max the Poet, drinking the house red at the other. The TV was on with the sound off, and the radio was tuned to an oldies station, and Eddie was polishing a glass and thinking how this was the time he liked best, when the place was empty and peaceful and quiet.

And that's exactly why you'll never amount to anything, a little voice told him. Because nobody makes any money working a shift like this. When you're jumping around playing catch-up with fifty thirsty maniacs, that's when the tips roll in. And that's when an ambitious bartender rises to the occasion, and loves every minute of it.

There were bartenders who wanted to make a lot of money so they could spend a lot of money—on cars, on travel, on the good life. They wanted a Rolex on their wrist and a babe on their arm, wanted to fly out to Vegas and leave their money on the craps table or stay home and put it up their nose. And there were others who wanted to make a lot of money and use it to get their own joint up and rolling, so they could put in even longer hours and make even more money—or bust out and start over, if that's how it played out.

And there were guys who were just doing this for a little while, waiting for a chance to quit their day job (or night job, or whenever the hell their shift was) and make it as an actor or a painter or a writer. And yes, he'd been one of those wannabes himself for a stretch, taking acting classes and getting headshots taken and making the rounds, even picking up small parts in a couple of showcases. But he was no actor, not really, and by the time he'd gotten a third of the way through a screenplay (about a bartender who got laid all the time, which was art improving on life, wasn't it?) he realized he wasn't a writer, either. One thing about paint, he didn't have to try it to know he'd be no good at it. He'd helped a girlfriend paint an apartment once, and that was plenty.

Nope, he was a lifer in the bartending trade. He knew that, and as of that particular weekday afternoon—he figured it was something like two years ago, though he hadn't marked the date on his calendar—he'd known he wasn't going to be a great success at it, either. The thought, which he'd instantly recognized as wholly true, had depressed him at first, and that evening he drank a little more than he usually did, and the next morning he felt a little crummier than usual, and took three aspirins instead of two, plus an Excedrin to keep them company.

By the time the hangover was gone, so was the depression. The fact of the matter was that he'd never really wanted to get anyplace. He just thought he ought to want to, like everybody else. But he didn't. His life was fine just the way it was. He never had to work too hard, he never worried much, and he got by. There were things he'd never have or do or be, but that was true for everybody. You could be the richest, most successful man on the planet and there'd always be one woman who wouldn't love

you back, one mountain you couldn't climb, one thing you wanted to buy
that nobody would sell to you.

He had a good life. Especially on lazy afternoons like this one, when
he didn't have much to do, and the perfect place to do it in.

The Mets were playing a day game in Chicago, and the set was on
with the sound off, so you could watch Mo Vaughn take the big swing
without some announcer telling you what you were seeing. On the radio,
the Beach Boys were proclaiming the natural superiority of California
girls. Max the Poet sat with his usual glass of red, reading a Modern Library collection of Chekhov's stories, and an older dude with a tweed cap
was at the corner by the window with a bottle of Tuborg, and two semi-
regulars, wannabe actors or writers, he couldn't remember which, were
drinking glasses of draft Guinness and talking about the woman whose
household goods they'd just moved from her ex-boyfriend's place in
NoHo to a studio apartment in the Flatiron district. She was nice, they
agreed, pretty face and a great rack, and the tall one said he got the feeling she liked him.

The other one shook his head. "That was flirting in lieu of a tip," he
said.

"She tipped us."

"She tipped us five apiece, which is the next thing to stiffing us altogether. In fact it's worse, because when they stiff you maybe they didn't
know any better, or maybe they forgot."

"You know Paul? Big Paul, got the droopy eyelid?"

"Only sometimes."

"What, like you only know him on months that got an *r* in them?"

"The lid only droops sometimes, asshole. And I know what you're
gonna say, because I seen him do it. He never gives 'em a chance to forget, or not know better, because he tells 'em in front that a tip's expected."

" 'Just so you know, sir, we work for tips.' Takes brass balls, but only
the first time. Only I have to say I've seen it backfire."

"I guess you got to know when to do it. He works it right, they're
scared of him, they overtip. The only thing is it feels like extortion, and
for chump change at that."

"Well, chump change is what we just got, all right, but maybe it's all
she could afford. I still say she liked me."

"You gonna make a move?"

"I might. Give her a chance to settle in first."

"Give her a chance to forget all about the studly moving man."

"You think? How long is too long, that's the question."

Jesus, Eddie thought, he could listen to this shit all day.

He turned to see how the guy in the cap was doing with his Tuborg.

The bottle was still there, the glass still filled to the brim, but the guy was gone. He'd come in what, half an hour ago? Sat there with his tweed cap halfway down his forehead and his plaid shirt buttoned up to his neck and his shoulders hunched forward, never spoke a word. There'd been a Tuborg coaster on the bar, and the guy had picked it up and tapped it with his forefinger. Eddie'd said, "Tuborg? Only got bottles," and the fellow nodded, and put a twenty on the bar. Eddie hadn't said anything when he brought the beer or when he came back with the guy's change, and whenever he'd glanced over there the guy was in the same position, and so were the glass and the bottle.

And now he was gone. Unless he was in the john, which was possible. He turned to the TV to see how the Mets were doing, and somehow the score had gotten to be seven to four, with the Mets on the short end of it. They'd been up four-three last time he'd noticed.

Maybe Sosa'd hit one out. When the wind was blowing out, your grandmother could hit the ball out of Wrigley. And Sammy Sosa, shit, he could do it when the wind was blowing *in*.

He watched the Mets go down in order, then went to refill a glass for one of the moving men, and he checked on the Tuborg, and it was still there, the bottle and the glass, and the guy was still missing.

And he wasn't in the john, because Max was just coming back from there, and there was only room for one at a time. He asked Max if he'd seen the man leave, and Max didn't know who he was talking about, hadn't even seen him come in.

He could have ducked out for a breath of air, or to buy a newspaper. Or cigarettes; the ashtray where he'd been sitting was empty, but that didn't mean he wasn't a smoker, and he could have discovered he was out and gone out to buy some.

But he'd been gone too long for that. And he'd scooped up the change from his twenty. Some people did that automatically, just as others left the change on the bar top until they were ready to call it a day or a night. This man, this fucking enigma in the tweed cap, had originally left the change in front of him, never touching it or his Tuborg, and now he was gone. Vanished into thin air, just like Judge Crater, except he didn't even walk around the horses first. Just plain disappeared.

The record ended, and there was a commercial, and on the television set someone hit one over the ivy. A Met, evidently, because they had the usual shot of one of the Bleacher Bums throwing it back. Remarkable, he thought, that people still did that, showing their disdain for balls hit by anyone but their beloved hometown losers. Suppose you were from out of town, suppose you didn't give two shits about the Cubs, and you caught a home run ball hit by the visiting team. Would they be able to pressure you into giving it back, the way Big Paul, Droopy-eyed Paul, pressured people into tipping him?

Another record played, the Stones with "Ruby Tuesday," and he looked over and the beer was still there and the guy was still gone. Something wrong with the beer? He went over and sniffed it, and it smelled like beer, and he was going to take a sip and thought better of it. He got a fresh bottle of Tuborg from the cooler and poured an ounce or two into a glass and held it to the light. Clear enough, and he took a sip and it tasted fine.

He got two clean glasses, divided the remaining beer between them, and set them in front of the two movers. "Taste test," he said. They gave him a look, shrugged, and sipped the beer.

"Well?"

"Tastes like Tuborg," the tall one said.

"Meaning you saw the bottle. It taste all right?"

"It's not going to win me over from the black stuff, if this is a marketing thing."

"I just wondered if the case was off," he said. "Guy ordered a beer, didn't touch a drop. Look at it, full to the brim."

"There a fly in it? That'd put a person off."

"No fly, and wouldn't you say something if there was?"

"This asshole? He'd drink it, fly and all."

"Protein," the other agreed. "You're gonna drink, you gotta eat. Maybe he quit drinking."

"He never even started," Eddie said. "Not one drop."

"Maybe he quit a while ago, and came in here to test himself. Ordered a drink and walked out without touching it."

"He must have stared at it for half an hour."

"There you go, man. Testing himself, proving he's stronger than a bottle of Tuborg."

"Anybody's stronger than that Danish piss," his friend said. "Let's see him try it with Guinness."

Earlier, when the papers were full of the Marilyn Fairchild murder, they'd had their share of curiosity seekers, drawn by the media attention. Corpse-sniffers, Lou called them. Lou had been on that night, and had served drinks to the woman and to Creighton, the man who'd walked out with her and later strangled her. (Or allegedly strangled her, as the papers were careful to put it, *allegedly* being accepted journalese for *We know you did it but we don't want your lawyer up our ass*.)

The corpse-sniffers came mostly at night, hoping Lou could tell them something they hadn't read in the tabloids. Funny thing was that Lou, working nights, never saw much of Creighton, who was more likely to come in and nurse a brew in the afternoon, a Beck's or a St. Pauli Girl, enjoying the peace and quiet the same way Eddie did. He'd stop in occasionally at night—otherwise he and Fairchild would have missed each other, to the benefit of both of them, unless you believed in karma and kismet and destiny. Anyway, Lou served them that night, but it was Eddie who'd shot the shit with him many times, and you wouldn't have figured him as a guy to do something like that, but then you never knew, did you?

One thing he did know, the mystery man in the cap wasn't coming back for his Tuborg. Eddie carried the bottle and glass to the sink, and poured them out.

Now if there was anything the least bit important about the mystery man, he thought, then he, Eddie Ragan, had his hands full of evidence. Because the guy had almost certainly touched the bottle or the glass, hadn't he? Eddie had set them both in front of the man, the glass topped with its creamy head, the half-full bottle beside it, and didn't the man then take hold of them and move them an inch or two closer? Everybody did, it was a reflexive response, even if you weren't going to take a drink right away.

Or, in this case, ever.

If he'd touched the glass or bottle, he'd probably left his fingerprints. Because he certainly hadn't been wearing gloves. The cap was an odd touch on a mild day, but there were guys who never went anywhere without a cap, they felt naked without it. Gloves would have been ridiculous, though, gloves would have stuck out like a sore thumb (he had to grin at that one), so the guy had clearly been gloveless, and would have left prints.

An ambitious bartender, he thought, might slip the bottle and the glass into separate plastic bags and set them aside for when the police came calling. Or he might even ring them up over at the Sixth Precinct—he knew a couple of cops there, as far as that went. Hey, got a clue, he could tell them. Give it to the forensics team, lift the prints, check the FBI computer, find out who this dude is.

He laughed, tossed the bottle with the other empties, plunged the glass into the sink. Rinsed it, took it out, polished it with the towel.

Not a bad life, he thought. You had time to let your mind wander, time to imagine all sorts of crazy shit.

FROM HIS BENCH IN the triangular patch of fenced-in greenery called Christopher Park, the man with the tweed cap had a good view of the entrance of the Kettle of Fish. In the course of half an hour he didn't notice anyone entering or leaving the bar, but he might not have noticed. His mind wandered, and what he saw, for much of that time, was a series of

images that had burned itself into his vision, and, he had to suppose, the
vision of everyone in the city, and beyond.

An airplane, gliding effortlessly, inexorably, into a building. A brilliant explosion of yellow at the left, like a flower bursting into bloom.

Two towers standing, their tops spewing smoke and flame.

Then one tower standing.

Then none.

THE HORROR.

The horror and the beauty.

The beauty . . .

HE HAD LIVED WITH his wife in a sprawling three-bedroom apartment
in a prewar brick apartment building at Eighty-fourth and Amsterdam.
They'd lived there for almost all of their thirty-five-year marriage. When
the building went co-op in the early seventies, they'd bought their apartment at the insider's price, paying a low five-figure price for what was
now worth well over a million dollars.

After he'd collected his Christmas bonus for the year 2000, he'd
opted for early retirement. He had headed the research department at a
Madison Avenue advertising agency, and they were just as happy to re-
place him with someone younger and less expensive. His health was
good, and he looked forward to years of leisure, to the foreign travel
they'd never had time for, to long walks in the city, to long evenings with
his books. They might take to wintering someplace warm, but they'd
never move to Florida or Arizona or the Caribbean. Their children were
here, and soon they would be grandparents. Anyway, he loved the city too
much to leave it.

He'd just finished breakfast that morning, and he was sitting in the
living room with the morning paper. The television set was on—his wife
had turned it on, then returned to the kitchen to do the breakfast dishes.
He wasn't paying attention to the television, but then it got his attention,
and he put down the paper and never picked it up again, because it might
as well have been from the last century, or the one before that, for all the
relevance it had.

Their windows faced north and east, and they were on the fourth
floor, so you couldn't see anything. At one point he took the elevator to
the top floor and climbed up onto the roof, but the building was only sixteen stories tall and there were any number of high-rises that blocked the
view of Lower Manhattan. He went back downstairs and sat in front of
the television set and they showed him the same shot over and over, the

second plane sailing into the South Tower, the bloom of fire and smoke, over and over and over. He couldn't look at it, he couldn't not look at it.

His daughter, twenty-seven years old, three months pregnant, was an administrative assistant at Cantor Fitzgerald. They'd joked about the name, how it sounded like an extremely ecumenical cleric, but that was before the plane hit the floor where the firm had its office and made the name a synonym for annihilation.

She could have been late for work. She had severe morning sickness, her husband had joked that she was preparing for the world's first oral delivery, but it rarely stopped her from beating the rush hour and getting to her desk by eight-thirty.

She'd have been sitting there with a cup of coffee when the plane hit. She wasn't supposed to have caffeine during pregnancy, but one cup in the morning, really, what harm could it do?

None now.

Her husband worked for the same firm, and in the same office. That wasn't a coincidence, it was how they'd met, and of course he was always early for work, often arriving at seven or seven-thirty. That was when you could get a lot accomplished, he used to say, but sometimes he'd wait so that he and his wife could share the walk to the subway and the ride downtown. So maybe he'd gone in ahead of her that morning, or maybe they'd been together. There was no way to tell, and what earthly difference did it make?

His daughter, his son-in-law.

His son, his baby boy, was with an FDNY hook-and-ladder company stationed on East Tenth Street between Avenues B and C, and lived with a young woman in a tenement apartment two blocks from the firehouse.

And was involved in rescue operations in the North Tower when the building came down on him.

For days—he was never sure how many—all he seemed to do was sit in front of the television set. He must have eaten, he must have gone to the bathroom, he must have bathed and slept and done the things one does, but nothing registered, nothing imprinted on his memory.

One day he went into the bedroom they shared and his wife was sleeping. He called her name twice, a third time, but she didn't stir. He went back and sat down again in front of the television set.

Some hours later he went to the bedroom again, and she hadn't changed position, and he touched her forehead and realized that she was dead. There was, he noticed for the first time, a vial of sleeping pills on the bedside table, and it was empty.

Her action seemed entirely reasonable to him, and he only wondered that she had thought of it first, and only wished she'd told him, so that he could have lain down and died beside her. Without disturbing her body, he took the empty pill bottle downstairs and refilled it at the CVS on Broadway. He took all the pills and got undressed and got into bed.

Twelve hours later he awoke with a splitting headache and a dry mouth and a bottomless thirst. The throw rug beside the bed was stained with vomit.

He got out of bed, showered, put on clothes, and went up to the roof, intending to throw himself off it. He stood at the edge for what must have been half an hour. Then he went downstairs and called a doctor he knew, and a funeral parlor.

His daughter and son-in-law had been vaporized, atomized. Their bodies would never be recovered. His son lay at the bottom of a hundred stories of rubble. He told the funeral director there would be no service, and that he wanted his wife cremated. When they gave him the ashes he walked all the way downtown, five miles more or less, and got as close to Ground Zero as you could get. There were barriers up, you couldn't get too close, but he did the best he could and found a spot where he could stand in relative privacy, tossing his wife's remains a handful at a time into the air. He stood there for a few minutes after he'd finished, then turned around and walked back the way he came.

Crossing Twenty-third Street, he realized he was still carrying the container for the ashes. He dropped it in the next trash basket he came to and walked the rest of the way home.

HE GOT UP FROM his park bench now and walked to Christopher and Waverly, where he walked counterclockwise around the little triangular block on which stood the little triangular building that housed the Northern Dispensary. He liked the lines of the building, the way it filled its space. He liked, too, that it stood at the corner of Waverly Place and Waverly Place. The street didn't just make a ninety-degree turn here, it actually intersected itself, and that had always appealed to him.

What's the most religious street in the world? he used to ask his daughter, when he'd take her walking in the Village on a Sunday afternoon. *Waverly Place* was the answer, *because it crosses itself*.

The Northern Dispensary had been there forever. There'd been a little café on the corner called Waverly & Waverly, but it hadn't been there for long. Something else had replaced it, and had been replaced in its turn.

Some things lasted, some things didn't.

He stood listening to the sounds of the city, breathing in the taste and smell of the city. Sometimes, drawing a deep breath, he would fancy that he was inhaling some of the substance of his daughter and son-in-law.

They had gone off into the air, and he was breathing the air, and who was to say he was not taking in some particulate matter that had once been theirs?

He turned, retraced his steps, crossed Christopher. Then came West Tenth Street, and then Charles.

Once all three streets were named for one man. Tenth Street, or at least a stretch of it, was then called Amos Street, and the man was Charles Christopher Amos, who'd owned a large tract of land there.

And West Fourth Street had been called Asylum Street. So, when you stood at the corner of West Fourth and West Tenth, you were at the erstwhile intersection of Amos and Asylum, and how many people knew that?

Of course it was no less interesting an intersection now, West Fourth and West Tenth Streets. What business did they have intersecting one another? Numbered streets ran east and west, numbered avenues ran north and south, that was how it was supposed to be, but here everything was askew, everything came at you on a slant, and West Fourth Street angled north even as Tenth and Eleventh and Twelfth Streets angled south.

He liked that almost as much as Waverly crossing Waverly . . .

He turned the corner on Charles Street and stood in a doorway across the street from where the woman had been killed. He remembered how the man and woman had left the bar together and walked side by side (but not arm in arm) along a more direct version of the route he'd just taken.

How he'd walked along in their wake.

He put his hand in his pocket and felt the cool surface of the object within, tracing its contours with his fingertips. He drew it from his pocket and held it in his closed right hand, and he stood in the shadows as they lengthened.

A couple passed—college age, the boy Asian, the girl a blonde with almost translucent skin. They were too wrapped up in each other to notice him, but then hardly anyone ever did. Then they were gone, and time passed, although he was barely conscious of its passing.

After a time he moved out of the shadows and walked back to Waverly, staying with it as it crossed Seventh Avenue and walking two more blocks to Bank Street.

This would have been the man's route home. There was his building, and was that his window, with the light on? Was he at home?

And would he be coming out soon? Maybe yes, maybe no. Time would tell.

He was still clutching the small object in his closed right fist. Like what? A talisman? A charm?

He opened his hand and looked at it lying in his palm, a little turquoise rabbit. There was something sweetly whimsical about it, something endearing.

He returned it to his pocket and drew back into the shadows, waiting.

eight

JOHN, **IF YOU'RE** home, it's Roz. Come to think of it, it's Roz whether you're home or not, but are you?"

She was in the middle of another sentence by the time he got the phone to his ear. "I've always liked that construction," he said. " 'If I don't see you before you leave, have a nice time.' And if you *do* see me before then, should I have a lousy time? Odd use of the conditional, if you think about it."

"Or even if you don't."

"Damn," he said. "I did it myself, didn't I? And in the same paragraph."

"You're sounding chipper, John."

"I am? Maybe it's the music. It's pledge week on the jazz station, so I switched to classical."

"What are you listening to?"

"Ravel," he said. "*Pavane for a Dead Infant*. What's so funny?"

"You're making this up, right?"

"Yeah. I don't know what the hell I'm listening to, Mozart or Haydn, one of those guys. And if I'm sounding better, it's probably not the music. Maybe I'm just getting used to being under house arrest."

"You're not getting out?"

"Not really. I did have a visitor the other day. Well, two of them. Maury Winters came over, and he brought along a private detective who's going to track down the real killer."

"Oh?"

"It sounds like OJ, doesn't it? Searching the golf courses of America for the real killer of Nicole and Ron. This guy, though, all he's likely to find is the next drink in the next gin mill, judging from the red nose and the matching breath. The idea is she went out right after I left and dragged somebody else home, which strikes me as not impossible, and maybe somebody saw her. It'd be nice if a witness turned up, but so far nobody has, so this joker's on the payroll to go look for one. And, since she picked me up in a bar, my guess is that's where he'll go looking, and there are enough bars in the neighborhood to keep him busy."

"Maybe he'll come up with something."

"Maybe he will. I'm inclined to belittle him, but maybe that's just me. The guy's a retired cop, twenty years on the job, and the fact that he likes his booze doesn't necessarily mean he's inept."

"But you don't have a lot of faith in the process."

"I can't say I do, no. I think he's just going through the motions."

"The detective?"

"Well, sure, but that's what they do. No, what I think is Winters is just going through the motions in hiring him, hoping to stir up something that'll muddy the waters. But as far as finding the guy, I think he thinks the guy's already been found."

"What makes you say that, John?"

"Impression I get. The cops quit looking once they got to me, and I think Winters figures they got it right. I suppose it's natural. What percentage of his clients are innocent of the crimes they're charged with? I don't mean how many get acquitted, I mean how many genuinely didn't do it?"

"That's true for any criminal lawyer, isn't it?"

"That's my point. And it shouldn't interfere with his ability to present the best possible defense. Still, you'd think he'd ask me."

"Ask you?"

"If I did it. That's the damnedest thing, Roz. Nobody asks."

"Nobody?"

"Well, aside from the cops, hoping I'd fall on the floor and confess. Nobody else. Not even Karin. She wanted to know if I was planning to skip to Brazil, but other than that she didn't seem to care if the man she bailed out was guilty or innocent."

"She knows you couldn't have done it, John."

"You figure?"

"Of course. Anybody who knows you knows that much."

Her words, delivered in such a matter-of-fact manner, moved him profoundly, and for a moment he was unable to speak. Then he said, "That's very good to hear, Roz."

"Well."

"Just for the record, I didn't do it."

"I know that."

"But you're wrong about one thing. I could have."

"How's that?"

"Anyone could have," he said. "Anyone's capable of it."

"Of murder."

"I think so, yes."

"Well, there's a sobering thought," she said. "Even thee and me, eh? God knows there've been times I felt like it. When that Carmichael cunt managed to work things out so that she stayed and I got the ax, I'll admit I had fantasies about killing her. I mean I thought about it, I ran it through my mind, but there was never a chance it was going to be real. And, of course, getting out of that rathole was the best thing that ever happened to me."

"And me."

"That and bringing Hannah back from China, and how could I have done that if I was serving twenty-five to life? So I'm certainly glad I didn't screw it up by letting Lesley Carmichael have it with her monogrammed Tiffany letter opener."

"Was that how you fantasized it?"

"That was one of several ways. But it was never real, and I honestly don't think I could ever do anything like that. I'm tough as an old boot, sweetie, and God knows I've got a temper, but it never gets physical. I never even throw things. Some women throw things, did you know that?"

"Fortunately," he said, "most of them can't hit what they're aiming at."

"I wonder if dykes throw things. All those games of softball, they could probably knock your eye out at thirty paces."

"The women who fling glass ashtrays at me," he said, "tend to be at least nominally heterosexual. I know what you mean, though, having fantasies and knowing that's all they were. But there was a time when it was more than a fantasy."

"For you, you mean?"

"For me."

"I don't suppose Lesley Carmichael was the designated victim?"

"No, I didn't even get pissed at her, actually. I'd figured they were going to drop me sooner or later. No, this was earlier. I was thinking about killing my wife."

"Jesus, the way you said that."

"How did I say it?"

"Like you were thinking of going to a movie, or taking a tai chi class. So, I don't know, dispassionately?"

"Well, it was a long time ago."

"And you were really thinking about it? Like, thinking of doing it?

Does Karin even know? I guess not, or she might not have been in such a rush to post your bail."

"It wasn't Karin."

"Hello? How many wives have you had, sweetie?"

"Two. I got married right out of college."

"I never knew that."

"Well, it's not a secret, but it doesn't come up all that often. It was over in less than a year, and not a moment too soon, let me tell you. We fought all the time, and neither of us wanted to be married, and least of all to each other. Nor did we have a clue how to get out of it. I swear I don't ever want to be that age again."

"I think you're safe."

"We were driving somewhere flat. I want to say Kansas, but it could have been anywhere in the Great Plains. Were we on our way to visit her parents? No, we'd already been to see them, they lived in Idaho, he ran a family-owned lumber mill. Her father, that is. Her mother baked her own bread and smiled bravely. You can imagine what a good time we had there."

"And then you were in Kansas."

"Or someplace like it, and in a motel for the night, and we'd been at each other's throats all fucking day. And the thought came to me that I was going to have this bitch around my neck for the rest of my life. And there was this voice in my head: *Unless you kill her.*" He frowned. "Or was it *Unless I kill her?*"

"Honey, it only matters if you're writing it. An inner voice, who cares if it's speaking in the first or second person?"

"You're right."

"Only a writer . . ."

"I guess. Point is I couldn't get the idea out of my head. Here was this impossible situation, and only one way out of it."

"Aside from walking out the door, which didn't occur to you."

"It absolutely didn't, and don't ask me why. All I knew was I was stuck for life unless she died."

"You're not even Catholic."

"No, and neither was she. Don't look for this to make sense. In my mind it was *'til death us do part*, and that was beginning to seem like a splendid idea. Here we were, in the godforsaken middle of the country, on our way to a teaching job I was going to take in western Pennsylvania. They were expecting a married guy, but if I wasn't married I didn't really have to go there at all, did I? I could tell them my plans changed and thanks but no thanks, and I could come to New York, which was what I'd wanted to do in the first place.

"And nobody knew me in New York, and if I ran into anybody I knew

I'd tell them the marriage didn't work out, that Penny left me and never said where she was going. Of course her parents wouldn't know where she was, and they'd get to wondering, but I had that figured out, too. I'd beat them to the punch by calling them with an address for them to give to Penny when they spoke to her. In case she wanted to get in touch, I'd say, sounding like a man with a broken heart."

"Wouldn't they eventually go to the police?"

"I suppose, but it would just be a missing person, not a homicide, and nobody would know where to look for her. They certainly wouldn't have any reason to start digging in a cornfield in Kansas."

"You were going to bury her in a cornfield?"

"I figured that was perfect. If you pick a recently plowed field, and go do your digging at night when nobody's around, all you'd have to do was make sure you dug deeper than they plow. The body could stay there forever."

"You had it all figured out."

"I couldn't fall asleep. I sat there in that piece-of-shit motel room while she was lying there asleep with her mouth open—"

"Which is always attractive."

"—and I thought about killing her. I didn't want to make anyone at the motel suspicious, so I had to avoid getting blood on the sheets, anything like that. I thought about strangling her or smothering her with a pillow, but suppose she put up a fight? What I settled on was I'd knock her out first by hitting her on the head. There was a tire iron in the trunk I could use, and if I wrapped a towel around it there'd be less chance of breaking the skin and causing bleeding."

"This is getting awfully real, John."

"Well, how real was it? This was twenty-five years ago, more than half my life. I can remember being in that room, working it all out in my mind, but how accurate is that memory? And how close did I come to flat out doing it?"

"Did you go out to the car for the tire iron?"

"No," he said, and frowned. "Hold on, I think I did. Jesus, this is weird. I remember it both ways."

"Wait a minute," she said. "Hang on here a minute."

"What?"

"John, I read this story."

"Yeah, I wrote about it. Turned it around some, the way you do, but that's where the story came from. The *Yale Review* turned it down and then *Prairie Schooner* bought it. I'm surprised you remember it."

"How would I not remember it? I published it, for God's sake, it was in *Edged Weapons*. Give me a minute and I'll come up with the title."

" 'A Nice Place to Stop.' It was the motel's slogan. In the story, that is, but either I made it up or it was some other motel's slogan. It seemed to fit the story, but I'm not sure it's the best title I could have come up with."

"It's not bad. In the story—"

"In the story the guy does go out for the tire iron, and he wraps the towel around it and swats her good, and then he realizes he can't go through with it. Strangling her, like he planned to do. And it dawns on him that he can just leave, he'll give her all his money and the car and say goodbye and hit the road, and what can she do? So he waits for her to wake up and he's going to tell her all this. He'd like to just split and let her figure it out for herself when she comes to, but he knows he'd better wait and tell her."

"But he can't, because she's dead."

"Right, the blow with the tire iron was enough to crack her skull and kill her, towel or no towel. So now he has to go through with it and bury her in a field the way he planned, and he does, knowing it's all unnecessary."

"And he gets away with it, doesn't he?"

"Well, we don't know that," he said. "He's still free and clear at the end of the story, but maybe that's just because they haven't caught up with him yet. But even if he gets away with it, what we get is that he's not really getting away with anything after all, because he's got her wrapped around his soul the way the Ancient Mariner had the albatross around his neck."

"Right."

"Maybe the title's better than I thought."

"Yes, I see what you mean. When did you write this one, John?"

"Not right away. Maybe a year, two years after the divorce, I started running it through my mind and it started to turn into a story. And of course I changed tons of things, and the guy in the story wasn't me and the woman wasn't Penny. But that's why I remembered going for the tire iron, and also remembered not going for the tire iron. One memory was from life and the other was from the story."

"Writers are strange people."

"You're just finding this out?"

"No, but I keep forgetting, and people like you keep reminding me. Oops, there's a call I have to take. Will you be around for a while?"

"Where would I go?"

"Nowhere for the next hour or so, okay? I'll get back to you."

HOW CLOSE HAD HE come to killing Penny?

It wasn't hard to remember the story's immediate origin, not where it came from but the spark that got him to write it. He was in New York, living in this apartment, and he was seeing someone new, a trainee copywriter at an ad agency. He'd decided he was getting more involved than he wanted to be, and made plans to tell her that he felt they should both be seeing other people. The person he thought she should probably be seeing was a trained psychotherapist, but he didn't figure he had to tell her that part.

He didn't look forward to the whole business, but at least it was early days for the relationship, and he'd be wise to nip it in the bud before he found himself married to her, and looking for ways to get rid of her.

Like, Jesus, that insane moment in the motel room when he'd actually contemplated killing Penny. And just suppose he'd taken the fantasy one step further, suppose he'd gone out and come back with a tire iron . . .

From there his imagination just ran with it. Striking the blow, Jesus, he'd regret it immediately, and the minute she came to he'd—but wait a minute, suppose she didn't?

The story was essentially complete in his mind by the time he sat down and started putting it on paper, but it morphed and evolved as he wrote it, the way they always did. Once it was done, though, all it needed was a word changed here and there and a fresh trip through the typewriter and it was done. He sent it out and it came back and he sent it out again and it stuck.

He thought of that blond bitch from the DA's office, had an Italian name. Fabrizzio? Hadn't wanted him out on bail, wanted him stuck in a cell at Rikers.

Would she think to read his books?

Well, if she didn't somebody else would. "A Nice Place to Stop" was just another story, a little more violent than most, maybe, but violence was often present in his work, and he'd already found himself wondering what the prosecution would try to do with that, and what a jury would make of it. People in the business knew to separate the writer from the writing, knew that the author of a sweet little juvenile book about cuddly bears and talking automobiles might indeed be a plump grandmother who smelled like cookie dough, but could just as easily be a grizzled old drunk with tattoos and a bad attitude. But were jurors that sophisticated?

They might be, here in New York, where everybody was an insider, at least in his own mind. Still, it would be easier all around if they didn't happen to know the precise origins of "A Nice Place to Stop."

He went to the refrigerator, gnawed at a slice of leftover pizza, took out a beer, hesitated, put it back. Sat down again and booted up the computer, opened the thing he'd been working on when—Christ, a million years ago, it seemed like—when those two refugees from the Jehovah's Witness Protection Program had turned out to be cops.

He read some, scrolled down, read some more. Shook his head.

Nothing wrong with it, really, and he sort of saw where he was going. But it felt like something he'd been working on in another lifetime. He was the same person who'd written these pages, he was in fact the same person who'd written "A Nice Place to Stop," the same person who'd stood in that motel room and contemplated—hell, call a spade a spade, forget *contemplated*—who'd planned murder.

The same person throughout, but he felt further detached from the writing on the screen than from that ancient short story. He frowned and tried to find his way back into it, writing a sentence to follow the last one he'd written. He looked at it, and it was all right, it fit what preceded it. He took a breath and let himself find his way, batted out a couple of paragraphs and stopped to look at them.

Nothing wrong with them. Still . . .

He went to the fridge, reached for the beer, put it back, checked the coffeepot. There was a cup left. Cold, but so what? He took it back to his desk and closed the file, opened a new one. Without really thinking, he let his fingers start tapping keys.

Fifteen minutes in, MS Word asked him **SAVE NOW?** He clicked the Yes box, and, when asked for a title, keyed in *Fucked If I Know* and clicked to save what he'd written under that title. Not quite in the same league with "A Nice Place to Stop," and maybe he should call this one *A Nice Place to Start*, and maybe it was. But *Fucked If I Know* was okay for the time being, and God knows it was accurate.

He reached for the coffee, found the cup empty. Couldn't even remember drinking it.

He put his fingers on the keys, went back to work.

ROZ SAID, "GIVE ME a reality check, will you? It wouldn't be for a couple of years yet, but do you think I ought to enroll Hannah in Hebrew school?"

"You're a lapsed Catholic," he said. "Don't tell me you're thinking of converting to Judaism?"

"No, why would I do that? I rather enjoy being a lapsed Catholic."

"And Hannah's Chinese," he said. "But you said Hebrew school."

"Right."

"Well . . ."

"If I don't send her," she said, "isn't she going to feel left out? She'll be the only Chinese kid in Park Slope who doesn't have a bat mitzvah."

He said, "Is that from some comic's routine? Did Rita Rudner try it out on Letterman last night?"

"I'm serious," she said. "At least I thought I was serious. Is it really that ridiculous?"

"What do I know? I don't live in Park Slope."

"Well, I've got a few years to think about it," she said. "How come you picked up before the machine? I thought you were screening your calls."

"Phone calls haven't been a problem lately. Maybe my fifteen minutes of fame are over."

"Don't count on it, honey."

"No," he said, "I guess not. When the case goes to trial is when it starts in earnest. Unless they catch the prick before then, and then the phone'll really start ringing off the hook. Not just reporters wanting to know how it feels to be vindicated, but the department head from the New School saying of course they'll want me back in the fall, plus all the old friends I haven't heard from, telling me they knew all along I was innocent. Jesus, I sound like a cynical bastard, don't I?"

"Actually," she said, "you sound like your old self."

He flexed his fingers, looked at the computer screen. He'd been at a natural stopping place when the phone rang, and had picked up without really thinking.

"My old self," he said. "That's pretty interesting."

"Not that the John Blair Creighton we all know and love can't be a cynical bastard. And ironic. Didn't *Kirkus* comment on your almost diabolical sense of irony?"

"Devilish, actually, but that's close enough."

"Devilish is better, it sounds more playful. Well, ironically enough, you old devil, this may not be an entirely bad thing."

"How's that?"

"I know what you're going through, to the extent that it's possible for anyone but you to know it, and I don't want to minimize it, but—"

"But there's a bright side? I'd love to know what it is."

"Well, don't take this the wrong way," she said, "but all in all it's not a bad career move."

He got a cigarette going and smoked it while she talked. She'd had a phone call from an editor at Crown, where his most recent book had been published. Sales had been disappointing, and his editor was no longer with the publisher, had in fact jumped ship before his book hit the stores, which certainly hadn't helped his cause. It was the second book in a two-book contract, and Crown had had no further interest in him, or he in

them, truth to tell, but this editor, whose name he didn't recognize, had
called Roz to talk about something else entirely.

"And then it just happened to occur to her to ask about you. I represented you, didn't I? She thought she remembered that. And of course
they'd published you, and people there had good feelings about your
books, in spite of the fact that sales hadn't been what any of us had hoped
for, quote unquote."

"Jesus wept," he said. "They want me back?"

"There was no reprint sale on either of the two they published," she
said. "No paperback, trade or mass-market, and this fact popped into my
head, and I said, you know, I was glad she'd called, because I'd been
meaning to call her to get rights reverted on the two books, considering
that they've long since gone out of print."

"And?"

"And I got some hemming and hawing, and the reluctant admission
that they'd had some recent interest in both books from a mass-market
publisher. So I vamped a little myself, and admitted with some reluctance
that you were hard at work on a major project, and that they should hold
off on any reprint sale for the time being. She was on that like a pike on a
minnow, John. As your loyal publishers, of course they want your new
book, and of course they realize on the basis of my description that it's
clearly a more commercial venture—"

"How did you describe it?"

"I didn't. *Major project* is what I called it, and how descriptive is
that? I know it's tacky, John, but in addition to being the designated suspect in a murder case, you're also a hot ticket. Now I know that right now
writing, or even thinking about writing, is the last thing you feel like doing, but hear me out, okay?"

He leaned back, blew a smoke ring. "Okay," he said, amused.

"You could use a few bucks, sweetie. I don't know what Maurice
Winters charges, but he's got to be billing at a base rate of six or seven
hundred dollars an hour, and it doesn't take long for that to add up. And
didn't you say something about a private detective?"

"Yeah, and the guy's bar bill alone . . ."

"The point is it would be good if you could make some serious
dough, and all of a sudden it looks as though you can. Soon as I got done
with your new big fan at Crown, I made a few well-considered phone
calls to a few top people here and there." She named some names. "I got
interest and enthusiasm from everybody I talked to," she said, "and they
didn't even bother trying to conceal it."

"And nobody found it unacceptably crass to cash in on a book by an
accused murderer?"

"No. You think I'm being crass, John?"

"No, not at all."

"You're my client," she said, "and you're on the spot financially, along with whatever else you're going through. If you can get a big transfusion of cash, it's got to take some of the pressure off." She stopped herself for a moment. "On the other hand," she said, "it's not as though I'm going to waive my commission. If you make a fortune I make fifteen percent of a fortune, so I'm very much acting in my own interest here, as well as yours."

"Nothing wrong with that."

"Makes the world go round, or so I'm told. One way to look at this, life handed you a lemon and we're opening a lemonade stand. Can I tell you what I want to do?"

"By all means."

"I want to get back to all these nice people who say they can't wait to hear more from me, and I want to put a package into play involving your next two books plus your backlist titles, the ones we control the rights to. I'll tell them I'm going to run an informal auction, but I'll be open to a really solid preemptive offer, and I wouldn't be surprised if I get one that's good enough to take."

"How good would it have to be?"

"High six figures. That surprise you?"

"No," he said, "not the way you've been talking. Ten minutes ago it would have surprised the shit out of me. Now it seems perfectly logical, in a cockeyed kind of way."

"Cockeyed's the word for it. Sweetie, before I start selling something, it would help to know if I've got something to sell. I'm sure writing's the last thing you feel like doing, the last thing you even think you'd be capable of doing, but it might get you through the days. At the least it'll give you something you can do without leaving the house, and it might even be therapeutic, and . . . what's the matter, did I say something funny?"

"Funnier than Hannah's bat mitzvah," he said. "After I got off the phone with you, I started writing."

"You're kidding."

"Scout's honor. Hold on a sec." He went to the Tools menu, selected Word Count. "Eight hundred and eighty-three words," he said, "and where would we be without computers? A few years ago I'd have said I was on the fourth page, but now I can apprise you of my progress with pinpoint accuracy."

"That's great, John. You went back to work on the book? That shows you can write, and if you're really into that book, well, you should stay with it, but . . ."

"But what?"

She took a breath. "I don't want to tell you what to write, John. That's something I never want to do. But if you were ever going to write a book with more deliberately commercial potential . . ."

"Now would be the time for it, huh?"

"From what you showed me of the book you're working on, now there's nothing wrong with it and a lot that's right with it, and it could certainly work as the *second* book in a two-book deal, but right now . . ."

He said, "Roz, that's not what I was just working on. I looked at it, I felt completely out of touch with it."

"Oh."

"So I started something new."

"Just now, we're talking about."

"Right."

"That you've got eight hundred words done of."

"Eight hundred and change."

"And does it have, how to put it, commercial elements? I know it's early to say, but is there any way it could be described as a thriller? Literary of course, anything you write is going to be literary, which is all to the good, but would it, uh . . ."

"Tie in with my present circumstances?"

"Thank you. Would it?"

"Remember the story we were talking about? 'A Nice Place to Stop'?"

"Of course."

"Well, that's it."

"The story expanded to novel length," she said thoughtfully. "I can see how that might work. Flashbacks to give you more of a sense of who the characters are, and—"

"No, that's not it. The novel's not an expansion of the story, it *starts* with the story. Only I'm rewriting the story, of course, in fact I just plunged right in without even re-*reading* the story, because I have a very different perspective on the characters now. I mean, look how many years it's been since I wrote the thing, plus all the time since the incident that inspired it."

"Of course."

"It starts with the story," he said, "and he knocks her out with the tire iron, and then changes his mind, but it's too late. So he does what he planned on doing, buries her deep and lights out for the territories, except he's in the territories, and what he lights out for is New York."

"And it's how he gets pursued and caught?"

"He gets away with it."

"And?"

"And I don't know what happens," he said, "because I'll find out by writing it, but it feels as though I *do* know what happens, all of it, except not on a conscious level. But it's all down there waiting for me to dig it out." He leaned back in his chair. "Anyway, I'm what, eight hundred words in? I'll be covering old ground for the first several thousand words, but it's all preface to his life in New York, and what it's like for him to create a life founded on having gotten away with murder. How that's empowering in certain ways and constraining in others. I guess sooner or later it all has to come back and bite him in the ass, but just what bites him and what part of his ass gets the tooth marks, well, I'll wait for the book to tell me that." He took a breath. "So? What do you think?"

"What I think," she said, "is that Maury Winters isn't going to have to worry about getting paid."

nine

IT WASN'T WHAT she'd expected.

It was an apartment, first of all, on the fifteenth floor of a thirty-story postwar apartment building on Tenth Avenue and Fifty-seventh Street. She'd known as much, really, but had somehow pictured the place as a ground-floor hole-in-the-wall with a hand-lettered sign over the door, T*A*T*T*O*O P*A*R*L*O*R in curlicued, over-elaborate script, and a window full of tattoo art and needles and scary-looking equipment. Inside it would be cramped and claustrophobic, with nothing more comfortable to sit on than those three-legged stools they gave you in Ethiopian restaurants.

And Medea would be a sort of cross between a pirate and a gypsy, oily and squat and swarthy, with a head scarf and a gold tooth and a trace of a mustache, perched on a stool of her own and assessing her with a cataract-clouded eye, sizing her up, deciding whether to pierce her flesh as requested or drug her and sell her into white slavery.

And of course it was nothing like that. The building had a concierge, resplendent in maroon livery, who called upstairs before directing her to an elevator. Medea, waiting in the doorway of 15-H, was about Susan's height, with a long oval Modigliani face and almond-shaped eyes. She was wearing a simple white sleeveless shift that stopped at her knees, and she had calves like a dancer's and arms like a tennis player's.

"You're Susan," she said.

"Susan Pomerance."

"I'm Medea." Her voice was low, and her speech at once unaccented and foreign-sounding. An exotic creature, Susan thought, and followed her into the apartment, which turned out to be a textbook example of minimalism—eggshell walls, pale beige wall-to-wall broadloom carpet, and,

along the walls, a couple of built-in ledges covered with the same carpet-
ing as the floor and equipped—ooh, a sumptuous touch—with beige
throw pillows. Overhead there was some track lighting, and, on the wall
to your left as you walked in, a single monochromatic unframed canvas
three feet by four feet, just one big yellow-brown rectangle. It was not art-
less, it had texture and tone that indicated the artist had labored over it,
but the whole business was so utterly different from what she'd expected
that she burst out laughing.

"I'm sorry," she said, and covered her mouth with her hand.

"It's the color," Medea said. "Primal, wouldn't you say? I probably
smeared mine on the wall myself, but I never could have made such a
neat job of it."

"My God, it's baby-shit brown. I hadn't even thought of that."

"Then why did you laugh?"

"Because I was expecting a gypsy souk," she said, "though I don't
guess you find many of them fifteen floors up. And because I'm scared
stiff, I suppose. I've had my ears pierced, of course, but this is different."

"Of course it is," Medea said, and reached out to touch Susan's earlobe. It took her a moment to recall which earrings she was wearing.
Teardrops, lapis set in gold. They'd been a gift, from and to herself, on
her last birthday.

Medea's earrings were simple gold studs. More minimalism, Susan
thought.

The almond-shaped eyes—their irises, she saw now, were a vivid
green, which pretty much had to be contacts, but who could say for sure
with this unique specimen? The eyes took her measure, sized her up.
"Scared stiff," she said, as if the phrase were one Susan had invented.
"But excited as well, I would say."

She felt a pulse in her earlobe where Medea had touched her. Was
that even possible? Was there a blood vessel there that could have a pulse?

"A little," she said.

"You want your nipple pierced."

"Yes."

"Why?"

"I don't know."

"And what is it you fear? The pain?"

"Is it very painful?"

"You'll feel it," Medea said.

Her complexion was darkly golden, though some of that might be
from the sun. She looked like a woman who spent a lot of time in the sun.
But there was also the suggestion of a mix of races, to the point where
race disappeared. Asian, African, European, swirled in a blender.

"I think," Medea said, "that you'd be disappointed if there were no pain. But then what exactly is pain? I've heard it said it's any sensation we make wrong. Do you like hot food?"

"Hot food?"

"Spicy, not thermally hot. *Picante* rather than *caliente*. Curry, chili, three peppers in a Szechuan restaurant, five stars in a Thai one."

Was this a test? "The hotter the better."

"The person who insists on bland food," Medea said, "experiences the identical sensation you do when she puts a chili pepper in her mouth. But, instead of savoring it, she finds it painful and unpleasant. She's afraid it's going to burn her mouth, or make her sick, or, I suppose, kill her. She makes it wrong."

Contacts or not, the green eyes were extraordinary, their gaze compelling. They held Susan's own eyes and kept her from glancing down at Medea's breasts. She couldn't help wondering if the woman's nipples were pierced. Her ears were, of course, once each in their lobes, but she saw no nose ring, no other visible piercings.

No tattoos, either. None that showed, anyway.

Maybe she wasn't into that. Maybe she was one who did, not one who got done. Were there tops and bottoms in the world of body piercing?

Who would pierce the piercer?

TWO WEEKS AGO HER part-time assistant, Chloe, had shown up at the gallery with a loopier-than-usual expression on her face. She looked as though she knew a secret, and it was a good one.

Susan noticed right away, but had no time to waste wondering what had the girl looking like the cat that swallowed the canary. In a pinch, she could probably guess what Chloe might have swallowed, with the choices narrowed down to illegal substances and bodily fluids. Or the occasional hot fudge sundae; Chloe, while by no means fat, had clearly escaped the heartbreak of anorexia.

But she had a string of phone calls to make, and she had the photos of Emory Allgood's work to go over, most of which were fine, but a few would have to be redone, and she made notes for the photographer, and Lois would complain, as usual, but would reshoot as requested, also as usual.

The sculptures were in storage; she'd booked an artist who owned a van and consequently doubled as a mover, and he'd rounded up a couple of auxiliary schleppers in paint-stained jeans, and somehow they'd found the house on Quincy Street just off Classon Avenue. She wasn't sure about the neighborhood, whether they were in Fort Greene or Clinton Hill or Bed-Stuy, but the address turned out to be a fine old four-story limestone row house, a little rundown but a long way from falling apart, and the Barron family had a whole floor, and Emory All-good, the eccentric uncle, had a large room at the rear, overlooking the garden.

It had been filled with his constructions, his sculptures, and they'd overflowed into the rest of the apartment. "I'm just glad to be getting these out of here," Reginald's mother had said, "except I suspect I'm gone to miss them, you know? You get used to seeing something, and then it be gone, and you miss it."

Reginald had assured his mom that Uncle Emory would be making more, and indeed she'd barely met him, a wild-eyed, wild-haired little man, all skin and bones and knobby wrists and a bumpy forehead, who'd grinned and mumbled and then scooted past her, taking an empty laundry cart with him, and bumping down the stairs with it. Out looking for more materials, Reginald had assured her, and eager to get to work on more projects.

And all the work at the Quincy Street house was now tucked safely away in her storage locker a few blocks from the gallery, all but one piece that, finally, Mrs. Barron had decided she couldn't bear to part with. Susan could see why the woman liked it. It was the most conventional and readily accessible piece of the lot, and for that reason it was the one she herself was most willing to leave behind.

Her uncle's very first piece, Mae Barron had said, and Susan could believe it. The poor devil was just starting to go nuts then, or just beginning to figure out how to make something out of his craziness. He'd come a long ways since then.

She took care of business, and when she came up for air she saw that Chloe still had the same expression on her face. "All right," she told the girl. "You're dying to tell me something. What is it?"

"I got another one."

"Another—?"

Chloe put thumb and forefinger together, as if gripping a needle, and thrust forward. "Another piercing," she said.

How was anybody supposed to notice? The child already had both ears pierced to the hilt, not just the lobes but all up around the outside of the ear, with a little gold circlet for each hole. And, inevitably, there was a stud in her nose, a little gold bead, which she could only hope Chloe would live to regret. Because one fine day, barring an overdose of Ecstasy or a losing bout with some virulent new sexually transmitted disease, young Chloe would wake up and find herself a fifty-year-old woman with fallen arches and varicose veins and a fucking ring in her nose.

She studied the girl, who maintained her enigmatic-and-glad-of-it expression. What had been added? Another gold circlet? Who could tell, and how could that be such a source of impish delight? There was still just the one ring in her nose—and thank God and all the angels for that—and she couldn't see any evidence of any further facial mutilation. Nothing in her eyebrows; she recalled one sweet young thing with multiple eyebrow piercings, each fitted with a little gold hoop, and you found yourself waiting for someone to add a little rod and hang curtains. No safety pin through the cheek and—

God, not a tongue stud? Those made her slightly sick to think about, and didn't they thicken your speech, or get in the way when you ate?

"Not your tongue," she said, and Chloe extended the organ in question, and no, it was whole and untouched, and, the way it stuck out, just the least bit provocative. The girl retracted it just before Susan would have had to tell her to do so.

"That's a relief," she said. "Okay, I give up. Whatever it is, I can't see it."

Chloe giggled, and yanked down the front of her scoop-necked blouse, and there were two plump and pert and very charming breasts, and one of them had a gold stud in the nipple.

She looked around in alarm, but the gallery's only customer, an out-of-towner with schoolmarm glasses and a fanny pack, was on the far side of the room, trying to make sense out of one of Jeffcoate Walker's monsters. By the time she looked at Chloe, the girl had tucked her treasures safely away.

She said, "When did you—"

"Friday, right after I left here."

"How on earth—"

"I know," Chloe said. "I didn't think I could go through with it. I thought, oh, shit, this is going to hurt like a motherfucker. But it wasn't as bad as I thought it would be."

"But why?"

"Well, she puts ice on it first, and that numbs it a little, and—"

"No, that's not what I mean. Why do it? Why have it done?"

The question seemed hard for the girl to grasp, as if she'd never learned to think in those terms. "I don't know," she said. "I've just been wanting to do it for ages. And I heard about this woman, that she's really good, and like *the* person to go to if you're serious about piercing."

"You're not concerned about infection?"

"I never had any problems before."

"But the location . . ."

"You just turn it once a day, same as with an earring, and, you know, put alcohol on it. It's easier, because you can see what you're doing."

She let it go at that, but later, when Chloe was getting ready to leave for the day, she told her she still couldn't understand why she'd had the urge to get her nipple pierced in the first place. It wasn't a fashion state-ment, after all, because in the ordinary course of things it would go un-seen, except perhaps at a topless beach, and—

"It's exciting, Susan. It's like this secret thing. But you could do your navel and it'd be just as much of a secret, but it wouldn't be the same thing."

"Why?"

"Because your tit's not the same as your navel, I guess. It's tender and intimate, so that makes it scarier to do in the first place, and it's not just a secret, it's like a sex secret."

"Okay."

"Plus," she said, "it's just plain hot."

"A turn-on for guys, you mean."

"Probably, if only because of what it says. *Hey, look at me, I'm hot.* But it's a turn-on just having it. Physically, I mean."

"Physically? Knowing it's there, I suppose, but—"

"No, *physically*, Susan. You know how it feels when someone plays with your nipple and it gets hard? Or you do it yourself? That's how you feel *all the time*."

SHE DIDN'T WANT TO miss anything.

And there were things she'd missed just by being born when she was. When she was a kid, *safe sex* meant your parents wouldn't find out what you did, or it meant being on the pill. But by the time she was old enough, out of high school and ready to check out the world, safe sex meant being careful what you did and whom you did it with, because there was sud-denly this new disease and if you got it you died. Penicillin didn't help, nothing helped, you just died.

When she was married, when it began to dawn on her and Gary that they both had urges that extended beyond their own double bed, they'd speculated about partying with other couples, about orgies, about clubs where you could just take off your clothes and have sex with strangers. There used to be clubs like that, there was Plato's Retreat, for one, and it was supposed to be a hip thing to go there in the late seventies and early eighties, before AIDS, before safe sex. She'd heard stories about it, in high school, in college, and there were different movie stars who were supposed to show up now and then, and by the time she'd have been ready for it, the place was closed.

Gary had wanted to see her with another woman, and somehow he found another couple similarly inclined, and she and the other wife spent an awkward half hour doing things, both of them for the first time, and she might have enjoyed it if it hadn't been abundantly clear that the other woman was just there to keep her husband happy.

The men didn't notice the difference, or didn't care, and when she and Donna had run out of new things to pretend to enjoy, Gary, fiercely tumescent, was on her at once, even as the other man—she couldn't remember his name—mounted his own wife. Gary would have been happier taking a shot at Donna, that was obvious, but that had not been part of the original game plan, and she was just as glad, finding Donna's husband singularly unappealing.

They'd met them through a personal ad Gary had answered (or perhaps he'd placed the ad himself, she was never sure) and of course they never saw them again. He was funny afterward, annoyed with her for not having gotten into the spirit of the thing, then concerned that she had been having such a good time with the other woman. Deep down inside, was she really a lesbian?

He was anxious, too, that someone in his office would find out, and what kind of behavior was that for an assistant district attorney, an officer of the court and member of the bar? She didn't see how that could happen; at his insistence they'd used false names, and of course at one point she'd called him Gary, which no one appeared to notice, anyway, but still he'd reproached her for it on the way home. Didn't she have any sense? Couldn't she even keep names straight?

Then two weeks later he wanted to meet another couple, he had their letter and photo, and he sulked and pouted when she said she wasn't interested.

The incident hadn't ended their marriage, it was going to end anyway, but the underlying issue was not the least of the forces pushing them apart. He'd long since remarried, and she heard they were happy, and tried not to wonder what their sex life was like.

Since then she'd slept with men she was attracted to. And she had gone to bed a couple of times with a woman, a canvasser for the local Democratic organization. They'd gone to the same college but hadn't really known each other then, and the lovemaking was good but the woman was too neurotic, and a couple of times was plenty.

When she was living with Marc, he'd taken her once to an S&M club he knew about at Greenwich and Gansevoort, in the old meatpacking district just below Fourteenth Street, and they'd worn leather to fit in and drunk fruit juice at the bar. Nobody was actually screwing, the activity was all role-playing, bondage and discipline, domination and submission. Some of it looked interesting, but in a curiously intellectual way. She felt disconnected from it, and, worse, was very conscious of being an intruder. Her spiked wrist bands and leather pants didn't change the fact that she was just a voyeuse.

"They don't mind," Marc had assured her. "They're exhibitionists, for God's sake. If they didn't want an audience they'd stay home."

She could understand that. She had a streak of exhibitionism herself, and much the best thing about her half hour with Donna had been knowing she was being watched. But she really didn't want to stand around like a tourist while a fat man with a too-long goatee had his buttocks whipped by a wraithlike woman in what looked like a black wet suit with cutouts. Nor, God help her, did she want to change places with either of them.

"I just thought it was something you should see," he told her later, and she said she was glad she'd gone, but wouldn't want to go again. No, he said, neither would he, but he had the feeling she'd make a dandy dominatrix.

What made him say that, she'd wanted to know. Was he interested in that sort of thing? Did he long to play slave and mistress, did he want her to tie him up, to do any of what they'd seen at the club?

"Not my scene," he'd said, "but I have to say I can picture you in the role. Maybe it's just that you'd look great in the costumes."

Was it something she wanted to do? She hadn't thought so, but knew there was something she needed to explore, some limits she had to test.

Once the museum in Lausanne had changed her life, she'd been too busy to find the envelope, let alone push it. The gallery took all her energy, and didn't leave her the time to have a relationship in which to grow restless. There were a few men she saw, two of whom were ideal for her purposes. They were both married, they both lived out of town (one in Connecticut, one in a suburb of Detroit), and she'd met them at the gallery, where they'd bought pieces of art from her.

When the first one had hit on her, the Detroit guy, she'd been concerned about the propriety of sleeping with a client, but she decided she was being overly scrupulous. She wasn't a shrink going to bed with a patient, or a studio boss nailing a starlet, or a matrimonial lawyer (like hers, for example, the shitheel) consoling an incipient divorcee. He'd fallen in love with Aleesha MacReady's take on Susannah and the Elders, and she'd sold it to him with the mixture of elation and despair that came from getting a good price for a work she herself loved and would never see again. What was there about the transaction to prevent them from having dinner together? And, afterward, why shouldn't she go back to his hotel room (the Pierre, a high floor, a view of the park, very nice) and fuck his brains out?

Her life worked, and the gallery was getting a good reputation, and even making a little money. Lately, though, she was feeling a vague restlessness. She couldn't define it, didn't know what it was, and found herself talking about it at lunch with an old school friend.

"Tick tock," Audrey had said. "You need to have a baby."

"What are you talking about?"

"Your biological clock, Suze. You're what, thirty-six?"

"Close enough."

"What does that mean, thirty-seven? And don't tell me about your lack of maternal impulses. Doesn't matter. Tick fucking tock, and you've got the urge whether you know it or not."

"Forget it," she'd said. "I don't want a baby. For God's sake, I'd rather have fibroids."

And it was true, the last thing she wanted was a baby, she didn't even trust herself with house plants, but the clock was ticking all the same, and it wasn't her fertility that was running out, it was her life. She didn't really expect to die soon (though people died whether they expected to or not, they got on planes that crashed or worked in buildings that planes crashed into). But the same friend who'd advised her that her clock was ticking had brought news of a classmate who'd died of breast cancer, and another struck down by one of the more virulent forms of multiple sclerosis. She was young, she was in the fucking prime of life, but that was no guarantee of anything, was it? Because there were no guarantees, and there never had been, but it took you a while before you realized it.

How long before she wouldn't want to have sex? How long before nobody much wanted to have it with her? She looked great, people looked at her on the street, and not just construction workers, who looked at everybody, but men in suits, men with briefcases.

If there was anything she wanted to do, now was the time to do it. If there was anything she was curious about, now was the time to satisfy her curiosity. That was what had moved her to crawl under the table at L'Aiglon d'Or and surprise Maury Winters with a blow job he'd be a long time forgetting. She'd always wanted to do something like that, she'd always wondered what it would be like, so what was she waiting for?

And if someone saw her, so what? So fucking what? The management wouldn't ask her to leave. They were a French restaurant, and hadn't a president of France died that way, carried off by a stroke or a heart attack, leaving some terrified little cupcake (or an éclair, *s'il vous plaît*) trapped in the well beneath his desk?

So why shouldn't she get her nipple pierced? How painful could it be? If she didn't like the result, she'd take the ring out and let it heal up. And if it really made you feel excited all the time . . .

SHE SAID, "HOW COME you don't have any piercings?" And, when Medea put a finger to an earlobe, "Besides that. I mean, everybody has pierced ears."

"The others don't show."

"Your nipples?"

"Would you like to see?"

There was the slightest smile on Medea's full lips, and Susan sensed that the woman was playing with her. She could resist, or she could let herself be played with. And what on earth would resistance gain her?

She nodded.

Medea reached behind her neck, unfastened a clasp, and let the white shift fall to the floor. She stepped out of it, and she was the same golden brown color all over, and Susan was sure that some of the color came from the sun, because she could smell the sun on Medea's skin.

The woman's figure was exquisite, slim at the waist, just full enough in the hips to be feminine. Her breasts were as firm as a girl's and of a size to fit the hand, and both nipples were pierced, and sported gold studs identical to the ones in her ears.

She felt lightheaded, felt a tingling in the palms of her hands and the soles of her feet. She had never been so moved by the physical beauty of another human being. She was responding to Medea as to a work of art. She felt foolish staring at her like this, but sensed the woman was willing to be stared at. And this was confirmed when Medea raised her arms over her head and pirouetted slowly around, like a slave girl displaying herself in an Eastern market.

The woman had no body hair at all, not on her legs, not under her arms, not at her crotch. There was the faintest trace of sun-bleached golden down on her arms, but that was all.

"I'd recommend studs," Medea said, touching her own for illustration. "Certainly at first, and for general wear. They don't show until you want them to. And you can always switch to hoops for special occasions. Do you like the way they look?"

"Very much."

"There's more, if you're interested."

"More?"

"More piercings."

But she'd seen the woman, front and back, top to bottom. How could there be more piercings?

A tongue stud? But wouldn't she have noticed it? And wouldn't she have simply stuck out her tongue?

No, it wasn't a tongue stud. Of course not.

"Are you interested?"

She nodded.

"You have to say so. You have to ask to see it."

"Please," she said.

"Please what?"

"Please show me."

Medea backed up, sat down on the carpeted ledge, a pillow beneath her bottom. She opened her legs to reveal gold hoops half an inch in diameter affixed to her labia. The sight was not a surprise, by this point Susan had guessed what she'd see and where she'd see it, but there was something so intimate about the display that emotion flowed over her like a wave. She thought she might cry, or cry out.

"Rings," Medea said, "because studs would sort of get lost here. And so you can do this."

And she took a ring between each thumb and forefinger and opened herself up.

Susan stood there. Her heart was pounding, tolling like a bell in her chest.

"Go ahead," Medea told her.

She sank to her knees.

THERE WAS ANOTHER ROOM where the piercing was done, and it looked like a surgery, with white walls and a white tile floor. There was a padded table one could lie on, a high-backed chair one could sit on. There was a shelf of books, and a copy of Gray's *Anatomy* open on top of a small metal cabinet.

She had undressed in the other room, even as Medea had donned the white shift again. She might have left her slacks on, but she took everything off, blouse and bra, slacks and panties.

She waited for Medea to indicate whether she was to sit in the chair or get up on the table, but the woman made no sign. The far wall, Susan noticed, was curtained, and something made her ask what was behind the curtain.

"Sometimes it's difficult to keep oneself still," Medea said. "Fear, pain, excitement—one moves, and it's better not to move."

"I can keep still."

"Sometimes it's a relief not to have to try to keep still, Susan. To be able to let go."

Medea drew the curtain. Behind it, in front of a windowless wall, stood a black metal frame in the shape of an X. There were black leather wrist and ankle cuffs attached to the four arms of the device. For a moment Susan experienced what she thought was déjà vu, until she realized that she actually had seen a similar apparatus at the club on Gansevoort Street.

Wordlessly, she stood with her back up against the cold metal and allowed Medea to fasten the cuffs. She hesitated for only a moment when Medea showed her a black leather hood, then gave a quick nod. The hood covered her entire head but was cut out in front so that she could breathe through her nose. Her mouth was covered, so she couldn't cry out, nor could she see a thing through the black leather. And, when Medea secured the hood to the upper arms of the cross, her head was immobilized.

She realized suddenly that she hadn't told Medea which nipple she wanted pierced, nor had Medea asked. And she knew that she was not going to be allowed to choose, that it would be Medea's choice, and something deep within her, something that had been wound tight, suddenly relaxed. It was her fear, she decided. She hadn't known she was afraid, hadn't permitted herself to feel it, and now the fear was gone.

There was a timeless moment, and then Medea was touching the tips of both of her breasts at once. Her touch was feather light, but hardly necessary to prepare her for the ordeal. Both nipples were already firm and fully extended.

The touching continued, and finally stopped, and then she felt Medea's mouth on one breast, and then on the other.

Making her choice, she thought. She gets to choose. You get to not choose.

She chose the right breast, and a moment later Susan felt what she at first took for fire, and then knew was ice. Odd how you could mistake the one sensation for its opposite, cold for hot. Odd how the ice, numbing her nipple, sent currents of energy coursing through the rest of her body.

Something brushed her nose. She breathed in the scent of oranges. Then she felt something pressed against the tip of her right breast, and then she felt the sensation she had planned to steel herself against. But she'd forgotten to do so, somehow, and now Medea had thrust a needle through her nipple, and she opened herself up entirely to the sensation, and God, it was too much, but no, no, it was not too much.

It was only fire and ice. It was only pain.

THE BLACK METAL X was a St. Andrew's cross, Medea told her. Her wrists and ankles were still fastened to it but the hood was off and she could look down and see the gold stud that had been thrust through her right nipple, with a little gold bead showing on either side.

Medea was asking her how she felt.

It took her a moment to realize she could speak now. "Good," she said. "What was the orange for?"

"To receive the needle. Otherwise I might stick myself."

"Oh."

"I'll cut it in quarters. We'll eat it."

She shook her head. "First do the other one."

"Today?"

"Please."

"Of course. Do you want the hood?"

Did she? She didn't need it, but it streamlined the process, taking away the options of sight and speech.

Before her mouth was covered, she said, "No ice this time."

MEDEA'S BEDROOM WAS ANOTHER surprise. It was Victorian, the bed a four-poster, the mattress soft, the sheets cool cotton. Susan lay on her side, enjoying the postlovemaking languor, feeling the sweat cooling on her skin, the soreness at the tips of her breasts.

She was thinking of Medea's hairless loins, and without preamble she said, "Isn't it a nuisance, having to have it waxed?"

"I do it myself."

"Really?"

"And it could be a nuisance, but I don't like body hair."

"I was so excited when I finally started to get some."

"I was excited when I got my first period," Medea said. "It ceased to be exciting some time ago."

"The most excitement," Susan remembered, "was one time when I didn't. If I'd had her, how old would she be?"

"It was a girl?"

"They never told me. I just always think of it as female, I don't know why." She rolled onto her back, looked up at the ceiling. "I've mostly been with men. How about you?"

"Some of each. I'm mostly by myself. When I do the waxing, I make a ritual of it. Music and candlelight, scented oils. I'll spend hours. So it's not such a nuisance."

"You did your own piercings, didn't you?"

"Not the ears. They were done ages ago. But everything else, yes."

They fell silent, and then Susan was surprised to find herself telling Medea about the incident at L'Aiglon d'Or. "I just wanted to do it," she said, "and I did."

"You're very bold."

"Am I?" She thought about it. "I don't know. Maybe I'm just a whore."

"You could be both."

She laughed.

"But you're not a whore," Medea said.

"I have to ask you this. Were you with Chloe?"

"Chloe?"

"My assistant, I mentioned her before. The blonde with the crew cut and the nose ring."

Medea laughed. "They're all blondes," she said, "and they all have nose rings. But I remember her, and no, all I did was pierce her and send her home. That's all I ever do. This never happens."

"Never?"

"Two, three times in as many years. Some repeat clients like to be immobilized and hooded, and of course it's sexual for them, but not for me. I wanted you. I don't know why. It won't happen again."

"If I wanted more piercings . . ."

"Where?"

"Like yours."

"Wait at least three months, dear. Give yourself time to integrate the piercing you just had."

"And if I decide I want a waxing?"

"I can give you the name of someone who's very good."

"I see."

Medea leaned over her, kissed her lightly on the lips, rose from the bed.

"ALCOHOL ON A COTTON ball several times a day," Medea told her. "Rotate the posts ninety degrees once a day. You can take aspirin for the pain."

She'd have stuffed her bra in her purse, but Medea suggested she wear it to prevent her sore nipples from rubbing against her blouse as she walked. When she'd finished dressing she realized she hadn't paid for the piercing. She reached for her purse, asked how much she owed.

"Oh, please," Medea said. "There's no charge."

"But that's not right. I took up a couple of hours of your time."

"I enjoyed the experience."

"And the gold studs, at the very least let me pay for the studs."

"They're a gift. You may feel like a whore if you like. But there's no need." And, when she hesitated, "We won't do this again. We're not going to become lovers. But I'll think of you when I masturbate."

Medea held the door for her, ushered her through it. She rode the elevator to the lobby, walked out onto Fifty-seventh Street.

And I'll think of you, she thought, next time I blow a lawyer in a restaurant.

Her nipples tingled.

ten

THE MAN WHO had registered at the Hotel Clinton as G. T. Strong, the man who had left his Tuborg untouched on the bar at the Kettle of Fish, the man who had lost his entire family in or after the 9/11 attack, stood in the shadowed doorway of an apartment house on East Twenty-eighth Street and watched the building directly across the street.

He was dressed differently, in clothes he'd retrieved from his storage locker. He was wearing a dark suit and a white shirt and a necktie, and he'd replaced his sneakers with lace-up black oxfords. He'd shaved that morning, as he did two or three times a week.

During the afternoon he'd found a leather briefcase in good shape at a thrift shop. A hardware store supplied a hammer, an ice pick, a large screwdriver, and a cold chisel.

It had taken him a while to get to this point, and there'd been some changes in the external circumstances of his life. He lived in a different hotel, and was registered under another name. He'd finished that volume of George Templeton Strong's diary and had exchanged it for another book, Herbert Asbury's *The Gangs of New York*. He liked Strong, but the man had been deeply interested in music, he'd taught it at Columbia, and the diary entries were full of music. He'd had enough music for the time being, and he always enjoyed Asbury, had read the book many times over the years. Picking it up was like taking up an old friendship.

Now he was three-fourths of the way through it.

For a week or more he'd been uncertain what to do, and so he'd followed his routine, walking, reading, taking his meals, waiting for the next action to reveal itself to him. Until early one morning, walking on Eighth Avenue in Chelsea, he'd seen a familiar face. It was the young man who'd discovered the body on Charles Street. Pancake, his name was. No, that was wrong, but he would wait and it would come to him.

He spent the whole day following the young man, and of course the name came to him as he had known it would. He'd seen it in the newspapers. Pankow, that was the name. He followed him to his home and returned the next morning to follow him on his rounds again.

Pattern, that was what he was looking for. Not the pattern of Gerald Pankow's days, that was evident enough, but the pattern that he himself was creating, had been creating since his wife and son and daughter and son-in-law had sacrificed themselves for the city.

Too long a sacrifice can make a stone of the heart . . .

The line came to him and he knew he'd read it somewhere once but didn't know where or when. Did he have a heart of stone? He put the tips of his fingers to his chest, as if to palpate the heart within, to determine by touch if it had calcified.

The three bars Pankow swept out each morning were possibilities, but, once he'd managed to determine the nature of the premises on Twenty-eighth Street, it was clear to him where he ought to direct his efforts. He stopped following Pankow and began spending his waking hours on Twenty-eighth Street.

The building was five stories tall, with a Korean nail shop on the parlor floor and a locksmith a floor below, several steps down from street level. The top three floors were residential, but the third floor was the one Pankow cleaned every morning. He'd known that from the first; the lights went on moments after the young man entered the building, and went off shortly before he left.

Watching the traffic in and out of the building, watching lights go on and off, he learned the nature of the business conducted on the third floor and the schedule on which they operated. After Pankow left, there was no activity for a couple of hours. Then, somewhere between ten-thirty and eleven, a middle-aged woman appeared and let herself in with a key. Over the next hour, five or six considerably younger women came and buzzed to be admitted.

Starting at noon, men came to the door, buzzed, went inside, and reappeared anywhere between twenty minutes and an hour later. Around ten in the evening, two or three of the girls would leave. At midnight or a few minutes after the hour, the lights would go out, and shortly thereafter the remaining girls and the older woman would leave the building and go their separate ways.

Three days ago he'd got the suit out of storage, shaved, put it on. He'd found out the telephone number—it wasn't difficult when you knew the address and knew how to use a computer at an Internet café—and he called it. He made an appointment, saying a friend had recommended the establishment. He was going to give his friend's name as George Strong, and his own as Herbert Asbury, but the woman who answered hadn't asked for names.

Instead she'd supplied one. When he rang the bell, he was to say his name was Mr. Flood.

He'd said he would come at ten that evening, and from nine o'clock he waited across the street, and at ten he rang downstairs, gave his name as Mr. Flood, and was admitted. There were two girls in abbreviated costumes in what he guessed you'd call the parlor, and the older woman who brought him there told him they were both available. To pick one was to reject the other, which bothered him until he realized how unlikely it was that it bothered them. One girl reminded him faintly of his wife as a young girl, and so he chose the other.

He hadn't had sex since well before the bombing. He and his wife had still had relations, but it had become an infrequent event. Sometime in July or August, he supposed, and it was July now, so it might have been a year since he'd had sex, or wanted to.

He still didn't want to, but when he and the girl were both undressed he found he was able to perform. He became detached during the act, and observed, disembodied, as his body did what it was supposed to do. She had put the condom on for him and she removed it and disposed of it, returning with a washcloth to sponge him clean.

He paid the madam a hundred dollars, tipped the girl twenty. He went straight to his hotel, and when the hall shower was empty he stood under the spray for a long time, washing her scent from his body.

Now, three days later, he'd shaved again and put on the suit again, and he'd called and made an appointment for eleven-thirty. "Don't be late," the madam told him. "On account of we close up at midnight."

At ten minutes past ten the door opened, and three of the girls came out and walked off together toward Third Avenue. He felt a stab of sorrow when he noted that the girl he'd been with on his previous visit was not among them. Of course she might not have come in at all that day, that was entirely possible, but he had a feeling he'd find her in the parlor when he went upstairs.

And he was right. "I know you had a good time with Clara the other night," the madam said, "so you could see her again, or Debra here's a very sweet girl herself, if you're a man who likes a change."

He was a man who liked things to remain the same. That, at least, was the sort of man he had always been. But things didn't remain the same, they changed irrespective of the sort of man you were. And nowadays he didn't know what he liked, or what sort of man he was.

He chose Clara. If he'd been told her name the first time he'd forgotten it as soon as he heard it, but he knew it now, and wished he didn't.

"You musta worked late," she said, when they were in the bedroom together. She nodded at the briefcase. "Came straight from the office, didn't you?"

He nodded.

"What you need now," she said, "is you need to relax."

He undressed, and she slipped out of her wrapper. Her body was familiar to him, and that made him wish he'd chosen the other girl, whose name he'd already forgotten.

He wished he could forget Clara's.

While she was hanging up his suit jacket, he opened the briefcase and drew out the heavy claw hammer, chromed steel with a black rubber grip. The price sticker was still on it. Her back was to him when he brought the hammer up and swung it as hard as he possibly could at the back of her head. It made an awful sound, but that was the only sound; she fell without crying out, and he caught her as she fell and eased her down.

Was she dead? Had the single blow been sufficient?

It was hard to tell. She lay face up, and she might have been sleeping but for the blood that welled from the back of her head. He took hold of her wrist but couldn't tell whether it was her pulse that he felt or the throbbing of his own heart. He had to be sure, and he didn't want to hit her again, wasn't sure that he could, so he got the cold chisel and stuck it into the left side of her chest.

He felt an awful aching in his own chest, as if he himself had been stabbed. He looked down at her and felt tears coursing down his cheeks and realized that he was weeping. He got a tissue from the box at the bedside, wiped the tears away.

Sacrifice—hers now, along with so many others—had not made a stone of his heart, not yet, not entirely. He could still feel. He could still weep.

AFTER THE DEATHS, THE four that were his, the three thousand that were his city's, all he could seem to do was read, and all he could read was the city's history. He took down his copy of the New York City encyclopedia, the huge volume that had been a surprise bestseller for Yale University Press, and sat down with it, reading it through like a novel. He'd browsed extensively in the book since it had come into his possession, but now he started at the first page and read through to the last.

Not everything registered. There were times when he would sit up, realizing he'd read his way through several articles, scanning the columns, turning the pages, and he had no idea what he'd just read. It didn't matter. He wasn't studying for a test. He went on reading, and turning pages.

From time to time he would pause and look off into the middle distance, and his mind would go all over the place.

When it was time to sleep, he slept. When he thought of it, he ate. When he was awake, he sat in his chair and read.

He had been reading about the Draft Riots in New York during the Civil War, when the city was essentially lawless for days, and when mobs lynched black men and beat policemen to death. The Draft Riots were a puzzle, an anomaly, and all the arguments trotted out to explain them—the animosity, born of competition for work, of Irish immigrants for freed African slaves, the resentment of white workingmen at being drafted to fight a war for black freedom, and others, so many others—all were valid, and all seemed beside the point.

But he'd looked at them in the context of the Civil War, or in the context of the city's ethnic and political realities, and he could see that he'd been completely wrong. The Draft Riots happened because they had to happen.

They were a sacrifice.

They were the city, New York, sacrificing itself for its own greater glory. They were a ritual bloodletting by means of which the city's soul was redeemed and renewed, rising from its own psychic ashes to be reborn greater than it had been before.

And the Draft Riots were not an isolated example. No, not at all. The city had been shocked over the centuries by no end of tragedies, great pointless disasters that were no longer pointless when viewed through the lens of his new perspective.

The *General Slocum* tragedy, for example, when a ship loaded to capacity with German immigrants and their children, bound for a holiday excursion, caught fire and burned and sank in the East River. Hundreds of men and women and children perished, so many that the Lower East Side neighborhood known as Little Germany ceased overnight to exist. So many residents had been lost that the survivors couldn't bear to stay where they were. They moved en masse, most to the Yorkville section of the Upper East Side.

Or the Triangle Shirtwaist fire of 1911, when 150 seamstresses, most of them young Jewish women, died when the sweatshop they worked in went up in flames. They couldn't get out, the fire doors were locked, so they either jumped to their death or died in the fire.

Sacrificed, all of them. And each time the city, reeling in shock, bleeding from its wounds, had rebounded to become greater than ever. Each time the souls of the sacrificed had become part of the greater soul of the city, enriching it, enlarging it.

When this great insight came, this revelation, he stopped his front-to-back reading of the encyclopedia and began skipping around, looking for further examples to support his thesis. They were there in abundance, tragedies great and small, from the city's earliest days to the eleventh of September.

The history of the city was the history of violent death.

The gang wars, from the pitched battles between the Bowery Boys and the Dead Rabbits to the endless Mafia palace coups and clan wars. Albert Anastasia, shot dead in the barber chair at the Park Sheraton hotel. Joey Gallo, gunned down in Umberto's Clam House. Throughout the five boroughs, blood seeped into the pavement. The rain couldn't wash it away. It only made it invisible.

And fires, so many fires. You thought of the city as nonflammable, a city of glass and steel and asphalt and concrete, but hadn't the world watched as buildings of glass and steel burned like torches until they melted and collapsed of their own weight? Oh, yes, forests could burn, and wooden houses could burn, but so could cities of concrete and steel.

ENERGIZED BY WHAT HAD emerged from his reading, he found it impossible to read. He would pick up a book only to put it down and pace the floor, consumed by the thoughts that came at him in battalions. He began to leave the apartment, walking for hours through the city's streets. His feet took him to Little Germany, where no Germans had lived for years, and past the one-time site of the Triangle Shirtwaist factory, and, more than once, to the barriers that still ringed Ground Zero.

And, walking, he had a further insight.

He was thinking of the fire in the unlicensed social club that had taken the lives of seventy or eighty Hondurans a few years earlier. It had been a great tragedy, certainly, but it had not come upon the poor people as an act of God. An embittered Honduran immigrant, furious over some real or fancied insult, had returned to the club with a container of gasoline and set the place on fire. He'd been caught and tried and convicted, and was serving a life sentence somewhere.

The people he'd killed had been sacrificed to the city of New York, he could see that clearly enough. They'd come to New York and died here so that others of their countrymen could follow them here and live and thrive and prosper. And the man who hurled the gasoline, the man who tossed the match, had surely been the architect of their sacrifice, and hadn't he sacrificed himself in the bargain? He was alive (unless he'd been killed in prison, for he did seem the type to get killed in prison) but what kind of a life did he have?

Perhaps . . .

Well, take the Triangle Shirtwaist fire. A horrible fire, certainly, bad enough to consume the entire building, but the great loss of life occurred because the doors were locked from the outside. Otherwise there would have been fatalities, certainly, but some, even most of the young women would have been able to get out alive.

Was it pure happenstance that the doors were locked? Was it, as some claimed, that the bosses locked the doors to keep the women at their sewing machines?

Or . . .

Or could the same hand have locked the doors and set the fire?

That's what had happened. He was sure of it. Someone had made the great tragedy happen, someone intent upon causing as much loss of life as possible. Maybe it was sheer villainy, as inexplicable as all evil is inexplicable, or maybe, maybe . . .

Maybe it was someone with a vision. Maybe it was someone willing to sacrifice those lives, and to give up his own morality in the process, his morality and his hope of eternal reward (for what fate but Hell could await a man who'd do such a thing?), to give up everything, to *sacrifice* everything, for the sake of the greater good?

Dulce et decorum est pro patria mori.

The Latin phrase came to him from somewhere in the past. Sweet and decorous it is to die for one's country. Or for one's city, and how would you say that in Latin? He'd forgotten everything he ever knew of the language, except for a few odd words and phrases. Still, the things you'd forgotten tended to come back to you.

Dulce et decorum est . . .

And the *General Slocum* disaster? There were all sorts of explanations advanced for the tragedy, several of them plausible enough, but were any as apt as that someone had sabotaged the ship, someone had set the fire, someone had deliberately made the whole thing happen?

And the Draft Riots. Spontaneous combustion, erupting naturally and inevitably out of social and political and economic realities? Or did circumstances merely provide a framework of logs and sticks and kindling, waiting for a knowing hand to strike the spark and fan the blaze? The history books spoke of neighborhood agitators who'd urged on the mob, only to lose control of it. But what if they'd never intended to control it? What if their sole purpose had been to unleash the whirlwind?

He saw them now, a long chain of men (and women, too, for who was to say it was an exclusively male calling?), not selling their souls but giving them up, sentencing them to perdition, committing unpardonable sins for the good of generations yet unborn.

Did many of them see the greater purpose? Probably not, but surely some did. Surely he was not the first to be consciously aware of what he had to do, no matter how great the cost to himself.

Walking home, he picked up a discarded newspaper. A man in a stolen car had gone berserk at the wheel, driving down Seventh Avenue at top speed, running red lights, caroming off other cars, and taking deliberate aim at pedestrians, trying to run down as many of them as he possibly could. He eluded police pursuit, then repeated the stunt on Eighth Avenue, hitting a few more pedestrians before he was finally taken into custody. He was perfectly calm, and told police he was angry, though he seemed unable to say what it was he'd been angry about.

He remembered how he'd taken the sleeping pills and lain down beside his wife. He had been ready to join her sacrifice, and his disappointment at surviving had been softened slightly by the thought that there must be something for him to do.

And now he knew what it was.

Dulce et decorum est . . . pro urbe *mori.*

See? It had come back to him.

IN LATE MARCH, A little more than six months after he'd scattered his wife's ashes to the winds of Lower Manhattan, he took the number 3 subway to the Bronx. He got off at the East 160th Street stop and walked north and west to an abandoned building on Cauldwell Avenue. He'd discovered it a week ago, and had visited it daily for the past several days. The windows were boarded up, but the piece of sheet metal nailed over the doorway had been pried up at the lower left corner to give access to the squatters—drug addicts, homeless people—who found the place an acceptable alternative to sleeping in the street.

He'd purchased half a dozen quart cans of charcoal lighter fluid, buying them one at a time in different shops in Manhattan to avoid arousing suspicion, and he carried them with him in a canvas tote bag that had belonged to his wife. It had been a gift from one of the children, a cloth sack with GOOCHEE stenciled on the sides, and the giver—it was his son, he remembered now, and he couldn't have been more than twelve at the time—had told her that he knew what she really wanted was a Gucci bag.

How they'd laughed, and how she'd loved that bag. She'd used it for years.

He fully expected someone, a cop or a local resident, to challenge him, to demand to know what he was doing where he so clearly did not

belong. He was oddly calm, quite unconcerned about what might happen
to him, but in fact nothing happened, and no one seemed to notice him.

Maybe he was dead, he thought. Maybe he was a ghost, and that was
why people paid no attention to him. They couldn't see him.

But no, he'd bought the charcoal lighter fluid. He'd handed over his
money, been given his purchases and his change.

He raised the sheet metal, crawled under it, and went into every
ground-floor room he came to, squirting the lighter fluid where he
thought it would be most effective. He emptied all six cans, lit a match,
set a fire, and walked away from the building.

Steps away from it, he remembered the GOOCHEE bag. He'd put it
down and neglected to pick it up. Well, the fire would consume it, and it
would be untraceable anyway. He kept walking.

In movies there would be a great whoosh, an explosion, flames shooting into the night sky, shock waves knocking him to the ground as he ran
off down the street. But there was nothing of the sort. He walked a block,
looked back, and saw a building that looked no different from the way it
had looked when he approached it. His attempt at sacrifice-by-arson
would seem to have been a failure.

He turned at the corner, walked a block, turned again. He kept walking until he came to a small storefront restaurant with signs in Spanish.
There were no tables, just a worn Formica counter with eight backless
stools.

He took a stool. The menu hung on the wall, chalk on slate, with several of the dishes rubbed out. Even if he read Spanish, it would have been
hard to make out. The woman behind the counter, assuming he didn't
speak Spanish, addressed him in strongly accented English, asking him
what he wanted. He pointed to the plate of the man two stools away on
his right.

"Arroz con pollo," the woman said. "Tha's cheecken an' rice. Tha's
what you wan'?"

He nodded. The food, when she brought it, was a little spicy for his
taste, but it wasn't bad. He wasn't hungry, he was rarely hungry, but realized he hadn't eaten since breakfast. And thirsty. Water was *aqua* in
Latin, and was it *agua* in Spanish? Or if he just made the gesture, raising
an invisible glass to his lips . . .

While he was considering the matter, she brought him a glass of
water.

He had eaten half his meal when he heard sirens. And this wasn't a
single ambulance, this was more than one siren. He tucked ten dollars under his plate and didn't wait for change. He'd lost his bearings, wasn't

sure which way he'd come from, but all he had to do was walk toward the
sirens.

The building was burning after all. He didn't see flames shooting, but
there was a lot of smoke, and a lot of activity on the part of the firefighters. A crowd had gathered to watch, and he joined them, but felt danger-
ously conspicuous. He managed to find his way to the subway and went
home.

It made the papers, because there were two fatalities—a young man
who'd evidently been sleeping, or comatose from drugs, and a firefighter,
thirty-two years old, the father of three, a resident of Sunnyside, Queens.
Both had died of smoke inhalation.

He mourned them, and honored their sacrifice.

A DAY AFTER THE Bronx fire, he set about reorganizing his life. He liq-
uidated his stocks and mutual funds and put everything into a money-
market account at his bank. The apartment was his most substantial asset,
but it seemed an impossible chore to list it for sale and wait for the co-op
board to approve a prospective purchaser. And how much money did he
need, anyway? A few dollars for rent, a few dollars for food.

In the end, he'd walked away from the apartment. Rented a storage
locker, ferried some possessions there a carton at a time, then packed a
small suitcase and left. Sooner or later, he supposed, his failure to pay
maintenance charges would lead someone to take some sort of legal action, and he'd eventually lose the apartment, but he'd never even know
when it happened, and wouldn't care if he did.

Since then, he had set a fire in a two-family house in Middle Village,
Queens (minimal damage, no loss of life) and sacrificed three people in
their homes, most recently Marilyn Fairchild, of Charles Street. Sometimes his actions seemed pointless to him. How could individual sacrifices revitalize the wounded city? As well, he thought, to try easing the
water shortage by spilling a bucket of water into the reservoir.

Then he'd spotted Gerald Pankow, and recognized him, and saw a
way to establish a pattern.

And now he rose from the body of the girl. He opened the door a few
inches and stuck his head out. He said, "Could one of you come here for
a moment? Something seems to be wrong with"—what was her name?—
"with Clara."

The older woman came, the madam, and she saw Clara lying on her
back, then registered the chisel planted in her chest, and looked up at him,
naked, advancing on her, and opened her mouth to scream, to cry out, but
before she could make a sound he hit her with the hammer. It was a glanc-

ing blow and it drove her to her knees. She held up hands curled into claws, she blinked at the blood flowing down her forehead and into her eyes, and he swung the hammer full force and smashed her skull.

Without checking if she was dead he bolted from the room. Debra was racing for the phone. She tripped over a footstool, righted herself, and had the phone in her hand when he reached her. He wielded the hammer and hit her on the shoulder and she dropped the phone and cried out, and he swung backhand and hit her just above the bridge of the nose. She went sprawling and he rained blows upon her, hammering at her face until her features were unrecognizable.

His own heart was pounding. He steadied himself, got to his feet, and had trouble keeping his balance because the room was spinning. His knees buckled, and the black curtain came down.

Later, when he got around to noting the time, he calculated that he had been out for the better part of a half hour. He had fallen beside Debra, and he had blood all over himself, and he must have left fingerprints all over the place, and she'd cried out between the first and second blows, and someone a floor above could have heard her, could have heard the noise the hammer made, could have heard him when he fell.

He might have awakened to bright lights and sirens. Instead he came to in the midst of silence and death.

He found the bathroom. He showered, used the liquid soap, used the Herbal Essence shampoo. He retrieved the hammer from where it lay beside Debra's body, the chisel from Clara's chest, and washed them both in the sink before returning them to the briefcase. He dressed, tied his tie until he got the knot right.

He put his hand into the pocket of his suit jacket and drew out the little turquoise rabbit. He'd been carrying it ever since he took it from Marilyn Fairchild's apartment, and now he walked over to Clara's body, got down onto one knee, and placed the rabbit so that it covered the hole the chisel had left in her chest.

What would they make of that?

He went around the apartment, using a hand towel to wipe surfaces he remembered touching and others he might have touched. But he'd touched the rabbit, hadn't he? He picked it up and wiped it off and decided he wasn't ready to leave it behind after all. He put it in his pocket and left Clara's wound uncovered.

The poor girl . . .

He had the towel over his hand when he turned the doorknob to let himself out, dropped it behind him before he drew the door shut.

He walked crosstown to his hotel. On the way he stopped several times to discard the tools from his briefcase, dropping them into three well-separated storm drains. He hadn't used the big screwdriver, had never even removed it from the briefcase, but he got rid of it just the same, and left the briefcase propped against a trash can. Perhaps someone would get some use out of it.

eleven

FROM THE MOMENT he'd found Marilyn dead in her apartment, the very apartment he'd been so blithely cleaning, opening doors ceased to be a carefree enterprise for Jerry Pankow. He couldn't turn a key without at least a quiver of anxiety over what he might find on the other side of the door.

Not so much with his commercial clients, the three bars and the whorehouse. But when he called on his once-a-week residential clients, he couldn't entirely banish the fear of finding a dead person on the premises. He rang the doorbell first, as he had always done, and then he knocked, as always, and then he turned the key in the lock and opened the door and called out *Hello!* once or twice, and stood still listening for a response.

And after that, after he'd assured himself that there was no one conscious within, he was very careful to survey the entire apartment, to look in every room. Not until he'd determined that he was alone did he set about doing his job.

So far the most unnerving moment had come one afternoon when, after he'd done his routine of ringing and knocking and helloing, he'd walked through a silent apartment to find Kyle Lanza, who worked downtown all day every day, not only home but sprawled flat on his back on his bed, his eyes closed, his arms at his sides. He was wearing sweatpants and a Bad Dog T-shirt—and, Jerry noticed, just in time to keep from losing it altogether, a giant set of earphones. Roused, he was full of apologies. And, thank God, alive.

Time passed, and the apartments he cleaned kept not having dead bodies in them, and he kept up the precautions but lost the apprehension.

It was possible to walk in on a dead client, it had in fact happened once, but that didn't mean it was likely to happen again.

Nor did that July morning come equipped with premonitions. All he felt was fine, and the sun was out and the sky was clear, and he didn't have a residential customer today, so he'd made a date with himself—after breakfast he'd be stretched out on a towel on the roof of his building, wearing nothing but sunscreen and Speedos.

He was looking forward to it as he mounted the half-flight of steps to the building on East Twenty-eighth. He gave a wave to the Korean woman in the nail shop, opened the door of the vestibule for the three upstairs floors, rang the third-floor bell, rang again, used his key. There was a bell beside the door leading to the apartment, and he rang that as always and knocked as always and used his other key, and as soon as he opened the door he knew this was going to be a bad day, and he could forget about working on his tan.

The smell hit him the instant he cracked the door. He probably would have noticed it under any circumstances, but he knew what death smelled like and recognized it immediately. He went in anyway and closed the door and threw the bolt, which was ridiculous, because he didn't have to fear the outside world, where the sun was shining and people were alive. Anything fearful was here, and he'd just gone and locked himself in with it.

Every odor was particulate. He'd heard or read this somewhere, and it was information he wished he didn't have, because it meant that, if you could smell it, you were breathing it in, you were taking it into your system. But in fact it wasn't that overpowering, it wasn't enough to make you gag. It was knowing what it was that made it so upsetting.

And then seeing it. One on the parlor floor, her face unrecognizable, and two in one of the bedrooms, one crumpled at the other's feet.

God, couldn't he just go? He'd been there only a few minutes, he hadn't touched a thing or met a soul, so couldn't he just slip out and rejoin the world of the living? This job, like all the jobs, was off the books, and he doubted that Molly (with her skull literally smashed in, Christ, who could have done a thing like that?) even knew his last name.

He'd waved to the Korean woman in the nail shop.

But would she remember? And what could she possibly say? *Yes, I see boy come to clean. He wave to me sometime. He nice boy.* She couldn't exactly tell them anything that would have them making a beeline for his door.

Lois would know what to do.

But he didn't need to call her to know what she would tell him. *For*

God's sake, Jerry, be a grown-up. You're a citizen and you just discovered three dead bodies, so what the hell do you think you're supposed to do? Butch up and make the call.

He reached for the phone, saw that the receiver was off the hook. That might be important, he thought. It might be a clue, there might be fingerprints or trace evidence on the phone.

God, he didn't want to do anything *wrong*.

He let himself out, found a pay phone at the corner of Third Avenue. It would be easy to keep walking, but he heard Lois's voice in his head, telling him to butch up, and he dialed 911 and gave his name and the address of the crime scene, and told the operator what he'd found. Yes, he said, he'd wait for the officers at the scene.

THE RESPONDING OFFICERS WERE two uniformed cops from the local precinct, a man and woman his own age or younger, and he answered their questions but held back the part he didn't want to mention. He'd have to, he knew that, but he might as well wait for the detectives to get there. Otherwise he'd only have to go through it a second time.

The detectives were older than he was, which was at once reassuring and intimidating. One was black and one was white, and both were balding and out of shape and looked uncomfortable in their suits and ties.

They went over the same ground the uniforms had covered, but more thoroughly. They wanted to know the routine at the apartment—when did they open, what time did they shut down, how many girls worked there, and did anybody stay on the premises overnight. He answered what he could, explaining that all he did was come in and clean the place when nobody was around. He didn't even know for sure what sort of establishment it was, insofar as no one had ever come right out and told him, although it did seem pretty obvious to him. They agreed that it seemed obvious, all right.

Then they wanted to know where he'd been during the past twenty-four hours, and how they could verify his whereabouts. He told them all that, and the black cop made notes, and the white cop said, "Pankow, what's that, Polish? You grow up in Greenpoint, by any chance?"

Hamtramck, he told them. And where was that, somewhere out on the Island? No, he said, it was a suburb of Detroit, and predominantly Polish.

A lot of Polish people lived in Greenpoint, the cop said, and he agreed that they did. You ought to go there for pierogi and kielbasa, the cop said. He sometimes did, he said, when he got the chance.

Then he said, "There's something else you ought to know."

Oh?

God, he didn't want to do this. But he'd already started, and besides they'd find out themselves and wonder why he hadn't said anything.

"Last month," he said. "I had a client in the Village, I used to clean her apartment once a week. Somebody strangled her, and I was the one who discovered the body."

They stared at him, and the black cop said, "The woman, she sold real estate? And they got the guy, some kind of writer. Aren't you the guy who—"

"Destroyed the evidence," he said. "She was in the bedroom so I started in the living room. I thought she was sleeping."

"Well, they got the guy," the black cop said, and the white cop said he hoped he hadn't done any cleaning this time. He assured them he hadn't.

"These women here," the white cop said, "you wouldn't make that mistake. You'd know right away they're not sleeping."

THE BLACK COP'S NAME was Arthur Pender. His partner was Dennis Hurley. Pender said, "That is one hell of a coincidence, wouldn't you say? You think you're hiring somebody to mop your floors, turns out he's the angel of death."

"They already got somebody for the one in the Village," Hurley said.

"Maybe it gave the kid ideas. Maybe he liked the attention he got finding a body and decided he'd like to find a couple more."

"He seem to you like somebody who was enjoying the attention?"

"Looked like he wished the floor would swallow him. Can't see him doing it, either, gentle guy like him."

"You're saying that 'cause he's gay."

"Well, yeah, I guess so."

"That don't make him gentle," Hurley said. "He's got that wiry kind of build, he could be a lot stronger than he looks. He could be a ballet dancer, and they're real strong."

"Ballet dancer. You're just sayin' *that* on account of he's gay."

"You think he killed them, Arthur?"

"No."

"We'll check his alibi, but what do you bet it holds up?"

"No bet. One in the Village was strangled, wasn't she?"

"And these three were beaten and stabbed."

"And besides," Pender said, "they already got the writer for the one in the Village."

"If he did it."

"Yeah, the man could be innocent. You ask him, bet that's what he says he is."

"As a newborn baby. Arthur, you see any connection between the two cases besides the Warsaw Whiz? Where'd he say he was from, Ham Sandwich or something?"

"Hamtramck. Don't ask me how to spell it."

"Outside of Detroit, he said."

"*Inside* of Detroit. It's an autonomous area within the bounds of the City of Detroit."

"How do you happen to know that?"

"No idea. One in the Village sold real estate?"

"Something like that."

"Be an easy thing to say you did."

"What do you mean?"

"Just looking for a connection besides Mop & Glo. Any chance she could have been a working girl?"

"Lived in the Village and tricked on Curry Hill? Be interesting to know."

"And not too hard to find out," Pender said, and reached for the phone.

"NO RECORD OF PROSTITUTION, no rumors she was ever in the game. Marilyn Fairchild didn't just call herself a real estate agent, she made a good living at it. Commissions in 2001 exceeded $150,000, and ninety percent of that must have been in eight months, because how many co-ops changed hands after 9/11?"

"It was worth a call," Hurley said.

"Plus she had a reputation for going out and dragging men home with her, which is the story on how she and Creighton wound up together."

"*That's* his name. It was driving me nuts I couldn't think of it."

"And working girls aren't like musicians, they don't finish up their paid gigs and then jam all night for free."

"You know what we're going to get, Arthur? It was some fucking john, he went with one girl and she didn't want to do what he wanted her to do—"

" 'No, no, not in the ass, what kind of a girl do you think I am?' "

"Or he planned it from the jump, whatever it was, but either way he went batshit. He killed everybody and went home."

"Must have planned it. Used a hammer and a chisel, according to the ME. You don't find those layin' around in your average whorehouse."

"Unless it's some kind of special whorehouse for carpenters. I'd say he brought his tools with him. Came late, too, after the other girls called it a night."

"Right."

"Probably fixed it so he was the last customer. Only had women to kill that way."

"Another reason why it's not the Polack. You kill what you want to fuck, basic principle of lust murder."

"If that's what this was."

"What else could it be? Madam wasn't paying the right people and this was to teach her a lesson?"

"Some lesson. How's she gonna pay now?"

"Even if someone in one of the families is pissed at her, nobody'd do it like this. A hammer and chisel?"

They batted it around, thinking out loud, trying out theories.

"I hate the coincidence part," Hurley said. "Creighton goes home with Fairchild and strangles her. Our perp—"

"The Feebs'd call him the unsub."

"Our perp goes to a quiet little whorehouse, picks up a hammer and chisel and thinks he's a kid again in shop class. And both premises, Fairchild's apartment and our whorehouse, have the same ballet dancer come by to do a little dusting and cleaning."

Pender said, "About Creighton."

"What about him?"

"They have an argument, he's half in the bag, next thing you know she's dead."

"So?"

"Lot more people get drunk than kill somebody."

"Where you going with this, Arthur?"

"Meaning he's most likely leaning that way from the start."

"Leaning toward murder."

"I been drunk a whole lot of times," Pender said. "I never once wound up with my hands around nobody's neck."

"So he killed Fairchild, and then what? He finds out he likes it?"

"Happens like that, sometimes."

"Yeah, but don't forget he got arrested. You figure they let him out nights so he can go get laid?"

"He's in a cell? Do we know that?"

MAURY WINTERS SAID, "**TALK** to him? Ask him questions? No way I'm gonna let that happen."

"Sir, three women were killed last night, and—"

"I'm sorry to hear that. If it was up to me everybody would live forever, and that goes double for women. The Mets lost, did you happen to notice? Mo Vaughn struck out three times and hit into a double play. You want to ask my client anything about the game?"

"Was he there?"

"What, at the game? They're on the road, they were in Houston. He's on bond, he had to surrender his passport, so how could he go to Texas?"

The lawyer had the cops grinning. Creighton, under strict instructions not to open his mouth, found the spectacle entertaining. At least until you considered the content, which was that they were trying to hang another killing, a triple murder, on him.

The white one, Dennis Hurley, big red-haired guy, map of Ireland on his face, said, "Mr. Winters, let me just tell you where we're coming from. We got a case with a possible link to Mr. Creighton here, and we'd like to rule him out."

"Go right ahead. Rule him out. While you're at it, tell your buddies to rule him out for Fairchild."

"If he can account for his time last night—"

"Why the hell should he? He's charged with one crime, he's under no obligation to help you with another one."

"That's understood."

"So?"

"If he was at the ball game," Arthur Pender said, "not in Houston, but did the Yankees play at home last night?"

"Against the Brewers, and Soriano homered twice. You fellows should follow the game. It's America's pastime, in case nobody told you."

"Nobody tells us anything," Pender said. "If he was there, with Senator Clinton on one side and Cardinal Egan on the other—"

"Isn't there a joke starts like this?"

"—then we could cross him off our list and be on our way."

"This was last night? What hours are we looking at?"

"Ten to midnight."

"Ten P.M. to midnight? The medical examiner working with a stopwatch these days?"

"There's more than medical evidence," Pender said. "That's our window, those two hours, and if your client can establish where he was during that time period we'll thank you for your time and leave you alone."

"Which I think you'll do regardless," Winters said, "because I don't know where he was last night. To find out I'd have to ask him, and do you know why I'm not going to do that?"

"I bet you'll tell us," Hurley said.

"Because if I ask him," Winters said, "and he can't prove where he was, and I tell you to go screw yourselves, I'd be telling you in the process that he can't establish an alibi, and why should you have any such information? Whereas if I tell you right off the bat to go screw yourselves, that's all I'll be telling you, and you can do it or not as you see fit."

"Do what or not?"

"Screw ourselves," Pender said. He shrugged, got to his feet. "It was worth a try. If you do talk to him, and if he does have an alibi you want to tell me about—"

"I never liked sentences with *ifs* in them," Winters said. "Tell me something. Why are you looking at him in the first place?"

"Can't tell you that."

"You don't give nothing, my friend, you're not gonna get nothing. You're telling me this man's a suspect but you can't tell me why he's a suspect?"

"He's not a suspect."

"He's not a suspect but you want to know has he got an alibi. Lovely. Why are you looking at him?"

The cops exchanged glances. At length Pender shrugged, and Hurley said, "The body was discovered by the same kid who discovered Fairchild."

"What, the faygeleh? That's your connection?"

"Same guy is first on the scene twice in a couple of weeks? What are the odds on that?"

"At the moment, my friend, they're a hundred to one in favor of it, because it already happened. I'm not saying it's a coincidence. There's a connection, but what it connects is Fairchild to the dead women, and can we stop pretending we don't know who they are? I listen to the news the same as everybody else. This was in the East Twenties, if I'm not mistaken, in what the girl announcer didn't quite call a whorehouse, but I got the distinct impression."

"East Twenty-eighth," Hurley said. "And yeah, it was a whorehouse."

"Three hookers?"

"Two and the madam."

"Ah, Christ, what a world. They said *bloodbath*, but they generally do with a multiple homicide. They exaggerate."

"Not this time."

"Without asking what the murder weapon was, may I conclude the women weren't strangled? Which I'd have concluded anyway, because for one man to strangle three women one after the other is a neat trick."

"They weren't strangled."

"Curiouser and curiouser," Winters said, "which sounds like a Dickensian law firm, doesn't it? Never mind. I've enjoyed this, believe it or not, but I think we're finished, so—"

He said, "Maury?"

All three of them turned to look at him, as if surprised that he could talk, or that he was there at all.

"If I could talk to you privately," he said.

"They were just leaving, which would have given us all the privacy anyone could want. But why don't you fellows wait in the hall for a moment?"

When they were out of the room with the door closed he said, "I was here last night."

"I'm not surprised. You're home all the time, from what you've told me. *Home Alone* is a movie, not an alibi. I don't suppose you had company?"

"No," he said, "but I think I can prove I was here. The window is ten to midnight, isn't that what they said?"

"Ten to midnight."

"I had a couple of deliveries somewhere around that time. Must have been close to ten when I called and had Two Boots send up a pizza. And I called the deli a little after that and ordered up a sandwich and a six-pack of Beck's."

"You had a pizza and a sandwich at the same time?"

"I was out of beer and I wanted one with the pizza. I don't like to call the deli just for beer."

"What, they'll think you're a drunk?"

"You're right, it's stupid, but I was just as happy a couple of hours ago when I had the sandwich for lunch. They should both have records of the delivery."

"They should."

"While I was eating the pizza," he said, "my agent called. She's working on a deal, she wanted to discuss strategy. She can confirm that we were on the phone for ten minutes, maybe closer to fifteen."

"And this was when?"

"Say ten-thirty."

"That leaves plenty of time for you to get in a cab and kill three women in a whorehouse. If I'm going to show anything to Frick and Frack, I'd like to show 'em enough to cover you past midnight."

"I was online," he said.

"What, the computer? They can take those things apart and find out what you had for breakfast, but—"

"No," he said, "I was online, Maury. This was after I got off the phone with Roz."

"Your agent."

"Right. Something she said, it doesn't matter, but I wanted to check something on Amazon. I logged on, I checked my e-mail, and I went to their website."

"How can we prove this?"

"I have a dedicated phone line for the computer. It's a local call to AOL when you log on. Won't there be a record?"

"Very good."

"And I wound up buying a couple of books from Amazon. I always do, it's impossible to visit the site without remembering some book you think you have to have, especially in the middle of the night. A couple of clicks and it's in the mail two days later."

"They'd have a record of a purchase."

"They send you an e-mail confirming it, with time and date on it. I downloaded that, it's on my hard drive."

Winters went over and opened the door.

"YOU'LL CONFIRM ALL THIS," the lawyer told the two detectives, "in about a minute and a half, give or take. You'll pull the LUDS and that should be enough, but you can go as far as you want. Put one of your computer people on it, talk to the pizza place, the deli."

"We had to check him out," Arthur Pender said.

"And you checked, and he's out. But as far as I'm concerned, you boys are on to something."

They looked at him.

"Fairchild and the three last night," Winters said. "They're as linked as they ever were. The same boy finds all the bodies, that was too good a coincidence twenty minutes ago and it's no different now."

"Meaning?"

"Meaning Ernest Hemingway here didn't do either of them. You just cleared him on one, you should go ahead and clear him on the other."

"Not our case," Hurley said.

"So why not talk to your friends at the Sixth, tell them talk to the geniuses in the DA's office."

"Yeah, right. I'm sure they'd love to hear from us."

"How could you not tell them? You just looked at this gentleman in connection with a homicide and cleared him a hundred percent. You don't think that's information they ought to have?"

"I suppose we could make a call."

"Of course you could," Winters said. "Thanks for coming, fellows. You've been very helpful."

WINTERS STAYED AND CHATTED with him after the two detectives had left. After the lawyer's departure, Creighton called his agent.

"Talk about highs and lows," he said. "I started out thinking I was going to be charged with three murders. Next minute Maury's talking about getting the original charges dropped."

"Really?"

"But he told me privately that's not going to happen. The DA's not going to withdraw an indictment just because I've been cleared in a case that may or may not be related to the original crime I'm charged with. They've still got the same evidence they had before. She still picked me up at the Kettle and I still went home with her."

"And she's still dead."

"The poor woman. You know, I've been angry at her all along, for getting me into this mess in the first place. Like it's her fault. But all she wanted was to get laid, and she wound up dead, and how is any of that her fault?"

"You're not angry with her anymore."

"No, and I can't understand why I was in the first place."

"You were afraid, sweetie."

"And now I'm not, because I'm beginning to see daylight. This won't get charges dropped, according to Maury, but what it should do is create a little doubt in the minds of Reade and Slaughter."

"The arresting officers?"

"Right. Even if they're still completely convinced I did it, they'll want to cover their asses in case it becomes clear I didn't. Which means they might look a little harder for witnesses who might steer them in the direction of another suspect."

"That would be wonderful. The only thing . . ."

"What?"

"This is going to sound like St. Augustine. 'Lord, make me chaste, but not yet.' "

"You lost me."

"Look, you and I both know you didn't do this thing, right? And we know you're going to be cleared."

"It's beginning to look that way."

"Well, that's the important thing, in fact it's the only thing that matters, but all things being equal . . ."

"What?"

"I'd just as soon it doesn't all clear up today or tomorrow," she said. "Or even next week or next month. God, that sounds terrible, doesn't it?"

"It might, except I think I see where you're going."

"The best thing for our purposes is if you're an accused murderer awaiting trial when we make the deal. Then, when the book comes out, you're a guy who was falsely accused of a horrible crime and has since been completely exonerated. I know you'd like to be off the hook as soon as possible, but I'm your agent and I used to be your publisher and I can't help seeing it from that standpoint."

"Don't apologize. I'm writing all the time these days, Roz. I'm completely into the book, and of course I want it to do everything it can. If I'm cooped up in my apartment for the time being, well, it's worth it. And I'd be cooped up anyway, putting words on the screen."

"And it's going well?"

"It's going beautifully."

"I turned down a couple of preempts, sweetie. One yesterday and one this morning."

"What were the numbers?"

"I'm not going to tell you. I'm auctioning on Friday. I told Esther at Crown what I want for a floor bid. That'll give them topping privileges. She's supposed to get back to me later this afternoon."

"What do you want for a floor?"

"I'm not going to tell you that, either, until I find out if I get it. Oh, that reminds me, I was going to call you about this. Esther had a suggestion, and whether or not we wind up going with them, I think it's worth thinking about. How would you feel about a name change?"

"You mean a pseudonym?"

"Jesus Christ, *no*! We've got all this publicity, why would we want to shitcan it?"

"That's what I thought, but—"

"You've always used *Blair Creighton*, but all the news stories have referred to you as *John Creighton*, so Esther suggested bylining the books, all of them, old and new, as by *John Blair Creighton*. Which I think has a very nice ring to it."

"I should have done it that way from the beginning," he said. "I've had the thought off and on for years."

"So that's a yes?"

"An emphatic yes."

"Jeez, that was easy. Every client I have should be like you, baby."

"Under indictment, you mean?"

"Get back to work," she said.

HE THOUGHT HE'D HAVE trouble getting back into the book, but he looked at the last sentence he'd written and remembered what he'd planned to write next, and once he'd put the words down there were more words to follow them.

He was on a break, cracking a fresh pack of cigarettes, when she called again to report Esther Blinkoff at Crown had come up with the floor bid. In return, she got to make a final offer when all the other participants had finished bidding.

"US and Canada only," she said, "because my guess is we'll get the

same dollars with or without foreign, so why not keep them for ourselves? Everybody's going to think the book won't do much overseas, because who gives a shit in Frankfurt if some woman gets strangled in New
York? What they'll forget is you're a novelist with a following overseas,
and we're not selling true crime, we're selling literature. They might not
get much abroad, but I will."

"What's the floor?"

"I was coming to that. One point one."

"Million."

"Duh."

"Jesus. Well, I guess my personal Philip Marlowe can order doubles
if he wants. It sounds like I'm going to be able to afford to cover his tab.
One million one hundred thousand. Where'd the *point one* come from?"

"It's coming from Crown, but it was my idea and I was ready to fight
for it. An even million sounds preemptive, even if everybody jumps up
and down and calls it a floor. The extra hundred thousand makes the
whole number sound like a step in the right direction."

The extra hundred thousand was substantially higher all by itself than
his highest previous advance.

"Plus," she said, "if all the other players keep their hands in their
pockets, we've got a hundred thousand more than we'd have otherwise."

"There's that."

"You know what's a shame? The world never knew you were a suspect in the whorehouse murders, and now they don't get to learn you've
been cleared."

"It'll probably come out. Everything seems to, sooner or later."

"Yeah, but after the auction."

"Ah," he said. "Not necessarily."

"Oh?"

"Not if somebody leaked it."

"Holy shit. Now why the hell didn't I think of that myself? I know
Liz Smith well enough to call her . . ."

"Or Page Six."

"Page Six first, to tell them the police have talked to you in connection
with the triple killing, di dah di dah di dah, and then Liz Smith so she can
rush to your defense and tell the world yes, they talked to you, and they
cleared you. I'll call right now. Wait a minute. Will I be breaking any laws?"

"You'll be pissing a few people off," he said, "but I can't see where
you'll be doing anything illegal. They didn't even ask us not to talk to
anybody."

"I'm sure they never thought they had to. What about your lawyer? Is
he one of the people I'll be pissing off?"

"What do you care? Anyway, he'll figure the cops leaked it."

"And they might, so I'd better get cracking. Bye, sweetie."

He put down the phone and went over to the window. Below his window, a black man in camo fatigues went through the blue garbage can, selecting aluminum cans for redemption. Recycling didn't seem to work in New York, all the trash wound up in the same landfill, but the law requiring you to separate it at least made things easier for the can collectors.

Across the street, a man with a clipboard was leading a dozen people on a walking tour of the Village. Willa Cather had lived on this block, and maybe he'd tell them as much and point out the house. They shuffled on by, leaving Creighton with a view of the old man leaning in the doorway.

He'd seen him before, in his plaid shirt and the pants from an old suit. Homeless, he guessed, or the next thing to it, but too proud or not desperate enough to root around in garbage cans.

Maybe he'd go downstairs, take the old fellow to the Corner Bistro and buy him a burger. One point one, Jesus, he could damn well afford it.

He went back to the computer first, to tinker with the last sentence he'd written, and when he looked up an hour had gone by and he'd written a page and a half. He stood up, rubbed his eyes, yawned.

One point one. He ought to call somebody, but who was there to call? And what kind of conversation could he have with someone he hadn't talked to since before Marilyn Fairchild's death had changed his life?

He could call Karin, tell her her money was safe, tell her the kids weren't going to have to worry about money for college. But shouldn't he wait until after the auction?

He was hungry, he was thirsty, he'd done a good day's work, and damned if he wasn't on the verge of genuine success. Blair Creighton had managed to get by, and that was no mean accomplishment in the field he'd chosen, but *John* Blair Creighton . . .

Look out, Grisham. Not so fast, Clancy. And you better watch your ass, Steve King.

He grabbed his cigarettes, checked to make sure he had his wallet, and got the hell out of there. When he hit the street he looked around for the old guy he'd seen earlier, but he'd drifted off, missing out on his chance for a Bistro Burger. And the Bistro could wait, because why not take the bull by the horns?

He started walking, and when people looked his way he looked right back at them.

EDDIE RAGAN LOOKED UP when the door opened, and he figured his face showed about as much as it did when he played poker. All in all, he did pretty well at poker.

"John," he said. "Been a while."

"Well, I've been busy, Eddie. Better let me have a Pauli Girl."

"You got it."

And he sat where he always sat and got a cigarette going and looked at the TV, where Gene Fullmer and Carmen Basilio were duking it out on the classic sports channel. Basilio was bleeding so bad he must have needed a transfusion afterward, and even in black and white it was pretty gruesome. Nowadays they'd stop it, but this was from before the sport got so candy-ass.

Creighton drank some beer, looked around, saw Max the Poet. "Max," he said.

Max looked up from his book, looked over the tops of his glasses at Creighton, said, "John. Haven't seen you in a while."

"No, it's been a while," Creighton agreed.

"Well, you didn't miss much," Max said. "Everything jake with you, John?"

"Jake indeed. And with you, Max?"

"Oh, I can't complain," said Max the Poet.

I love this job, Eddie thought.

twelve

O N THE FLIGHT home from Dallas–Fort Worth, his seat companion in the front cabin was a ruddy-faced Texan with a GI haircut and intelligent brown eyes under a heavy ridge of brow. Buckling up, the man said, "If there was no other reason to hate the goddamn Arabs, and there's plenty, what they've done to air travel would do for me. The airport security measures just drive a man crazy. Anything under five hundred miles, I get in the car and drive."

"It's a difficult situation," Buckram said.

"I know, but it'd be comforting to think there was a guiding intelligence behind it all. I saw them pull a woman out of line for one of their random searches and I swear she was eighty years old and used an aluminum walker. Meantime how hard is it to get a gun onto an airplane? All you have to do is tuck it in your turban."

"They're afraid to get criticized for racial profiling."

"There's a difference between stopping cars because the drivers are black and paying extra attention to people who flat out look like terrorists. I'll tell you, my doctor wanted to schedule me for an MRI last week. Don't bother, I told him. I'm flying to New York in a few days, I'll ask airport security to send you the results."

He hadn't heard that one, and laughed.

"Listen," the man said, "I like to talk, but I hate to inflict myself on someone who'd rather read, so if you brought a book along . . ."

"It's in my checked luggage, and I'd rather have human company anyway."

"Well, I'm not sure I qualify," the man said. "Some would argue otherwise. Name's Bob Wilburn, from Plano."

"Fran Buckram, from New York."

"I already knew that."

"Well, all I have to do is open my mouth and people know I'm from New York."

"I expect they do, but I already knew your name, too. Recognized you from your photographs. You're the fellow who made New York a nice place to go to."

"I had a lot of help."

"Can I ask what brought you to Texas? And you could make me real happy by telling me you're coming down to run the police department in Dallas."

"Hardly that. I was giving a talk last night to a roomful of business-men in Arlington."

"Not the Pericles Club? Damn it all, I go to that more months than I miss, and I'd've been there last night if I paid attention to my mail and knew who the speaker was. I'm sorry I didn't get to hear you."

"You didn't miss much," Buckram told him.

IT HAD GONE WELL enough. They'd flown him first class on American, met him at DFW in a limousine, put him up at the Four Seasons. The club premises were Texas opulent, with a lot of dark wood and red leather, and western art on the walls that included several paintings by Charles M. Russell. Dinner was good, and his talk went well enough. They paid at-tention, they asked questions at the end, and the applause was more than just polite.

Now he was on his way home, $3,500 to the good, less a third to the lecture bureau that made his bookings. That meant he'd net $2,366.67 (and he wished they'd raise his price a hundred dollars, just so they'd be dealing in round numbers) which was not bad compensation for being well treated and fussed over while he gave a talk he'd given so many times he could do it in his sleep.

It changed, of course, according to circumstances and what was on his mind, and, he supposed, the phases of the moon. But it didn't vary much, and the fact that it got an increasingly favorable reception bothered him. He was getting good at it, but what he was becoming good at was performance.

He felt like an actor in a long run of a Broadway show. He thought of Carol Channing, touring forever with *Hello, Dolly*, playing the same part in the same show a couple of hundred times a year. How could she stand it? Why would she want to?

And the conversations over cocktails, the chatting with his dinner partners, the smiles and handshakes and photos taken, they were all part of the performance, ad-libbed for the occasion but nevertheless the same.

The hardest part used to be during the Q&A, when he had to answer a question without letting on that he'd been asked it a few hundred times. But he'd learned how to do that, too. It had felt phony at first, but now it just felt like part of what he did, and what did that make him?

"ONE THING I HEARD," Bob Wilburn said, "is you might be the next mayor."

"You heard that all the way down in Plano, Texas?"

"Heard it in New York, matter of fact. I'm up there every couple of months. But I could as easily have heard it in Texas. There's a whole lot more folks in Dallas can name the mayor of New York than there are New Yorkers who can tell you who's mayor of Dallas. You fixing to run?"

"That's a long ways off," he said.

"And that's a good way to answer the question, or to not answer it. Here's another question—why in the hell would anybody want the job?"

He laughed. "Beats me, Bob."

"What was it that fellow said? His name slips my mind, but you know who I mean. Talks like he swallowed the dictionary."

"William F. Buckley."

"That's the fellow. Ran for mayor of New York, didn't have a snow-ball's chance, and some reporter asked him what he'd do if he won. Said he'd demand a recount."

"It's a good line."

"It's a damn good line. You want the job, Fran?"

"I don't know."

"That sounds honest."

"It is."

"It's an important job. Somebody's got to do it, and when you know you'd be good at it—"

"I'm not as sure of that as I used to be," he said. "After 9/11, I looked at Rudy and watched him do everything right, and I don't know if I could have done that well."

"A time like that, a man finds out what he can and can't do. I don't know, Fran. Politics? I pay too much money to too many politicians to have a lot of illusions about the whole business. God knows I've never wanted to go into it myself."

"Neither have I," he said. "All I ever wanted to do was be a cop."

THAT WASN'T ENTIRELY TRUE. His father was a cop, and when he was a little kid of course what he wanted was to wear a blue uniform and carry a gun and do what his daddy did. But that changed, and he grew up knowing a cop was the one thing he definitely did not want to be. "It's steady," his father told him, "and a man can take some pride in it, but it's no life for a kid with a head on his shoulders. You're cut out for something better, Fran. You don't want to wind up like your old man."

Francis X. Buckram had come home from World War II and traded a khaki uniform for a blue one and never got out of it. He was a beat cop for the rest of his life, on his feet most of the time, and those feet had never been right since the Battle of the Bulge. He'd come home at the end of his shift and sit on a stool in the bathroom with his feet in a tub of water. "Hit those books," he told his son. "Pay attention to what the nuns teach you. You don't want to wind up like this."

Then, two months before he could have watched his son graduate from Colgate, Frank came home from work and told his wife he didn't feel so hot. "I'll call the doctor," she said.

"It's nothing," he said, and sat down in his chair. His eyes widened, as if he saw something that surprised him, and then he slumped in his chair and died. It was, they told his wife, a massive myocardial infarction, which was another way of saying a heart attack. At least he didn't suffer, they told her, and she said, *Oh, a lot you know, for didn't that man suffer his whole life?*

Fran flew home for the wake and the funeral mass, then hurried back to finish school. He'd delayed choosing among the law schools that had accepted him, and now he wrote them all and said he'd be unable to come. He didn't want to be a lawyer. He wanted to be a cop, under it all he'd always wanted to be a cop. When his father's friends—cops, all of them—came up to him at the wake, many of them said, *You're making something of yourself, you're going to be a lawyer, your dad was so proud of you, that's all he talked about.*

When he caught a break, parlaying a good arrest into a promotion to detective, his mother was there to see him get his gold shield. She kissed him and said, *Oh, Fran, if he could see you now.* Later, he wondered how to take her words. If Frank Buckram could see him now, then what? Would he shake his hand or shake his head? Slap him on the back or across the face?

When he came back from Portland and was installed as police commissioner in a public ceremony at One Police Plaza, with him in a uniform with a ton of brass on it and Rudy presenting him with the commissioner's badge, his mother was there in her wheelchair. She'd turned into a little old lady, she had less than a year and a half left, and her voice was so faint he'd had to bend down to catch what she was saying.

"So proud," she said. "Your poor father, how proud he'd be. His heart'd be bursting, he'd be so proud."

And now? He was flying first class, he was staying in good hotels, he was getting paid good money to say the same thing over and over. Men with too much money were willing to give some of it to him so he could try to get a job nobody in his right mind would want.

How proud would the old man be now?

BUCKRAM WAS INDEED AN Irish name, he told Wilburn. It was also an English word, meaning a stiff cotton fabric used in bookbinding, and he'd checked the etymology once and learned the word had antecedents in Middle English and Old French, and derived ultimately from *Bokhara*, in Central Asia.

The Irish had no connection to that part of the world, unless they were indeed one of the Ten Lost Tribes. The name was an Anglicization of a Gaelic name that started out *Buccrough*—and ended in any of several unpronounceable ways. It wasn't a common name in Ireland, but he'd checked the directories during a visit to Ireland, and there were Buckrams in County Monaghan, where his father's people had come from. He'd thought of looking them up, but Monaghan was in the Midlands, well out of his way, and what would he say to them, anyway?

Wilburn said, "There was talk that you might get your old job back. That the new fellow might appoint you."

"We discussed it," he said, amazed to be talking so openly with a stranger. He'd had a Bloody Mary shortly after takeoff, but when did one drink ever loosen his tongue? He'd always been able to knock them back with the heavy hitters without fear that the slightest indiscretion would pass his lips. No, he evidently felt like talking, and he didn't think the drink had anything to do with it.

"You didn't want it or he didn't want to offer it?"

"I wanted it, and he'd have liked to give it to me," he said, "and we both realized it wasn't a good idea. Rudy'd hired me and fired me, and Rudy's endorsement put him in Gracie Mansion, even if he doesn't actually live there—"

"Likes his own place better, does he?"

"—and he couldn't start off his own term putting me back in as commissioner without biting the hand that fed him, and publicly at that. He's in an awkward position anyway, coming in on the heels of a hero, and one who'd still have the job if the voters had anything to say about it."

"Never did understand the logic of term limits. But it's all politics, isn't it?" The Texan shook his head. "Politics. Why would a man want to involve himself in all of that?"

THERE WAS NO CAR meeting him at JFK. He got his bag from the carousel and waited in the taxi queue for a cab. The driver's name ended in -*pour*, which probably meant he was an Iranian. Whatever he was, he drove like a cowboy on crystal meth.

His apartment was on East Sixty-seventh, in one of the white brick monstrosities he'd proposed for landmark status. His weekly cleaning woman, a cheerful young Nicaraguan with about twenty English words at her command, had shown up in his absence, and the place was immaculate. He unpacked, checked the mail, and returned phone calls, then ducked around the corner to drink a cup of coffee and read a newspaper.

There was more on the triple homicide on East Twenty-eighth Street. The *News* had taken to calling the killer the Curry Hill Carpenter, because forensics had determined that he'd used a hammer and a chisel to murder the three women. He had a feeling the name would stick; it had an ominous quality, suggesting the murderer was a craftsman, workmanlike in his attention to details, and the alliteration didn't hurt. And wasn't the *k* or hard *c* sound supposed to be effective? Wasn't there a whole riff to that effect in *The Sunshine Boys*? *Cucumber* is funny, *radish* is not. *Kokomo* and *Cucamonga* are funny, *kumquat* is funny. *Fort Wayne*? Not funny.

Nothing funny about the murders. What was funny—funny peculiar, not funny ha-ha—was the illusion of a link to the murder last month in the Village, the real estate agent who got her neck wrung by the writer. Both premises were cleaned regularly by the same individual. That wasn't much of a stretch, but when you added in the fact that the individual was also the first person on the scene at both venues it became dramatically more significant.

Funny, too, was the fact that the information had gotten out. Maury Winters, whom he'd last seen getting his pipes cleaned under the table at L'Aiglon d'Or, was the writer's lawyer, and he supposed Maury must have leaked the story to a press contact. It was the kind of thing that could cloud the open-and-shut case against what's-his-name, Creighton, and you could be sure Maury would bring it up in court.

He was done with the story, done with a sidebar column playing up the human angle, when something clicked and he checked the names of the victims. The madam was one Mary Mulvaney, forty-four, with an East Side address a few minutes from the UN. But the columnist in the sidebar had referred to her as Molly, and had spun a theory about a propensity for raffish behavior in those whose names ended in -*olly*. He'd cited Polly Adler, the legendary Prohibition-era madam, and Holly Golightly, the fictional good-time girl in *Breakfast at Tiffany's*. It didn't seem like much of an argument to Buckram, not even if you tossed in Ollie North, whom the writer had failed to add to the mix. But now, putting the nickname with the last name—

Jesus, he knew Molly Mulvaney. Had known her, anyway. She'd

been a witness twenty-plus years ago, she'd been one of three high-ticket hookers who'd been partying in a Kips Bay penthouse with Tiny Tom Nappi, a midlevel mob guy whose sobriquet derived not from his stature, which was neither tall nor short, but from his sexual equipment, which was rumored to be in the same league with John Dillinger's and Milton Berle's. Nappi had said he wanted to die in a room full of booze and pussy and cocaine, and he got his wish, though probably not the way he had in mind. He'd gone to answer the door, and was shot through the peephole. The large-caliber slug went in through his eye and blew out most of the back of his head.

Molly hadn't seen anything, and was bright enough to have kept her mouth shut even if there had been anything to see. Buckram had caught the case—which they'd solved in the sense that they knew who'd ordered the hit and had a pretty good idea who'd pulled the trigger, but never had enough to charge anybody. And he'd interrogated Molly Mulvaney at length, and liked her. They'd even flirted a little, although he'd made sure it didn't go beyond that. She wasn't really in the game, she'd told him. She just liked to party, and the life was kind of exciting, but this was more excitement than she'd signed on for, thank you very much, and what she thought she'd do was get the hell back to Fordham Road and marry a fireman. *Or maybe a cop*, she'd said, *if I knew where to find a real cute one.*

If she'd gone back to the Bronx she hadn't stayed, and if she'd married her fireman it hadn't worked out, but she'd evidently found the right way to be in the life, moving into management and letting younger bodies do the heavy lifting. Kept regular hours, made a decent living, lived in a good neighborhood. Nothing wrong with that, the illegality of it aside, until somebody beat her brains out with a hammer, and why in God's name would anybody want to do that?

They'd be checking everything out, and of course they'd checked Creighton and of course he'd been cleared, and the coincidence of the Pankow kid threw a big monkey wrench into the middle of things, but they'd check Molly's book, and that would probably upset a lot of citizens and screw up a few of their marriages. And they'd track down the other girls who worked for her, or had worked for her in the recent past, and they'd look for somebody with a grudge. If Molly was mobbed up—and she had to be to some extent or other, she was too hip to try riding bareback—they'd look for the OC connection, and lots of luck to them on that one.

Would they close it? The easy ones broke for you in the first forty-eight hours, and that hadn't happened, but that only meant it wasn't going to be easy, not that it wasn't going to be closed. He sat there, in the Joseph

Abboud suit he'd worn to Texas, and after a stretch of staring off into space he pulled himself up short, suddenly aware what he'd been doing.

He'd been figuring out what he'd be doing if it were his case. And, he realized, that's what he really wanted. Not to run around the country telling people what they already knew. Not to hold office, whether it was mayor or commissioner of police.

What he wanted was to be out there on the street, running an investigation, working a case.

THERE WAS A PHONE call he'd tried to return earlier, to a cop he'd known years ago by the name of Jimmy Galvin. They'd lost touch, and the message on his voice mail hadn't indicated the reason for the call. Probably to tell him somebody had died, he figured. More and more, that's what a call from the past meant. Somebody else was gone, and somebody wanted to make sure you got the news.

He called back and got a machine with a canned message, not even Galvin's voice, and he left his name and number and forgot about it, and he was trying to decide where to go for dinner when the phone rang, and it was Galvin. They exchanged pleasantries, and he scanned his memory for the name of Galvin's wife and came up empty. If he'd ever known it, he didn't know it now.

"How's Mrs. G.?" he asked.

"Well, there you go," Galvin said. "I retired a little over three years ago, figuring I'd get to spend a little more time around the house, and it turned out she liked me better when I wasn't around so much. So she went and got herself a divorce, and I'm living in Alphabet City in a coat closet that I can't afford."

"I'm sorry to hear that," he said. "I'd heard you retired, but I hadn't heard about the divorce."

"It's not so bad, Fran. I have to do my own wash and fix my own meals, but you get used to that. The hard part is now I have to break my own balls."

"Trust me," he said. "You get used to that, too."

They talked a little about being divorced and learning to be single again. Galvin said he figured it would be easier if he had a real job. He was working on a private license, and the dough was okay, what with the pension he got from the city. But the work was irregular, with long stretches of nothing to do, and the inactivity got to him.

"I don't know, Fran. I was thinking, but you probably got things you have to do. I mean, you had the top job, you're an important guy . . ."

"Jim, I was important for fifteen minutes. Now all I am is out of work."

"Yeah? What I was thinking, you feel like getting together for a drink?"

Just what he needed, a boozy evening with a cop who put in his papers just in time to see his life disintegrate. But he found himself saying that might work, that he'd enjoy it.

"There's this place," he said. "I been dropping in there, you might like it . . ."

He thought, Jesus, not a cop bar. He tried to think of an alternative to suggest, but Galvin surprised him.

"It's called Stelli's," he said. "Up on Second Avenue in the Eighties. The food's Italian, if you want to have dinner, or we could meet afterward. Entirely your call."

What the hell, he'd been trying to figure out what to do about dinner. "Dinner sounds good," he said. "Say eight o'clock?"

"Perfect. I'm trying to remember the cross street, Fran. It's in the Eighties, and above Eighty-sixth, I know that much—"

"I know the place," he said. "We'd better have a reservation."

"I guess we'll need one, if we're gonna have dinner."

"I'll make the call, Jim. Stelli's at eight. I'll look forward to it."

HE WAS OUT THE door at six-forty-five and caught a cab right away. This time the driver was a black man with a French name. Haitian, he supposed, or possibly West African. Wherever he'd come from, the guy'd been doing this long enough to know the city. He didn't have to be told where Stelli's was. The name was enough. He drove right to it.

thirteen

GREGORY SCHUYLER WAS a dear man, and, as chairman of the board of the Museum of Contemporary Folk Art, an important frog in the small pond Pomerance Gallery swam in. Whenever Susan suggested lunch he was quick to select an impeccable restaurant, and wouldn't hear of her picking up the check, or even splitting it. And there was no question of the museum reimbursing him. Not only did he volunteer no end of unpaid hours to the museum, but he also gave them an annual donation in the $50,000–$100,000 range, depending upon the fortunes of the Schuyler family trust of which he was the principal beneficiary.

He'd taken her to Correggio and insisted they have the Chilean sea bass. *Because it may be our last chance, you know. The Australians say it's being fished out and want everyone to observe a moratorium. But that doesn't mean we shouldn't order it this afternoon. Ours have already been caught, haven't they?*

He was going on now about some really exciting quilts, and she smiled and nodded in the right places without paying a great deal of attention to the words. Had she ever seen what she would regard as an exciting quilt? She understood quilts, she could tell the outstanding from the merely expert, and she could appreciate the whole folk tradition of quilting. She responded to the better examples of a wide variety of quilts, from the pure Amish work (geometrically precise blocks of unpatterned fabric) through the various complex patterns of American folk tradition, to the sometimes astonishing painterly works of appliqué and embroidery produced by sophisticated contemporary artists.

The quilt that had come closest to stirring her was a crazy quilt, entirely handmade, by an unknown Pennsylvania quilter. Odd shapes of discordant fabrics overlapped one another in no pattern at all, held together by oversize stitching in a vivid orange that clashed with everything. Sometimes the woman's needle seemed to have gone out of control, piling up whirls of orange as though trying to spin itself into the ground.

She didn't *like* the quilt, didn't see how anyone could like it, really, but it had that touch of inner turmoil that had changed her life the day she saw it in Lausanne. The woman had surely been mad, but madness in and of itself was no guarantee of artistry. Lunatics could produce perfectly predictable and pedestrian paintings, they could turn out smears as devoid of interest and excitement as the fingerpainting of a dull child. Not every spoiled grape had been touched by the noble rot that could produce a Trockenbeerenauslese; not every deranged artist blossomed into a Jeffcoate Walker, an Aleesha MacReady, an Emory Allgood.

Was it time to let Gregory Schuyler know about Emory Allgood?

She waited for a conversational opening, then eased into it. "Have you been traveling, Gregory? So many people seem to have lost their appetite for it."

"Oh, I know," he said. "Friends of ours were planning on a camel trek across Jordan earlier this year. In March, it must have been. Is that when you trek across Jordan?"

"A cold day in hell," she said, "is when *I* trek across Jordan."

"My sentiments exactly, my dear, but these friends of ours are intrepid travelers. Leif and Rachel Halvorsen, do you know them? They go everywhere, they sleep in places one wouldn't want to drive past. After last September, they decided that this might not be the year to go trekking anywhere in the Middle East. Jordan is supposed to be better than most, but still."

"Where did they go instead?"

"That's the whole point, they stayed home. Rachel told Caroline there was no end of places they'd have been comfortable going, but they just wanted to be in New York right now. And I must say I can relate to that. We were going on a South Seas cruise this winter, we had it booked and mostly paid for, and we didn't go. Now that was because it was one of the cruise lines that went out of business, but we could have rebooked on another line and gone *some*where. And instead we stayed home."

"And this summer?"

"Well, next month is Mostly Mozart, and Beverly would have my head if I wasn't here for it." He was on the festival board. "But we'll go somewhere in September, I think, or the beginning of October. I wonder what the anniversary will be like."

"Of—?"

"Of the bombing. I'm sure there'll be ceremonies, and something awful on television, but I wonder if . . ."

"If something will happen?"

"It's funny, I didn't want to speak the words. Let's get off that subject, shall we? I do think we'll travel in the early fall, but I really don't know where. Caroline always wants to go to London, and that's certainly a possibility, but I find myself drawn to Scandinavia."

"Just so you're home the beginning of November."

"Oh, I'm certain we will be. But why?"

"Or even late October, so you can have an early look. I've got a show coming up that I'm over the moon about."

"Oh, how exciting! New work by one of my favorites?"

He was mad about Jeffcoate Walker, buying for his own collection as well as the museum's, which had led Susan to speculate that he had depths no one suspected. As it was, Gregory Schuyler was an enigma, married for years to a beautiful woman but fitted out with the sensibilities and refined elegance of a homosexual. His manner was distinctly gay, but his energy was not, and she'd often caught him looking at women in a way she'd never seen him look at men.

The common wisdom with such men was that they were so deep in the closet they didn't even know it themselves, and she supposed it was possible, and how could you disprove a premise like that, anyway? Until they invented an instrument to read a man's unconscious mind, the argument would remain moot.

"New work," she said, "by an artist I know you haven't seen before, because no one has. He's my own discovery, Gregory, and I'm sure he's mad as a hatter, but what he's done with it is absolutely incredible."

"That *is* exciting. A painter?"

"A sculptor. An assembler, really, and unlike anyone you've ever seen."

"African-American?"

"Yes."

"I won't say they seem to have a gift for it, that's as patronizing as prattling about a natural sense of rhythm, but much of the best work in that vein is African-American, isn't it? How ever did you find him, Susan? Did you go down to Mississippi and poke around little black towns in the Delta?"

"He's local."

"He's a New Yorker?"

She nodded.

"Oh, I almost wish you hadn't told me. Now I can't wait until the fall. Do I absolutely have to wait, Susan? Can't I have a sneak preview?"

"You can have an early look," she said, "but not this early. Nobody's seen the work yet, and nobody's going to see it for at least three months."

"That's what? The middle of October?"

"As soon as I finish with jury duty."

"Oh, dear. Suppose you get on a case?"

"I won't. Maury Winters told me how to make sure that doesn't happen. I'll just have to spend three days sitting around a courthouse and being bored."

"Knowing you," he said, "you'll run into somebody who does paintings on black velvet of Elvis Presley turning into a werewolf. Does your new discovery have a name?"

"He does, and I just wish I could remember it."

"Susan, Susan, Susan. You're an impossible tease. I hope you know that."

"I know," she said, "and it's completely unintentional. I wasn't going to mention him at all, but—"

"Oh, please. That's why you wanted to have lunch in the first place."

"Only to make sure you'd be in town for the opening."

"I want first look, Susan."

"You'll be one of the very first."

"That's not quite the same, is it? Susan, you're impossible. How can you build up my excitement and then leave me like this?"

The implied sexual metaphor could only be intentional. And how would he react, she wondered, if she were to crawl under the table right now and take his cock in her mouth?

"Susan!"

"What?"

"You just had a wicked thought, didn't you? You did! Tell me."

"Oh, no," she said. "I couldn't possibly."

HER NIPPLES TINGLED.

But then they always did. At first, when the soreness wore off and left only the tingling, she thought this was going to be too much to bear, walking around all the time in a state of low-level stimulation. But then she found out that she got used to it, and felt a little bit disappointed. But there was no cause for disappointment; what you got used to, she came to realize, was being slightly excited all the time. It didn't stop working, you were still excited, but that degree of excitement became your normal condition.

Which was sort of fun.

At first she couldn't wait to make another appointment and go get labial rings like Medea's. She positioned herself in front of a mirror and pretended she already had them and used her fingers to open herself up. You could see better, she thought, without the hair, and three days later, the earliest appointment she could get, she was getting waxed by the woman whose number Medea had given her. There was nothing sexual about the experience, except for the idea of it, but she couldn't wait to get in front of the mirror again. And of course she couldn't stop touching herself, and couldn't stop watching herself touching herself, and when she was through she lay there, feeling utterly wiped out, and her nipples were still tingling.

And she decided to wait on the next piercing. There was no hurry, she decided, and it would be good to explore one level before rushing on to the next one.

What she couldn't get over was that she felt sexy all the time. She couldn't credit this entirely to the physical changes she'd recently made. That was a part of it, but there'd been something going on before or she'd never have even considered the piercing in the first place.

Every day, some thought or presence would trigger an impulse not unlike the one that had put her on her knees under the dinner table at L'Aiglon d'Or.

But she wasn't crazy. She could have an impulse without having to act on it. She could imagine herself doing certain things—and her imagination, she was just beginning to realize, was as vast and as eccentric as the imaginations of the artists she was drawn to. But she could enjoy the fantasy without having to transform it into reality.

And wasn't that how you distinguished the sane from the insane? Not by their thoughts but by their actions.

In her imagination, for example, she seduced Chloe.

She couldn't believe it would be terribly difficult. *Come into the back office,* she'd say. *There's something I'd like to show you.* And, with the door closed, she'd open her blouse. She'd have gone braless that day in preparation for this, or she'd have ducked into the loo and removed her bra, so she could bare herself as artlessly as Chloe had when she pulled down her scoop-necked blouse and showed her treasures. *Look what I've done, Chloe! You inspired me. I kept thinking how lovely your breasts looked and the next thing I knew . . .*

Or she'd say, *Do you like the way they look? Yours are bigger, aren't they. Could you show me yours again, Chloe?* And she'd make a fuss over them, and maybe reach out and cup the girl's breast, she could feel it in her hand right now, just thinking about it. Or she could lean forward and press her breasts against Chloe.

And she'd say something like, *Oh, do you know what else I did?* And she'd drop her skirt and step out of it, and take off her panties, or better yet have removed them in advance, or not worn them at all that day. And she'd show herself to Chloe, and Chloe would be stunned, she wouldn't know what to say or do or even think, but she'd be turned on a little, even if she'd never done any girl-girl stuff, even if she'd never even thought about it.

Now show me yours, Chloe.

Oh, I couldn't.

Oh, please, I want to see it.

But I have hair.

I don't care, I want to see it . . .

And she'd have her, right there in the office.

EXCEPT SHE WOULDN'T. NONE of it would happen, she wouldn't allow it to happen. She'd be inviting disaster, ruining a satisfactory working relationship, and, if by some chance life didn't happen to follow her script, messing things up with results she could only begin to imagine.

And you didn't have to seek adventure. If you prepared yourself for it, it would come to you.

Days after her waxing, the phone rang, and it was the man from Detroit, in town overnight for a closing. He knew it was short notice, but was there a chance she was free for dinner. "Someplace terrific," he said. "Price no object, because I'll expense it, and it damn well ought to cost them when they tell me at nine in the morning to be at the airport by ten."

They met in SoHo and had the world's most expensive sushi. She sat across the little table from him and pictured him spread-eagled on her bed, his hands and feet fastened to the bed frame with cords of rawhide. His head hooded, but the hood a modification of the one she'd worn at Medea's, with an opening for the mouth as well as the nose.

He couldn't see, wouldn't know what to expect, and she'd lower herself onto him. He'd smell her sex first, and then she'd be sitting on his face . . .

"You're different," he said.

The words startled her, fitting in so perfectly to her reverie. She recovered and asked what was so different about her.

"I don't know, Susan, but something's changed. Is your hair the same? You're smiling, you look like the fucking Mona Lisa. It's not your hair. You look sensational, but you always look sensational. What is it?"

"You'll see."

He was staying at the Pierre, as usual, and they went straight back to his hotel. She told him she had a surprise for him, that he had to play along with her, had to do as she said, had to keep his eyes closed until she said he could open them. She had him undress and lie down on his back on the cool sheets. She undressed and sat on the bed beside him and stroked him with one hand and herself with the other.

No restraints, no hood, but she could still act out her fantasy. She teased him a little longer, then moved to squat on her haunches, positioning herself over his face. "You can open your eyes now," she said, and she let him look at her for just a couple of seconds before she lowered herself onto his mouth.

Afterward, he couldn't get over the nipple rings, the waxed loins. "I knew something was different. I thought you were going to show me a tattoo, a butterfly on your thigh, something like that. I had no idea you were so kinky."

"I'm a work in progress," she told him.

He made her stay the night, which was a first, and demonstrated a propensity for kinkiness all his own. The next day she skipped lunch and went on a buying spree at the Pleasure Chest. The sales clerk was a gay man with a physique straight out of Muscle Beach, and he was delighted to put names to all the different items on display, and explain their functions.

He helped her get everything into a cab. "Have fun," he told her. "But, uh, don't use everything at once."

SHE WAS A WORK in progress. The phrase had sprung glibly to her lips, but later she realized how appropriate it was. A work of mad folk art, perhaps, but very much a work in progress.

And not off-the-wall mad, because she was able to choose what was to remain fantasy and what was to be enjoyed in the flesh.

So she didn't dart under the table at Correggio, or let the lunch conversation amount to anything more than the lightest sort of flirting. Gregory Schuyler's good opinion was far too important for her to jeopardize it for whatever rewards his pale body might provide.

She was back at the gallery in time to receive a call from Reginald Barron. Uncle Emory had completed another piece, and would she want to include it in the show?

"And he's working on another. He'll do like that, one right after the other, and then he'll just stop for a spell. I know you were talking about having a catalog prepared, so you'd need to have everything by a certain date."

She thought of his youth, his broad-shouldered masculinity, his adorable shyness. *I have gold studs in my titties, Reginald. I have a hairless pussy. Do you want to come over and play?*

"That's very thoughtful," she told him. "Suppose we use the end of the month as a cutoff date? I'll arrange to come by then and pick up whatever's completed." And then she'd make another run to Brooklyn a week or two before the show; the catalog would already be closed by then, but if there was any Emory Allgood work outstanding, she wanted it in her storage locker, not where some smooth opportunist could snatch it out from under her.

After she'd hung up she had a thought. Suppose she rang him back, asked him if he could possibly come in today with the piece he'd called about. If it wasn't too big, if he could get it into a cab . . .

No, the only reason she thought of that was because, if he brought the piece to the gallery—or, even better, to her apartment—she could have him out of his pants and into hers in nothing flat. And that was something she was determined not to let happen.

Not until after his uncle's show.

SHE SENT CHLOE HOME at five, stayed on herself for another hour and a half. She walked home, detouring to pick up half of a barbecued chicken at Boston Market. She ate it at her kitchen table—she had an eat-in kitchen, Marilyn Fairchild had found her a sweetheart of an apartment—and then drew a tub and soaked in it. Lying there, she felt herself stirred, and touched herself. Just a little.

She dried off and got in bed and played some more. Not all of the paraphernalia from Pleasure Chest required a partner, so she tried out some of her new toys. But she reined herself in, didn't let herself climax, because it was Friday night and she felt adventurous and you could have a good time all by yourself, you could have an orgasm as powerful as the best anyone else could give you, but what you couldn't have was an adventure.

She thought about the men she could call, and a woman or two she could probably call, but none of them were what she wanted, not tonight. She wanted a stranger.

Marilyn Fairchild had found herself a stranger, one who'd turned out to be a little stranger than she'd bargained for. God, what an awful thing. And what could it have been like for her, those last few moments?

Maybe she was unconscious, passed out. Maybe she never saw it coming, maybe it was over before she knew it.

But maybe not.

She imagined hands on her throat, a weight pressing down on her. Asphyxiation was supposed to have an erotic element, God only knew how many idiots died every year hanging themselves to intensify their orgasms. It was probably safer with a partner—if you wanted that kind of thing, and if you trusted the person to know when to stop.

Maybe Marilyn had wanted Creighton to choke her—just a little, just to get her over the edge. Maybe his hands had had a mind of their own.

Maybe she came and went, just like that.

She should run it by Maury. Maybe he could try it as a defense strategy if all else failed. Except lots of people had tried variations of that, hadn't they? *It was rough sex, that's the way she wanted it, and it just went too far.* Had any jury ever bought that one? If so, she couldn't remember it.

Well, she didn't want to get what Marilyn got. But she wanted some excitement, a stranger if not a strangler. Where should she go looking for him?

She put on makeup and perfume. Changed her earrings for her amethyst studs. Put on a little black dress with not a thing under it except the gold in her nipples. Slipped on a pair of Blahniks, changed her mind, went with the Prada pumps. Like it mattered, like anybody was going to be looking at her shoes.

She had to wait ten minutes for a cab. "Stelli's," she told the driver. "Do you know where that is?"

fourteen

AUCTION TIME.

He didn't see why he should feel anxious. He remembered something Lee Trevino had said in response to talk about the pressure involved in trying to sink a putt in a tournament playoff: *Pressure? If you make it you get a million dollars, but if you miss it you still get half a million. That's not pressure. Pressure's when you're in a two-dollar Nassau with five bucks in your pocket.*

And where was the pressure for him? Esther Blinkoff at Crown had already given a floor bid of more money than he had ever expected to find on a contract with his name on it. The worst that could happen, the absolute worst that could happen, was that the other four prospective bidders would hear the numbers Crown had put on the board, shrug their shoulders, and go home. And he'd get an advance of $1,100,000.

He'd been up late the night before, fooling around on the computer, then channel surfing. AMC was running *Casablanca,* and he told himself he'd just watch it for a few minutes, but he'd never been able to turn that film off and couldn't this time, either. He got misty when they played "La Marseillaise," the way he always did, and he was still there and still paying attention when Bogart told Claude Rains that it looked like the beginning of a beautiful friendship.

It must have been close to three when he got into bed, and not quite eight when he rolled out of it. He was working on his second cup of coffee when the phone rang at ten after nine, and it was Roz.

"The horses are at the starting gate," she said. "Actually they're just leaving the paddock, because I don't start making calls until ten o'clock. Is this your first auction, John? Well, do you know how it goes?"

"The high bidder gets me."

"I mean the mechanics of it. They're all at their desks, and I call one of them and tell them where the bidding stands, and they go into a huddle and get back to me, and then I call the next one. It's not like sitting in the gallery at Christie's and *bing bang boom* it's over. It can take all day, and sometimes more than a day."

"So this could be continued on Monday?"

"No," she said, "because everybody's on notice that today is the day, and by five o'clock you're going to have a new publisher. Or a new old publisher, if you wind up with Esther."

"At one point one."

"Or at *x*-point-*x*, if she exercises her topping privileges, which she got by giving us the floor."

"Do the others all know about the floor?"

"Honey," she said, "everybody in America knows about the floor. It was in *Publisher's Lunch* yesterday. Believe me, all four of them know they can't play for less than seven figures."

Publisher's Lunch was a daily e-newsletter, full of industry news and gossip and free on request. He'd subscribed for a while, then unsubscribed when he realized how much time it was draining out of his day. The fact that they'd reported the floor bid somehow made it more real.

"John," she was saying, "what I want to know is whether or not you want me to keep you in the picture. I can call you whenever somebody bids or passes, but I know you're working on the book, and maybe you'd rather not be interrupted, in which case you won't hear from me unless there's something I need to clear with you. Or until the auction is over, whichever comes first."

He said the latter sounded like a good idea. She agreed, and they wished each other luck, and after she rang off he realized she'd sounded faintly disappointed by his choice. And why wouldn't she be? She was sitting all alone in her office, running a drawn-out auction over the phone, and he was telling her no, he didn't want to share the excitement with her.

Far as that went, she wasn't the only one he'd just disappointed.

He rang her back. "Changed my mind," he said. "Yes, keep me posted."

"If it's gonna interfere with your writing—"

"Who are we kidding? What am I going to get written today, whether or not the phone rings? You know what I realized? I'm in a profession that's supposed to be glamorous, and maybe it is, if you're sitting upstairs of a garage in Moline, Illinois, typing away and dreaming of someday seeing your words in print. But when you're doing it, all it is is a combination of daydreaming and word processing."

"And?"

"And here's the one time in a writer's life when it's genuinely exciting, and the horses are leaving the paddock, and I've got a fistful of tickets, and here I am telling you I don't want to watch the race, just call me when it's over. So I changed my mind."

HE'D FIGURED WORK WAS out of the question, but decided there was no reason why he couldn't tinker with what he'd written earlier that week. He went over what he'd printed out, noting typos, finding and fixing the occasional infelicitous phrase. He was entering his changes on the computer when she called at ten-fifteen.

"I drew lots," she said, "and called Putnam first, and they didn't have to go into a huddle, they'd already gone into their huddle because they knew what the floor was. They bid one point two."

"That's more than one point one."

"You could have been an accountant, did anybody ever tell you that? The important thing is they're in. I'd rather have a slight increment from them than a big jump now."

"Why's that?"

"Psychologically I think it's better at this stage. Anyway, I knew Gloria wouldn't try a preemptive overcall, if you don't mind a bridge term in the middle of an auction, because it's not her style, which is why I called her first."

"I thought you drew lots."

"No, why on earth would I do that? I know what order I want them in. I said I drew lots, because that makes it sound fair, and they pretended to believe me, but I didn't and they know I didn't."

"Wheels within wheels," he said.

"Now I'm waiting to hear from St. Martin's. Having fun?"

"Uh-huh. Are you?"

"Time of my life," she said. "Stay close to the phone, okay?"

IN THE BEGINNING, A rejection slip with a handwritten *Sorry!* on it was encouraging, while an actual note saying that they'd liked his story (albeit not enough to publish it) was cause for minor celebration. His first sale was to a little magazine that paid in copies, but it was his first sale, for God's sake, and what difference did it make how much they did or didn't pay him?

It was never about the money. He hadn't gotten into the business to get rich—and, indeed, hadn't thought of it as a business when he got into it. It was what he wanted to do, and he had the unwarranted self-assurance to believe he'd be able to make a living at it.

And, one way or another, he had. Somebody (he was pretty sure it was James Michener) had said somewhere that a writer could make a fortune in America, but couldn't make a living. It was a great line, and there was truth in it, because the men and women who hit the bestseller list did make a fortune, and the overwhelming majority who ground away at it, and who were good enough to publish one book after another, had to have professorships or day jobs or trust funds to get by.

But there were others who didn't hit the list or line up for food stamps, people like him who came out with a new book every year or two, and wrote short stories, and did some reviewing, wrote the occasional article. Picked up a few dollars running the odd workshop at a writers' conference, critiquing manuscripts, looking good for the wannabes. Knocking out a novelization of a film, or a TV tie-in, or whatever someone would pay you to write quickly and under a pseudonym.

Writing, and turning a buck at it. Never getting rich, always getting by.

But it had gotten harder in recent years, and not just for him. Increasingly, the top and bottom grew at the expense of the middle. Michener's half-truth was becoming unqualified fact. You could make a fortune as a writer, but you couldn't make a living.

And it was beginning to look as though he was going to be one of the ones who made a fortune. Of course, whether or not he would get to spend any of it was an open question.

"ST. MARTIN'S JUST BID one point three."

"A subtle pattern begins to emerge."

"Next up is Simon & Schuster, then Little, Brown."

"This could be a long day."

"Jesus, let's hope so," she said.

TREVINO MIGHT BE RIGHT about pressure, but there was a difference between pressure and excitement. He wasn't under any pressure right now, there was nothing he had to do, nothing expected of him. After the deal was done, when he had to sit down and produce a book to justify an advance of one point one or two or three or four million dollars, that's when the pressure would come in.

Right now it was exciting. He couldn't work on the book, not even on polishing what he'd written. As edgy as he felt right now, he'd wind up changing things for the worse.

He stood up, paced the floor, went over to the shelf with his books, and took down a copy of *Edged Weapons*. He read the front matter—the dedication, the acknowledgments, and an epigraph quote from "The Death of the Hired Man," by Robert Frost. He'd paid something like a hundred dollars for permission to use it—authors had to pay for permissions themselves, he'd been chagrined to learn—and, reading it now, he wondered why he'd spent the money. He loved the poem, he'd reread the whole thing not that long ago, but the lines he'd quoted didn't seem to him to have much to do with his stories.

Maybe he'd just wanted Robert Frost's name in a book of his, and maybe it was worth a hundred bucks to make it happen.

"JOHN? HOW ARE YOU holding up?"

"I'm fine," he said. "I was just reading my favorite author."

"John O'Hara, if I remember correctly."

He laughed out loud. "Well, you're right," he said, "but I was reading a guy named Blair Creighton."

"Ah, *my* favorite author. But not Simon & Schuster's, I'm afraid. They decided to pass."

"Oh."

"I'm not surprised. Claire was hot to trot, but she didn't get the support she wanted upstairs. Don't be disappointed."

"Okay."

"Because I called Geoffrey at Little, Brown, and he didn't have to go into a huddle, he knew what he was going to bid. You want to hear?"

"Do I want to hear? No, why on earth would I want to hear?"

"Two million dollars. John? Are you sitting down?"

"I am now."

"That's why I wanted to call him last, I figured he'd jump. My guess, that's as high as we're going, unless Esther exercises her topping privileges. Are you okay? You're not saying anything."

"I'm speechless."

"You have a right to be. My next call's to Putnam, but everybody'll be at lunch now."

"Is it lunchtime already?"

"It's almost one o'clock. Make yourself a sandwich. Or pick up the phone and order something."

"I don't think I can eat."

"Ha! Neither can I. If you go out—"

"I'm not going anywhere."

"Well, if you do, be back by two-thirty, okay? And keep the line open."

THE ACKNOWLEDGMENTS PAGE OF *Edged Weapons* thanked the magazines in which each of the stories had previously appeared. He couldn't remember what each had paid him, but one $5,000 sale to *Play-*

boy accounted for well over half the total. (They'd never bought another, and the one they took wasn't particularly sexy or, he thought, especially strong. He guessed the editor had just liked it.)

He'd received a $5,000 advance for the collection, and it had earned that and a few thousand dollars more, between the hardcover and trade paperback editions. And there'd been some foreign sales, and every once in a blue moon someone would reprint one of the stories in an anthology, and he'd get a check for one or two hundred dollars.

Of course he got some reviews, he drew some attention. One of the stories, about a young man concerned about his sexual identity, drew several fan letters, all of them from young men with similar concerns. He hadn't written back, or kept the letters, but he'd been glad to receive them.

"PUTNAM JUST WEIGHED IN with two point two."

"No kidding."

"They surprised me. I thought Geoffrey's bump would knock Gloria out of the game. It's not horse races or bridge anymore, did you notice? All of a sudden it's poker."

"And now it's up to . . ."

"St. Martin's. They'll have to think about this one. Last thing they knew they were looking good at one point three, and that was a whole nine hundred thousand dollars ago."

WHEN HE GOT TO the contents page he remembered how he'd agonized over it, arranging and rearranging the stories, trying to put them in the perfect order. He'd first considered arranging them chronologically, but in the order they were written or the order they were published? Then it struck him that no one cared about the chronology, that there should be a flow to the collection. He'd shuffled the poor stories like a deck of cards, and couldn't remember why he'd settled on the final lineup.

If he had it to do over again, he'd put them in alphabetical order. It was clear-cut, it was wonderfully arbitrary, and how could you argue with it?

That would have put "A Nice Place to Stop" first, if you counted the *A*, and a title like that on the book's leadoff story was sort of a setup for the critics. *Creighton's first story is called "A Nice Place to Stop," and believe me, you'll be glad you did . . .*

Of course it was the story he wanted to read, but he'd avoided doing so ever since he started work on the book, and didn't want to change things now. He read the one *Playboy* liked, and followed it with the only story in the book that hadn't managed to have a magazine appearance.

Maybe it was the contrarian in him, but he liked the unpublished one better.

"TWO POINT FOUR."

"From St. Martin's?"

"From St. Martin's. And a very regretful pass from Little, Brown."

"Really?"

"I expected it, John. Geoffrey made his best offer at the start. He loves your work, he liked it before all of this, and he told me to congratulate you on finally getting the kind of money you've deserved all along. He just can't see how they can make money paying out any more than two million. He thought that would be enough to get it, and frankly so did I."

"I almost wish . . ."

"I know. He genuinely likes your work, and they'd publish you right. But anybody who pays this kind of dough will publish you right, because they'll have to. And they'll like your work, too. They'll love it. They all get into the business so that they can sell the books they like, and they all wind up liking the books they can sell. I think it's going to be St. Martin's, and I think it's going to be two point four. Can you live with that?"

He said he'd force himself.

HE READ ANOTHER STORY, one of the earlier ones, and decided it wasn't bad. He'd do it differently now because he'd learned a lot, he'd probably compress some of the earlier material and enlarge some of what came later. And there were elements that seemed simplistic, but that might be nothing more than the judgment of middle age upon his youthful self.

Not bad, all in all. But if there was anything that hinted the author would one day be in line for a seven-figure advance—nine, if you counted the two zeroes that came after the decimal point—well, he was damned if he could see it.

"PUTNAM'S OUT."

"You figured they would be."

"I never thought we'd get that last bid out of them, but once we did I couldn't really guess which way they'd jump. But they're out, and wish you well."

"So it's St. Martin's."

"Unless Crown decides you're worth that plus fifteen percent. That's what they have to come up with to top the auction and take you home with them."

"In other words, they have to pay your commission."

"Hey, I never thought of it that way. I like that. Now let's see if Esther likes it."

WHILE HE WAITED, HE called the deli. He was out of cigarettes, and it was no wonder, he'd had one going pretty much throughout the morning and afternoon. He told them to send up a carton, and while he was at it he ordered a sandwich and a six-pack.

While he waited, he tried to figure out how much to tip the kid. He usually gave him two bucks, which seemed to please him well enough. But this was a special day. He could give the kid five bucks, or ten. Jesus, why not give him twenty? All of a sudden he could afford it.

And what would the kid make of a twenty-dollar tip? In this neighborhood, a man tipped you twenty dollars, he probably wanted more than beer and cigarettes. And how would the kid feel next time he came by and got the usual deuce? Confused? Disappointed? Pissed off?

By the time the kid showed up, his philanthropic impulses had passed. Here you go, he said, and handed him two dollars.

"LISTEN," ROZ SAID, "WE'VE got to celebrate. I hope you haven't got any plans for tonight."

"You're kidding, right? I haven't got any plans, ever, until they set a trial date."

"You do now. I'm taking you out to dinner."

"Well . . ."

"No arguments, sweetie. Tonight, and my treat, and it's got to be someplace elegant, someplace break-the-bank swank."

"I gather the auction's done."

"Oh," she said, with studied nonchalance. "Oh, didn't I tell you? Yes, it's all wrapped up."

"And the winner is St. Martin's at two point four."

"Wrong twice," she said. "The winner is Crown, and the price is precisely . . . hang on a minute, I've got it written down here somewhere . . ."

"They topped the bid, then?"

"They did indeed. I guess Esther Blinkoff really is your new biggest fan. Here we go. Three point one oh five, oh oh oh."

"Three?"

"Three million, one hundred five thousand dollars."

"You know," he said, "when it got above six figures, which it did the minute they gave us the floor, the numbers stopped being real. Do you know what I mean?"

"Uh-huh."

"But this is . . . I mean it's all more money than I can get my mind around, but two million is more than one and three is more than two."

"My little number cruncher."

"I'm not making any sense, am I? Three point one oh five. Wait a minute, that's wrong."

"It sounds kind of all right to me."

"St. Martin's bid two point four, right? Plus fifteen percent—well, I'm not going to figure it out, but it doesn't come to over three million dollars."

"You're right about that, and I'll explain over dinner. And it's your birthday, bubbeleh, so where would you like to go?"

"We could go to a diner and it would feel like a celebration to me. I haven't been out of the house."

"You haven't? Literally?"

"I took a walk yesterday, down to the corner and back. And the other day I went out for a beer. To the Kettle of Fish, if you can believe it."

"Isn't that where . . ."

"That's where. It felt weird walking in there, but that was me. Nobody else seemed to notice, and this one old fart said I hadn't been around lately, had I."

"I know where I'm taking you. At first I thought it should be someplace like Le Cirque or Lutèce, or maybe Union Square Café—"

"Any of those would be great."

"—but this isn't about food, this isn't about putting on the Ritz. This is about going out in the world in triumph."

"Meaning?"

"Stelli's."

"God, I haven't been there in ages."

"Is it all right? Because if it's not—"

"No, it's perfect. What time?"

"Nine o'clock? We'll make an entrance. Can you hold out that long?"

"I've got a sandwich in the fridge. If I get hungry between now and then I'll work on that. Let me see, Stelli's. I guess I'll take the One train to Eighty-sixth and catch a crosstown bus, or am I better off . . ."

"Very funny. Take a cab, you funny man. You funny rich man."

fifteen

ESTELLE SAFRAN, KNOWN to one and all as Stelli, sat on her stool at the corner of the bar nearest to the front door. It was indeed her stool, and it was not only reserved for her but had been designed and built for her. It was larger than the others, to accommodate her girth, and had a power switch, rarely used, that would raise or lower the seat several inches.

She weighed, well, none of your business, and stood five foot three in flats, which were all she ever wore. *Honey, if I wore heels, I'd make holes in the sidewalk.* Her round face was capped with a pile of unconvincing blond curls, and her eyes, always elaborately framed in mascara, were a startling guileless blue.

She'd been a chubby child who grew fatter in her teens. *Such a pretty face,* her mother's friends said, and it was a phrase she would hear or overhear for years. *Such a pretty face, and isn't it a shame . . .*

Diets hadn't worked, and Fat Girl Camp hadn't worked, and by the time she graduated from the High School of Music and Art she had said the hell with it. At Cornell she hung out with the writers and the theater majors and got a reputation for a savage wit and a deft hand in the kitchen. She wrote ten short stories and two-thirds of a novel, played Tony's wife in a student production of *A View from the Bridge*, and realized she couldn't write and she couldn't act, and, more to the point, she didn't really want to do either. What she wanted to do was hang out with people who did—and maybe whip up a little something.

She somehow knew that a man would come along who loved her for herself alone, loved her in spite of her weight, and she met the guy shortly after she graduated and married him four months later. Unfortunately he turned out to be a spoiled child-adult, a mean-spirited emotional cripple who'd picked out a fat girl so he could feel superior to her, secure in the knowledge that she'd never leave him, because where could she possibly go? She divorced the son of a bitch in less than a year, kept the apartment, and started having an open house every Sunday.

Friends and their friends would start to turn up around four in the afternoon, bringing a bottle of wine or whiskey, and there'd be nuts and homemade party mix to nibble on, and around seven she'd go into the kitchen and bring out big bowls of pasta and salad. Everybody ate, everybody drank, and everybody talked at once, and at midnight she threw out the last hangers-on and went to bed.

Monday mornings she went off to work, and when she came home the apartment was always immaculate, every dish and glass washed and put away, the floors vacuumed, the kitchen gleaming. That was her one indulgence, having someone clean up for her on Mondays, and it was worth it. Her shrink had suggested it, when she'd said for the tenth or twentieth time how she hated cleaning up afterward. Then hire someone to do it for you, he'd said, and for years she would say that therapy was worth every penny, if only because it got her to hire a housekeeper.

But that was only half of it, because the shrink made one other suggestion, and this one changed her life. She was working the fifth or sixth in a long series of pay-the-rent jobs, currently handling phone orders for an East Side florist, and complaining about it, not for the first time. "I need a career," she said, "instead of a fucking job. But what? I can't write, I can't act, my degree's a bachelor's in English, what the hell am I supposed to do?"

"What do you enjoy?"

"What do I enjoy? Having people over, listening to them talk, and watching them eat. That's great if you can live on the half-bottles of booze they leave when they go home. I've got two cupboards full of open bottles and a job that makes me want to vomit."

"You're running a salon," he said.

"And if this was Paris in the twenties, they'd write books about me."

"Add an *o*."

"Huh?"

"Change the salon," he said, "into a saloon."

She knew instantly that he was right, and told him that he was brilliant, a genius. She only wished she was thin and gorgeous so she could take off her clothes and show her appreciation. When she left his office she phoned her employer and quit, then went to work finding the right location and lining up backers.

Neither proved difficult. Her apartment was in Yorkville, in one of the big prewar apartment buildings on East Eighty-sixth, and she figured that was where they were used to coming on Sunday nights, so why not stick

with it? Besides, she wanted to be able to walk to work. It was a pain in
the ass getting in and out of the back seat of a cab.

She found the perfect spot, a restaurant that had gone under when the
owner retired and his nephew took over and ran the place into the ground.
Her lawyer negotiated a lease with a clause that gave her the option of
buying the building anytime during the term of the lease. She made phone
calls as soon as the lease was signed, looking for backers, and the first
person she reached said he'd always wanted to own a piece of a restaurant, and he'd put up fifty grand.

But she didn't want a partner, didn't want to owe important money to
anyone. Five, she told him, was the maximum she would take from any
one person. And he wouldn't own a piece of the place, she'd own all the
pieces. If the place was successful, he'd get double his money back. If it
went in the toilet, well, he could afford to lose five thousand dollars,
couldn't he?

She raised all the money she needed, and on her terms, and the next
time she saw the shrink she told him again that he was a genius, and she
had one more question. What the hell should she call it?

"What do people call it now?"

"It doesn't exist yet," she said, "so nobody calls it anything."

"On Sundays," he said, "when they're getting ready to go to your
apartment, your salon, where do they say they're going?"

"What do they say? How should I know what they say, they're not
there yet for me to hear." She thought a moment. "They say they're going
to Stelli's."

"So?"

"A genius," she said.

Stelli's was a success from the night it opened. Her Sunday night
freeloaders, most of whom had invested from $500 to $5,000 in the
restaurant, showed up not only for the opening but several nights a week.
She never hired a publicist, but got in the columns without professional
assistance. And why not? The most interesting people in New York were
regulars at Stelli's, and spent their most interesting evenings in conversation at her bar.

She drew writers, of course. They'd been the core of her Sundays,
and they were her favorites, not just because she respected their work but
also because they had the best conversation. It was important for them to
be original. An actor would find a story that worked and use it over and
over, delivering it a little better each time. But it was the same shtick, and
if you'd heard it once, that was plenty. A writer, though, felt compelled to
think of something new.

She got actors, too, and liked them, if only because they were so determined to be liked. And they were decorative, too, and drew the eyes. But she also got politicians, both local and national, and a small international contingent from the UN. She didn't get the Wall Street guys, or the crowd from Madison Avenue, and she didn't get the ladies who lunched or the pinky-ring cigar smokers. But she got a few of the more sophisticated cops and the hipper gangsters, and an occasional Met or Yankee. And lawyers, of course. Everybody got lawyers.

She learned how to keep the help from stealing and her suppliers from cheating her. She learned how to avoid serious health violations in the kitchen, and how much to schmear the inspectors to overlook the less-than-serious ones. She refined the menu, dropping the items that nobody ordered. She made money, and by the end of the first year she'd paid back her backers, and six months later had paid them back double. She invested her profits in CDs and T-bills, and six months before her lease was up she bought the building. Now nobody could raise her rent and nobody could make her move and Stelli's could go on being Stelli's forever.

Such a pretty face. She put on a few pounds every year, just a few, and she was resigned to it, most of the time. But once, not long after she'd exercised her option and bought the building, she got inspired and went on an Oprah-type diet and lost a lot of weight. She didn't shrink all the way down to a size three, but she did get to be the size of a normal person, and everybody oohed and aahed over her.

And she discovered that, with the extra flesh gone, she didn't have such a pretty face after all. Maybe the observation had been true when she was a girl, but since then her features had matured in an unflattering fashion, and she had a big nose and a big mouth, and the face that looked back in her mirror, the face that appeared at the top of this new almost-slender body of hers, looked like it ought to be peering over the parapet of Notre Dame. She looked like a fucking gargoyle, and for this she was eating salad with no dressing? For this she was passing up pasta?

She put the weight back on, and then some, and she felt a whole lot better, and never again thought about taking it off.

Now, on this Friday night, she sat in her custom-built seat with the first of the four or five Chardonnay spritzers she would consume in the course of the evening, greeting her guests as they arrived, with smiles for all and kisses for a few. Her tables were all booked, except for the two she'd hold back in case a cherished regular arrived hungry without a reservation. (Once a Pulitzer Prize–winning novelist, a Sunday salon alumnus and $5,000 backer, had gotten off a flight from the Coast and come straight to Stelli's, and all her tables were taken. "Hey, it's all right," he'd insisted. "I'll just sit at the bar, and you know what I'll do? I always have martinis with a twist, but tonight I'll have them with olives." She'd served him a full meal at the bar, and started a trend. Now several of her regulars ate at the bar on nights when they came in by themselves. But she always held back two tables, just in case.)

A smile, a nod, a kiss. The out-of-towners got nice warm smiles, too, because their money was as good as anybody else's, and for all she knew so was their company. Half her regulars had been out-of-towners once, until New York got in their blood and became a part of them even as they became a part of it.

Two men in sports jackets. One she'd seen a few times recently, a cop or ex-cop, and if you gave her a minute she'd come up with the name. "Jim," she said, "it's good to see you." And his companion, a familiar face, damn good-looking, nice clothes, and the minute he gave her a smile she placed him. "Fran! You look terrific, and where the hell have you been keeping yourself? I saw more of you when you were living in Seattle."

"Portland," he said.

"Same difference. It's great to see you, Fran, and you, Jim. I hope you gentlemen made a reservation . . ."

"Two at eight," Fran Buckram said.

"That's easier than eight at two, which is what I had the other night. Or would have had, if I hadn't told them to get lost. Go to Madrid, I told them. They eat late there, you'll feel right at home. They thought it was a restaurant, they wanted to know how to get there. It's in Spain, I said. Just walk to Paris and take a right. Philip? Be sure you take good care of Jim here, and the commissioner."

"HERE I WAS TELLING you how to find the place," Jim Galvin said, "and she greets you like the prodigal son. 'Take good care of the commissioner.' "

" 'Take good care of *Jim* and the commissioner.' "

"I gotta say I'm surprised she could come up with my name. It's not like I've been coming here that much."

"She's good. Next time she'll know your last name, too."

"How do you know she didn't know it now?"

"Either way," Buckram said, "it would have been *Hello, Jim.* But then when she handed you off to Philip it would have been *Take good care of Mr. Galvin.*"

"And the commissioner."

"Well, titles are for life, as far as the public is concerned. You run into Clinton, you're not going to call him Bill."

"*How ya doin', Mr. President?* Except not everybody gets that treatment, Fran. It's still Mayor Koch and Mayor Giuliani, but how about Dinkins? And it stopped being Mayor Beame ten minutes after Koch got sworn in."

"So I'm the commissioner for life, is that what you're saying?"

"Unless you get to be something else that trumps police commissioner."

No, he wasn't going to have that conversation again. "The mix is what makes this place work," he said. "I started coming here after I got my gold shield, not all the time but every couple of weeks. You remember a wise guy named Teddy Kostakis? We had him for something, I forget what, and he rolled over and was gonna make all kinds of cases for us. And we brought him here one night, we're feeding him, we're buying him drinks, and he's feeling like a pretty important guy, like a celebrity. And it turns out Teddy's one of those guys, the alcohol messes with his volume control. More he drinks, louder he gets."

"There's a lot of guys like that."

"And they're usually sitting at the next table, but not this time. And here's Teddy, telling his stories so they can hear him out in the street, and you can't get him to pipe down. Now this is a nice place, you know that—"

"Sure."

"And they get a decent crowd, but more often than not there's a couple of made guys in the joint, and if they're hearing what he's saying, and if they've had as much to drink as he's had, well, I don't mind that much if Teddy gets shot, but I'm sitting right across the table from him, and whatever misses him could hit me."

"Wha'd you do, yank him out of there?"

"You remember Phil Carnahan? A sweet guy, retired to Florida and lasted about six months down there."

"Couldn't take it?"

"Loved it, but he had one of those kinds of cancer that gets you out in a hurry. He called me to tell me he had this boat, I had to come down and go fishing with him, and then he called two weeks later to say he'd been to the doctor and got some bad news. And the next call I got was from his wife. I'm sorry, I didn't mean to get off on this track. Where the hell was I?"

"He was sitting next to Teddy."

"Oh, right. So he takes him by the shoulder, he shakes him, gets his attention, which isn't the easiest thing in the world at this point, and he says, 'Teddy, Teddy, you got to watch what you say. Don't you know where you are?' And Teddy looks at him, like *Huh?* And Phil says, 'This is Stelli's, Teddy. The fucking place is crawling with writers. They'll steal your material!' "

SHE READ STELLI'S FACE as she entered, and decided to improvise. "Hi, Stelli," she said. "Did Maury Winters get here yet?"

And she saw the woman's expression soften. She'd greeted her by name, she'd mentioned a prominent local figure who was an occasional if not frequent patron of the restaurant's, so she must be okay. Stelli told her that the lawyer hadn't made a reservation, which didn't surprise Susan greatly because she happened to know he was in Amagansett for the weekend.

"We made a very tentative date," she said. "I'll be at the bar if he comes in. It's Susan Pomerance."

"Of course, dear."

Yeah, like you recognized me, she thought, moving to the far end of the bar, where there were several seats open. That's fine, dear, she thought. I'll pretend I'm waiting for Maury and you pretend you know who I am, and we'll both pretend your first take on me wasn't that I was a hooker.

She ordered a Cosmopolitan and watched the bartender prepare it. He set it down and waited while she took the first sip, and she smiled her approval. He smiled back and moved off, and he was cute, a little young but that was all right. But you had to wait around all night if you wanted to fuck a bartender, and even then there was no guarantee. He could be gay, he could have a wife or girlfriend. Too bad, she thought, because he *was* cute.

To her left, a man and woman were deep in conversation. To her right, two men were telling Tallulah Bankhead stories. That was before her time, but it was before their time, too, and it was the sort of place where you could horn in on a conversation if you had something to contribute.

She said, "The line of hers I always liked was *My daddy warned me about men and whiskey. He never said a word about women and cocaine.*"

They liked that, and at once turned to include her in the conversation. The one closer to her signaled for another round, and asked her if she was ready for another Cosmo. She smiled and shook her head, she'd hardly touched hers. "Next round," she said, and when their drinks came she raised her own glass.

The man farther from her said, "To men and whiskey? Or women and cocaine."

She thought about it. "It's probably déclassé to admit this," she said, "but I never much cared for cocaine."

They liked that, too, and the man next to her introduced himself and

his friend. He was Lowell Cooke, he told her, and his friend was Jay Mc-
Gann, the writer.

"But don't pretend you've heard of me," McGann said, "because nobody has."

"But that'll change very soon," Cooke said, "as soon as your book
comes out."

"He has to believe that," McGann said. "He's my editor. And you
are . . . ?"

"Susan Pomerance," she said. "I have an art gallery in Chelsea."

"A woman of substance," McGann said. "I have to confess, I'm partial to women of substance. They're so . . ."

He turned to his friend for help.

"Substantial," Cooke supplied.

"That's it, they're so substantial. You see? I need an editor."

If she had to choose, which one would she pick? Neither was male-
model gorgeous, though McGann had a rugged Marlboro Man quality to
him that she liked. Cooke had a nice sensuality about him, though. When
he moved his hands, she could feel them on her body.

Pie or ice cream? But why couldn't she have pie à la mode?

God, she was wet at the very thought of it, and maybe it hadn't been
such a brilliant idea to go out without underwear. But it felt sexy, Jesus
did it ever feel sexy, with her nipples (and they tingled, they always tingled now) rubbing the inside of the dress when she moved, and no cloth
to bind her bare and dampened loins, and what if she did go home with
the two of them? What if she fucked them both, one after the other or, better yet, both at once?

She'd never done that. Gary, that asshole husband of hers, with his
oh-let's-be-swingers number, had never really arranged anything interesting. And men who drooled at the thought of two girls and a guy got
uptight at the idea of two men and one woman. Afraid they'd be shown
up as less virile than the other guy, she supposed. Or, worse, scared of
having some kind of sexual contact with him, and terrified that they might
enjoy it.

Men . . .

ROZ HAD MADE THE reservation for nine, and he was ten minutes late.
Stelli was there to greet him, and he said he was with Roz Albright.

She took his hand in both of hers, which surprised him. "She's waiting for you in back," she said. "I don't know where Philip is, but go ahead
back, you'll find her. And John?" She was beaming. "I heard the news.
Congratulations."

He walked the length of the restaurant, feeling as though every eye in the place was on him. Roz was at a center-rear table, and there was an ice bucket on a stand next to the table, with a bottle of champagne chilling.

JIM GALVIN INTERRUPTED HIMSELF in the middle of a war story. "Oh, Jesus," he said. "You're not going to believe who just walked in."

"Who?"

"Don't turn around. Shit, he's coming this way."

"Who is it?"

"My fucking client, and how did he even know I was here? Wait a minute, he didn't, and he doesn't even see me. The champagne's for him, and what do you figure he's got to celebrate?"

Buckram could see him now, giving the big blonde a hug and a kiss, then sitting down opposite her. The guy's face was familiar, but he couldn't think why.

He said, "Who is he, and what are you doing for him?"

"I'm doing jack shit for him, which I guess is why it spooked me to see him walk in like he's gunning for me. Who is he? He's John fucking Creighton is who he is."

"The writer?" And he put his hands together and mimed wringing an invisible neck.

"Yeah," Galvin said. "That writer. I'm supposed to turn up a witness that'll help the defense. Like what? Somebody who saw him not kill her?"

"Be a neat trick."

"I got one guy, says he's pretty sure the two of them left the bar separately. But hell, there's evidence puts him in the apartment with her. Maybe this muddies the water some, maybe Winters can do something with it, but—"

"Maury Winters? That's who you're working for?"

"Yeah, and I never thought I'd see the day. I'll never forget how he made a monkey out of me in court one time. Anything comes of this, the DA'll be trying to make me look stupid, and Maury'll be objecting left and right. Funny how it comes around, isn't it?"

"Maury Winters."

"Is that the magic word, Fran? You and him got a beef or something?"

"See the brunette? Fourth stool from the end?"

"Changing the subject again? Yeah, I noticed her when she walked in. She's a beautiful woman, I wouldn't mind seeing more of her, but what's she got to do with my boss?"

"The last time I saw Maury," he said, "was in a fancy French restaurant."

"Yeah, well, I guess he can afford to eat anyplace he wants."

"He was all by himself at a table, and she was under it."

"Come on, Fran."

"Cleaning his pipes. Swear to God."

"Jesus. If she pulled something like that here . . ."

"She couldn't, Jim. She'd never get away with it. She'd have to do everybody."

"I ALMOST DIDN'T RECOGNIZE you," Roz said. "I was trying to remember when I saw you last. When did you shave?"

"About an hour ago."

"I mean when did you lose the beard, not when did you last run a razor over your face."

"Same answer," he said. "It needed a trim, and I got carried away. I feel slightly naked, but I probably would anyway, being suddenly out in public. And Stelli recognized me. She even congratulated me. She couldn't be referring to the indictment, or the shave, so I can only assume she heard about the deal. You told her, right?"

"I did," she said. "I couldn't help myself. But if I hadn't, someone else would have before the evening was out. Word gets around in nothing flat, you know that. When you get home, I'll bet you'll have congratulatory messages on your machine. Which reminds me, did Esther call?"

"Right after I got off the phone with you. I swear I've never met the woman, but the way she talked you'd have thought at the very least we shacked up once for a week in Cancún."

"If you'd ever seen her, you'd know how funny that is."

"Right now," he said, "she's the most beautiful woman in the world, as far as I'm concerned. Next to you, of course."

She grinned. "Goes without saying. Oops, here's somebody."

He turned as a tall silver-haired man, wearing a seersucker suit over a black T-shirt, approached the table. Creighton recognized him, got to his feet.

"John Creighton? I'm Roger Delacroix, I heard your good news and I just wanted to extend my congratulations." They shook hands, and Delacroix lowered his voice to add, "And my support. I can imagine—no, actually, I *can't* imagine what you're going through. But I know you'll come out of it all right."

He sat down, watching as Delacroix rejoined his party at a table on the far side of the room. "I'll be a son of a bitch," he said. "Roger Delacroix."

"And half the town just saw him come over and shake your hand."

"Roger fucking Delacroix. I wouldn't have thought he knew I was alive, and this morning he probably didn't. But that was a hell of a nice thing he just did, and with no ulterior motive that I can see. I mean, it's not as though I can swing a couple of votes in Sweden and get him the Nobel he's had coming for the past twenty years."

"I wish somebody could."

"So do I, especially now. Did you hear what he said at the end? Just to me, not to the whole room. Not ignoring the murder charge, but acknowledging it and dismissing it. Essentially saying he knows I'm innocent, and how the hell can he?"

"I can think of slightly more than three million reasons."

"Is that it, do you figure? I can't possibly be guilty if I'm worth all that money? And speaking of which, you were going to tell me how it got to be three million."

"I was wondering when we were going to get to that."

"St. Martin's bid two point four," he said, "and that plus fifteen percent comes to exactly two point seven six. Which is nothing to sneeze at, but it's not where we wound up."

"I was a pretty good editor," she said, "but I'll tell you something. I'm a better agent."

"And?"

"Before I called Esther," she said, "I called Joan at St. Martin's and told her she was the last one standing."

"At two point four."

"At two point four, and I reminded her Crown had the right to top that with a bid of . . . what did you just say it came to?"

"Two point seven six."

"So, I said, I wanted to give her a chance to raise her own bid, because this was her last chance, and I had the sense she really wanted the book—"

"If not, she was bidding like a lunatic for no good reason."

"—so maybe she'd like to edge it a little bit higher and make it that much harder for Esther to top. She thought about it and said what did I think about two point six."

"And I bet you thought it was dandy."

"Now here's where I'm really proud of myself, sweetie. What I said was it was a step in the right direction, but if she went one notch higher to two point seven, then Esther would have to go over three million dollars to beat her out, and she was a lot less likely to get clearance at that figure."

"And she went for it."

"She thanked me. Pour us some more champagne, why don't you? You want to know the best part?"

"You just told me the best part."

"No, this is even better. I called Esther, not really thinking she'd top, because you have to remember we haven't heard from her since it was her floor at one point one. I kept her in the picture, I told her what level we were at, but she never said anything, because what was there for her to say? Now we're at two point seven and she's got to say something, and what she said was yes."

" 'Yes I said yes I will yes.' "

"Her exact words. No, as a matter of fact her exact words were *I'm glad we wound up where we did, so we can announce a sale in excess of three million dollars*. The more they spend, the more important the deal is to everybody, and the more ink they'll get for it, and the ballsier Esther looks for throwing all those dollars on the table."

"What did you say to Joan?"

"That she gave it her best shot, but that frankly I didn't see how anybody was going to get you away from Crown. And she said evidently two point seven wasn't enough, and maybe she should have gone to three herself. And we both told each other that three probably wouldn't have worked either, and I said I'd better get off and call you, because you were probably climbing the walls."

"As indeed I was."

"No, because I'd already spoken to you, I wasn't going to make you wait until I called her. I'm telling you all my secrets, and from now on you're probably not gonna believe a word I say, are you?" She put a hand on top of his. "Saved by the bell. You don't have to answer that, because here's somebody else to congratulate you."

"OH, DEAR," SUSAN SAID. "It's beginning to look as though I've been stood up, doesn't it?"

"I can't believe that," Jay McGann said. "Whoever he is, the man's probably dead."

"Or kidnapped by terrorists," Lowell Cooke offered. "Or he's a damned fool. Which is what I feel like, because I'm afraid we have to desert you."

She'd seen this coming. When McGann had ordered the last round of drinks, Cooke had reminded them that they had to roll, that they were running late.

"I've enjoyed this," she said.

"So have we," Cooke said, "but his wife'll kill me if I don't get him home to her in a hurry. Mine'll kill me anyway. Susan, tell me your last name again, I've got a mind like a sieve."

"Pomerance."

"And the name of your gallery?"

"The Susan Pomerance Gallery."

"Duh," Cooke said, and McGann asked what hours she was open. She told him, and added that she could certainly arrange a private appointment after hours if that would be more convenient. He said he wouldn't want to put her to the trouble, sending a little message with his eyes, and she said it wouldn't be any trouble, and sent the message right back to him.

And they were gone, and Jesus she was hot, and the bartender really did look awfully cute, but she didn't intend to waste half the night waiting for him. She took a wee sip of her Cosmo, then turned to survey the room.

She looked, not for the first time, at the big man at the center table on the rear wall. She'd noticed him when he came in, noted with approval the athletic stride, the strong jawline, the don't-care masculinity of his corduroy jacket and black jeans. But he was with a woman, and they were drinking champagne and talking a mile a minute, so she'd put him out of her mind.

Then the word filtered down the bar that he was John Creighton, John Blair Creighton, which made him the man who'd gone home with Marilyn Fairchild and strangled her. But that wasn't the news, she learned. The news was that he'd just signed a book contract for over three million dollars.

She wouldn't have recognized him, he'd had a beard in the photo that ran in the newspapers, but she could see now that it was the same face, the same strong presence.

She looked at him now, saw him moving his hands as he talked, and she could feel those hands on her body, taking hold of her, turning her, positioning her the way he wanted her. Taking her from behind, splitting her like a melon, his big hands gripping her shoulders, then moving to grip the sides of her head, then settling on her throat . . .

But he was with someone. Her eyes moved from him, and found those of a man a table away from Creighton. She'd seen him before and known he looked familiar, but now she was able to place him. And he was looking back at her.

She held his gaze, just for a moment, then turned for another sip of her drink.

JIM GALVIN WAS SAYING something, but Fran Buckram had stopped paying attention when the two men at the bar left and the woman in the black dress remained behind. He watched her, trying to figure her out, and then she caught him, her eyes locking on his. It was such a damned cliché, eyes finding each other across a crowded room, but he felt something. Fifty-three years old (a youthful fifty-three, you could say, but when you used the word *youthful* it meant you had to) and he could feel it just the same, a stirring, a quiver of excitement.

He was on his feet without having consciously decided to get up. Jim had stopped in midsentence and was looking up expectantly, waiting for an explanation. Well, he'd have to wait.

He walked straight across the room to her, threading his way among tables, pulling himself up short to avoid bumping a waiter with a tray. She had turned away from him, she was facing forward, drinking her drink. He stood at her shoulder, close enough to breathe her perfume, and groped for an opening line.

"They're not coming back," she said, without raising her eyes from her glass. "Have a seat."

"I've been sitting all night."

She turned to him, smiled. "Me, too," she said.

"Can I buy you a drink?"

"I don't really want another drink," she said, and he felt rejected for an instant before she smiled again and extended her hand. "I'm Susan Pomerance."

Her hand was warm and soft, her grip firm. "Fran Buckram."

"I know. You were pointed out to me."

"Oh?"

"Not tonight. Sometime last month, it must have been, in a French restaurant called—"

"L'Aiglon d'Or. You were with Maury Winters."

"You know Maury? He's a dear man."

"Good lawyer, too."

"And you remember me from just seeing me that night?"

"I couldn't take my eyes off you. Except for when you weren't there to be seen."

"I dropped my earring."

"I remember."

"It took me a while to find it. Of course it was dark there."

"It must have been."

"And there were diversions. You're a very attractive man."

"You're a beautiful woman."

"Thank you, Fran. Do they ever call you Franny?"

"No."

"I might. Would that upset you?"

"No."

"Turn toward me more. And stand closer. Now put your hand under my dress. Go ahead, nobody can see. Yes, that's right. What are you thinking?"

"That your barber's a lucky man."

"Oh, thank God. You're witty. I'd fuck you even if you weren't, but this way it's so much nicer."

"Let's get out of here."

"First make me come."

"I'll make you come later."

"You'll make me come all night long, but I don't want to wait. Do me now, with your fingers. That's right."

She sat perfectly still, she didn't move, and her face didn't change expression. Her eyes held his, and when he felt a trembling in her loins she caught her breath almost imperceptibly, and something changed in her eyes.

After a moment she said, "That was lovely. Franny? You were the police commissioner. You're used to being in charge, aren't you?"

"I haven't been commissioner in a long time."

"But you're still used to being in charge."

"I guess so."

"Tonight," she said, "I'm in charge."

"All right."

"No," she said firmly, "*I'm in charge*. We do what I say. If you want to come home with me, those are the rules."

"Fair enough."

"You have to promise."

"I promise."

She looked at him as if to determine what his word was worth, and nodded shortly.

"Wait for me outside."

"I have to take care of the check."

"Go ahead, and then wait for me outside."

Back at the table, he palmed two fifties to Jim Galvin and asked him to take care of the check. Galvin was saying something, but he acted as if he hadn't heard, clapped the man on the shoulder, and headed for the door. Stelli caught him on the way out, told him not to be a stranger, presented her fleshy face for a kiss.

He turned at the door, and saw her walking toward his table. Had Galvin called her over? But no, Galvin didn't even see her, he was holding his glass of whiskey and looking into it as if it were a crystal ball. And Susan Pomerance wasn't going to that table anyway, she was going toward John Creighton's.

Or for all he knew she was looking for the ladies' room, because someone stood and blocked his view, and what was he standing there for, anyway?

He went outside and stood on the sidewalk in front of a shop that sold mineral specimens and semiprecious stones. He wondered if she'd come out, wondered if he'd get to go home with her. Wondered what in the hell he was getting himself into.

I don't want to wait. Do me now, with your fingers.

Wherever it went, he thought, it had to be more fun than running for mayor.

ROZ WAS SAYING THAT she'd felt all along they were better off with Crown. "Now we don't have to fight with them over those two backlist titles. As a matter of fact, they're going back to press on both of them. They'll be back in print by September. By *John* Blair Creighton, this time around."

"If they promote the new book right—"

"Honey," she said, "they'll have no choice, not with what they're spending already. And it's gonna be easier to sell than umbrellas in a shit storm. Oh, I was shameless hustling this one, John, but it's easy when you've got something good to sell. Imagine if OJ could write like Faulkner, I told them."

"I don't write like Faulkner."

"No, and neither does OJ. Imagine if Mailer hit an artery the night he stabbed his wife."

"Imagine if Nabokov did Jon-Benet Ramsey."

"God, you're worse than I am. Imagine if he caught her in a net and mounted her like a butterfly. And speaking of lepidoptera, here comes yet another moth drawn to the lamp of your genius."

A woman in a black dress, whom he'd noticed earlier at the bar. She rested a hand on his shoulder, leaned in toward him. She said, "Mr. Creighton? It's awful to intrude, but I can't help myself. My name's Susan Pomerance, and I'm a very big fan of yours."

"You are?"

"Huge," she said. "And I heard your good news, and I couldn't be happier for you." She slipped a business card into his hand. "I hope you'll call me," she said, and smiled gently at Roz. "I'm sorry," she said, and turned from them.

" 'The Susan Pomerance Gallery,' " he read aloud. " 'Folk and Outsider Art.' With an address in Chelsea and a phone number, and the URL for a website."

"Everybody's got a website. Except you, now that I think of it. Don't worry, they'll have one built for you. There's something on the back."

He turned the card over, shook his head, passed it to Roz.

" 'I'd love to get to know you better.' Yes, dear, I'm sure you would.

Signed Susan. And there's another number, no doubt for the phone on her bedside table."

"Amazing," he said. "What was that all about? I figured she had to be a reporter, but not many of them own art galleries. Well, she did say she was a fan."

"And she wants to discuss the color symbolism of the stories in *Edged Weapons*. Why do writers turn into morons when you get them away from their keyboards?" She leaned forward. "John, wake up and smell the champagne. She wants to fuck you."

"I thought of that, obviously, but . . ."

"But what? You couldn't believe your good luck?"

"Roz, I can't believe *any* of my good luck."

She sighed and patted his hand. "It's a lot to take in," she said. "Don't try to make sense out of it right now. Just relax and enjoy it. Meanwhile, do you want me to get rid of this for you?"

"No," he said, reaching to take the card from her. "No, I might as well keep it."

sixteen

T HESE ARE THE rules. You do what I say. You speak only to answer questions."

"What's your side of the bargain?"

"I won't shed any of your blood. I won't do any lasting damage. And I guarantee this is going to be the best night of your life."

"I don't know," he said. "I've had some pretty good nights."

"Not like this one."

There was a moment when he might have decided this was all too weird for him. Maybe she shouldn't have said anything about blood, maybe the phrase *lasting damage* might have an anaphrodisiacal effect on a man who'd seen a lot of permanent damage in the course of his professional career. But she'd wanted to give him an idea in front just what he was letting himself in for.

Still, she really didn't want to lose him now . . .

He took a moment to think about it. Then, slowly, he nodded.

Good.

"Take off your clothes."

They were in the living room of her London Towers apartment. She made herself comfortable on the sofa while he undressed, folding his clothes and placing them on the chair. His body, she was pleased to note, was trim and athletic, with good muscle tone. He had a little hair on his chest, none on his back. His penis was small, but it was flaccid; you couldn't really tell what you had until it was erect.

"You're circumcised," she said. "You can't be Jewish. No, don't say anything, that wasn't a question."

She touched the tip of her index finger to the tip of his penis. "So I guess I won't need the pinking shears this time," she said, and watched his expression until he realized she was kidding.

"This way," she said, and led him into the bedroom.

JUST TWO BLOCKS EAST of London Towers, on Twenty-third Street a few doors west of Seventh Avenue, the man who had most recently been calling himself Herbert Asbury was sitting in the window of a coffee shop, watching the establishment across the street. It was a bar called Harrigan's, housed in a four-story industrial building that, like its neighbors on either side, had been converted to residential lofts.

This was not the first time he'd watched it.

He'd ordered a cup of coffee, and he'd only drunk a third of it when it seemed to him to be time to leave. He set a quarter beside his saucer, paid his check at the register, walked to the corner and waited for the light to change before he crossed the wide street. He hadn't actually been inside Harrigan's, and he wanted to get the feel of the place.

Because this was a Friday, there was live music in Harrigan's, with four tables in the rear occupied by people listening to the jazz duo of piano and amplified guitar. Up front, four men and two women sat at the bar. There were three empty stools in a row not far from the entrance, and he took the middle of the three stools and ordered a beer. The bartender, a rawboned girl with her light brown hair bound up in a kerchief, asked him what brand he wanted. When he looked blank she named several brands, and he nodded when she said Heineken. She said, "Is that a yes? You want a Heineken?" and he nodded again and she brought him one.

She brought a glass, too, but left him to pour the beer for himself. He sat there for what must have been twenty minutes, although he hadn't checked the time when he came in and had no sense of its passage. At some point he put a ten-dollar bill on the bar, and at some point she took it away and brought back change.

Then he left, scooping up all of his change but a dollar, and leaving the untouched beer on the bar.

THE HANDCUFFS WERE THE standard police type of stainless steel. She cuffed Buckram's hands behind his back, then had him lie faceup on the bed with his bound hands in the small of his back. After she'd anchored his feet to lower corners of the bed frame, she ran silk ties under his arms and secured them to the frame's upper corners. He remained calm throughout, and she noted with interest that his penis had grown to a respectable size during the course of this procedure.

In one fluid motion she drew the black dress up over her head and tossed it aside. She watched his eyes as they studied her, the breasts with gold-studded nipples, the hairless loins he'd touched but hadn't seen.

The hood surprised him.

He didn't like the idea, she could see that right away. She stroked his chest to gentle him. "You'll like this," she assured him. "Shutting out one sense heightens the others." And, when the hood was on and fastened, covering his eyes and mouth, covering everything but his nose, she said, "Besides, there's nothing you can do about it."

The sense of empowerment she felt was remarkable. It was beyond sex, it was a new energy that surged through her entire being. She could do anything to this man. She could hurt him. She could kill him. He couldn't do a thing to stop her. He could, if he wanted, make a snorting noise through his nose, but it wouldn't carry beyond the room. He was helpless, and she was all-powerful.

She knew he had to be coming to a similar realization, and she watched his penis soften as the perception drained his excitement. That gave her an idea, and she fitted him with a leather cock ring that circled the base of the organ. It was, the clerk at Pleasure Chest had explained, a sort of Roach Motel for penises. The blood got in, but it couldn't get out—and neither could the semen.

She played with him for almost an hour, using her hands, her mouth, her breasts. She said, "Franny, Franny," and sucked his nipples. She did all the things she'd thought of in recent weeks, and other things she'd never thought of until now.

She touched herself, too, and rubbed herself against his leg, but she stopped short of letting herself come, waiting until she was seated astride him, riding his cock, rolling and thrusting, moving however she wanted to move, until she came with a fierce wordless cry and collapsed upon him.

CHEEK WAS ON EIGHTH Avenue at Twentieth Street, next door to a Cuban-Chinese restaurant and downstairs from a travel agency. The top three floors of the building had apartments, four to a floor.

The bar was gay. Or, more accurately, the bar's clientele was gay. He'd determined as much right away by noticing the men who went in and out of it. There were no women patrons, which was an indicator in it-self, but you could tell just by looking at the men. While a good many of them were not discernibly gay as individuals, collectively they couldn't possibly be otherwise. They were mostly young, and they were mostly slender, and even the older ones tended to look young, at least from a distance.

He might well have suspected Cheek was a gay bar without seeing any of its patrons, simply because it was in a neighborhood where most of the bars were gay, and because you couldn't see in the windows. They looked to have been painted black on the inside.

It didn't bother him that they were gay. He didn't know that he'd ever been in a gay bar, but he felt comfortable enough at the idea of going. He supposed that he could even have sex with one of them, if for some reason it should be necessary to his purpose. He'd been able to have sex with Clara without feeling the slightest bit of desire for her. He could probably have sex with anyone, or anything, and his body would perform while his mind remained apart, the disinterested observer.

He wasn't dressed right, though. He was older than everybody else, and he looked his age in a way that they did not. He could choose more appropriate clothes than his black trousers and short-sleeved sport shirt, he could dye his hair, but he didn't want to do any of that.

He didn't absolutely have to get inside the place, but it seemed to him as though he ought to. It would be good to know if the windows were opaque from within as well as without, or if they were like one-way mirrors. And it would be good to have a beer there, as he'd had one at Harrigan's.

Men turned to look at him as he came in, and stared at him candidly in a way he wasn't accustomed to. They wouldn't have looked at him that way on the street, but he had come in here, and was thus available to be looked at and appraised. Eyes sized him up, then looked away.

There was only one open seat at the bar, and when he took it the man to his left (young, blond, tanned, wearing a black silk shirt with the top three buttons undone) said hello, and that his name was Leo. When he didn't respond, Leo looked amused and turned away. He said something to the fellow on his other side, and Herbert Asbury (or George Templeton Strong, or what you will) heard the words *tourist* and *uptight*.

You couldn't see out the windows. The black paint was thick, and no light got through it.

He ordered a beer, left it untouched. When he didn't come back, Leo drank it.

HIS COCK WAS STILL in her, still fully erect. The tip was a deep brownish purple, and she knew it wasn't safe to leave the ring on too long. Nor was it possible to get it off other than by cutting it, which she did with a pair of blunt-nosed scissors.

"Poor Franny," she murmured. "Don't worry, I wouldn't leave you like this." She cupped his balls, planted a light kiss on the tip of his cock. "Now it's going to be your turn."

She told him not to move, then unfastened the cords that held him in place on the bed. He was still cuffed and hooded. She told him to roll over on his stomach, and fitted a bulky pillow under his middle before once again fastening the cords. The pillow elevated his hips enough so that she could reach around and get hold of him.

First, though, she got out some more of her toys. She put them within reach, then stroked his buttocks. He had a nice ass, small and well muscled. She cupped his buttocks, drew them apart, pressed them together.

She slipped a finger between them, felt his sphincter tighten to resist the intrusion. She said, "Franny? Think of all the men you sent to prison. Do you know what happens to them when they get there?"

She dipped two fingers into a jar of lubricant, worked it into him. She talked to him all the while, telling him he was her little Franny, her little girl, and she was going to fuck him. She got her other hand underneath him and held his cock while she probed him, and she felt it grow in her hands.

Then she let go of him and strapped on the harness. It was tricky, she'd had trouble when she tried it on the first time, but now she got it right, and attached the dildo. The smallest one, because she didn't want to hurt him, not more than a little.

Just as she was about to enter him, a thought came: *Wait, am I allowed to do this?* She registered the thought and overrode it, slipping easily into him, and the thought went away.

She became the man, somehow, and he the woman, and the rubber dildo became her own stiffened flesh. Every thrust stimulated her clit and sent tremors through her whole pelvic area, but that was the least of it, really. It was the idea of it, the reality of it: he was helpless and she was fucking him, fucking him, fucking him like a girl.

DEATH ROW WAS GOING to be a problem.

He could see that right away. The bar was on Nineteenth Street near the Hudson, not far from the facility where he had his storage locker. It was a gay bar, too, but of a different sort from Cheek. A huge man stood at the entrance, his arms corded with muscle, his belly hanging over his belt. He was wearing black leather pants, a black tank top, and studded leather wristbands, and his head was shaved, with a large hoop earring hanging from his right earlobe. He was letting some people in and sending others away, and a pattern was not hard to discern: the ones permitted to enter were all wearing either denim or leather.

He didn't own appropriate clothing. He could buy some, though not

at this hour, but sensed that he wouldn't pass muster no matter how he
dressed.

Nor was there a window, blackened or clear. The ground-floor facade
was whitewashed brick sporting spray-painted graffiti and, over the door,
the name of the establishment. A drawing on the black door showed a
skeleton, a ball and chain on one ankle, within a prison cell.

He positioned himself so that he could get a glimpse of the interior
when the door opened, but all he saw were dangerous-looking men entering or leaving, with no indication where they got to once they entered, or
where they were coming from before they left. He went around the corner
and sat down in a doorway and thought things over.

When he returned, he walked up to the doorkeeper, who sized him
up, called him Pops, and told him he couldn't come in. "You're not
dressed right," he said, and pointed to a sign that spelled out the dress
code, in addition to banning weapons, hazardous materials, and illegal
drugs. The dress code, he somehow knew, was more rigorously enforced
than the other provisions.

He let his shoulders slump forward, heaved a sigh.

"Pops," the fellow said gently, "do you know what kind of a place
this is?"

"I think so."

"Believe me, you wouldn't feel at home here."

"My son did."

"Say what?"

He drew a breath, let it out. "My son used to come here. He was . . .
he liked the company of men, he liked to dress in leather."

"And you're trying to find him?"

"He's dead."

"I'm sorry."

"He died of . . . that disease."

"Yeah, well, lots of people did. I lost a lot of friends."

It was interesting, he thought. The man looked so intimidating, with
his big shaved head and his muscles and his dress, but underneath he was
gentle.

"I just wanted to . . . to see some of the places he liked. That was a
whole side of his life I couldn't share with him, and I just . . ."

He let his voice trail off, waiting.

"I can't take you downstairs," the fellow said. He drew the door open,
motioned for him to come over and look. Inside, a flight of stairs de-
scended, lit by low-wattage bulbs. Downstairs, music played, almost
drowned out by the sound of men talking and dancing.

"That's the best I can do, Pops. I'll tell you what you'd see down-stairs. There's a big room with stuff hanging on the walls, and a lot of men in leather and denim drinking and talking, maybe dancing a little. And there's a back room, but we don't need to get into that."

And what were the hours?

"He said sometimes he would stay all night," he said. "The sun would be up by the time he left."

"Yeah, well, maybe we don't always close when we're supposed to. But we're usually locked up by six, anyway."

"Thank you," he said. "Thank you very much. I'm sure my son would have liked you."

"Maybe I knew him. What was his name?"

"Herbert," he said. "Herbert Asbury."

"Doesn't ring a bell," the fellow said, "but there's a lot of guys I know by sight, that I never get their names. So maybe I did know him. One thing, I'll bet he was a nice fellow."

HE WAS LYING ON his back, his arms at his sides. She had removed the hood and the restraints, and he'd been entirely passive during the process, neither helping nor resisting.

She asked him how he felt.

He thought it over, then told her he didn't know.

Then he said, "You know, I thought I'd been around. I've never experienced anything remotely like this. If anybody told me I'd consent to this, I'd have said they were crazy."

"And if they told you you'd love it?"

"You think I loved it?"

She dipped her fingers in the pool of ejaculate, held her hand in front of his face. "This didn't come from me," she said. He was silent, and she said, "I should make you eat it."

He made a face.

"But I'm too greedy," she said, and sucked her fingers clean. "There's more, you know, in case you change your mind. You came enough to start your own sperm bank. I tied you up and fucked you in the ass and you loved it."

"If I could have gotten loose—"

"But you couldn't."

"No."

"So there was nothing to do but enjoy it."

"That doesn't mean I want to do it again."

"Ever?"

Again, he considered the question. "I don't know," he said. "God knows I don't want to do it again now. I hope you didn't break anything up there."

"You didn't bleed."

"Yeah, I seem to recall that you promised me I wouldn't."

"I used a lot of lubricant. And I used the smallest one."

"That was the smallest one? Well, thank God for small favors. I don't want to think what it would have been like with the big one."

"But you will think about it," she said. "Later, you won't be able to keep from thinking about it. You'll wonder."

"Jesus, who are you? The devil?"

"Just a woman."

"You really own an art gallery? You're not—"

"Not what?"

"Someone who does this for a living?"

"Someone told me I would make a good dominatrix. But she was wrong. I couldn't possibly do that."

"What was that we were just doing?"

"But that was because I wanted you," she said. "I took one look at you and I knew just what I wanted to do with you, and that you'd love it. And that *I'd* love it."

"Whatever you are," he said, "you're something. Well, I guess I'd better—"

He started to get up, but she stopped him with a hand on his chest.

She said, "You're released from your promise. You're under no restraints, and of course you can go if you want to. But wouldn't you like to stay awhile?"

"And do what?"

"Look at me," she said. She cupped her breasts, opened her legs. "You can probably think of something you'd like to do with me."

"And if I was eighteen years old I could probably do it, but—"

"You don't have to be hard, Franny. You don't have to use your cock. You've got a beautiful mouth, you've got lovely hands, and I've got a whole closet full of toys for us to play with. Unless you don't think that would be any fun."

For answer he rolled over and took her breast in his mouth. He sucked her for a while, then stopped for a moment. "I was just thinking," he said. "I was trying to think if I ever had sex with a woman without kissing her, and I don't think I ever did."

"Even whores?"

"I never went with one."

"Not even once?"

"Never had the urge."

"And you always kissed your wife?"

"Maybe waking up in the middle of the night, you know, and just going into it straight from sleep. But aside from that, no."

"And you think we should kiss, Franny?"

"I don't know. Maybe not. What do you think?"

"Maybe another time," she said. "When we know each other better."

seventeen

IT WAS, NO question, the best day of his life.

First the auction. It had been genuinely exciting, in a way a writer's life never was.

Oh, there was pleasure in the work itself. That was where the real satisfaction lay. You imagined something and put words together, and you opened a door in the imagination and walked down an untrodden path, and it led to another door. And you opened that, and went off to see where it led, and day by day and page by page an entire alternate universe manifested itself before you.

Sometimes you struggled, and stared for hours at the empty page that reflected the barren imagination. Sometimes, like Flaubert, you spent the morning inserting a comma and the afternoon taking it out.

Sometimes you were able to write, but the words tasted like ashes in the mouth. You tapped at the keys like a field hand chopping cotton, like a factory worker on the assembly line. Somehow the words got on the page, and afterward they turned out as often as not to be as good as words that sang as you typed them, but they weren't much fun to write.

And sometimes, sometimes, the book came utterly to life and wrote itself. The words came too quickly for the fingers to keep pace with them. Characters spoke their own perfect dialogue spontaneously, and you were the court stenographer, dutifully recording everything they said. Plots, hopelessly tangled, worked themselves out before your eyes, like the Gordian knot magically untying itself. It was you doing it of course, or otherwise you wouldn't walk away from the keyboard exhausted, drained, empty. But it was a part of your consciousness that consciousness knew nothing of, and it was sheer joy when it took over and ran the show for you.

But was it exciting?

Maybe, maybe it was. But not like this.

And it had been the best sort of excitement, because the exhilaration of climbing higher and higher was not balanced by a fear of falling. Each bid brought another roll of the dice, but he wasn't going double or nothing, he wasn't risking anything. He was already a winner. The only question was the amount of his prize.

And wasn't it remarkable how each increase raised the threshold of his own greed? Weeks ago, before any of this had happened, before he had ever heard Marilyn Fairchild's name, he'd really wanted only two things—to finish his book, and to find someone willing to publish it. He'd want a five-figure advance, certainly, because he had to eat, he had to pay the rent, but he wouldn't expect much, and it wouldn't have taken much to make him content.

Once they started bidding, once the numbers started to climb, he kept wanting more. Two million? Someone actually wanted to pay him two million dollars? That's amazing, that's wonderful, that's miraculous—now how about two point five? How about three?

When it was over, when Crown had topped St. Martin's, when even that price turned out to be higher than he thought it would be, all the delight he felt could not entirely silence one small voice. A voice of disappointment, wishing it didn't have to be over, wishing somehow it could have been more.

An eternal truth, he thought. The more you get, the more you want.

For the first time he felt that he understood how a man could have a billion dollars and want more, how an executive could take his hundred-million severance package and use it to bankroll a new company. The more they had, the more they wanted—not because of what they could do with it, but for the sheer joy of getting it.

HE TOOK OFF HIS jacket, hung it in the closet. He turned on his computer, thinking he'd check his e-mail, then changed his mind and shut it down again.

He'd keep this apartment. He wasn't sure how much three million dollars was, but Roz's commission would come out of that, and taxes, federal, state, and local. He'd probably net somewhere between one and two million dollars, and that would come in over a period of a couple of years, with most of it deferred until he delivered the two books, and some payable on publication. It was still a lot of money, no matter how they paid it and how much the government skimmed off the top, but it didn't mean he could go out and buy himself a penthouse on Central Park South.

Even if he could, he'd still stay here. He liked it, it suited him. It was only one room, but it was room enough for him and his things.

Maybe he'd travel more. See a little of the world, or at least the parts
of it that you could still go to. Take a house in Sag Harbor for a season,
spend a winter in the Caribbean.

Take more cabs, he thought. Eat in nicer restaurants. Buy top-shelf
booze. Speaking of which . . .

He put a couple of ice cubes in a glass, poured some whiskey over
them. They'd had that bottle of champagne at Stelli's, and afterward she
had an Amaretto and he had an Armagnac, and liked it well enough to
have a second. And then, when he'd finally gone outside with Roz and put
her in a cab, a writer who'd come over to the table earlier followed him
out to the street and insisted he come back for a quick one. The quick one
had turned out to be three or four slow ones, taken at Stelli's long bar with
eight or ten of New York's brightest people, and nobody talked about his
deal or anybody else's deal. They talked instead about the Yankees and
the Mets and the mayor and the governor and the affair a talk show host-
ess was having with the husband of a CNN anchor and the shake-up in the
Catholic church and the shake-up in the FBI and the shake-up at the *Daily
News* and, well, just about everything.

And nobody made a fuss over him, thank God, but nobody ignored
him, either, and they listened to what he had to say and laughed at his better lines and treated him, all in all, as if he belonged there. And that was
as it should be, because, now, he did.

What an incredible evening.

HE HADN'T REALLY WANTED to go. He wasn't exactly surprised when
Roz had suggested—no, better make that *insisted on*—a celebratory dinner. And there'd been no way to refuse, not after the job she'd done for
him. But he'd figured it would be at best anticlimactic and at worst uncomfortable. He'd been feeling self-conscious going down to the corner
for a pack of cigarettes, so how was he going to like being out in public?
And at Stelli's, yet.

What he'd discovered was another eternal truth, the day's second,
right up there with *The more you get, the more you want.*

And it was a beauty: *Nothing succeeds like success.*

Like everyone else on the planet, he'd heard the line a million times,
and it had always struck him as a tautology. What the hell was it supposed
to mean? Nothing succeeds like something that is successful. Well, sure.
Who could argue with that?

But that wasn't what it meant at all. It was success itself, the fact of
success, that gave rise to further success. The first cause of the initial success—the accomplishment, the lucky break, whatever it was—didn't
have anything much to do with it. If you were a success, the world threw

laurels at your feet, your reward for . . . for what? For being a success, dimwit. What else?

Roger Delacroix, *the* Roger Delacroix, had made a point of coming to his table to shake his hand and congratulate him. He couldn't really say he read Delacroix, but by God he respected the man's work. (And there were other writers he didn't respect, didn't think much of at all, whose books he bought and read as soon as they came out.) Delacroix's act tonight had been generous and selfless, but it was his seven-figure deal that had brought the man to his table. His success had drawn Delacroix and the others, and had fattened on their attention.

He carried his drink over to the window, looked out at the city. There were no lights burning in the building directly across the street, and only one, on the top floor, in the building to its immediate left. A bald man in a suit walked the careful walk of the man who does not want anyone to know he's drunk. A woman walked her dog, an Irish wolfhound, an enormous galumphing creature. He recognized the woman, but wondered if he'd do so if she hadn't had the dog with her.

The air seemed clearer than usual, his vision sharper.

Nothing succeeds like success. He'd finish the book, buoyed by the success it had already enjoyed. That would sweep the anxiety and self-doubt from his path, and he'd write it and polish it and turn it in, and Esther would love it because she'd come to it eager to love it. And the sales force, charged up in advance at the knowledge that they'd have this eminently promotable, eminently saleable book to push, would read it with great enthusiasm and make sure all their accounts loaded up on it. That would guarantee the stores had big piles of the books, and the publisher's advertising dollars would further guarantee that the piles wound up on the front table at Borders and the front octagon at Barnes & Noble, so that you couldn't walk in the door without it smacking you right in the face.

And so on.

The critics might like the book or they might not. But either way they'd give it more space than they'd ever given his previous work, and take it more seriously, and express their enthusiasm or distaste more fervently. It was the length and placement of a review, that and the heat it generated, that impacted sales far more than whether the critic did or didn't like what was between the covers.

And the public would run out and buy it. In the chains, in the independents, from the online booksellers, they'd buy the book as enthusiastically as if Oprah had told them they had to. Enough of them would buy it to get it on the bestseller list, and then tons more of them would buy it simply because it was on the list, and—ready now?

Nothing succeeds like success.

And here was the capper, here was the one thing that made it all just perfect. All of this success, this wild hitherto-undreamt-of success, was on its way to him notwithstanding that no one, repeat no one, not his agent or his publisher or any of the wonderful fellows who'd been in such a hurry to shake his hand, no one on the fucking planet had read one fucking word of the book.

He'd been working away at it every day, and it was coming along just fine, thank you. Some days were diamonds and some days were stones, as John Denver used to sing, and there was a guy who had it all until his plane crashed, which showed that even success had its limits. And yes, some days were diamonds and some days were stones and some days were little better than mouse turds, but each day the book got a little bit longer, and it was going to be a good one. He knew that, and he'd told Roz, but nobody else knew a thing about it except for the fact that he was working on it.

So it wasn't the book. That's what the publisher would sell and that's what the readers would buy, but that's not what the success was about. They weren't paying him three point one oh five because of what was in his computer. They were paying because of what was on his rap sheet. The whole reason, the sole reason for his success was that everybody was dead certain he'd strangled a woman.

Figure that one out. Go on, fucking figure it out.

He drank his drink.

AND SUPPOSE THEY FOUND him guilty?

That wasn't something he wanted to think about. He was able to get up every morning and sit down at the computer and get work done because he was able to put the whole matter out of his mind. Denial, he figured, was given to man for a purpose. You were crazy if you didn't make use of it.

But he could think about it now. On a night like this, flushed with triumph, high on success, he could afford to think about it. What if there was a trial, and the prosecution presented their case and his lawyer did his best to refute it, and the jurors came back and he heard the words *Will the defendant please rise?* and he rose, and he heard all the other words, so familiar now to everybody from *Law & Order* and Court TV. All those words, and the last one: *Guilty.*

It could happen. He hadn't done it, but they didn't know that and he couldn't prove it. And all of them—Esther Blinkoff and all the other bidders, and all the people in the upstairs offices who green-lighted the bidders and told them how far they could go, Jesus, they all knew it could happen, and they went ahead and placed their bids just the same.

Because it didn't matter.

Just as it didn't matter to his own lawyer, Maury Winters, whether he was in fact guilty or innocent. It didn't matter and shouldn't matter because the lawyer's job was to get him off, and his guilt and innocence were consequently irrelevant.

So why should they be any more relevant to Esther Blinkoff, whose job was to generate revenue for her employer? She did this by publishing books that would sell, and his book would sell because of who he was and what he might or might not have done.

His book might very well be out before the jury came in. That would make the verdict moot, wouldn't it? Or, if the trial began and ended before publication day, all it would do was generate publicity for the book. A guilty verdict wouldn't make the public yawn and turn aside. If anything, an acquittal might diminish their interest somewhat, in which case it would be his job to go on all the talk shows and stir things up again.

Either way, though, Crown was looking good. Either way, John Blair Creighton, Author, was a success. Hell, if they sent him to Sing Sing or Attica or some other state-sponsored Xanadu, somebody would make sure he had a PC in his cell, or at least a typewriter. Book Two of his famous seven-figure two-book contract could be a prison novel. Always a popular staple, and the film prospects should be terrific.

This seemed to call for a drink, and he could skip the ice this time.

ANOTHER REVELATION, MORE BRACING than the whiskey:

He wasn't going to be found guilty.

It was possible, because nobody knew how a trial would go or what a jury would do. But it wasn't going to happen, and not because he hadn't killed Marilyn Fairchild. That only mattered if he could prove it, and he couldn't.

There was a very simple reason why they'd come back and say *Not Guilty*, and that was because, as of today and forever after, he was a success.

And that was why Roger Delacroix, *the* Roger Delacroix, had not only congratulated him on his book deal, had not only shaken his hand, but had also taken the trouble, quietly, graciously, discreetly, to tell him he knew he was innocent. Not because he knew squat about the case, or about him. But because he knew, deep in his gut, way down in his bones, that no writer with a three-million-dollar contract could be guilty of splitting an infinitive, never mind wringing a woman's neck.

Imagine if OJ could write like Faulkner . . .

They wouldn't convict him. They wouldn't be able to, any more than they'd been able to with OJ. Not because he had money. The rich had an

edge in court, but they didn't get a free pass. Look at the Menendez brothers, look at Michael Skakel. Once in a while, even the rich got the judicial
shaft.

It wasn't OJ's money, or his Dream Team of lawyers, or the inept
prosecution or the flaky judge. It wasn't because he was black and so
were most of the jurors. None of this hurt, but that didn't explain why he
got off, and it seemed so clear now.

He got off because he was OJ Simpson.

He was a success, he was a star, he had that glow, that magic. How
could twelve people get in a room and convict him? They must have
known he did it, or else they were the only twelve people in America who
didn't, but it didn't make any difference. They couldn't help themselves.
He was OJ Simpson and they had to cut him loose.

THE GLASS WAS EMPTY, but he wouldn't fill it up again. He was feeling the drinks. The alcohol had carried him through the long evening. It
wasn't fuel, but it worked as if it were, lifting you on its wings, keeping
you from feeling your exhaustion. He'd had just enough to keep that
edge, and now he was ready to put himself to bed.

Undressing, he came across the card the woman in black had given
him. *I'd love to get to know you better / Susan.* She was a beauty, too,
self-possessed and radiant. If she were here right now, he thought, she
could get to know him in a hurry.

Should he have made a move? She was out the door before the possibility had even occurred to him, so it had never been an option, and it
didn't take much thought to realize it would have been a bad idea. He was
with Roz, for one thing, and although there would never be anything romantic or sexual in their relationship, that didn't mean he could abandon
her and trot off after some tail-wagging cupcake. But even if the timing
had been different, even if Susan had turned up as he was putting Roz in
a cab, it still would have set the evening off in the wrong direction.

This wasn't the night for a romp with a starfucker, however classy
this one might be. This was a night to be spent exactly as he had spent it,
first at the bar at Stelli's, sharing laughs and insights with men who had
suddenly become his peers, and then at home, by himself, to taper off
with good whiskey and think through and relive the best day and night of
his life.

He'd keep her card, though.

But where? It was all too easy to misplace things in his roomful of or-
ganized clutter, and he didn't want to let it slide until calling her would be
awkward. His memory might be spotty in the morning, and he might be
like a squirrel who buried nuts and forgot where he'd buried them. You

got a lot of trees planted that way, but in this instance, if you'd pardon the expression, he was more interested in getting his nut.

So the idea was not to make a point of remembering where he put the card, but to put it where he'd find it anyway. He could leave it on top of the computer keyboard, that would work, but then it would be in the way and he'd have to stick it somewhere, and he'd be back where he started from. But if he left it where it would not be in the way, but where he'd see it every day . . .

He opened his sock drawer, propped it on top of a pair of navy socks, and closed the drawer.

That did it, and now he could go to bed and dream whatever sort of dreams successful men dreamed. He wouldn't set a clock, he'd wake up whenever the sun or his bladder woke him, and—

Wait a minute.

He'd seen something, got the merest glimpse of something, in his sock drawer. Or imagined it, some chimera hovering on the edge of thought and the periphery of his vision.

Forget it, he told himself, and go to sleep.

But it was still there in his mind's eye when he got into bed, just a patch of color, really, but of a color that didn't belong in a drawer full of socks that were almost all black or navy, with the rest brown or maroon. His white socks were in another drawer, with gym gear, because that was pretty much the only time he wore them. He was, you'd have to say, a dark socks kind of a guy, although—who knew?—he supposed that might change with success. He might turn out to be the sort of man who wore argyles, but up until now he'd been Mr. Dark Socks, so what would a hint of bright color be doing in his sock drawer?

He got up, switched on the light. Opened the drawer, and yes, Jesus, there it was, sitting between two pairs of socks as black as a murderer's heart.

He drew it out and looked at it, a little turquoise rabbit, expertly carved by some fucking Indian with too goddamn much time on his hands.

eighteen

THERE WAS NO dearth of information. You could sit in an Internet café and surf the Web for a modest hourly fee, and leave there knowing how to make nerve gas and botulin, how to construct all manner of bombs and incendiary devices. Even a nuclear bomb. Secrets that earned the death sentence for the Rosenbergs were readily available to anyone who knew how to use a computer and consult a search engine.

But what good did it do to know that a truck packed with a particular fertilizer and a particular detergent could bring down a building? If you were an older gentleman, living alone in a fourth-rate hotel room, how could you possibly assemble those components? Where would you get a truck, let alone its explosive contents?

A constitutional amendment guaranteed him the right to bear arms, and there were groups of men throughout the country who exercised that right to the fullest extent, equipping themselves with machine guns and automatic rifles, with bazookas and grenade launchers, with enough so-phisticated weaponry and ammunition to unseat the government of Brazil. But could he walk into a store and buy a gun? Well, perhaps, if he rode a train to Virginia or North Carolina and back.

Practically speaking, though, he couldn't buy a gun, he couldn't pur-chase dynamite. He didn't have access to a lab where he might produce some sort of biological or chemical weapon, or the opportunity to pur-chase the raw materials for them.

He had hands that could encircle a throat. There were stores that would sell him hammers and chisels and screwdrivers and charcoal lighter fluid. But now it was time for sacrifice on a larger scale, and the tools for such a sacrifice were impossible to obtain.

Fortunately, he was resourceful.

. . .

THE GLASS JARS, SIX of them, had each held a quart of apple juice. He'd bought them two at a time at supermarkets, brought them back to his room, and poured the contents down the sink.

The gasoline had been slightly more difficult to obtain. To get it you had to go to a gas station, and you needed a car for them to put it in. But suppose a man's car was several blocks away from the station, and he needed gas to get it started?

"I got no container," the station owner told him. "You need an approved container. What do you think, you can cup your hands together and I'll fill 'em up with five gallons of gas?"

It was a Wednesday night when he had the conversation with the gas station man, and stores that might carry such containers were closed. He thought of getting a length of plastic tubing and siphoning the gas from parked cars. But he might be noticed, and anyone who saw him would know at once what he was doing. Besides, if he did siphon the gas, he'd need a container to put it in.

In the morning he found a hardware store on Twenty-third Street, not far from Harrigan's. They had five-gallon and two-gallon containers, and the smaller one would fill all six jars, with two quarts left over. He bought it and took it to a different gas station from the one where he'd had the conversation. This one was the Getty station on Eighth Avenue and Horatio. A man he assumed to be a Sikh filled the can for him and took his money. He thought of saying *Thank you, Mr. Singh,* thinking to surprise the man by knowing his name. All Sikhs, he knew, had the last name of Singh, though he didn't know why. *Thank you, Mr. Singh,* he might have said, but of course he said nothing at all.

The rags with which he stoppered the jars were wadded-up strips torn from a plaid cotton flannel shirt. He didn't have to buy the shirt but instead had fetched it from his storage locker. He never wore it, it was too large for him yet short in the arms, a bad fit altogether. He'd taken it from the apartment only because it had been a Father's Day gift once. That was why he had never discarded it over the years, and why it was among the few articles he took when he left. His son had given it to him, and how appropriate to put it to use now, to sacrifice this remembrance of his son even as his son had himself been sacrificed.

The lighters were disposables, the Bic brand, better than matches because you could operate them easily with one hand. They sold them everywhere. He'd bought three, at three different stores, just to be on the safe side.

The hammer was very much like the one he'd used on East Twenty-eighth Street, and might have been the same brand, though he'd purchased it at a different store.

The straight razor he'd happened upon in the Salvation Army thrift shop on Eighth Avenue. It was similar to the one that had been among his father's effects, although he couldn't recall the man ever shaving with anything but a safety razor. Maybe it had been his grandfather's before him.

He could have bought the razor from the thrift shop, they only wanted five dollars for it, but he thought it might be a worthwhile precaution to slip it into his pocket.

HE WAS BACK IN his hotel room by 1 A.M., and it took him just twenty minutes to fill the jars with gasoline, stuff their mouths with the flannel rags, and pack them into a large canvas tote bag he'd bought from a homeless street peddler with his wares spread out on a blanket. When he asked the price, the man said, "I usually get five dollars, but I'll take two."

He used his pillowcase to keep the jars from banging against one another. That was the one thing he'd forgotten, not realizing it would be a problem until he started putting the jars in the tote bag. He should have gotten some rags, or some extra clothes from his locker, but the pillowcase was a good improvisation. Loaded, the tote bag had some weight to it, but it wasn't too heavy to be manageable, and the hammer fit neatly along one side, handle down.

Ever since he stole it, he'd kept the straight razor in his pocket. He'd drawn it out many times, in the privacy of his room, and had practiced with it, returning it each time to his pocket. He checked, and it was there now.

His first stop was Harrigan's. When he'd initially planned this, he thought he would hurl his gasoline bombs, his Molotov cocktails, through the window. But plate glass wasn't that easily shattered. Suppose his jar bounced off the window and exploded harmlessly on the sidewalk?

With that in mind, he'd bought the hammer. But when he got there he saw that the door was wide open, a hook securing it. Maybe the air-conditioning wasn't working, maybe the room was too smoky.

It did make things easier. He walked in the door, stood in the doorway, put his tote bag on the floor at his feet. He drew out one of the cocktails, lit the rag, and hurled it toward the back of the room, where the musicians were playing. There was a loud noise and a burst of flame, but he was too busy repeating the process with a second jar, which he lobbed over the people drinking at the bar so that it exploded against the back bar mirror.

He picked up his tote bag, hurried out the door.

. . .

HE COULDN'T SEE IN the window at Cheek, but neither could they see out. He stepped up next to the window, waited for traffic to die down on the avenue, waited until there was no one around to see what he was doing. He tucked two Molotov cocktails under his left arm, took the hammer in his right hand, and smashed the window.

He ignited both wicks at once, sent them sailing one after another through the opening he'd created. Tossed the hammer in, too, because he didn't need it anymore. There was no window at Death Row.

HIS FRIEND WITH THE shaved head and the earring was still on duty, and smiled in recognition when he saw him. "Hiya, Pops," he said. "A little past your bedtime, isn't it?"

He came closer, muttering something about being unable to sleep.

"Why I work nights," the fellow said. "I've had trouble sleeping all my life. What's in the bag? You got something for Buddha?"

"Is that your name?"

"It's what they call me. You bring me a sandwich?"

"Better," he said, and held the bag so Buddha could see it, but down low, so that he had to bend down and forward for a good look. The razor was in his free hand, open and ready, and in a single smooth motion he drew it across Buddha's throat. Blood gushed as from a fountain, and he didn't draw back quickly enough to keep from getting some on himself, but it couldn't be helped.

Poor Buddha collapsed onto his knees, trying to raise a hand to hold back the gouting blood, his eyes wide in disbelief. His mouth worked but no sounds came out of it.

That was the hard part. Now it was child's play to open the unattended door, to walk to the head of the stairs, and to put to use the last two Molotov cocktails, lighting their wicks, hurling them into the void at the bottom of the stairs. He dropped the two Bics into the tote bag—he'd lost the third somewhere, evidently—and tossed it down the stairs.

Shouts, cries, flames leaping . . .

Outside, he looked for the razor. He'd dropped it earlier, and saw now that Buddha had collapsed upon it. He spotted the tip of the handle protruding from beneath the fellow's bare shoulder. Blood had pooled around it, and he decided not to bother. The razor couldn't be tied to him, anyway, because no clerk could remember selling it to him. So he'd done the right thing when he took it without paying.

BACK AT HIS HOTEL, he showered and shaved. He used a disposable razor, made by the same company that produced the disposable lighters.

He wondered how men had managed to shave every day with straight razors like the one he had used on Buddha.

He remembered the man's kindness, the gentle nature lurking beneath the rough macho exterior. Tears welled up, and he had to interrupt his shave because they blurred his vision. He blinked them back, and bowed his head for a moment, honoring Buddha's sacrifice.

Back in the room, he saw that there was blood on his shirt, blood on the sleeve of his jacket. Probably on his shoes, too. He'd wash off the shoes, and he could sponge the jacket so nothing showed. There'd be traces that would show up if they tested it, but if things got that far it wouldn't matter, would it?

The shirt wasn't worth salvaging. He'd get rid of it in the morning. And the two-gallon container of orange plastic, with two quarts of gasoline still in it. Or should he keep the container? He might very well need it again.

No, he could buy another if and when he required one. Better to be rid of it for now.

He got into bed, and immediately regretted the loss of the pillowcase. It had been in the tote bag when he disposed of it. He'd meant to retrieve it, but it had slipped his mind. Probably just as well, because it would very likely have smelled of gasoline, but now he had to sleep on the bare pillow, covered in a rough striped fabric like mattress ticking. And right after he'd shaved, too.

nineteen

IN THE DAYS after he'd walked in on the leavings of the Curry Hill Carpenter, Jerry Pankow had wanted nothing more than to call his remaining clients and tell them to find someone else. He even found himself considering a return to Hamtramck for the first time since he had the good fortune to leave the place.

"How can I stay here?" he demanded. "People are dying all over the place."

"Nobody lives forever," Lois told him. "Not even in Hamtramck, although I grant you it must seem that way. Not counting roaches and waterbugs, have you ever killed anything?"

"No, but—"

"Or spiders. That's what women need men for, you know. To kill spiders. The day she saw me kill a spider in the kitchen, Jacqui knew we had a chance of making it together. You've had some bad luck, Jerry. One of your customers went home with the wrong guy, and another one opened the door to the wrong guy, but they were two different guys. They're sure the writer killed Marilyn, and they're just as sure he had nothing to do with the mess at the whorehouse."

"Mess," he said, "does not begin to describe it."

"Don't quibble, Jerry. Stay with me on this. And bear in mind one of the lessons sobriety teaches us. Your lifelong conviction notwithstanding, you are not actually the piece of shit the world revolves around."

"Meaning?"

"You tell me."

He thought about it. "Meaning I'm the only connection between Marilyn and Molly, and that's just coincidental. They're not dead because they had the bad luck to hire me."

"Very good. Now go to a meeting."

"I just came from a meeting."

"So?"

"I guess another one couldn't hurt just now. Lois? Suppose it happens again?"

"Happens again? I don't . . . oh, you mean if you walk in on a third dead body?"

"It would be a fifth, actually. A third, what did you call it? A third mess."

"I'll tell you what," she said. "If that happens, you can go back to Hamtramck. I'll even pay your plane fare. But Jerry? No matter how many dead bodies you find, you still can't drink."

IN THE END, HE didn't even take a day off. He couldn't really afford to; the closing of the whorehouse represented a serious drop in his income. So he got up each morning and took care of the three bars, then serviced whatever residential customers were on his schedule. And went to as many meetings as he could fit in.

This morning, Saturday, the forecast was for near-record levels of heat and humidity, and you could already feel both indicators starting to climb by the time he got outside. Saturdays and Sundays were light days, morning days, with nothing on his schedule but the three bars. They were apt to be grungier than usual on Saturday mornings, after the intensity of Thank-God-It's-Friday celebrating, and sometimes a bartender, eager to get out of there after an especially late night, would slack off on his part of the deal, leaving the chairs on the floor, say, and unwashed glasses on the bar top.

He walked to Death Row, and long before he got within sight of the place he was breathing in the smell of it, the strong odor of a fire that had been put out with water. He paid no attention, because it was something you smelled a lot in that part of town. The Hudson piers would catch fire, especially on the Jersey side, and the creosote-soaked timbers would send up plumes of black smoke for hours.

Then he drew closer and saw four or five people gathered on the sidewalk across from Death Row, which was unusual at that hour, when the block was almost invariably deserted. And he looked at what they were looking at, and saw the windows all broken out on the building's upper floors, and the streaks of soot and fire damage on the lintels.

He joined the four men across the street. They were quick to tell him what had happened, although they had slightly different versions. There'd been a fire, certainly, and it had started in the basement leather bar, Death

Row, and pretty much gutted the entire structure before the firefighters got it under control.

"They threw one rough trade type out, and he came back with a gun and opened up on everybody, and then he started a fire."

"I didn't hear anything about a gun. Just some queen with a resentment, and Buddha was killed trying to keep her from getting in the door."

"Please. It was bashers, it had to be."

"Every time a gay man stubs his toe somebody calls it gay-bashing."

"Well, what do you call it when three gay bars go up in flames on the same night? Do you think they were struck by lightning?"

"I felt so wonderful during Gay Pride Week, and now this has to happen. I heard there were over thirty people killed at Death Row alone."

"I heard forty."

"I heard twenty-seven, including some of the people who lived upstairs."

"People actually lived upstairs of that hole?"

"A friend of mine, he's a nurse at St. Vincent's in the Burn Unit, and he said they brought in men with third-degree burns over eighty percent of their body. When it's that bad you're not expected to live, and it's probably better if you don't."

"I can never remember, is it first-degree that's the worst?"

"Only with murder. With burns, third-degree is the worst."

"There's no fourth degree?"

"Only what the firemen call *Crispy Critters.*"

"Oh, gross."

"I heard it was worse at the other bars."

"No, I heard Death Row was the worst."

"I just hope the cops get them. It must have been two or three of them, because they spilled a whole fifty-gallon drum of petrol down the stairwell."

"The drums hold fifty-five gallons, and when did you turn into an Englishman?"

"I beg your pardon?"

"Petrol? She thinks she's Camilla Parker-Bowles."

"It would have taken at least three men to get past Buddha."

"Or one man with a gun, and is there a law that says every big man with a shaved head has to be called Buddha?"

"His name was Eric, and he was a good person."

"You knew him?"

"He was my friend."

"Then I'm sorry. I didn't mean . . ."

"That's all right."

He knew the answer, but asked anyway: "The other bars . . ."

Cheek, he was told. And someplace farther east that nobody had heard of, Harriman's, something like that.

He could have corrected them on the name, and told them it wasn't a gay bar, but why? Why do anything?

He turned away and walked back home.

THE FIREBOMBINGS OF THE three Chelsea bars were immediately gathered into a single case file, and the death toll alone—seventy-three killed, plus twelve so seriously injured they were not expected to recover—ensured the investigation would wind up in the hands of the Major Cases squad. Although it took a few hours for the FDNY investigators to officially label the fires as arson, the cops had it listed that way from the beginning. The eyewitness testimony, confused and contradictory as it was, all agreed on one point: each establishment had been deliberately attacked with explosive and/or incendiary devices.

With 9/11 less than a year old, and with suicide bombings almost a daily occurrence in Israel, there was widespread agreement that terrorism couldn't be ruled out. Accordingly, FBI investigators coordinated with the team from Major Cases, and the Office of Homeland Security flew up an expert from Washington.

According to one theory, the virtually simultaneous attacks on the three targets bespoke a high degree of organization. Furthermore, at least one witness at Death Row reported that the attackers wore camouflage gear.

In response, others argued that the attacks were by no means simultaneous, and that as much as three-quarters of an hour might have elapsed between the first attack, on Harrigan's, and the third, at Death Row. Even on foot a perpetrator could easily cover the required distance in that amount of time. As for the camo gear, it turned out to have been worn not by a team of attackers but by two of those in attendance; evidently their garb, complemented by paratrooper boots, had been deemed sufficiently in keeping with the bar's ambience as to be allowable under the dress code.

Both of the camouflaged individuals, one a fashion photographer during daylight hours, the other a stockroom manager, were in Death Row's notorious back room at the time of the bombing. Like almost everyone trapped in that cul-de-sac, they died there.

Saturday afternoon, a little more than fourteen hours after the initial assault on Harrigan's, the cops got a break.

. . .

DENNIS HURLEY LIVED WITH his wife and three sons in a detached
ranch house (an emotionally detached ranch house, his wife's smartass
brother called it) just over the Queens line in Nassau County, near the
Hempstead Turnpike and within walking distance of Belmont Race
Track, which would have been handy if he cared for horse racing, but he
didn't. He liked to go out in a bluefish boat when they were running, and
he liked to watch sports on television, even golf, and he liked to roast corn
and grill steaks and chops in the backyard, which is what he was getting
ready to do when his wife came out to tell him Arthur Pender was on the
phone.

"Tell him to come on over," he said.

"Tell him yourself," she suggested, but when he got on the phone
Pender didn't want to talk about backyard barbecues, or Tiger Woods's
chances of a Grand Slam.

"Those firebombings," he said. "You hear about them out where you
are?"

"I'm less'n a mile from bein' in Queens," he said. "The only difference is the schools, and it's not as much of a difference as we were hoping. Yeah, of course I heard. We get New York One out here, not to
mention it was all over CNN this morning."

"You happen to notice the names of the places got hit?"

"I noticed where they were. A few blocks to the east and they'd be
our headache."

"Be Major Cases either way, but that's not the point. I'll give you the
names. Harrigan's, Cheek, and Death Row. Ring any bells?"

"I don't think so. Gay bars, right? And the last one sounds like it must
have been a charmer, but . . . wait a minute, Arthur."

"Dingdong, huh?"

"That Polish kid, one we thought linked our case to Charles Street.
Except it didn't, because What's-his-name was home all night and he
could prove it."

"Creighton."

"Yeah, and we didn't like him for it anyway, once we met him. These
joints, Death Row and the rest, they were all on his list, weren't they? Not
Creighton's but the kid's."

"Pankow's his name."

"Tip of my tongue, Arthur."

"They weren't just on his list. They *were* his list. Went and mopped
their floors seven days a week. Only other customers he had were private
residences that he went to once a week."

"Jesus. You know, I heard the names myself, but I was watching TV with half my mind on the sports pages in *Newsday*. I should have caught it."

"You would've, next time you heard the news."

"Yeah, maybe. Shit, Arthur, we got to go in, don't we? I mean, we can't phone it in, and it won't wait till morning."

"Afraid not."

"Wouldn't you know I just lit the fucking charcoal. Well, she can grill. She never gets it right, but if I'm not here I won't know the difference, will I?"

"We'll go to that Malaysian place you like."

"That's if we even get time to eat. You want me to come by for you?"

"No, I want to have my car with me," Arthur Pender said. "I'll meet you there."

THE FOCUS OF THE investigation shifted when Pender and Hurley raised the possibility of a direct link between the firebombings and the activities of the Curry Hill Carpenter. The immediate result was an expansion of the task force investigating the bombings, with the inclusion of personnel from the Thirteenth Precinct previously assigned to the Curry Hill investigation.

Evidence began to accumulate, and the argument that the killings were linked was bolstered significantly with the discovery of a stainless steel claw hammer with a black rubber grip among the burned-out wreckage of Cheek. Witnesses had reported the window was smashed before the first Molotov cocktail was thrown, and investigators theorized that the hammer might have been used to break the glass. While there was no way to tie the hammer to the Curry Hill murders, forensics determined that it could well have been the implement used to beat the women to death. "If it wasn't this hammer," a technician said, "it was one a lot like it. It might not have had a claw on the back of it, because he didn't use the claw, but this is what the business end of it would have looked like."

Eyewitness testimony was difficult to sort out, but there were plenty of police personnel assigned to the task, and some common elements began to emerge. Reports accumulated of an older white male, of medium height and slightly built, ordinary in appearance and unremarkable in dress, who had been observed both in and around the targeted premises. At both Cheek and Harrigan's, persons who'd been on the scene hours earlier recalled an older man who had ordered a drink and left it untouched.

A waitress in a coffee shop across from Harrigan's thought she might have had a customer fitting that description; on that Friday night, he'd lingered over a cup of coffee for a long time, and she seemed to recall he'd looked out the window a good deal of the time. He'd had some of his coffee, but he never finished it, and if he ever said a word she couldn't remember it. He hadn't even asked for coffee, had ordered by pointing to another patron's cup, then nodded when she asked if that was what he wanted.

Other cops canvassed the immediate environs of the whorehouse, coming up in short order with a manager in another coffee shop who reported similar behavior, although he couldn't furnish even a general description of the customer in question. He remembered him because a waiter had asked him to check the coffee and see if anything was the matter with it. He'd checked, and it was no better or worse than usual. The customer, whoever he was, had already paid without complaint, and left the premises. The manager might have seen the man, he was behind the register and had presumably taken his money, but had no sense of which customer he'd been or what he looked like. The waiter might remember, but he was away for several days visiting family in Philadelphia.

FDNY inspectors established that the propellant was ordinary gasoline. Anyone with an automobile had ready access to gasoline, but one detective noted that the perpetrator had never been linked to a motor vehicle, and could quite easily have covered the distance from Harrigan's to Cheek to Death Row on foot. This prompted him to check with attendants at nearby gas stations, and on Eleventh Avenue he turned up an excitable fellow who remembered a man who'd wanted to buy gas for a stalled car. "But I didn't sell him nothing," he insisted. "I told him you gotta have an approved container. He went away, I never saw him again."

The man was only able to furnish a vague general description, but it was encouragingly close to the one then in circulation—white, middle-aged or older, medium height, slight build, no visible distinguishing marks. It led him to widen his search, and a few blocks below Fourteenth Street he stopped at a Getty station—the last one left in the world, as far as he could tell—where the proprietor, one Khadman Singh, remembered selling two gallons of gas—regular, unleaded—to a white man perhaps fifty-five or sixty years old. Sometime in the middle of the week this was, he recalled. This was not unusual, people paid no attention to gauges, they ran out of gas all the time. This man had a container and paid cash for his gas, which was not unusual either, because who would bother with a credit card for a three-dollar sale? But what was unusual, in Singh's experience, was that the man had approached from the right, which is to say from the south, or downtown, and had walked off in the opposite direction, heading uptown on Eighth Avenue.

. . .

WHILE MOST OF THE task force worked from the crime-scene evidence, a small group focused on the common denominator of all four venues, the three bars and the whorehouse. Which is to say Jerry Pankow.

He was interrogated at length, over and over. No one suspected him of any conscious involvement in the perpetrator's scenario, but it seemed entirely possible he knew something, even if he didn't know that he knew it. The series of layered interrogations aimed at unearthing unconscious knowledge, and while they didn't lead anywhere, it wasn't for lack of trying.

Another possibility lay in anticipating the next outrage. No one thought the man who'd just scored what a *Post* columnist called a hat trick for terrorists would call it a day and rest on his laurels. He looked to be that classic urban nightmare, the serial terrorist. Reporters were writing sidebar columns on George Metesky, the Mad Bomber of a half century ago, who'd planted explosive devices in public places in an unfathomable private vendetta against Con Edison. Others, by no means convinced that the whorehouse murders were his first venture, were looking at every unsolved crime since the calendar ticked over to start the new millennium.

And policemen, trying to get ahead of him, staked out the apartments of Jerry Pankow's remaining clients.

"I don't have any clients," he told them. "I called them all, I told them I'm through. I'm out of business anyway, it was the commercial clients that paid the rent. The rest, there were five of them, twenty-five dollars a day, you do the math. I want a real job, I want to work in an office or something. With other people around, living ones."

They staked out the residences of his customers—his former customers—just in case. And sat back and waited.

THE RAZOR WAS ANOTHER source of leads.

It lay beneath the dead body of Eric "Buddha" Kesselring, twenty-eight, of Ludlow Street, whose throat it had been used to slash and whose blood had pooled around it. Thus it presented a challenge to the lab technicians who examined it; they had to remove the blood without destroying any trace evidence it might conceal. When they were done, they had two good fingerprints and one partial, which they turned over to an investigator who sat down with them at her computer.

The computer search came up empty. The perpetrator (if that's whose prints were on the razor, which seemed a fair working assumption) had never been fingerprinted. This meant he'd never been arrested, had never applied for a government job, and had probably never served in the military. It meant, too, that the prints on the razor couldn't point him out now, but might help confirm his guilt if and when he wound up in custody.

Prints aside, the razor presented some interesting possibilities. The first was that it was the killer's own razor, that he'd owned it for decades, that he kept it either for sentimental value or because it was what he preferred to use on his whiskers. If that was the case you could probably forget about tracing it, but suppose he'd acquired it recently, for the express purpose of cutting a throat?

There were still men who bought straight razors, detectives discovered, and still manufacturers that produced them. The majority of customers were barbers. Not many men still went to the barbershop to be shaved, but those who did were looking for an old-fashioned shave, with a shaving brush and a straight razor, not a noisy buzz with an electric shaver or foam from a can and a disposable plastic device. A straight razor, the kind the barber honed on a leather strop, that was what they expected to be shaved with.

It turned out there was a wholesaler on Atlantic Avenue in Brooklyn who sold barber supplies, including straight razors. He identified the razor as one made in Solingen, Germany, by a firm that had gone out of business (or at least stopped producing razors) some twenty years ago. That didn't make the razor an antique, just an old razor, and, since straight razors didn't change much from one decade to the next, it was possible that there were still retailers who had similar razors in stock. It was also very possible that some local barbers, who kept their razors for a lifetime, had razors like this one.

The wholesaler's own retail accounts included two not far from the perpetrator's field of operations. Both were drugstores, and both carried a wide line of homeopathic remedies and old-fashioned devices. One was on Third Avenue at Nineteenth Street, the other on Sixth Avenue in the Village, between Eighth and Ninth Streets.

Neither had sold a straight razor to anyone within the past month.

Someone thought of thrift shops. There were quite a few in the immediate area, and two police officers worked their way down the list, finding quite a few that had a straight razor or two for sale, but none that had actually sold one. Then, in the Salvation Army store on Eighth Avenue, a woman with mean little eyes in an otherwise grandmotherly face said that no one had bought a straight razor from her, but one man had stolen one.

"If I'd seen him," she said, "I might have stopped him on his way out and suggested he pay for it. Or perhaps not. After all, he was armed, wasn't he? Though I can't say he looked terribly dangerous."

If she'd seen him? If she hadn't seen him, how did she know he'd taken the razor? How did she know whether or not he looked dangerous?

"The security camera. We have two of them and they're running all the time while we're open. At the end of the day I review the tapes. Most of the time there's nothing to look at, you can fast-forward through vast stretches of nothingness, but I'll slow it down when I see anybody behaving furtively. Or quite boldly—they're bold as brass, some of them."

It was useful to review the tape in order to keep shoplifters from returning. When an offender turned up after he'd been caught on tape, he was simply turned away at the door, which was safer all around than trying to stop a suspected thief on his way out. No one could sue you for false arrest that way. And the value of the goods stolen was pretty much beside the point; they were all donated, after all, and the few items of real value got snatched up early on by dealers.

And did she by any chance still have the tape of the man pocketing the straight razor?

She did. They had thirty tapes for the two cameras, and rotated them, so that each day's taping erased what had been recorded two weeks previously. She had to scan several tapes to find the right one, but she was able to go through them at great speed because she knew precisely what she was looking for. When she got there she slowed the tape to normal speed, and the two cops watched over her shoulder as an aging white man wearing a plaid shirt and dark pants picked a razor off a shelf, flicked it open, closed it, flicked it open a second time, rubbed it with his thumb to test it for sharpness, closed it again, looked around casually, and just as casually slipped it in his pocket.

They gave her a receipt for the tape and took it to a technician who tinkered with it electronically to sharpen the focus and increase the definition, then printed out copies. You couldn't see the face very well, the camera was placed high and to the side, but it was something to work with.

The Sikh at the Getty station looked at one of the prints and said that it looked like the man to whom he'd sold the two gallons of gas. The witnesses who remembered a man who ordered a drink and left without touching it said it was hard to tell, but it was certainly possible that this was the man they'd seen. A man in the burn unit at St. Vincent, who'd gotten a glimpse of the man when he'd been about to launch the second Molotov cocktail at Harrigan's, said he couldn't tell; when he pictured the face, it morphed into the features of Satan, horns and all. Maybe it was him, maybe not. He couldn't tell.

A patrolman, months out of the academy, came up with a suggestion. Collect surveillance tapes for the forty-eight hours preceding the massacre from every available source in the neighborhood—ATMs, liquor stores, check-cashing services, building lobbies, everywhere. Security cameras were all over the place nowadays, you couldn't pick your nose anywhere outside your own house without a good chance of having the moment recorded. Nobody ever looked at all those tapes unless something happened—except for the gimlet-eyed lady at the Sally Ann thrift shop, who evidently had time on her hands. They got recycled, over and over, but maybe there were some that hadn't been recycled yet, and maybe the Carpenter—the newspapers were still calling him that, and consequently so were the cops—maybe the Carpenter had gotten his picture taken somewhere down the line.

A dozen cops went around collecting tapes. Armed with prints made from the thrift shop tape, they and others sat in front of video screens and looked for the Carpenter. A veteran patrolman named Henry Gelbfuss spotted him, on a tape from a Rite Aid drugstore, and everybody agreed it was the Carpenter. He was the man on the thrift shop tape, no question.

The Rite Aid tape, enlarged and sharpened and defined, was still a far cry from a Bachrach portrait, but it was good enough to release to the media, good enough to show on television, good enough to print on every front page, along with a number to call if you recognized the man in the photo.

A lot of people did.

NAILED!

That was the headline in the *Post*, accompanied by an artist's rendition of the man whose security camera photo had appeared prominently throughout the media the day before. The drawing showed a disembodied hand holding a claw hammer, which had evidently been used to drive a nail through the man's forehead, pinning him to the wall.

The *Daily News* showed their artist's rendition of the photo, with the Carpenter, a hammer in one hand and a Molotov cocktail in the other, pinned against a similar wall, but held there in this case by searchlight beams. **GOTCHA!** cried the headline.

The implication seemed to be that the Carpenter had been captured. This may have been intentional—before they got to the newsstand, many New Yorkers would already have learned from radio or television that the city's most wanted criminal had been at least tentatively identified. They'd be quicker to buy a paper if it appeared to promise a further development in the story.

The text explained that the Carpenter had been nailed, or gotten, only to the extent that authorities now knew who he was. A variety of callers (*our readers*, the *Post* labeled them, staking a claim) had agreed that the man pictured in the press and on TV was one William Boyce Harbinger, sixty-two, the recently retired director of research at Lister Durgen Augenblick/Advertising.

Several of the callers were men and women who had worked with Harbinger at LDA. All had lost touch with him since his retirement in late 2000, and none could offer a clue as to what might have sent him off on a murderous rampage. He was described as a quiet man ("It's always the quiet ones," readers all over the city murmured), and none of his coworkers reported having had any contact with him outside the office.

Other callers recognized him from the Upper West Side neighborhood where he had lived for decades, and some were neighbors of the Harbingers in the Amsterdam Avenue apartment building. They agreed that he was quiet, almost reclusive, and no one seemed to recall having seen either Harbinger or his wife in some months.

Police cars from all over Manhattan congregated at the intersection of Eighty-fourth and Amsterdam. Cops surrounded the building, blocked off the exits, filled the lobby. The superintendent, summoned from an evening in front of the television set, said that he hadn't seen Mrs. Harbinger since sometime late the previous year, when she'd been taken from the building on a stretcher. "They didn't use no siren," he said, "so maybe it was too late."

And he hadn't seen Mr. Harbinger for a long time, either, though he couldn't say how long. He hadn't paid his monthly maintenance charges in a long time, but he'd owned the apartment since it went co-op thirty years ago, and paid rent there before then, and the apartment was a very valuable piece of property, owned free and clear, no mortgage, so you knew he'd pay the maintenance sooner or later.

The super had keys to all the apartments, and at one point, concerned that something might have happened to Harbinger, he'd knocked on the door, then let himself in. There was nobody home, and no signs that anything might be amiss. The place was dusty and the air stale, as if no one had lived there recently.

The super thought maybe he'd gone to Florida, something like that. And maybe he was back by now, because the super hadn't been in the apartment since. His mailbox was never jammed up, it was always clear, so either he was living in there now, keeping to himself the way he did, or at least he was coming by to collect his mail.

The super let the cops into the apartment, and they found it as he'd described it. There were additional bills from the co-op association for the monthly maintenance charges, slipped under the door every month, and there was the usual array of menus from Asian restaurants, and the air was stale and the horizontal surfaces coated with dust.

What there was not was any sign of William Boyce Harbinger, or any indication of where he might have gone.

twenty

HARBINGER OF DOOM, the papers called him. Harbinger the Carpenter.

There but for the grace of God, thought Susan Pomerance, go all my favorite artists.

She wasn't following the unfolding story that intently, the way the rest of the city seemed to be. Chloe, for one, seemed capable of talking of little else. Every new development, every further revelation about the city's greatest nightmare, informed the girl's every utterance. The losses the man had suffered, his son and daughter and son-in-law, all killed when the towers came down. And then his wife dying, probably of a broken heart, and was it any wonder he cracked?

Without reading much of the newspaper coverage, without spending much time watching television or listening to any radio news beyond WQXR's hourly summary, she nevertheless found herself aware of most of the story's developments.

She heard about the increasing body of evidence suggesting he'd simply walked away from his apartment, turned the key in the lock, and disappeared. He hadn't collected his mail, after all; instead, he'd rented a post office box and had all his mail forwarded to it. He'd paid rent on the box for three months in advance, and never paid anything further, nor was there any indication that he'd ever visited the box to collect his mail. After several past-due notices went unanswered, a clerk opened his box, marked the first-class mail to be returned to sender, and discarded the rest.

He'd evidently lived in a series of flophouses, all of them in the general vicinity of Penn Station. Why, people wondered, would a man walk

away from a comfortable apartment, filled with his furniture and the possessions of a lifetime, to live in a squalid furnished room with the bathroom down the hall?

Susan didn't find it that incomprehensible. That was one of the things
people did when they were in the process of withdrawing, of turning inside. For a fortunate handful, the energies that made them turn inward
were somehow magically channeled into art. Instead of walking onto a
factory floor with an AK-47, instead of taking off all their clothes in the
subway, instead of murdering their children in their beds, or drinking
oven cleaner, or lying down in front of the Metroliner, they painted a picture or fashioned a sculpture. They made art.

And wasn't all art created to preserve the artist's sanity? Didn't they
all make art the way oysters made pearls? A grain of sand got into the
oyster's shell, which was to say under his skin, and it irritated him, it
chafed him. So the oyster secreted something, squeezed out some essence
of its own self, and coated the offending grain of sand with it, just to stop
the pain. Layer after layer of this mystical substance the oyster brought
forth, until the grain of sand and the pain it had occasioned were not even
a memory.

The by-product of the oyster's relief was the shimmering beauty of
the pearl. And every pearl, every single luminous gem, had at the core of
its being a grain of irritation.

If William Boyce Harbinger, Harbinger the Carpenter, had been able
to so channel his own furious energies, then the roots of his discontent
might have brought forth life instead of death. And yet, she thought, you
could argue that Harbinger was making his own kind of art, composing it
of death and destruction.

He knew so many unusual facts about New York, a neighbor had told
a CNN reporter. How the streets were named, and some forgotten event
that had taken place on a certain corner a hundred years ago. And a former coworker had confirmed that Harbinger's only after-hours pastime
that he knew of was the study of the city's history. "He loved New York,"
an op-ed columnist theorized, "and the city betrayed him, taking his
loved ones from him all in a single horrible morning. And now he is getting his horrible twisted revenge."

Perhaps, she thought. But perhaps not. Perhaps the city he loved was
his canvas, and he was striving to paint his masterpiece in blood and fire.

WHATEVER THE FOUNDATION FOR the Carpenter's acts, it was unar-
guable that the man was obsessed. He hadn't just suddenly lost his temper. He was, if not an artist, unquestionably a craftsman, from the
planning of his projects through the selection of his tools to the execution

of the finished work. And he managed all this because he was a man obsessed.

She knew a little about that.

She found herself these days in the grip of not one but three obsessions; rather than conflict with one another, they seemed to her to be complementary. Honoring all three of them, serving all three of them, she maintained her sanity.

The first, and surely it was the one that would be most easily justified to the world at large, was her increasing obsession with the works of Emory Allgood. She'd set firm dates now for the one-man show she was giving him. It would open on Saturday, November 2, and would be up for two weeks.

In preparation for the show, she found herself making frequent visits to her storage space, sometimes with no apparent purpose beyond that of familiarizing herself with the work, of absorbing its essence. She had responded unequivocally to Allgood's constructions from the beginning, and her certainty of its merit only grew greater over time.

One piece drew her more than the others. This didn't mean it was better, only that it had something special about it that worked particularly well for her. The central element of it had begun life as a spool, shaped like a spool of thread in a sewing cabinet but much larger—precisely thirty-two inches high, with the flanges twenty-one inches in diameter. The core, itself some ten inches thick, was of pine, the flanges of half-inch fir plywood.

Once it had held wire or cable of some sort, wrapped around its core like sewing thread around an inch-long spool. Now it held—what? The sins of the world, that would be her guess.

He'd mounted it on what must have been the steel base of some sort of low stool, and had driven all manner of objects into the wooden spool. The effect was not unlike that of West African nail fetishes, where an upended log, sometimes but not always carved into a human form, was pierced hundreds upon hundreds of times with nails—or, in one example she'd seen at the Brooklyn Museum, with the blades of knives, all of them rusted.

Like most African tribal pieces, the nail fetishes were art only in the Western viewer's perception; like the masks and shields and drums that filled museums and important collections, they were purely functional in the eyes of those who made them. She'd long since forgotten the purpose of the nail fetishes, if she'd ever been clear on it in the first place, and she couldn't hope to guess what had prompted a wild-eyed little black man in Brooklyn to stab knives and forks into the wooden spool, to pound nails and screws and miscellaneous bits of hardware into it, to screw in a brass

doorstop here, the wooden knobs from a chest of drawers there. Why had
he done it—and, most mysterious of all, how had he managed in the process to create not a mad jumble, not a discordant conglomeration of junk,
but an artifact of surpassing beauty?

The Sins of the World—that's what she would call it, and it would be
on the cover of the exhibition catalog and on the postcards as well. She
was positive someone would snatch it up, couldn't imagine Gregory
Schuyler letting it get away from him, but she didn't know if she could
bear to part with it. She might find she needed to hang on to it.

In the meantime, it had migrated from her storage bin to her living
room, where it occupied a place of honor. There she was able to confirm
that it wasn't just her, that others responded to it in much the same way
she did. You couldn't just walk past it. It grabbed your lapels, demanding
attention.

And it received rather more attention these days than it might have at
an earlier time, not because it had changed, not even because the world
had changed. It was simply seen by more people now, because her apartment was receiving more visitors than it had in the past.

And that, of course, was the result of her second obsession.

HER SEX LIFE, SHE was quite certain, was sane and manageable. She
had to keep reassuring herself of this, however, because it was without
doubt a far cry from what society regarded as either sane or manageable.
She was having sex when she wanted, with whomever she wanted, in
whatever fashion she desired.

If she were a man, she sometimes thought, what she was doing would
be seen as demonstrating no end of good, even wholesome male qualities.
The only way a man could engage in sexual behavior that the world
would deem excessive was if he forced himself on others, took his pleasure with children, or caught a fatal disease in the course of his adventures. (And even the latter was only punishment for his transgressions if
he caught it from another man; if he got it from a woman, it was just the
worst kind of bad luck.)

On the other hand, it was easier to do it in the first place if you were
a woman. If you were reasonably attractive, and if you presented yourself
well, you really weren't going to have a great deal of trouble finding
some man who would like nothing better than to go home with you and
fuck your brains out. He might not be terribly good at it, and he might
never call you again, but if all you were looking for was to get laid, well,
how hard was that?

Women knocked themselves out trying to attract men, and all they really had to be was available. A man did not care who made your shoes, or

if they matched your bag, and if he even noticed such matters he was probably not in any event going to be the man you wanted to take home. A man did not pay attention to your earrings (unless you were wearing them someplace other than your ears) and had no idea what you paid for your dress. His concerns were more basic. Did you have tits? Did you have an ass? Did you have a mouth? Did you have a pussy? Were any or all of these available to him? Fine. I love you. Let's go to bed.

The night with Fran Buckram, a delicious experience in its own right, had given her a sense of her own power. Here was this man, this unquestionably manly man, this leader of men, and he had let her do whatever she wanted with him. *Franny* she'd called him, and made a girl of him and fucked him like a girl. And made him like it. And afterward, with the rules suspended and her dominance put aside, she'd gone on calling him *Franny*, and he hadn't asked her to stop.

"I'll see you next Friday," she had told him at the door. "I don't think we need to meet anywhere, do you? Come here at eight. And, Franny? Don't bring flowers."

TUESDAY AFTERNOON SHE HAD a call at the gallery. "Susan? This is Jay McGann, we met at Stelli's the other night."

"I remember."

"I've been working all day and I need a break. I thought I might come over and look at some art."

"That would be nice," she said. "Why don't you bring your friend?"

"My friend?"

"Your editor. Isn't he your friend as well?"

"Oh, Lowell? Yes, friend and editor, but the poor guy's got to work for a living. I don't think he can get away from his desk at this hour."

"Come this evening," she said.

"Are you open nights?"

"I could arrange to be," she said, "but actually I have some of the best work at my apartment. You'd be getting a look at something the public doesn't get to see."

"I'd like that," he said. "And I could get away tonight."

"Call Lowell. See if he can make it."

He couldn't figure it out, and she was in no rush to help him. After a pause he said, "Uh, actually I'd hoped we could get acquainted."

"Yes, I feel the same."

"So it would really be more convenient, you know, if it was just the two of us."

"It was so nice meeting the two of you the other night," she said. "The way you interacted was very pleasing."

"Yes, but—"

"So I think it would be really nice to get intimately acquainted with both of you."

"Oh. Uh, whew. Uh, would you want one of us to bring a girlfriend?"

"Whatever for?"

"Uh . . ."

"Jay," she said, "don't you think I can make you both very happy all by myself?"

She went home and showered and put on the same dress she'd worn Friday night, knowing it looked good with nothing under it. They showed up together at a quarter to seven, a whiff of Scotch on their breath from the drink each had needed to get that far. She knew they wanted her, knew they couldn't believe it was really going to happen. And, of course, they had to be possessed by the usual performance anxiety, magnified by the need to perform in front of another male, and a friend in the bargain.

She began by showing them the art, and was pleased by the intelligence and perception evident in their reactions. They didn't need to be aesthetes, she just wanted to fuck them, but it made things better when there was a mind operating the body. All the standard fantasies about brutish macho studs notwithstanding, bright and sensitive men were almost always better in bed.

Emory Allgood's piece drew the most interest, and one of them wanted to know the price. She explained that it wasn't for sale, but that the artist had a show opening in the fall. She'd make sure they got invitations to the opening.

Enough, she thought.

"It's so nice to see you both," she said, and brushed the back of her hand across Jay McGann's crotch, then flung her arms around Lowell Cooke's neck and gave him a lingering openmouthed kiss. She thought Jay might grope her while she was kissing Lowell, but no, he was just standing there politely, waiting his turn. She turned from Lowell and kissed Jay, and felt Lowell's hands on her ass.

In the bedroom, they gaped at her when she got out of the black dress, gaped again at the gold at her nipples and the hairless pubic mound. They stripped without embarrassment, and there was another round of kissing with hands reaching everywhere, and then they were all three in her bed.

Men always wanted a threesome with two women, it was the closest thing they had to a universal fantasy, but what was the sense of it? A man only had one cock, and could only put it in one place at a time. Oh, yes, there were possibilities in foreplay, and then he could eat one girl while he fucked the other, and in the process cheat each out of the benefit of his full attention. It could be interesting for a woman, being with a man and woman at once, but for a man how could the reality ever be a match for the fantasy?

With two men and a woman, on the other hand, the physiology was equal to the fantasy. She had a mouth, she had an ass, she had a cunt— there was more than enough of her to keep them occupied.

It was divine, and utterly different from her night with Buckram. (Sweet Franny!) She'd got things going, then was able to be essentially passive and let them use her as they wished, turning her this way and that, learning her body with their hands, their mouths. Lowell slipping into her, Jay offering himself to her mouth.

In the end, she did manage to fulfill a longstanding fantasy. The night before, alone with herself and her thoughts and her toys, she'd slipped the smallest dildo into her ass, a larger one in her pussy. And now it was happening again, but this time her toys were alive, and she didn't have to manipulate them, she could give herself up utterly to the pleasure of being taken and used, being fucked fore and aft.

But she couldn't get them to do anything to each other.

Men were so funny. Caught up in passion and need, still they were careful not to touch one another, careful that each made physical contact with her and only with her.

After they'd finished their sexual sandwich, as she lay on her back between them with their seed oozing out of both her holes, she took one of them in each hand and said, "You know what I would love? I would love to see one of you suck the other. I would absolutely love that."

God, you'd think she'd suggested they dismember a child, or strangle their mothers with a rolled-up American flag. And it was so silly. Moments before, both of them buried in her flesh, they'd been able to feel each other's cocks through the thin membrane that separated her two passages. That had contributed to her excitement, and, she felt sure, to theirs as well, could they only acknowledge it.

"It would make me so excited," she said. "I get wet just thinking about it. If you just did that, you could get me to do anything you wanted, anything you could think of."

But there was the problem—they didn't want anything from her, now that they'd pumped the last drop of their passion into her. All they really wanted was to shower and dress and go home to their wives, and hope to God the women didn't pick tonight to feel passionate.

She'd planted the seed, though. She'd given them something to think about. And, when they came around next week, she'd propose some sort of game, some last-to-come contest, with the loser required to give the winner a blow job. And the loser would be a good sport about it, because

being a good sport was even more important than being a hundred percent
heterosexual, and he'd give in gracefully, and before they knew it they'd
both be doing it, and loving it.

What fun.

SEX WAS WONDERFUL, AND the more you did it and the more people
you did it with, the better it got. It was readily available, it didn't cost
anything, and it was even good for you. She might have found it impossible to keep it in proportion, and it definitely helped that she had a third
obsession.

John Blair Creighton.

She hadn't realized at first that her fascination with the man who'd
strangled her real estate agent, and who seemed to have been rewarded
with a multimillion-dollar book contract, was anything more than a desire to go to bed with him. There was, certainly, a healthy (or not) sexual element to the obsession. He was a big, broad-shouldered guy,
good-looking but not excessively handsome, and he had a sexual energy
she'd have been aware of even if she hadn't known who he was. She
wanted to fuck him—and would, she was sure of it—but there was more
to it than that. She was, well, yes, *obsessed* with the man, and she
wasn't sure why.

But it wasn't just sexual desire that made her spend hours online,
checking out the results of a Google search and downloading everything
she could find about him. And sent her to abebooks.com and alibris.com
to order copies of all his out-of-print books. And led her to read the
books, all of them, one right after the other, to read them cover to cover
not just for the stories (which were involving) or the characters (the men
convincing, the women a little less so) or the writing (excellent, simple
and straightforward, always clear as glass, and with a ring like Water-
ford). That made reading enjoyable, but it didn't make it a necessity,
something she felt honor-bound to do every night when she wasn't in bed
with somebody.

It couldn't be because she'd met him. She'd met any number of writers, and the fact of acquaintance was no reason to read their books. She'd
not only met Jay McGann, she'd fucked him walleyed, and she was in no
great hurry to read anything he'd written.

It had to be because he'd been charged with murder, but that by itself
could only take her to the first book. After that, she kept reading because
of something in the work itself, and she'd already established it wasn't
the writing or the plot or the characters, so what was left?

The sense that came through of the author. Wasn't that what made any work of art effective? You got little sidelong glimpses of a soul, and, if it resonated in a certain way with your own, you wanted more.

He was going to be important to her. She knew that much, and, when she thought about it, she had to admit that it was a little scary.

I mean, what if he actually did kill that woman?

twenty-one

HAT IF HE'D done it?

He woke up Saturday morning, and it wasn't until he was standing at the toilet, halfway through an endless pee, that he remembered the glimpse of blue in his sock drawer, the second look, the stunning reality of the turquoise rabbit. But had it happened? Or was it, please God and all the angels, a dream?

He brushed his teeth, showered, dried himself, then looked in the mirror and decided he ought to shave. Wielding the razor, he marveled at his own transparent foolishness. He'd shaved for the first time in years what, fifteen hours ago? And he wasn't going anywhere today, wouldn't be seeing anyone, and what was wrong with having a day's stubble on his face?

Anything to put off opening the sock drawer.

He further delayed the moment of truth by making the coffee, and it wasn't until he'd poured the first cup and had the first sip that he went over to the dresser and opened the drawer.

And of course the rabbit was there, in the same spot he'd left it the night before. It hadn't hopped around, nor had it disappeared as mysteriously as it had arrived. He picked it up and held it in both hands and wondered what the hell he was going to do now.

How had they missed it? Those two clowns, Slaughter and Reade—except they weren't clowns, they'd struck him as disturbingly competent, and not without some imagination. Still, they'd come to his apartment with one mission, to search for a missing turquoise rabbit formerly in the possession of one Marilyn Fairchild. They'd looked everywhere, certainly in the drawers of his dresser, and specifically in his sock drawer, because didn't he remember one of them—Slaughter? Reade?—picking up and squeezing each rolled-up pair of socks in turn, just in case he'd thought to hide the thing that way.

But did he actually remember that? Or did he in fact remember Chris Noth squeezing socks on an A&E rerun of *Law & Order*, playing Mike Logan to Jerry Orbach's Lennie Briscoe? (Or Paul Sorvino's Phil Cerreta, or what was the name of the character George Dzundza played? Jesus, if he couldn't remember *that* . . .)

The best day of his life, better than any night of sexual passion (and he'd had a few, and some of them, let's not kid ourselves, were pretty great). Better than either wedding, even better (har har) than either divorce. Substantially better, if the truth be told, than the days his children were born.

Which reminded him. He had to call Karin and the kids, had to give them the good news. It would be in the papers, Roz had told him the Crown publicists would see to that, but they ought to hear it from him first. The kids would be excited, and Karin would be relieved, and not just because it meant they weren't going to take her house away from her. She'd be relieved because she cared about him, even as he cared about her; that didn't necessarily stop when a marriage ended. And, pragmatically, she'd be happy to know that the kids' college educations were assured.

And by the way, he could add, *I found the cutest little bunny in with my socks. And do you know what that means? Well, you remember that nice woman who lived on Charles Street? It means Daddy killed her.*

BUT DID IT?

It meant he'd been to her apartment, but they knew it, and he knew it, he'd even admitted it. They could prove he'd been there, and the most the little blue rabbit could possibly do was confirm something he'd never troubled to deny.

Still, he'd exulted when they'd failed to find it, and he'd been devastated when it turned up after all. So what did it mean?

Well, it hadn't gotten there by itself. If the cops had found it, he could have tried telling himself that they'd planted it themselves. But that would have seemed unlikely, a real Dream Team stretch, and the obvious conclusion, the only plausible conclusion, was that he'd taken the creature from her apartment, stashed it with his socks when he got undressed, and forgot the whole thing by the time he awoke the next day.

It wasn't like him to steal something. He weighed the rabbit in his palm, trying to imagine why he would have taken it. Out of spite? Out of sheer cussed alcoholic meanness?

Maybe he'd meant to ask her about it, where she got it or who'd

carved it, some damn thing, and took it into the bedroom to show it to her.
And then forgot about it until he got home, and figured he'd find some
way to return it to her in the morning, and . . .

It seemed more likely that he would have picked it up on his way out
the door. Hadn't they argued? They'd had some kind of drunken sex, and
followed it with some kind of drunken argument. But he couldn't remember the details, and didn't know what he could trust of what he did seem
to remember.

Suppose the worst.

Suppose the argument got out of hand. Suppose she slapped him, or
said something that got to him. Suppose he got his hands on her throat,
just to shut her up, just to let her know she'd crossed a line, and suppose
she taunted him, said he wouldn't dare, called him an impotent cripple,
and suppose his hands tightened.

He'd have been drunker than he realized. Drunk enough to do it, too
drunk to remember it. Drunk enough, certainly, to take something with
him as he left, for a souvenir of the occasion, say, or just because it caught
his eye. Most pet shop sales, he'd read somewhere, were to men who got
drunk and suddenly decided that they had to bring home a puppy. Could
he have felt a similar need for a bunny rabbit?

He looked at the thing again. Much as he wished he'd never seen it,
he had to concede it was not without appeal. And he'd admired Zuni carvings in the window of Common Ground and other local shops. He'd never
felt the need to own one, but they were the sort of thing that, seized suddenly by a fit of drunken kleptomania, he might have reached for.

And, God help him, he'd have been capable of killing. How close had
he come, really, to killing Penny all those years ago? He'd never laid a
hand on her, but in the story that sprang from the nonincident, and in the
book he was writing now, the wife had died; the young husband had
changed his mind, but too late.

In the novel, the man got away with murder. But he hadn't really gotten away with anything, for all his life from that day on was shaped and
colored by that simple act of murder. And, as the story unfolded on the
page (or unscrolled upon the screen), it was becoming evident that the
protagonist was still a murderer, that he still sought solutions to problems
without regard to their moral implications, and that, before the book was
done, he would kill again.

But that was just a book, wasn't it? It was his attempt to construct out
of his imagination a logical series of consequences to an event that had
never taken place. It didn't prove anything, did it?

Christ, suppose he killed her.

. . .

THERE WAS REALLY NOTHING like denial. It was a powerful tool; used wisely, it could get you through a lot of bad days.

He spent the weekend cloaked in it, acting as if nothing had changed since he'd seen an unwelcome bit of brightness in his sock drawer. It meant nothing, he told himself, and acted accordingly. He made some phone calls, answered his e-mail, and worked on his book. He'd thought it might be hard to slip back into the alternate universe of the novel, thought the blue rabbit might have understandably thrown him off stride, but all he had to do was sit down at the keyboard, and a few mouse clicks took him out of his world and into the far more comfortable world of Harry Brubaker. Comfortable for him, because he was there as an observer and reporter. It wasn't all that comfortable for Harry, and it was going to get a lot worse.

While he worked, the rabbit sat on a shelf, next to the thesaurus, which he never used, and the dictionary, which he used less now that his word-processing program had a good spell-check feature. (Beside them stood *Bartlett's Familiar Quotations*, which he used far too frequently; he would grab it to check something, and the next thing he knew an hour had gone by.) Now and then he would glance over at the rabbit. It was ridiculous, even dangerous, to keep it—but he sort of liked having it there.

By Monday, when Tracy Morgensen called, he knew about Friday night's three firebombings. Tracy was a senior publicist at Crown, and told him she'd be his publicist, and how did he feel about doing some early publicity now? Because they did have his two books scheduled to ship in September, *The Goldsmith's Daughter* and *Nothing But Blue Skies*, and the sales reps would be taking orders for both titles this week, so a little publicity wouldn't be a bad thing. There wouldn't be a tour, because there wasn't enough time to set it up, and besides these weren't new books, and he'd probably toured when they were first published, hadn't he?

Well, no, he hadn't. But he couldn't really tour right now anyway.

"Because you're working on a new book. Yes, I know, and we're all excited. They didn't tell me the title. Do you know what it's going to be?"

He said he didn't. She ran down a list of things she was working on. All local, she said, so he wouldn't have to travel, in order to keep any interference with his writing time to a minimum. He told her that was just as well, because he wasn't sure if he was allowed to leave the state, given that he was currently out on bail and charged with homicide. That stopped her right in her chirpy little tracks, but only for a minute, and then they were back to work, figuring out what shows he would go on, what reporters would get to interview him.

By Thursday, when he went downtown to be Lenny Lopate's guest on WNYC radio, the police had released a photo of the Carpenter. Friday's papers carried the **NAILED!** and **GOTCHA!** headlines, and he'd watched coverage on New York One and read a long story in the *Times* before he walked over to Jones Street to meet a *Daily News* reporter at the Vivaldi. They sat outside, where they both could smoke, and ordered cappuccino, and she fumbled with questions, asking him what he as a novelist made of a person like the Carpenter, and how did incidents like those of the previous week affect his use of New York City as a canvas for his novels.

The questions didn't make sense to him, but that wasn't the point; they were in this together, she trying to write something that would pass for news, he looking to get some ink and sell some books. And, while he was at it, to give the public at large the impression that he was one of the good guys.

Maury Winters had made the latter point when he'd asked the lawyer if it was all right to go on the air. "It's a godsend," Winters told him. "Anything about Fairchild, the charges, the trial, you smile and explain you're not allowed to talk about it. You get some prick won't leave you alone on the subject, you stand up and walk out. Anything else, you're helpful, you smile a lot, you think crime's a terrible thing, you think the police do an outstanding job, you'll be glad when this Carpenter *momzer*'s locked up and the city can get back to normal. As for you, all you want to do is sit home and write books. And John? They want to interview you, you meet them somewhere. They'll want to come to your apartment, they'll want to photograph you at your desk, or in front of a wall of your books. Your apartment's off limits. You don't want 'em nosing around in your things. Meet in the park, meet for coffee. They keep asking the wrong questions, you can get up and leave. That's not so easy to do when you're already home. You meet a cute one, you want to fool around, go to her place. If she's married, go get a room."

The *News* reporter was cute, in an angular, hard-bitten sort of way, but she wasn't his type, nor did he sense that he was hers. At the end she turned off her tape recorder and put away her notepad and said that was fine, she'd be able to get a nice feature out of what he'd given her.

They both lit fresh cigarettes, and he asked how long she'd been at the paper, and how she'd decided on journalism. And she said what she really wanted was to write fiction, and that she'd almost enrolled for his workshop at the New School.

"You'd have been shortchanged," he said. "They canceled the last two classes."

She said, "Why?" and then winced when she figured it out; they'd canceled the classes because the teacher had been arrested for murder. "I'll bet I wouldn't have felt shortchanged," she said, recovering nicely. "I'll bet you're a good teacher."

"I didn't do much," he said. "Teaching writing is like practicing medicine. The Hippocratic Oath, I mean—*First, do no harm.* Mostly I just encouraged them to write. The good ones, that's all they need. The others, well, nothing's going to help them, and at least they're writing."

She got out her pad and made him repeat all that and wrote it down. Then she said she guessed he wouldn't be doing any more teaching, and he agreed that he was probably done with that. She paid for the coffee and they shook hands and he went home.

A FEW DAYS LATER, he had lunch with Esther Blinkoff. He met her at the Crown offices, where she took him around and showed him off to ten or a dozen people whose hands he shook and whose names he promptly forgot. The younger ones seemed a little in awe of him, and he wasn't sure whether it was the size of his contract or the fact that he was going to be tried for homicide. Young or old, they all told him how excited they were at the prospect of working with him.

At an elegant French-Asian restaurant on East Fifty-fifth Street she told him she felt guilty taking him away from his work. "I won't ask how it's coming," she said, and he told her it was coming along quite well, that he felt good about what he'd written and optimistic about the part he hadn't done yet. Was there any chance she could hope to see some of it sometime soon? He said he never liked to show anything to anybody until he was done.

"Roz said as much," she said, "but I thought I would try. Actually, I think you're right not to show work in progress. The only reason writers do it is it gives them a chance to stop work while they wait for a reaction from us, and the only reason we want to see chapters along the way is to assure ourselves that the writer's actually doing something, not just drinking up the advance." She patted his hand. "Present company excepted, I hardly need add. Oh, I have some good news. We just increased the print order on both books, *Daughter* and *Blue Skies*. They're good solid books, John, and I'm afraid we underpublished them the first time around. Of course we've had some personnel changes since then."

"For the better, as far as I'm concerned."

"Thank you, and I have to say I believe you're right. I think it's wonderful that those two books are getting a second chance in hardcover, and Tracy's going to make sure that they're received like new books. In other words, reviewed, but more than that we're hoping they'll generate the

kind of sidebars and feature articles that will serve as a launching platform for the big one. Did you say you had a working title?"

He'd long since decided against *A Nice Place to Start*, and had had
several working titles since, tentative successors to *Fucked If I Know*. The
current favorite was *Darker Than Water*, and he mentioned it with some
reluctance; if she didn't like it, they weren't off to the best possible start,
and if she loved it he was stuck with it.

"Meaning blood," she said immediately. "As in *thicker than water*,
but *darker* instead. John, I think it's very good. It sounds dark, obviously,
and it has the feel of a thriller title, but at the same time it's subtle enough
so that there's a literary feel to it. And it's short enough so that the art director won't have a hard time getting it to look good on the mass-market
paperback."

She'd heard him on *New York & Company*, and said he'd come across
well. Lopate made it easy for his guests, he told her, and she agreed, but
said he was effective in his own right. "And that's important," she said. "It
didn't used to be, and maybe it shouldn't be, but the business has
changed. How do you feel about touring? Not this fall, we've ruled that
out even if it were possible, but for *Darker Than Water*."

"If I'm free to tour, I'm all for it."

"Free to tour. Let's see now. In the most tentative way, because the
last thing I want to do is put pressure on you, we've sort of penciled the
book into our schedule for October of 2003. I know there's going to have
to be a trial—do you mind talking about this?"

"No, of course not."

"Well, we're certainly not going to publish *before* next October, and
wouldn't you think the trial will be over by then?"

"It seems likely," he said. "And if I'm acquitted, I'll be happy to go
anywhere you send me."

"If you're acquitted. John, I don't think there's the slightest doubt
you'll be acquitted."

"I think there might be a little doubt over on Hogan Place."

"At the Manhattan DA's office? I honestly don't know why they don't
drop the charges. I'm sure that lunatic killed her. He seems to have killed
everybody else who died in the past six months."

They'd collected a full set of Harbinger's fingerprints from the Upper
West Side apartment he'd abandoned, and someone had matched a thumb
print to a previously unidentifiable print left on a quart can of charcoal
lighter found in the ashes of a blaze in the Bronx back in the early spring.
That was strong evidence that the Carpenter had already been plying his
trade well before the Twenty-eighth Street whorehouse murders, and just

when he'd begun and how many times he'd struck were the subject of endless speculation.

As were his whereabouts. The Carpenter had stayed at the same Midtown flophouse for several days after his attack on the three Chelsea bars, moving out only a day or two before his picture was on every front page. He left without telling anybody, just walked off and didn't come back. By the time a tip brought the police to the hotel, his room had long since been given to another man. He'd left nothing behind, aside from fingerprints that made it certain he'd been there.

Since then there'd been no end of sightings, no end of squad cars dispatched to locations throughout the five boroughs. But nothing had panned out. William Boyce Harbinger, aka the Carpenter, had vanished from the earth or into it.

OVER COFFEE HE SAID, "Actually, there's a possibility the charges might be dropped. That's what my attorney's pushing for."

"I should hope so. That's Maury Winters, if I'm not mistaken? Now there's a man who could write a book. Of course his best stories are probably ones he's not allowed to tell."

They traded Maury Winters stories and then Creighton felt sufficiently at ease to raise a question that had been bothering him. "If there was no case," he said. "If it turned out Harbinger somehow got into the woman's apartment and killed her—"

"Which I'm convinced is what happened."

"Well, would it be harmful from a publishing standpoint? If there was no trial, and the story more or less petered out?"

"And would we consequently drop you like a hot rock? John, you don't need to go on trial for your life in order to become a star. You're a star already."

"That's very nice, but my sales figures—"

"A, never amounted to much, and B, are meaningless at this point. You're a man who's been the focus of considerable attention, and on the strength of that plus your unquestioned talent and ability and, I must say, an agent with more savvy than most, you've become a writer able to command a three-million-dollar advance. Which I was thrilled to pay, and not because I had hopes that you'd say something poignant on Court TV, or have a second career as an astronaut and be the first man to set foot on Mars. As far as promotion and publicity are concerned, you're already as hot a ticket as you have to be."

"I wasn't sure."

"Well, be sure. John, I didn't just make a deal for one book. I bought your whole backlist, which we'll bring out in paper a month before we do *Darker Than Water* in hardcover, and I like that title more and more, I hope you go on liking it yourself. Where was I?"

"The backlist."

"The backlist, which we'll sell the hell out of, trust me, but let me remind you that we also bought *Darker Than Water* plus the book that comes after it. You're not even thinking about that second book, and there's no reason why you should be, but I'm thinking about it, and I'm thinking of the books you'll write after that, which we haven't contracted for but will when the time comes. I want you at Crown until the end of time, John, or until I retire, whichever comes first, and that's not because I think I can milk a few sales out of a few newspaper headlines. So all I want is for you to live and be well and write some terrific books, and if that lunatic walked into a police station tomorrow and confessed to everything from the Lindbergh kidnapping on, and said that oh, by the way, there was a woman he strangled on Charles Street, John, I'd be the second happiest person on the planet."

"The second happiest? Oh, because I'd be the happiest."

"Wouldn't you? And I'll tell you something else, just from a purely promotional standpoint, and that's to have a best-selling author who it turns out was falsely accused of a crime committed by the notorious Carpenter—John, if you were a publicist, do you think you'd have much trouble getting a little media coverage for somebody like that?" She sighed. "But first they have to catch the son of a bitch, and the sooner the better. How he must hate us!"

"Us?"

"New Yorkers. For living when his children died. And his wife, or do you think he killed her himself?"

There'd been speculation to that effect; the physician, long the Harbinger family doctor, admitted under questioning that he'd signed the death certificate without looking too closely. It had looked like a suicide to him, and out of sympathy to the widower he'd written *cardiac arrest* in the space for cause of death. Which was true enough, in that the woman's heart had indeed ceased to beat.

The cremation, and the subsequent disappearance of the ashes, made it forever impossible to determine whether Carole Harbinger's death had or had not been at her husband's hands. Whether it was part of his problem, in other words, or part of his solution.

He said, "I don't know if he hates us. I don't know what it is that drives him. The Curry Hill murders, the bloodbath that got him his name, that looked like a thrill killing, but that's not what drives this guy. I don't see him as having any fun."

"God, I should hope not!"

"I can sort of imagine what somebody like that might be going through. Feeling so much pain, so much loss, and having to do something about it. I'm not presuming to guess how it is with this particular guy, but I can imagine how it might be."

Esther Blinkoff sat back, folded her hands. "There's your next book," she said.

HE FELT A LITTLE silly buying the cornmeal.

He picked it up at the Gristedes on Hudson Street, and had to decide between the white and the yellow. Both were stone ground and both cost the same, and he actually found himself checking the nutritional information box on the packaging, as if a higher vitamin C level in one might make all the difference. He decided yellow was a more traditional color of cornmeal, and that seemed reason enough to go with it.

The smallest package was eight ounces, and he figured that would last awhile.

He'd been walking home from another coffee shop interview, this one at Reggio on Macdougal Street with a reporter from *People* magazine. She'd brought a photographer, a very tall dark-skinned young man who never made a sound, but who somehow communicated a desire to photograph Creighton in Washington Square Park. He'd changed film and cameras several times, taking endless shots until Creighton told him that was going to have to be enough.

On the way home, a shop window caught his eye. Someone had arranged a desert diorama, with sand and cacti and, incongruously, quartz crystals and other mineral specimens. But what got his attention was a group of stone carvings of animals, fetishes similar to the turquoise rabbit. There were no rabbits, but there were several bears (unlikely in a desert, you would think) along with some dogs and other creatures he couldn't identify.

He entered the shop, and found a glass case with a great many more fetishes, some an inch long that could have been stamped out with a cookie cutter, others very elaborately and realistically crafted, including an eagle whose every feather was defined and a snarling bobcat or lynx that looked positively fierce.

The shop attendant, a black girl with her hair fixed in blond cornrows and rings on six of her fingers, explained what the fetishes were. The bear was a powerful figure in the Native American cosmology, he learned, and thus was the most common subject for carvers, even in areas where actual bears could not be found. And what he'd taken for dogs were in fact coyotes, and the coyote was the great trickster of Indian folk myths.

"Wile E. Coyote," he said.

"Except he's the one who gets tricked all the time. This one's probably a badger, and of course you get owls and birds. Here's a rabbit, an owl, a frog. A buffalo, you see plenty of them."

And would he like to take one of them home and feed it? He said he didn't think so, that a friend had given him a fetish and he just wanted to get some sense of what it was and what to do with it. Did you pray to them?

"I don't think so," she said. "I think you sort of honor their spirits, you know? And absorb their energy. And of course you have to feed them." And she'd explained about the cornmeal, and showed him a selection of small shallow dishes suitable for the purpose. The nicest one was a piece of lustrous black pottery, and he was astonished to learn they wanted forty-five dollars for it.

"It's Santa Clara," she said, "or San Ildefonso, I can't always tell the difference. See, this bowl here is Santa Clara, and this one's San Ildefonso, but on a small piece like this one, it's harder to tell. Oh, wait, it's signed, Maria Sojo. Well, she's a well-known potter, and she's Santa Clara, so now we know it's a Santa Clara piece, and that's why it costs that much. Some of these others don't cost half that much and"—she grinned—"I don't think the little animals can tell the difference."

But he liked the black one, and said he'd take it. While she was wrapping it he said he bet there was a lot she could tell him about the fetishes and pottery, and that he'd really like to take her to dinner and learn more.

She smiled, her whole face lighting up, and touched one of the rings on her left hand. "Now this gets sort of lost in the shuffle here," she said, "but it's a wedding band." He started to apologize, but she told him not to, that she was flattered. "You ever see me without the ring," she said, "ask me again, okay?"

A FEW DAYS AGO he'd moved some books to create a niche for the rabbit. Now he spooned cornmeal into the black dish and placed it in front of the little animal.

He checked his messages, returned a call from Roz. She was holding off on foreign sales until she had *Darker Than Water* in hand, but reported that his French publishers wanted to renew contracts on his earlier titles, and to acquire one book they'd passed on first time around.

Nothing succeeded like success.

There were two other messages, but not ones he wanted to respond to. He erased them and sat down at the keyboard, and the book drew him in almost instantly, and the next thing he knew it was dark outside and he was hungry. He saved his work, ran spell-check, and printed out the day's pages. While they were printing he picked up the phone and ordered Chinese food.

He could have gone out, but he hardly ever did, except for interviews. The phone rang more frequently these days, with old friends who'd avoided him after the arrest now eager to pick up where they'd left off. He was cordial enough, but found himself turning down dates, pleading the pressures of work. He gave the same excuse to a couple of new friends, if that's what they were—people he'd met that magical night at Stelli's, who hadn't dropped him earlier because they hadn't even known him then. He didn't bear resentments toward the old friends—at least he didn't think he did—and he didn't want to reject the overtures of the new friends. But he really didn't feel very social.

He wondered how much the rabbit had to do with this.

Not its mystical energy, nothing like that. Just the enormous fact of its presence, because until he'd come upon it in his sock drawer he'd been looking forward to an expansion of his social activities, to nights at the Kettle and the Corner Bistro, to field trips uptown to Stelli's. Dinners at fine restaurants, and night games at Shea, and the company of women.

He looked at the rabbit, serene enough in front of its dish of cornmeal. He heard Bogart's voice in his head, speaking in haiku:

> *Of all the sock drawers*
> *In all the towns in the world*
> *You hopped into mine . . .*

Hitting on the girl who'd sold him the little black dish had been spontaneous, and more of a surprise to him than to her. It was probably just as well she'd had a husband, or invented one. Jesus, she was half his age, and what would they talk about when they ran out of Zuni fetishes and Pueblo pottery?

And suppose she'd come back to his apartment, and wanted to see his fetish? Suppose she recognized it, suppose she'd sold it to Marilyn Fairchild? That wasn't as far-fetched as it sounded; Tenth Street was just a block from Charles Street, and the woman could very easily have shopped there.

He went over and took another look at the rabbit. Was he supposed to name it? That was something he could have asked the girl. He wasn't inclined to think of a name for it. He had to name characters, every little walk-on in Harry Brubaker's life needed a name and a history, and that made him think of the biblical folk tale of Adam in the garden, required to assign names to all the animals. It felt presumptuous, like playing God, when he arbitrarily assigned names and back stories to characters, but maybe it was more a matter of playing Adam.

The first day or two, he'd figured he had to get rid of the rabbit. It was dangerous to have it in his possession, and he was just lucky beyond belief that the cops hadn't found it when they'd come looking for it. How likely would they be to overlook it a second time?

He thought of ways to dispose of the rabbit, simple things like dropping it into a sewer, more elaborate strategies like walking a few blocks west and tossing it off a pier into the Hudson. You wouldn't have to weight it down, like a body. It would, appropriately enough, sink like a stone.

But for some reason he wanted it.

He liked the thing, and wasn't that nutty? Although, if you thought about it, it wasn't all that surprising. If he'd liked it enough to swipe it in the first place, why shouldn't he go on liking it?

Had he somehow killed her for it? Had she caught him taking it, and called him on it, and had that triggered the fight that left her dead? He could see how that might have happened, but that was the trouble, he could imagine anything and everything.

He'd keep it, he decided. At least until it was time to buy more cornmeal.

HER CARD WAS STILL in his sock drawer.

Susan Pomerance, who sold folk and outsider art, and what was a turquoise rabbit if not folk art? Probably not the sort of thing she dealt in, but she very likely knew something about the art of the southwestern tribes.

Come up and see my fetish—how was that for an opening line?

Did he even need an opening line? She'd made her interest clear enough. All that had been required of him was that he call her the next day, or the day after, and they could follow her script.

But he hadn't called. He'd found the rabbit, and walked around in a daze for a few days, and then forgot about her and her calling card, and now far too much time had elapsed. *Hi, this is John Creighton, I've had better things to think about than you, but I'm horny as a toad right now, so why don't you come on over?* Yeah, right.

She was good-looking, too, and more age-appropriate and culture-appropriate than the girl he'd hit on. But he'd waited too long, and that was that.

Might as well throw her card away.

Then again, it wouldn't hurt to hang on to it.

. . .

MAURY WINTERS SAID, "BEEN a while, boychik. I feel like we've been in touch on account of I keep reading about you in the papers."

"Have I been overdoing it, Maury?"

"No, it's good, the publicity. The more you show up as an important figure in the arts, the more absurd it is that you should be accused of a crime. Listen, you remember Fabrizzio?"

"Vividly."

"Yeah, she makes an impression. She also made an offer."

"Oh?"

"And I report it to you because I have to, but I also have to advise you very strongly to turn it down. What she offers is for you to plead to second-degree manslaughter, with a sentencing recommendation of three to five years. You'd do the minimum and be out in under three."

"I see."

"Now the only interesting thing about this offer," Winters said, "is that she made it, and believe me, she had a tough time getting the words out. The only reason she'd offer a plea to Man Two is her case is looking a little worse every day, and what she wants and what her boss wants is for it to go away. And the reason I'm even bothering you with it is because I'm going to turn it down, thanks but no thanks, and then she'll ask me what I want, and I'll say I want her to drop the charges altogether, and she'll make another offer."

"Which will be what?"

"My guess? Involuntary manslaughter, a year or two, whatever the code calls for, and the sentence suspended so you got no time to serve."

"Really."

"That's my guess. And that's where we have a decision to make."

He thought for a moment. "I'd have to allocute," he said.

"That's exactly correct, but how do you even happen to know the word, if you don't mind my asking?"

"TV."

"Of course, how else? Now everybody can talk like a lawyer. Yes, you'd have to allocute. You'd have to stand up in front of God and everybody, which includes the judge and the media, and tell how you happened to kill Fairchild."

"Which I didn't do."

"Which you have always maintained you didn't do, but you'd have to say you did. Now I can't advise you to lie, but someone in a similar position could say that his partner had been choking on something, had appeared unable to breathe, and consequently he'd taken hold of her and tried to assist her by shaking her, and it so happened he was holding her by the neck, and the shaking didn't help, and the next thing he knew . . . well, you get the point."

"Yes."

"If she offers it and if we take it, which is a lot of ifs for one sentence, you do no time whatsoever. That's the good news, but the bad news is you're on record as saying you did it. Anybody on the inside'll know it's a formality, but the general public's only going to know that you stood up in court and admitted you killed the woman. You've got a felony conviction on your record, and yes, you're free to walk around, but so's OJ, and there's not a whole lot of people inviting him over for dinner, or trying to fix him up with their sisters. Other hand, when it comes to prison, there's a world of difference between being inside and being out."

"What would you advise, Maury?"

"At this stage," he said, "I wouldn't, because what's to advise when there isn't an offer on the table? This is just a heads-up, John, so you can start thinking about it. Meanwhile, remember that green rabbit those bozos came around looking for?"

"Blue."

"Huh?"

"It said blue on the warrant."

"I stand corrected. Let's hope they find that Carpenter putz, and they search him head to toe, and when they look up his ass, lo and behold, there's the rabbit. Then you won't have to decide what to do about the offer Fabrizzio hasn't made yet."

COULD HE STAND UP in court and say he'd done it?

If he was innocent, could he proclaim himself guilty? If he was guilty, could he admit it, make it a matter of record?

And suppose he didn't know? Suppose he couldn't really say one way or the other?

twenty-two

HE HAD BEEN the hunter. Now he was the hunted.

It had changed so suddenly.

The Carpenter, they called him. At first it had been the Curry Hill Carpenter, when they had no idea who he was or what he'd done beyond the triple murder on East Twenty-eighth Street. He didn't like the name much, but appreciated the reference to the neighborhood, because that name, Curry Hill, embodied the city's resourcefulness in matters of nomenclature. Here was an area that didn't really have a name, that had never been thought of as a discrete geographical entity. It was south of Murray Hill and north of Gramercy, east of Kips Bay and west of the Flatiron district, so how to refer to it if you were trying to sell or lease property there? Well, it was adjacent to Murray Hill, that section named for the Murray family, and Indo-Pak restaurants abounded, so why not Curry Hill?

Just the Carpenter, now. After that Friday night, after they'd been clever enough to see that the firebombings were his work as well, one newspaper referred to him as the Curry Hill–Chelsea Carpenter, but that was cumbersome and not as catchy.

Since then, of course, they'd matched a fingerprint and knew about the Cauldwell Avenue fire in the Bronx. And they knew his name, and played off that in their stories and headlines, but mostly they called him the Carpenter, perhaps recognizing that his name (which he no longer used) and his address (where he no longer lived) were of far less significance than what he did.

The Carpenter. He'd disliked the name initially, irked at the way they were fixated on the physical implements he'd used on a single occasion, the hammer and the chisel. (They didn't even know about the screwdriver.) He grew more accepting of the sobriquet as he came to see it as pointing up the workmanlike nature of his efforts. And then one day it struck him that the word was more appropriate than they could consciously realize, for wasn't a carpenter more than a worker, more than the simple practitioner of a trade? Wasn't he, first and foremost, a builder?

Reading the stories, one realized that they missed the point, that they saw only the destructive aspect of what he was doing. They had no way of knowing that he tore down only to rebuild, took life only to renew life. They had no understanding of sacrifice, his or anyone else's.

And yet they must, on some unconscious level. That wasn't why they named him the Carpenter, that was the natural result of his use of the tools, reinforced by the happy alliteration of craft and neighborhood. But perhaps that was why the name stuck, why they clung to it after they knew his name. He was a carpenter, a builder, and he was building their city, and would go on with his mission while he had breath in his body.

YOU'D THINK THEY'D HAVE caught him by now.

At the beginning, he took it for granted he'd be caught, and didn't expect it would take long. When he watched firefighters battle the blaze on Cauldwell Avenue, he'd have been unsurprised if some inspector had picked him out of the crowd, had walked right up to him and taken him into custody. *All right, mister. We know you set the fire. Care to tell us why?*

And he'd have told them why. They might not have understood, but he'd have made the effort.

But no one approached him, or even looked twice at him. And in the weeks that followed he realized that no one ever looked twice at him, that he might have been invisible for all the attention he received.

When he was a boy he used to like a radio program about a character named Lamont Cranston, alias the Shadow. *Who knows what evil lurks in the hearts of men? The Shadow knows.* The Shadow, an announcer explained each week, had the power to cloud men's minds so they could not see him.

And didn't he have that power?

Except he achieved it through no exercise of will. And he wondered if it might not be an effect of the losses he had sustained, the four sacrifices that had set him upon his own sacrificial mission. Could not those deaths, coming one upon another as they did, have taken away bits of his own very self? He had not felt the same since then, and knew he never would. Was it not possible that part of what he'd lost had been that quality that commanded attention from others? He was not literally invisible, like Lamont Cranston, but when people did see him he didn't make much of an impression on their awareness. They took no notice of him and retained no memory of him.

As time passed, he came to take his invisibility for granted, to view it as a protective shield that would guarantee him invulnerability while he did his terrible work. He'd continued to take precautions, he'd made sure no one was looking when he hurled his jars of gasoline and when he wielded his razor, but he no longer expected to be captured, or even seen.

He hadn't even thought about security cameras. Nor had he fully appreciated the nature of the manhunt that would be an immediate result of the three Chelsea bombings, or that they'd be tied almost immediately to the triple murder on Twenty-eighth Street. He should have assumed the latter, he'd deliberately constructed a pattern, choosing the three establishments because they, like the whorehouse, were cleaned every morning by the very same young man who'd discovered the body on Charles Street.

It was hard now to recall why he'd established that pattern in the first place. He'd seen and recognized the young man; following him, it seemed as if he was being specifically led to the sites of his next sacrifices. It hadn't occurred to him to question this at the time, and now, looking back on it, he failed to see what his purpose might have been. You couldn't say it had no rhyme or reason. It had rhyme, certainly, but the reason was less readily apparent.

No matter. It was done.

HE SAT AT THE window, watching the city.

The apartment was a comfortable one, light and airy, comfortably furnished, with two window air conditioners that kept the place almost too cool throughout an August heat wave. It was spacious as well, occupying the entire top floor of a narrow three-story frame house on Baltic Street, in the part of Brooklyn known as Boerum Hill. He remembered Baltic Street from Monopoly; it and Mediterranean were the cheapest properties on the board. This Baltic Street was nicer than that, although he imagined the neighborhood had been marginal twenty or thirty years earlier. Now, like so much of Brooklyn, it had benefited from gentrification, and was attracting middle-income New Yorkers, unable to find space they could afford in Manhattan, or in long-desirable parts of the borough like Brooklyn Heights.

Evelyn Crispin, the woman whose apartment this was, was one such person. She was fifty-one years old, and worked as a legal secretary at a Wall Street law firm. She had been married in her twenties, and a wedding picture in a frame on her dresser showed her as a young and pretty bride, standing beside a beaming groom. He'd died a few years later, killed in an automobile accident, and shortly thereafter she'd moved to New York to start a new life. It had evidently been a solitary life, and for the past fifteen years she'd led it in this Baltic Street apartment, which she shared with a cat whose name William Harbinger did not know.

The cat, nameless or not, demanded periodically to be fed. It did so now, weaving itself around his ankles, rubbing its body against him to attract his attention. He went into the kitchen, got a can of cat food from the cupboard. There were only two left on the shelf, and when they were gone he'd have to figure out what to do about the cat.

He opened the can, spooned the food into its dish, placed the dish on the floor. Watching the animal eat, he was reminded that he ought to eat something himself, and opened a can of lentil soup and another of roast beef hash, which on balance did not look all that different from what he'd just fed to the cat. He heated the soup in a saucepan and the hash in a frying pan, transferred the contents to a bowl and a plate, and sat at the kitchen table to eat his meal. When the cat hopped up onto the table to investigate, he took it by the scruff of the neck and tossed it across the room. That would do for now, but next meal it would try again; the beast was capable of learning, but not of retaining what it learned.

When he was finished eating he washed his dishes in the sink, wiped them dry with a red-and-white checkered dishtowel, and put them away. He was, he thought, the ideal tenant. He washed the dishes, made the bed, and fed the cat. He even watered the plants, although he suspected he was overwatering at least one of them.

He checked the refrigerator's freezer compartment, and it had obligingly made ice of the water he'd put in the ice cube trays. He filled a bucket with the cubes, refilled all four trays with tap water, and dumped the bucket of ice cubes in the bathtub. Then he closed the bathroom door and returned to the front room and his chair by the window.

HE MISSED HIS BOOKS, his histories, his diaries of old New Yorkers. As far as he knew, they were still in his storage locker in Chelsea, but that wasn't a safe neighborhood for him. In a sense, no neighborhood was especially safe. His picture had been in all the papers and on all the news programs, and *America's Most Wanted* had shown it to the whole country. (*Let's get this coward off the streets!* had been the urgent message of the show's intense host, and he'd found this puzzling. He didn't expect the public to understand what he was doing for them, but in what respect could he be seen as cowardly? Evil, perhaps; he could see how they might view his actions as evil. But certainly not cowardly.)

In Chelsea, though, the residents could be expected to feel more personally connected to what he had done, and to have looked more intently at his photograph. He couldn't expect to pass unnoticed there. Nor could he be certain that the police had not already traced the storage locker, in which case they were very likely keeping it under surveillance. He missed his books, but he didn't need them, and didn't care to risk walking into a trap.

The phone rang, and he let it ring. There was an answering machine, but he'd disconnected it, not wanting people leaving messages. There weren't many calls, and this was the day's first. There'd been a call early on from her office, and he'd returned that call the following morning, explaining that Ms. Crispin had been called out of town suddenly for a family emergency, that she'd asked him, a neighbor and friend, to notify them, and that it was impossible to say when she might return. Two days later he called them again to report that her aunt had in fact died, that Ms. Crispin was the woman's sole heir, and would remain in Duluth. "She's not even coming back for her things," he said, sounding aggrieved himself. "I'm supposed to pack everything and ship it to her. She must think I don't have anything better to do."

So there wouldn't be any more calls from the office.

She had a bookcase full of books, mostly paperback novels, but one illustrated volume called *Lost Brooklyn*, filled with photographs of buildings, many of them quite magnificent, which had fallen to the wrecking ball. He liked looking at the pictures and pondering the transitory nature of all things, even buildings. But he couldn't get transported by pictures as he could by text.

HE HAD PLENTY OF money. Before they'd identified him, before they put his picture in the paper, he'd realized that his days of anonymity were over. Accordingly he'd used the ATM, drawing the $800 daily maximum for three days in succession. His expenses were lower now, too, since he couldn't go to a hotel, or eat in a restaurant. The $2,400 he'd drawn would last him for the time that remained to him.

Before he found the Baltic Street apartment, he'd had to be resourceful. He didn't dare sleep on park benches, fearing he'd wake up to a patrolman tapping the soles of his shoes with his nightstick, then taking a good look at him when he sat up and opened his eyes. He didn't need much sleep, though, and got what he required an hour or two at a time in air-conditioned movie theaters. He rode the G train to Greenpoint and bought shirts and socks and underwear at a bargain store on Manhattan Avenue, which seemed safer to him than Fourteenth Street, and ate in ethnic enclaves in Queens, where the residents were more caught up in tensions over Kashmir and civil war in Colombia than the doings of white people in gay bars in Manhattan.

Then he found Evelyn Crispin's apartment, and his life became less of a struggle. She had a cupboard and refrigerator full of food, and a soft bed for him to sleep in, and a comfortable chair and a television set with cable reception. She had neighbors, too, but he never saw them. He left the apartment after two A.M. and returned before five, and never encountered anyone.

Every day that he stayed out of sight, the likelihood of their capturing him diminished. The hunt would go on indefinitely, but the public, with its eight million pairs of eyes, had a notoriously short attention span. Look how quickly they'd forgotten all about the man who'd sent anthrax through the mails. Other stories were already competing for their notice, and the Carpenter's facial features, not that sharply delineated in their photo to begin with, would blur and soften and recede from the forefront of their collective memory.

Before long he would be invisible again.

SOMEONE WAS RINGING THE doorbell, knocking on the door.

He'd been drifting, lost in reverie, not asleep but not entirely awake, either, and now he sprang from his chair and turned toward the door. Someone had a key in it and was turning the lock. They couldn't get in, he'd thrown the bolt, but he had to do something.

He picked up a knife in the kitchen, then went to the door, called, "Yes? Who is it?"

"It's Carlos," a voice said. "Come to check on Miz Crispin. You want to open the door?"

"I can't," he said. "I was in the shower and I heard you banging on the door. You've upset the cat terribly."

"I don't want to upset nobody," Carlos said. "Where's the lady? Been days now and nobody's seen her."

"She's out of town," he said. "Didn't you get the note she left?"

"What note?"

"She's in Duluth," he said. "Her aunt passed away, she had to go there. Are you sure you didn't get the note?"

A woman's voice said, "Duluth?"

"In Minnesota. I'm a friend of hers, I'm taking care of her cat until she comes back. She asked if I'd stop in and feed the cat and water the plants, and I said I'd move right in, because my air conditioner died and just try to get them to come in the middle of a heat wave."

"I know she's from Minnesota," the woman said.

"I just wanted to make sure she was all right," Carlos said.

"She's fine," he said. "I had a postcard from her the other day. Come around tomorrow and I'll show it to you."

"No, I don't have to see no postcard. I just . . ."

"Listen," he said, "the water's still running in the shower. You're good to be concerned. She's fortunate to have such good neighbors."

"I'm the super. This building and three others on the block. I'm sort of responsible, you know what I mean?"

"I do," he said, "and I appreciate it."

He stood there, gripping the knife, until he heard their footsteps reach the bottom of the stairs.

HE WAS GOING TO have to decide about fingerprints.

To leave them or to wipe them away? There were persuasive arguments on both sides. If they found his fingerprints, and thus knew he'd taken refuge here on Baltic Street, he'd be catapulted back into the headlines. Of late there'd been little about him, some of it speculation that he might have left the city, might be in Mexico or Brazil or seeking refuge in some Arab nation (*with his terrorist brothers*, one columnist suggested), or that he might even be dead. His fingerprints would end such speculation, and would lead authorities to widen their search from Manhattan to the outer boroughs. The invisibility he'd begun to regain would afford less protection.

On the other hand, he'd be far from Boerum Hill, far from all of Brooklyn, by the time they even saw the need to look for fingerprints. Safety aside, might it not be advantageous to let the city know that the Carpenter was alive and well, and still devoted to his work? Fear was a powerful emotion, and had already served him well.

He could picture Carlos on *Live at Five*, interviewed by a vacuous reporter on the steps of the Baltic Street house. He hadn't seen Carlos, hadn't even tried to look through the peephole at him, but he was sure he knew what he looked like—short, stocky, a full head of curly black hair, pockmarks on his cheeks. "I go and check on her, you know? And he tells me he's her friend, she went home on account of her aunt died, he's staying there to feed her cat. And it sounds okay to me, you know?"

Yes, let them find his prints. Let them dread the Carpenter. It wouldn't make things that much more dangerous for him, and he didn't have to stay away from them for that much longer.

It was already well into August.

IN THE MORNING, HE thought, Carlos would start to wonder. Perhaps he should meet Evelyn Crispin's friend face to face, instead of having to talk with him through a door.

Time to be going.

He undressed, and put all of his clothes in her washing machine, sitting patiently at the window until it was time to switch them to the dryer. When they were dry he laid out the clothes he would put on when he awoke, packed the rest into a navy-blue backpack he'd found in one of the closets.

One of the small drawers in the kitchen held hardware—pliers, regular and Phillips-head screwdrivers, a hammer, a tape measure, a jar full of assorted nails and screws. He took out the hammer, and went through the jar to select the largest nail. It was a formidable thing, three inches long, and thick. He put the hammer and nail on the kitchen counter and closed the drawer.

The freezer had done its work, and the ice cubes had hardened. He collected the cubes in a bucket, refilled the trays, dumped the bucket in the bathtub. He wet a washcloth and gave himself a sponge bath, then got into her bed. The air conditioner, running full blast, had the room like an icebox, and he used both blankets.

He awoke at a quarter after two, dressed in the clothes he'd laid out, moving quietly to avoid disturbing the neighbor a flight below. The cat, whom he'd locked out of the bedroom, was busy rubbing against his ankles, signaling its hunger. He glanced down at the cat, then over at the hammer he'd left handy on the kitchen counter.

He opened a can of cat food, fed the animal, and had a look at the ice cube trays, but the thin skin of ice yielded to his fingertip when he tested a cube.

He watered the plants, except for the one that showed signs of overwatering, and freshened the water in the cat's bowl. Then he picked up the hammer and the nail and went into the bathroom, where Evelyn Crispin lay faceup in a tub of water in which some ice cubes, still not entirely melted, lay floating. He'd started with bags of ice from a bodega on Nevins Street, supplemented with his own ice cubes as fast as the freezer could make them, and, with both air conditioners running night and day, it had worked well enough. But it was a holding action at best, and he sniffed the air and knew it would have been time to leave whether or not Carlos had come knocking at the door.

There were bruises on Evelyn Crispin's cheek and temple, where he had struck her, and marks on her neck, where he had strangled her. He gazed down at her and felt something for her, but he couldn't say exactly what it was. Pity? Perhaps.

He knelt at the side of the tub, and his lip curled in distaste for what he was about to do. He took no joy in the act, but, like everything he did, it was not without purpose.

He pounded the nail into the very center of her forehead.

Shortly after three, he donned the backpack and slipped out the door, careful not to let the cat follow him out. He locked the door behind him, and made his way silently down the two flights of stairs. No light was visible under the doors of his neighbors on the lower two floors. He guessed they were sleeping soundly, and was careful not to interrupt their sleep.

Baltic Street was quiet and deserted when he let himself out the front door. He walked to Smith Street. There was a subway entrance three blocks to his right, at Bergen Street, and another at Carroll Street, six blocks in the other direction.

It was a nice night for a walk, and he was in no hurry. He turned left, and walked at a brisk but unhurried pace through the summer night. The backpack, he decided, was better than a suitcase, better than a tote bag or shopping bag. It left his hands free, and seemed less a burden altogether. He was glad he'd noticed it in the closet, glad he'd decided to put it to use.

Just a few more weeks, he thought.

Waiting on the deserted subway platform, he tried to think what he would do—not right away, but when it was time. The Carpenter's final action, the triumphant event in which he was part of the sacrifice, was his bid for greatness, and he couldn't think what it might be. He knew when it would happen, but not what form it would take.

But it wasn't something you could think of, was it? He had a seat on a bench, folded his hands in his lap, and, waiting for his train, he waited, too, for the answer to be revealed to him.

twenty-three

F

OR THE FIRST time, the Carpenter had signed his work.

The *Post* called it a direct response to their headline. They'd depicted him with a nail in his forehead, and he'd left his latest victim mutilated in just such a fashion. While quick to take credit, if that's what it was, the newspaper was just as quick to absolve itself of any responsibility in the matter. Medical evidence, they pointed out, established beyond question that the woman had lain dead for days in that tub of ice water before her killer had added his final grisly touch.

The *News* called it a challenge to the authorities. The Carpenter was taunting the police, daring them to catch him. No doubt he blamed the police for failing to prevent the 9/11 tragedy that took his family from him, and this was his revenge.

The *Times* interviewed a forensic psychiatrist, who pointed out that the Carpenter, who had always sought anonymity in the past, had now gone public, seeking the credit for his latest murder. He had now reached the stage where he actively desired to get caught, and would no doubt behave accordingly, taking greater risks, making less effort to avoid arrest, and very likely raising the stakes by committing crimes on an increasingly grand scale.

Fran Buckram first learned of the Boerum Hill murder from a TV newscast. He went out and bought all three papers and read the coverage in each, then turned on New York One to see if there'd been any further developments. There were none, then or in the days that followed, but the story continued to get a lot of play in the media despite the lack of anything you could call news.

Different experts contributed theories and observations, and reporters polled ordinary citizens throughout the metropolitan area to get their remarkably uninformed opinions. Everyone with even a passing acquaintance with Evelyn Crispin, at the law firm where she'd worked and in her Boerum Hill neighborhood, was encouraged to offer an appraisal of the woman's character and lament her horrible death.

How had the Carpenter picked her? What was it in her life that made him choose to end it? Why, having evidently killed the woman immediately upon gaining access to her apartment, had he cohabited with her corpse for well over a week? (This had not been intended to infer, the *Times* explained the following day, that there had been any sexual contact between Ms. Crispin and Mr. Harbinger, either before or after her demise, such contact having been specifically ruled out by postmortem examination. The day after that, the paper printed a second Corrections notice, stating that the word *infer* in the previous day's follow-up should of course have been *imply*.)

Buckram, who made it his business to read everything printed on the subject, thought that they were missing the point. He had a pretty good idea how the Carpenter had selected his victim. He hung out in the neighborhood and kept his eyes open, which seemed to be something he was good at, and painstaking about. He looked for someone who lived alone, whose apartment he could go to and from without passing through a lobby. He'd picked her out for convenience, and had killed her not because her death was part of his plan (whatever his plan might be), but because he wanted her apartment.

So he could hide out in it.

You didn't need to be a Feebie profiler in a cheap suit or a Freudian with a Viennese accent to work it out. You didn't have to think like a psychopath, either. It was, as far as he could make out, pretty much a matter of common sense. The son of a bitch was so hot he was on fire, with a whole police force turning the city inside out looking for him. They'd found his bank account and frozen it, found his storage locker and cleaned it out. He had no access to money or possessions, and nowhere to sit down and think about it.

The birds of the field had their nests, but a police task force was making sure the son of a bitch had no place to lay his head. Every desk clerk in every flophouse and cheap hotel had his picture, and got frequent follow-up visits from the cops. Homeless shelters, lounges at all three New York airports, waiting rooms at Penn Station and Grand Central—all were under close police scrutiny. Transit cops checked the benches on the subway platforms and went from car to car through the trains, eyeballing the sleepers. Even the drunks and druggies sleeping it off on sidewalks, normally regarded as part of the urban landscape, got a second look these days.

So he'd found an apartment to sublet. He couldn't do it the usual New York way, by checking the ads in the *Voice* or paying a broker or bribing a super, so he'd improvised, picking out some poor lonely Eleanor Rigby type, following her home, and throttling her. He'd fed the cat because that was simpler and quieter than killing it, and he'd watered the plants—well, who knew why he'd watered the plants? Maybe he just liked plants. The ice water bath, which puzzled some analysts while others saw it as some exotic form of torture, was just the guy's way of keeping the apartment livable. The ice helped to keep the stink down.

And the nail in the forehead?

Well, that was puzzling. No getting around it, that was a poser. If it was anything other than a signature, a way to claim this death as one of his own, Buckram couldn't think what it might be. And why would he want to do that?

To play a game with the police?

He didn't think so. The man had suffered extraordinary losses. His whole family had vanished in the blink of an eye, and not in a fire, not in an auto accident, not in a train wreck or plane crash, but in the course of a deliberate attack upon the entire city. That didn't seem likely to turn a quiet gentleman, almost reclusive in his retirement, into some cackling schemer intent upon making fools of a police department. No, Harbinger had a purpose. It might not be rational, couldn't be rational, but there was probably logic to it. Not that anybody could crack the code from a distance and read the poor bastard's mind.

As far as the tabloids were concerned, he was evil. Sick, twisted. And his acts were evil, no question about it, but something in Buckram resisted the demonization of the man. He'd run across a lot of people over the years who'd done evil things, and some of them knew their deeds were evil, but others did not. The woman who smashed her daughter's skull because she was sick of changing diapers was categorically different from the man who sat on his son's chest, effectively crushing the boy to death, because that was the only way he could think of to expel the devil that made the child cough all night long. Both were criminally unfit parents, and both could be placed in a space capsule and rocketed into orbit without making the world a poorer place for their absence, but one was evil in a way that the other was not.

He wished he could figure out what the Carpenter was trying to accomplish.

Because if you could do that, maybe you could figure out what he was going to do next. And he was going to do something. The nail in the forehead, if it did nothing else, served notice that the Carpenter wasn't ready to hang up his tools.

Until then, he'd thought the man might be done. He wasn't a lifelong career psychopath, had lived an apparently blameless life until 9/11 unhinged him, and it had seemed entirely possible that the level of carnage he'd achieved in Chelsea might well have shocked him out of his madness. Buckram had half-expected the man to turn himself in, or kill himself. They might recover his body from the river, or scrape him off the subway tracks.

Or he might just stop what he was doing and disappear. The common wisdom held that pattern criminals and serial killers never stopped until they were caught or killed, that what drove them continued to drive them to the end. But he knew this wasn't always so. Sometimes the bad guys seemed to lose interest. When they'd achieved a degree of notoriety, like the Zodiac nut job in San Francisco, the speculation about them went on forever. When their tally was lower and less publicized, their retirement went unnoticed; if, say, three prostitutes are abducted one after another from truck stops in Indiana and Illinois, and found brutally murdered in Interstate highway rest areas, it's news; when it doesn't happen a fourth time, it stops being news, and people forget to wonder why the guy stopped.

They wouldn't forget about the Carpenter, but he could have stopped. He could have wiped up his fingerprints and left the hammer and nail in the hardware drawer and gone off into the night, and no one would have linked this latest killing to him. And the next time he went to ground he might have worked out a way to do it without killing anybody.

But he'd used the hammer, used the nail. He wasn't done. He had something planned, something that would dwarf the Chelsea firebombings. Buckram could think of all sorts of possibilities. The city had no end of icons—the skyscrapers, the bridges, the great statue in the harbor. Anyone could compile a list, and, after 9/11, nothing seemed off limits to madness. But what good was a list when you couldn't read the bastard's mind?

He couldn't think his way to a solution, nor could he think of anything else. He wished to God there was something he could do. He'd thought of offering his services to the cop who was running the case, but realized what an embarrassment that would be all around. Even if he did it quietly, who could avoid the assumption that he was grandstanding, positioning himself for a 2005 run at Gracie Mansion? And, if he somehow convinced everybody otherwise, what possible help could he provide? As far as he could tell, they were doing everything there was to do, and doing a reasonably good job of it in the media hothouse that was New York.

He thought of the drawing room mysteries of the twenties and thirties, with the gifted amateur sleuth who volunteered his services to the

baffled police and solved intricate murders for them. And here he was, all
set to present himself as a latter-day version of that amateur sleuth. Because that was all he was now, his professional experience notwithstanding. He was a private citizen, and nothing changed that—not the awards
and commendations boxed up in his closet, not the courtesy cards in his
wallet, not the monthly pension check he drew after twenty-plus years of
service. Not the revolver in a locked drawer in his desk, or the carry per-
mit for it.

So he sat around reading about the case, and calling old friends to
talk about it. And he thought about it, and tried to figure some useful way
he could play a lone hand, somehow out-thinking the Carpenter and
tracking him down on his own. It was an appealing fantasy, but that's all
it was. A fantasy.

Yet he stayed with it. Because, for some goddamned reason that, like
the Carpenter's scheme, he hadn't yet managed to figure out, there didn't
seem to be anything else he could do.

IT WAS THE WOMAN, of course. Susan Pomerance. Seeing her at
Stelli's, remembering her from L'Aiglon d'Or, he'd seized his opportunity and picked her up.

Right, like a moth picking up a flame.

Next thing he'd known he was spread-eagled facedown on her bed
and she was calling him by a girl's name and treating him like a girl. He
thought she was going to rip him open, thought he'd bleed to death shack-
led to her bed and hooded like a trained falcon. And then he came so hard
he thought he'd die of that.

Afterward, dismissed and sent home, he took a long shower, then
drew a hot tub and soaked in it. He tried to put the evening in some sort of
perspective, but couldn't get a handle on it, swinging back and forth between excitement and revulsion. He'd sleep on it, he decided. A lot of
things made more sense after a good night's sleep.

He wondered if he'd be able to sleep, but dropped off almost immediately and didn't stir for almost nine hours. He awoke with a sense of
having dreamed throughout the night but no recollection of any of the
dreams. He ached physically, not only where she'd penetrated him but in
muscles throughout his body that he'd tensed in unaccustomed ways. And
he winced at the memory of what he'd done, or rather of what he'd allowed to be done to him. And at the recollection of his own response.

Come see me Friday, she'd said. Yeah, right, he thought. The only
question in his mind was whether he should call and let her know he
wasn't coming or just not show up and let her figure it out for herself.
With her looks and her morals, she wouldn't have trouble finding another

partner; with her toy chest, she wouldn't be hard put getting along without one.

Maybe he'd send flowers, with a note saying he'd decided not to see
her again. *Once, a philosopher* . . . the note could say.

Would she get the reference? A professor at Colgate had loved to tell
the story. Voltaire had accepted an invitation from a friend to go to a spe-
cialized brothel—young boys, something like that. He'd gone and had a
good time, and the friend invited him again a few weeks later. Voltaire de-
clined. But you had such a good time, the friend said. *Mais oui,* said
Voltaire. Once, *un philosophe*. Twice, a pervert.

Flowers and goodbye. That would be nice, the sort of mixed message
that might even appeal to the dizzy bitch. Or, to keep it simple, he could
skip the flowers and skip the note and just never see her again. She'd get
over it, and so would he.

He checked his book, and saw that it was moot. He couldn't go Friday anyway, he had to speak at a dinner in Connecticut. That would be his
second speech of the week—he had to fly to Richmond Tuesday morning
to talk at a luncheon.

He spent the weekend at his apartment, letting the machine take his
calls. Monday morning he called the lecture bureau and said something
had come up, to cancel his appointments for the week. Both of them, the
lunch in Richmond and the dinner in Hartford. The woman he spoke to
was clearly rattled and obviously wanted him to be more specific about
his reasons for canceling, but he didn't have the energy to invent something, and she evidently couldn't bring herself to press him for a reason.

Wednesday he was supposed to get together with a writer who came
highly recommended. They were just going to have lunch and explore in
the most general fashion the possibility of their working together to de-
velop a book proposal. Tuesday he called the writer to cancel. Did he
want to reschedule? Not now, he said. He had the writer's number, he'd
call him when things cleared up a little.

Wednesday he had lunch alone at a diner in the neighborhood, then
walked in Central Park for hours, pausing now and then to sit on a bench
and stare off into space. Thursday he went to the gym, gave up on the
treadmill after five minutes, gave up on the weight machines halfway
through his cycle. Sat in the steam room for longer than he should have,
and was dizzy and dehydrated when he got out of there. Went home,
drank a whole bottle of Evian water, and went to bed.

Friday he picked up the phone to call her and tell her he wasn't coming. He had her number at the gallery and dialed six of the seven digits,
then hung up. Picked up the phone again, dialed three digits, quit.

Jesus.

At eight that night he gave his name to her doorman, praying that she wouldn't be home. The doorman called upstairs, then nodded to him and pointed to the elevator. He knocked on her door and she called out that it was open.

He went in. There was no one in the living room. He walked on through to the bedroom and found her dressed in a black leather garter belt and black mesh stockings and high-heeled black shoes. Nothing else. The outfit should have looked absurd, but didn't.

"Hi, Franny," she said, almost gently. And smiled.

"Susan."

"No, don't talk. The hood will come later, but for now I don't want you to speak. Do you understand?"

He nodded. She was crazy, he thought, and he was crazy to be here, he ought to leave right now. And he was getting a hard-on, and who the hell was he kidding? He wasn't going anyplace.

"I waxed myself, Franny." She touched herself, showing him. "It was starting to grow back, so I took care of it. You use hot wax, you pour it on and let it cool and rip it off. It's painful, and very erotic. But it's pretty." She held herself open for his inspection, asked him if he didn't think it was pretty. He nodded, and she told him to get undressed.

"Look at you, Franny, you're hard as a rock. What's a sweet little girl like you doing with such a gorgeous cock? One of these times I'm going to wax you. Everything, your chest, your armpits, your cock and balls and ass. Everything. You'll be so silky smooth everywhere, and you'll wear silk underwear and you'll be hard all the time. Get on your knees, Franny. I'm all sensitive from the waxing and I want you to lick me. I want you to make me come."

When she sent him home later that night he felt at once gloriously alive and determined he would never see her again. He went home and had another night full of unremembered dreams, waking with a furious erection and a strong urge to relieve himself, which he resisted.

Sunday night he had a sandwich and a beer at a good deli, and around eleven he went over to Stelli's for a drink. He joined some friends at a table but hardly said a word, and didn't stay long. Early night, Stelli told him on the way out. Big day tomorrow, he said.

But all he did the next day was read the papers and watch TV news. Tuesday after breakfast he called his lecture bureau and told them to cancel all his scheduled engagements and not make any future bookings for him. He wasn't surprised when the phone rang ten minutes later and it was the head of the bureau, demanding to know what was the matter. Was he disappointed with their service? Was he going with a competitor? And, even if he was, didn't he realize he had to honor the bookings they'd made for him?

He said it wasn't that, he'd lost his taste for public speaking, he just couldn't do it anymore. He fended off further questions, and noted that she didn't close by telling him to give her a call if he changed his mind.

When he got off the phone he went through his book and canceled everything but a dentist appointment. Then he got out of the house and went for a walk in the park.

Friday he was back at London Towers. This time she hooded him immediately, pinned him on his back on the bed, and kept him on the edge of climax for an eternity. Finally she told him she was going to apply heat, that he might think it was going to burn him, but that it would not do him any damage. Then he felt something red-hot pressed against the base of his scrotum, then jabbed into his rectum. He smelled burning hair and thought he was going to die.

After a long moment the sensation changed, and he realized it wasn't hot at all, it was cold, and that she'd rubbed him with an ice cube that even now was melting inside him. He lay there while his breathing returned to normal and she gentled him with a hand on his chest and abdomen, stroking him lightly, calming him down.

What he'd smelled, she told him, was a feather from her pillow, held in the flame of a candle. For verisimilitude, she said. Her lips touched the base of his scrotum, where she'd first touched him with the ice cube.

Next time, she said softly, you'll be expecting ice. And you'll get fire.

THE FOLLOWING AFTERNOON, SATURDAY, he looked up a number and called a woman he hadn't seen in several months. Her name was Arlene Szigeti, and she worked at Carnegie Hall, in the Planned Giving division. Her job was to convince rich people of the value of making substantial bequests to the organization in their wills. She would take prospects to dinner and a concert, making them feel like members of an exclusive club. "I go out several nights a week with people a great deal more well off than you," she'd told him once, "but you're different. You pick up the check."

"Fran," she said. "Well, it's been a while."

"Too long," he said. "Are you free for dinner Wednesday?"

She had plans Wednesday, but Tuesday was open. Maybe a show first, he suggested, and dinner afterward. They agreed on a couple of plays neither of them had seen, and he got good orchestra seats to their first choice. She met him at the theater, looking even lovelier than he remembered. She was in her midforties, with fine-spun blond hair and elegant features. Her father, a Hungarian with ties to the Esterhazy family, had come over after the 1956 revolution, her mother's parents were Jewish refugees who got out of Germany just in time.

After the play they had a light supper down the street at Joe Allen's, then walked to her apartment on Fifty-fifth Street, five minutes away from her office. It was a foregone conclusion that they would go to bed— they always did—and that the relationship would not lead to anything. They enjoyed each other's company, in and out of bed, but the emotional chemistry wasn't there.

In her apartment she offered drinks and he said he was fine, and she came into his arms and they kissed.

He still hadn't kissed Susan.

In bed, his passion for her was stronger than it had ever been, and she was an apt and eager partner. At the end she lay with her head in the crook of his arm and her hand cupping his groin.

"Whew," she said. "If I knew you were that hot, we could have skipped dinner."

"Just so we had our dessert at home."

FRIDAY NIGHT HE WAS at Susan's again, naked, bound. "Now," she said, "tell me all about your date."

The previous week, just before he left, she'd asked him if he was sleeping with anyone else besides her. He said, "Sleeping? When did we ever sleep together?" Fucking, she said. Was he fucking anybody?

Not lately, he'd said, and she said that was no good. She was fucking other people, and he should do the same. During the coming week, she said, she wanted him to call some woman and go to bed with her. She expected a full report on Friday.

"But not on Thursday," she'd told him at the door. "I want you fully recovered."

Recounting the evening with Arlene, he realized that part of the excitement he'd felt with her came from knowing he'd be reporting in detail to Susan.

She listened intently and asked questions throughout. She wanted a full description of Arlene's body, wanted to know just what he'd done and how he felt. When he was done she told him he deserved a reward, and she got out her kit of wax and cheesecloth. She trimmed his hair with a scissors, waxed his chest and underarms and groin, then rolled him over and did his backside.

The wax was hot, but not too hot to bear. The removal of the hair was painful, but also bearable. When she'd finished she made him touch himself and sat cross-legged while he stroked himself.

When he was close to climax she moved his hands away and took him in her mouth, then climbed onto him and kissed him full on the mouth, giving him his seed, commanding him to swallow it.

"Oh, Franny," she said. "Our first kiss. Isn't it romantic?"

HE WOULD SEE HER again this Friday, and every Friday. He no longer entertained the notion of giving her up. He was, he supposed, enslaved, and it might be said that their relationship gave new meaning to the term *pussy-whipped*. He didn't care. It didn't seem to matter.

Once she'd asked him if it was true that he'd never been with a whore. Not until this summer, he said.

I'm not a whore, she said, and he said he hadn't meant it as an insult. She said she hadn't taken it for an insult, but that it was inaccurate. He said he knew that, that she didn't take money, that he hadn't meant it that way, but she cut off his explanation. She wasn't talking about money, she said. Money aside, didn't he know what a whore was?

A whore, she told him, would do anything he liked. She was entirely different. She would do things he didn't like, and make him like them.

HE DIDN'T CALL ARLENE again, or any of several other women who might have been available to play a similar role. Even if he'd been interested, the thought of trying to explain his sudden lack of body hair was daunting.

When he went to the gym, he skipped the steam and sauna, waited until he got home to take his shower. He didn't like the idea of anyone seeing him like this, and yet he was not entirely sorry she'd done it. He liked the smoothness of his skin, its sensitivity. And, while he didn't want to expose his hairlessness, when he walked about with clothes on he felt like a man with a delicious secret.

It was strange, all of this, and he didn't know what to make of it. He'd always taken it for granted that he knew who he was, and she kept showing him a side of himself the existence of which he hadn't even suspected. She couldn't have created this dark side, it would have to have been there all along, and he supposed it was better to know about it than not.

Or was it? William Boyce Harbinger (did his wife call him Bill? had his mother called him Billy?) must have had an unsuspected dark side of his own, forever hidden from view until the towers fell and shined an awful light on it. Harbinger, reborn as the Carpenter, must have been astonished by the acts he was capable of performing. Could anyone argue he was better off for it?

He kept coming back to the man, because he could think of nothing else besides his weekly descent into—into what? Depravity? Madness? His own unplumbed depths?

Better to think about the Carpenter. Maybe, somehow, he'd come up with a way to catch him.

twenty-four

THE CARPENTER SAT on a bench in Riverside Park, not far from the Rotunda, and the Boat Basin Café. It was getting on for midnight. The café was closed, and a light rain an hour earlier had cleared the park of the few walkers and sitters who'd shared it with him. The Carpenter didn't mind the rain. He scarcely noticed it.

From where he sat, he could keep an eye on one of his city's greatest anomalies, the Seventy-ninth Street Boat Basin. This little complex of docks and piers at the Hudson's edge allowed a favored few New Yorkers the privilege of mooring their boats there for an essentially negligible annual fee. Anyone who had a slip at the Boat Basin clung to it as if it were a rent-controlled apartment, and in fact it was that and more. If you were a boater, it afforded you economical dockage far more convenient than marinas like the one at City Island, way up in the remote northeastern region of the Bronx. But most of the boats moored at Seventy-ninth Street never left their slips, and many of them didn't even have working engines, running their lights and appliances off propane generators. They were houseboats, with the stress very much on the first syllable, and their lucky occupants were able to live a raffish Bohemian life in wave-rocked comfort for considerably less than it would have cost them to park a car anywhere in Manhattan.

The great wonder in the Carpenter's mind was that it had taken him this long to think of it. What better place to pass unnoticed than in a derelict boat on the Hudson? His own apartment was ten minutes away, and he knew the Boat Basin well enough. Once, when his children were young, he'd had fantasies of keeping a boat there. It would have been pleasant to take them all boating on a summer afternoon, then walk on home through the twilight . . .

He'd been coming to the park now for several nights, keeping out of the way of the occasional cop on patrol, always choosing a bench out of the reach of the streetlights. Now and then, in the hours between midnight and dawn, he'd go for a closer look at the dark and silent vessels.

The Basin dwellers, he knew, were a close-knit group, in the manner of a gathering of outcasts. They respected one another's privacy but stood united against a common enemy—i.e., the real estate interests and municipal authorities who periodically conspired to get rid of them. It wouldn't do, he knew, to take over the home of some gregarious houseboater, some pillar of the floating community.

Better to supplant a part-time resident, to slip like a hermit crab into the empty shell of a pleasure boater with an apartment somewhere else. And that way he'd be assured of a seaworthy vessel, one he could take out onto the water if he wished.

So he waited, looking for an opportunity. And he was watching patiently that evening when a boat pulled in and docked. It was a nice-looking one; he'd seen it the night before, noticed earlier this evening that it was not at its slip. He'd seen fishing poles on hooks above the cabin, and supposed the fellow had gone out for a night's fishing, or just to get out on the water and look up at the stars.

The lights went out, the engines ceased to throb. A man, wearing a brass-buttoned blazer and a Greek fisherman's cap, walked from the pier and headed east through the park.

The Carpenter followed him.

OVER THE NEXT THREE days the Carpenter learned that the man's name was Peter Shevlin and that he lived in one of the fine prewar apartment buildings on West Eighty-sixth Street between Columbus and Amsterdam. The lobby was attended around the clock, and the Carpenter never even considered entering it.

Shevlin worked in a high-rise office building on Sixth Avenue in the Fifties, and rode to and from his office on the subway. He seemed to live alone, and to spend much of his time alone. One evening he stopped on his walk from the subway to pick up dinner for one at a taco stand on Broadway, and that reinforced the Carpenter's conviction that he did not share his apartment with a wife or lover.

Years ago he'd been inside Shevlin's building, and knew the apartments there were all quite sizable. He guessed that Shevlin was widowed; if he'd been divorced, his wife would very likely have wound up with the apartment, and Shevlin would be sleeping on his boat, if indeed the courts didn't take that away from him as well. And he was of an age to be a widower. He was, the Carpenter realized, about his own age, and it struck him—for the first time, oddly—that the two of them were not that far apart in appearance. If you stood them side by side they'd look entirely different, but they were about the same height, and similarly built, they both had gray hair, and to describe one was to describe the other.

It was, he thought, as if the man had been sent to him. Another widower, a man who lived just two blocks from the Carpenter's old apartment. A man who'd lived the Carpenter's dream, owning a boat and mooring it at Seventy-ninth Street. A man ready for sacrifice.

The Carpenter slept during the day, turning up at one of the multiplex movie houses in time for the first show of the day. He took the senior discount, bought popcorn, and went into one of the theaters. The clerks were all young people working for minimum wage, and they hardly even looked at their patrons. The Carpenter, his head lowered, his shoulders drooping with age, never got a second glance.

He'd go to a theater, breakfast on popcorn, and doze off, sleeping lightly, and always waking up when the feature presentation ended. When he was a boy you could go to the movies and sit there all day, you could watch a double feature three times over if you were so inclined, but now they had lengthy intermissions between showings and you had to leave when the picture was over.

But there were eight or ten or a dozen or more screens under a single roof, and what was to prevent you from going from one to another? It was illegal, your ticket only entitled you to a single performance of a single film, but on weekday afternoons none of the films played to as much as a quarter of capacity, and often he was one of a half dozen patrons making up the showing's total audience. Why waste an attendant's time to keep a lonely retiree from double-dipping?

The Carpenter got plenty of sleep. Sometimes, when he couldn't sleep anymore, he watched the movie.

AFTER THREE DAYS OF movies and as many nights of following his quarry, the Carpenter tailed Peter Shevlin from the Eighty-sixth Street IRT station to a Vietnamese restaurant on Broadway, where he ordered a take-out dinner. Instead of heading for his apartment, he continued downtown on Broadway. He crossed Broadway at Eighty-fourth Street, which a street sign designated Edgar Allan Poe Street, then turned right and walked west to Riverside Drive. Flights of steps led down to an underpass, and the Carpenter followed him through it to the strip of park edging the Hudson.

The Carpenter waited in the park while the man boarded his boat, waited while the boat sat at anchor long enough for Shevlin to eat his dinner, and remained where he was when Shevlin cast off and took the boat out onto the river.

He wished it would rain. Rain would bring Shevlin back sooner, and would clear the park of other pairs of eyes.

But the good weather held, and the Carpenter got to see the sun set behind the buildings on the Jersey shore. It was past eleven by the time Shevlin's boat returned, and by then the Carpenter had picked his spot and was waiting. He'd reached into his navy-blue backpack—its load had increased in the past few days, with purchases he'd found it advisable to make—and he drew out a steel tire iron he'd picked up at an auto supply store on Eleventh Avenue. He'd have preferred a hammer, but suspected that hardware clerks were looking closely at older men who came in to buy hammers.

Shevlin passed without seeing him in the shadows. He stepped out, said, "Mr. Shevlin?"

The man turned at the sound of his name, and the Carpenter pointed to the ground and said, "You dropped something." Shevlin lowered his head, tried to see what he might have dropped, and the Carpenter stepped forward quickly and struck him full force with the tire iron, catching him just behind the ear. Shevlin dropped like a felled ox, and the Carpenter hit him again at the back of the neck, then grabbed him and dragged him into the bushes.

He checked for a pulse and wasn't surprised when he failed to detect one. Just to make sure, he clapped a hand over Shevlin's mouth and pinched the man's nostrils shut, and stayed like that for several minutes. If Shevlin hadn't been dead from the blows, he was surely dead now.

The park was deserted, but it was still too early for what the Carpenter had to do. First he returned the tire iron to his backpack, pleased with the way it had performed. Then he wrapped Shevlin in a pair of black plastic lawn and leaf bags, tucking his legs into one, pulling the other down over his head. Anyone noticing him now would see a trash bag, or perhaps some plastic mulch for the shrubbery, rather than human remains.

When he was satisfied with his work, the Carpenter found a bench from which he would be able to tell if anyone discovered the body. No one came any closer to it than the joggers who breezed by every now and then, and they were far too intent on their efforts to notice some dark form twenty yards away.

At two-thirty in the morning, when twenty minutes had passed without a single human being coming into that part of the park, the Carpenter resumed his labors. He stripped off all of Shevlin's clothing, filling one of the leaf bags with his jacket and trousers, shirt and socks and shoes and underwear. He removed his watch, but couldn't get his wedding ring off his finger, and decided it didn't matter.

He'd bought a boning knife and a saw at a restaurant supply house on the Bowery, and he used them to dismember Shevlin's corpse, cutting the man into manageable-size portions. The work was distasteful, but the Carpenter was not overly surprised to discover that it didn't bother him. It was a job, and he performed it as quickly and efficiently as possible, inserting each severed portion of the man into a plastic bag, securing the bag with tape, and setting it aside while he tackled the next part of the job.

Earlier, he'd located a Dumpster on Seventy-seventh between West End and Riverside Drive. He walked there carrying a taped-up plastic bag in each hand; each contained one of the man's thighs. He placed the packages in the Dumpster, which was full of what looked to be the debris from the gut rehab of a brownstone. He buried his packages under some broken bricks and loose plaster.

He put some of the smaller parcels in garbage cans, and walked all the way to Broadway to empty the bag of clothing into the Pembroke Thrift Shop's 24-hour collection box. The final two parcels went into his backpack. A key from Shevlin's key ring got him through the gate to the Boat Basin, and another admitted him to the boat's sleeping quarters.

He took off his shoes, stretched out on the bunk. The cabin was tiny, but he found it cozy, and quite comfortable. He wouldn't sleep, he'd had plenty of sleep earlier at the Lincoln Plaza multiplex, but it was pleasant to stretch out and feel the gentle rocking motion of the anchored boat.

There were things he would have to do. Shevlin's hands and head would have to be disposed of properly. He didn't care if someone found the other body parts, although it would be fine with him, and not all that unlikely, if they escaped detection and spent eternity in a landfill. But it didn't matter, really, if the city discovered that one more of its residents had died. His sole interest lay in keeping them from knowing to whom the various body parts had once belonged.

Fingerprints and dental records made the hands and head considerably more identifiable than the rest of the man. He could knock out the teeth, toss them in the river. Weight the toothless skull and sink it somewhere. Slice the flesh from the palms and the tips of the fingers before disposing of the hands.

A call to Shevlin's office would keep his absence from setting off any alarms. If someone did miss him and got the doorman to check his apartment, they'd find nothing suspicious within. He didn't think anyone would think to check the boat, certainly not for a while.

And he only needed it for a while.

The motion of the boat was restful, even hypnotic. He dozed off and slept for a little while, then woke up and stayed where he was, enjoying the gentle rocking motion, enjoying the tight quarters, enjoying everything about his new home.

He felt wonderfully at peace.

twenty-five

THE CALLER, WHO'D given his name as if she ought to recognize it, had a straightforward request. Would she, as a gallery owner in Chelsea, be willing to donate a piece of art to be auctioned for the benefit of Chelsea Remembers?

What, she wondered, was that? It couldn't be the first thing that came to mind, which was a memoir by an ex-president's daughter. But what the hell was it?

She confessed to an unfamiliarity with the cause, and the caller explained that Chelsea Remembers was an organization formed to raise funds for a memorial to the neighborhood residents, male and female, gay and straight, who had lost their lives in the Carpenter's savage firebombing spree.

She said, "A memorial? Like a statue?"

"There's been no decision yet as to what form the memorial might take. A statue is certainly a possibility, but there have been suggestions ranging from special streetlights in front of the three sites to an annual release of doves."

Ravens, she thought, would better suit the men who'd perished at Death Row. Ravens with just a touch of polish on their talons.

Just say yes, it's a worthy cause, I'd love to help, she told herself. But something made her say, "Maybe I'm missing something. What's the point, exactly?"

"The point?"

"I mean, do we have to throw up a monument every time somebody steps in front of a bus? How much bad public sculpture does a city need? I mean—"

The voice turned to ice. "Miss Pomerance, our small community lost

eighty-seven members in one utterly horrific hour. The lucky ones were
burned to death at once. The others spent hours or days in agony and then
died. Still others recovered, and after a few years of skin grafts some of
them may actually look halfway human. The point, if you will, would
seem to be implicit in the organization's name. The point is that Chelsea
remembers."

"I—"

But he hadn't finished. "We can only show our remembrance by doing something. Few of the victims had dependents, so aiding the families
of the victims would indeed be pointless. Many were estranged from their
families, if they had families at all. This neighborhood was their family,
Miss Pomerance, and some memorial, some bad and surely unnecessary
piece of public sculpture, would seem to some of us to be a good deal better than nothing."

"I am terribly sorry," she said. "Please tell me your name again."

"It's Harwood Zeller."

Oh, God, she did know who he was. He owned several buildings on
Ninth Avenue, and operated a restaurant in one of them and an antique
shop in another.

"I have to apologize," she told him. "I don't know what got into me.
Actually I do, I just got off the phone with my mother, and—"

"Say no more. When I get off the phone with *my* mother, I'm apt to
bite people."

"You're very gracious, and of course I'll want to contribute something."

She got the particulars, made notes, and by the time she got off the
phone they were on Woody and Susan terms. She pushed back her chair
and tried to figure out what her misplaced burst of candor was going to
cost her. If she'd just said yes in the first place she could have made them
perfectly happy with one of her mistakes, perhaps a Lynah Throp water-
color. She had a dozen of them moldering in her storage bin, bold primi-
tives of fanciful animals that had impressed her on first sight and had
never impressed anyone else, not even a little. She'd never sell them—
she'd never display them again, so how could she?—and the chance to
unload one and get a tax deduction in the balance was a godsend.

But now she had to give them something decent, something that was
certain to bring upwards of a hundred dollars at an auction where most of
the bidders wouldn't pay thirty-five cents to see Christ ride a bicycle.

Hell.

Well, it was her own damn fault. She'd think of something.

HER MOTHER HAD DIED almost five years ago, and she offered up a
silent apology at having taken her name in vain. It had seemed like the

perfect excuse to turn aside the wrath of a pissy little queen like Harwood Zeller, and she had to say it had worked like a charm. But if she'd had any sense she'd never have needed it in the first place.

The real reason for her pique, and one she thought Zeller might well have understood, was even more clichéd. She'd been waiting for a phone call from a man, and it never came.

Her obsession with John Blair Creighton hadn't ended when she'd run out of books to read. She emerged from his work with the conviction that she knew the man, that they were mated on some sort of psychic level. In Stelli's, even as she'd apologized for intruding, she'd sent him a message with her eyes, and she knew he'd received it. He'd liked her looks, he'd responded to her, he'd taken the card she'd handed him—and then nothing. He hadn't called.

And wouldn't, now. Weeks had passed, and he'd have called in the first few days if he was going to call at all.

She could send him an announcement for Emory Allgood's show, an invitation to the opening. She could add a handwritten note urging him to come. But he probably got a steady stream of those, like everybody else in Manhattan with a vague interest in or connection to the arts, and would probably discard it without even recognizing her name. Or he'd make a face, thinking *Here's a dame with a lot of crust, first she interrupts my meal, and now she wants to sell me some junk sculpture.*

Besides, that wasn't until November. Why did she have to wait that long?

On the nights when she was alone, she'd developed a ritual that she recognized as pathological even as she found it irresistible. She would bathe, and perfume herself. She'd had enlarged photos made from her two favorite dust jacket pictures of him, one taken outside Village Cigars on Sheridan Square, where he looked marvelously butch in a denim jacket and boots and a beard, the other a studio shot twenty years old, a portrait of the author as a young man, fresh-faced and innocent. These she placed on her bedside table, and lit the little lamp so she could see them.

Then she would touch herself while her mind occupied itself with the fantasy she had selected during her bath. Sometimes it was simple enough—she was Susan and he was John, and they loved with a love that was more than love, di dah di dah di dah.

Other times she became one or another of the female characters in his books, and played out scenes that departed from those he'd written, until she and her partner du jour were drawn into a maelstrom of passion.

More than once she was Marilyn Fairchild, with her auburn hair and her hot throaty voice, meeting him in a dingy Village bar and taking him home to her apartment. In that fantasy the two of them made fitful, angry love, moving from one position to another, snarling at each other while their bodies thrust away. At the end she lay writhing on her bed, a butt plug in her ass and the largest dildo deep in her cunt, while she strummed her clit with one hand and gripped her throat hard with the other.

That scared her, the first time she did it. Because in the fantasy it was two hands, not one, and his hands, not hers, and his grip didn't loosen with her orgasm. She was imagining herself dying at his hands, and the notion evidently thrilled her.

But it was just a fantasy. It wasn't really anything to worry about, was it?

IT WASN'T AS IF she lacked for sexual outlets. Nor was her growing fascination with Creighton taking the joy out of her real encounters with real people. If her initial experiments had been designed in part to empower her sexually, then she'd succeeded beyond her wildest dreams. She seemed to grow more powerful every day, able to get almost anyone to do almost anything.

She remembered what she'd said to Franny, drawing a distinction between her own acts and whoring. She didn't do what people liked. She did what they very definitely didn't like, or at least didn't know they liked, and made them like it.

Had Franny ever dreamed he'd like being treated like a girl, his body smooth and hairless, his flesh perfumed with scented oils? Every Friday night she took him to places he'd never been and showed him parts of himself he'd never imagined.

The other night she curled up beside him and sucked on his nipple, her cupped hands fashioning a breast from the surrounding flesh. *All smooth and hairless like a girl,* she'd murmured. *Franny, wouldn't it be nice if you got hormone shots? You could grow tits, Franny. I could take off your bra and suck your titties.*

Franny the tranny, she thought, knowing that in fact it would never go that far. He wouldn't go out looking for a sex-change doctor, and she didn't think she'd really like it if he did. She liked his manly chest, his firm pectoral muscles. But her words would stay with him, and he'd grow breasts in his mind, and when she stroked his chest and sucked his nipples he'd respond as urgently as if he did have breasts.

No reason she couldn't get him to have his nipples pierced. She'd send him to Medea—no, she'd *take* him to Medea. She hadn't gone back herself, wasn't so sure she wanted labial rings after all, but if she took Franny, and hooked him up to that St. Andrew's cross of hers, and if she could blow him while Medea did the piercing, at least for the first one, and then if she could talk Medea into letting her do the second, urging the needle through the stiffened flesh . . .

HER THREESOME WITH JAY McGann and Lowell Cooke was going through interesting changes. Lowell, the loser in a who-comes-last contest (which could be as easily viewed, she thought, as a victory of her left hand over her right hand) had been a good sport, giving his promising young author what he'd previously only given him metaphorically. She'd rubbed against him while he performed the act, murmuring encouragement, adding a caress or two of her own to his.

Now, several weeks later, any inhibition they'd had about inadvertent contact was long gone, and their hands were as apt to be on each other as on her. The sandwich remained their finale, and it never ceased to thrill her, having one at her back and one at her front, being impaled fore and aft. She sensed, though, that it wouldn't be long before she now and then yielded her central role, and took a turn as one of the pieces of bread.

Meanwhile she was still the meat in the sandwich. Or, as one of them had told her, *You're in the middle, fucking a writer and a publisher simultaneously. You know what that makes you, Susan? The agent!*

THE ALLGOOD SHOW WAS shaping up. She'd hired a small van and picked up the artist's new work, four of the five pieces he'd made since her earlier visit. He kept one, managing to communicate that he was not sure it was finished, but beamed happily as the rest were carried off.

Lois Appling photographed the new pieces, although they wouldn't be in the brochure, or in the show itself. They'd be held in reserve, for private sale to select customers after the sold-out show was down, or as a start toward her next show sometime a year or two down the line. And she sent Lois out to Brooklyn to photograph the artist. Lois normally worked in her studio, but understood that this particular artist was too nuts to come into Manhattan to have his picture taken. She brought back some good shots of the man at work, capturing not only his eccentricity but also his passion.

With all that done, she'd decided there was no need to deny herself. She got Reginald Barron to come into the city, met him for a drink at Chelsea Commons, took him on a walking tour to show him where the Carpenter had thrown his firebombs, and brought him up to her apartment and fucked the daylights out of him.

He was, as she'd anticipated, a beautiful boy, with a classical physique and a beautiful penis. His skin was like velvet, and his abiding innocence was delicious. He was not without experience—how could he be, looking the way he did?—but it was clear that she was something new to him, worldly and sophisticated, a woman his mother's age with a girl's hairless body.

For all of that, there was something oddly disappointing in the experience. She knew that she could enmesh him in an affair, that she could lead him across new frontiers as she led the others, but she knew that wasn't something she wanted to do. Afterward, when he came out of the shower, she brought him a glass of iced tea and told him she certainly hadn't planned for this to happen, but that she was just as glad that it did. It was a barrier they'd had to cross once to ensure a smooth working relationship, she told him, and he nodded thoughtfully, as if the gibberish she was spouting made perfect sense. And it had been lovely, she went on, but now there'd be no need for them to do this again. In fact, she stressed, it was important that they *not* do it again.

He nodded again, told her he supposed she was right. And, if he was a little disappointed, it was clear to her that he was also more than a little relieved. If he'd been just a few years older, she thought, he'd have known to keep the relief from showing.

She felt a similar admixture of disappointment and relief when he was out the door. Part of what bothered her was that she'd planned on waiting until after the November show. She'd jumped the gun by three months, and for no good reason beyond libidinous curiosity. She wasn't lacking for lovers, nor had she been driven by a particularly urgent yen for Reginald.

It took her a while, but she figured out what it was. She had an itch, and couldn't reach to scratch it, so she'd scratched somewhere else, where it didn't itch.

The itch was Creighton, and she couldn't have him. So she'd used this boy, in a way that had proved pleasurable but unsatisfying for them both, and now he was gone, and she felt worse than when she'd started.

She bathed, put on a robe, turned on the television set. The news was bad, the way it always was. She switched channels, and landed in the middle of some special on terrorism, just in time for them to show her for the thousandth time the plane striking the tower, and the burst of yellow flame shooting out the other side.

"What's the difference?" she said aloud. "What does it matter what anybody does? We're all going to die."

AFTER HER UNFORTUNATE (not to say costly) conversation with Harwood Zeller, after she'd called three different people to arrange a lunch date and found them all otherwise engaged, she skipped lunch and took a class at Integral Yoga, thinking it would calm her down. As far as she could tell, it had no effect whatsoever.

So she returned to the gallery and seduced Chloe.

At least that was what she thought she was doing. But it played out a little differently than she'd planned.

She'd waited until the gallery was empty, then surreptitiously locked the door. She went over and sat on the edge of Chloe's desk, swinging her leg, and asked the girl if she'd had any more piercings since she'd gone to Medea.

"Well, I got the other nipple done," Chloe said. "Want to see?"

They went into the back office, and Chloe cheerfully bared her breasts, and there was a stud in each, and how large and well formed they were.

"I went to Medea myself," she said, and Chloe said No, really? You're kidding me, right? In response she'd unbuttoned her own blouse, unclasped her bra, and held her breasts in the palms of her hands, offering them for inspection.

"Oh, they're beautiful, Susan!"

"Tiny, compared to yours."

"Oh, I'm a cow. Yours are so pretty."

Could anything really be this easy? "I have something else to show you," she said, and quickly got out of her slacks, removing her panties in the same motion.

Chloe gaped, reached out a hand, touched. With her other hand she grabbed Susan behind the head and kissed her full on the mouth. Below, the girl's fingers were busy.

"We can go to my apartment," she managed to say.

"First we're each gonna get off," Chloe said, "and then we'll go to your apartment."

So it was by no means clear who had seduced whom. Chloe, it turned out, had had plenty of experience with women, and had originally shown Susan her breasts not out of sheer exhibitionism but in the hope it might lead somewhere. "But you were so cool," Chloe said, "I just figured you were straight as a gate. So I let it alone."

At one point, lying on top of Chloe, tasting her own sex on Chloe's mouth, her own breasts cushioned by Chloe's breasts, she fitted her hands lightly around the girl's neck, lacing her fingers, putting her thumbs together.

She thought, What are you doing? Stop it!

NOT THE NEXT DAY or the day after, she left the gallery and walked down to the Village. Like some demented stalker, she went first to Charles Street, where she stood gaping at the brownstone where Marilyn Fairchild had lived and died, and then to Bank Street, where John Blair

Creighton was presumably hard at work on the book that would make him rich.

She got lost looking for the Kettle of Fish, but found it, and went in and had a glass of white wine, hoping he'd walk in. He didn't, and it was hard to see why anybody would. A collection of drunks and losers, she thought, with most of them able to claim membership in both groups. She finished her wine, fended off the halfhearted overtures of a man with the emptiest eyes she'd ever seen, and went home.

His number was in the book. That was how she'd found his address. She dialed his number and it rang and his machine picked up. She heard the message all the way through before ringing off.

She'd done this before. It was a way to hear his voice. But she wasn't about to leave a message. What could she say?

There had to be some way to get him to call her, some way to get past the velvet rope and into his life. That was all she needed. If she was right in what she sensed, he'd be drawn to her as fiercely as she was to him. If not, that would be almost as good; she'd get over her obsession and be free to live her life.

All she had to do was get one small foot in the door. But how?

In the morning, when the answer came to her, she couldn't believe it had taken her so long to think of it.

SHE GAVE HER NAME to the receptionist, and seconds later Maury Winters was on the line. "Your jury duty's not until October," he said, "and yes, you can get out of it. All you have to do is move to Australia."

"They've got all these poisonous spiders there."

"Spiders? I thought kangaroos."

"Kangaroos I wouldn't mind. Spiders I can live without."

"What's your source for these spiders that I never until this minute heard about?"

"The Discovery Channel."

"If they say spiders," he said, "there's spiders. Don't move to Australia. Go do your civic duty. Three days and you're done."

"That's not what I called about, Maury."

"It figures."

"I'm interested in one of your clients."

"I've got dozens of clients," he said, "and believe me, you're not interested in any of them. And if they were interested in you, you know what I'd tell you? Go to Australia. Spiders, schmiders, go to Australia."

"John Creighton," she said.

"Oh, him," he said. "The gambler."

"Does he have a gambling jones? I didn't know that. Because there's no hint of it in his books."

"As far as I personally know," he said, "he couldn't tell you if a straight beats a flush. No, this is a different kind of gambling. The DA's office offered him an easy out. Plead to involuntary manslaughter, do no time, case closed. He turned them down."

"He wouldn't have to go to prison? Is he crazy? Why did he turn it down?"

It made sense when he explained it. By taking the plea, he'd be stating for the record that he'd killed Marilyn Fairchild. He couldn't take the deal and go on maintaining his innocence.

"My opinion," he said, "it's a good gamble. Odds are they'll drop the charges if he doesn't take a plea and give them an out. Everybody'd be just as happy to put this one on the Carpenter's tab, and there's a lot of circumstantial *chazerai* to support it. The connection with Pankow, the kid who cleaned all three bars and the whorehouse, and also cleaned for Fairchild and discovered her body. Cleaned the whole apartment first, incidentally, which is why they didn't find any of the bastard's fingerprints there. One print in that apartment and they'd drop all charges and shake his hand in public."

"That's what it would take?"

"To make this go away? That, or a couple good sightings of the son of a bitch in the right place at the right time. I let my detective go, he couldn't come up with anything, but he tried. Went to the bar, the Fish Kettle, showed the picture, like they haven't all seen the schmuck's picture a thousand times already. There are plenty of people who think they saw him in the Village, but nobody can put him in the bar."

"But you think they'll drop the charges anyway."

"I think so, and if we have to go to trial I think we'll get a Not Guilty, but it's still a gamble. Now I've got a question. Why the hell do you care?"

"I want to meet him."

"You want to meet him. Creighton? Or the Carpenter?"

"God forbid. Creighton, of course."

"You said you read his books."

"All of them."

"They any good?"

"You haven't read them yourself?"

"I'm his attorney, not his editor. What does he need me to read his books? Are they any good?"

"They're excellent."

"I'm relieved to hear that. Maybe he'll be able to pay my fee."

"You must know about—"

"About the contract he signed, yes, of course I know about it. He'll be a rich man, which makes it that much more of a gamble. Most prisons, they don't let you take your computer with you. Some of 'em they don't even give you a pencil. Why do you want to meet him?"

"Actually," she said, "I did meet him. He was at a table at Stelli's last month and I went over and introduced myself. I gave him my card, said I'd like for him to call me."

"And he didn't."

"No."

"And you could call him, but how would that look?"

"Exactly."

"Susan, what? You read his books and you fell in love with him?"

"Maybe."

"Are you serious?"

"I don't know."

"So I call him and tell him what? Here's this girl, take her to a restaurant and you'll get a nice surprise."

"You can tell him that if you want."

"I can tell him anything, just so he calls you."

"Yes."

He was silent for a moment. Then he said, "Susan, he swears he never killed nobody, and he's my client, so of course he's telling God's own truth. But just between you and me, and the fact notwithstanding that nobody's gonna prove this in court, it's entirely possible he killed that woman."

"He didn't kill her, Maury."

"You know this because you read his books."

"Yes."

"If it goes to trial," he said, "I'll subpoena you, and you can read these wonderful books to the jury. I'd ask you if you know what you're doing, but the answer is you don't, and that's beside the point, isn't it?"

"Yes."

"I'll make the call, and I won't ask him to call you, I'll tell him to call you. And you'll owe me, which would mean I'd take you out for a nice dinner, but how can I do that if you're in love?"

"I could never be too much in love for that," she said. "And Maury? You don't have to take me to dinner, either."

"All I have to do is whistle, huh? But you're not old enough to remember that movie. I'll call him right now. You're at the gallery?"

"I'm home, I didn't go in yet."

"Stay by the phone. I'll make sure he calls."

twenty-six

SHE WAS BEAUTIFUL, and he'd almost let her get away.

He'd called her the minute he got off the phone with Maury. The conversation had been stilted, it could hardly have been otherwise, but it got them here, in the rear garden of Caffè Sha Sha, an Italian coffeehouse on Hudson. He'd suggested the place, then couldn't remember exactly which block it was on, between Christopher and Tenth or Tenth and Charles. It didn't matter; she knew the Sha Sha and said she'd meet him there.

"The thing is," he said, "I was going to call you. Then it got a little crazy for a couple of days, and then it slipped my mind, and then it was too late to call. Do you know what I mean?"

"I thought that was what happened. But I didn't want to phone you, that would have been awfully pushy—"

"It would have been all right."

"Well, I wouldn't have felt okay with it. Then I remembered Maury was representing you, and I thought, well, that'll work. You can't call the man himself, but how can it be a breach of etiquette to call his attorney?"

"How do you happen to know Maury?"

"We had an affair."

"Oh."

Her eyes held his. "A very casual now-and-then affair over a lot of years. You know, this is funny, John. I was going to say something simple, that we were old friends, and that would have been true enough, but with you I have the feeling I can say what I mean."

The waiter broke the moment, setting their cups of coffee in front of them. Creighton waited until he had withdrawn, then said, "Maury said you read my books. I think you told me that yourself at Stelli's."

"I did, and it was a lie. I hadn't then, not yet. I went home and ordered them online. I had to hunt around for some of them, but you can find anything online."

"They'll all be back in print before long."

"That's wonderful. I'm glad, but I'm also glad I didn't wait. You're a wonderful writer, John. You don't need me to tell you that, and I'm not Michiko Kakutani, but they spoke to me in a very personal way."

She talked about various books, and she remembered characters' names, remembered scenes, and gave him something infinitely more to be desired than praise.

One of the questions writers got asked was for whom they wrote their books. The answer he usually gave was that he wrote for himself, and it sounded up to here with artistic integrity, but he'd never been entirely happy with it because it wasn't altogether true. If it was just for himself, why bother writing it down? Why not work it all out in his mind and leave it at that? And, if he really was writing for himself, he'd have to say he was a failure at it. Because how often did he sit down with an old book of his own and read the damn thing?

No, there was someone he wrote for, but unfortunately it was a person who couldn't exist. He wrote for the reader he himself would be if he didn't happen to have written the book in the first place. He wrote for someone who would understand at once everything he did or tried to do, who would always know what he meant, and who would be intellectually and emotionally in tune with every word.

And there she was, sitting across a rickety little table from him. And she was gorgeous, and she was looking at him as if he were a god.

They talked. They sipped their coffee and talked, ordered more coffee and talked, sat over empty coffee cups and talked. Finally he got the check, put money on the table, and asked her what she'd like to do next.

She put her hand on his. She said, "Do you think they'll rent us a room? If not, we'd better go back to your place."

IT WAS LIKE HIGH school or college, it was like being young again. They sat on his couch and kissed. He got hard right away, but there was no urgency to it; he could happily sit there forever, holding her in his arms, feasting on her mouth.

They were like that for a long time. Then they moved as one, disengaging. She stood up and slipped out of her blouse and skirt, and he wasn't surprised to see that she wasn't wearing anything under it. He was surprised, though, by the gold at her nipples, the hairless delta.

She said, "John, I'll do anything you want, and you can do anything you want to me. Anything at all."

. . .

AFTERWARD HE GOT A cigarette, asked if it would bother her if he smoked. She said it wouldn't.

"You don't smoke," he said.

"No."

He lit the cigarette, took a drag, blew out the smoke, and watched it drift to the ceiling. He took another drag but didn't inhale, blowing a couple of smoke rings, then pursing his lips and blowing out the rest of it. He reached across her body and stubbed out the cigarette in an ashtray.

She asked if there'd been something wrong with it. He said, "Maybe I'll quit."

"Why?"

"Lately," he said, "I keep finding new things to live for. That makes it harder to justify committing incremental suicide."

"And you can quit just like that?"

"I don't know," he said. "I never tried before. I'm close to the end of the book, and this may not be a good time to go through withdrawal, but I can get a patch to keep from climbing the walls. You know what? I just decided. I quit."

He got up, grabbed the half-empty pack from the bedside table, got the carton with six packs still left in it. Outside the window, the neighborhood recycler was rooting in the trash for cans and bottles. "Hey, buddy," he called, and tossed the cigarettes to him. "Have a smoke," he said. "Live a little."

He got back in bed. "If I have them in the house, I might light up without even thinking about it. The patch will take care of the physical withdrawal. I might miss the oral gratification, though." He looked down at her. "Maybe I'll think of something," he said.

THEY THOUGHT ABOUT GOING out for dinner, wound up ordering from Hunan Pan. He put on a record, Thelonious Monk, solo piano. They sat cross-legged on the bed, eating off paper plates, listening to the music. Afterward he pulled up a chair and asked her how she knew. "Before you read the books. What made you order them in the first place?"

"When I met you," she said, "I felt something."

"So did I, though it didn't register consciously. I was high as a kite on the auction and everything that went with it. I told you what Roger Delacroix said."

"Yes."

"But there had to be a reason why I kept your card. It's still in my sock drawer. I missed my chance to call, but I wasn't going to throw away your number. What made you come over to the table, though? The whole room must have been talking about my book deal. *From a jail cell to the bestseller list, ladies and gentlemen.* You wanted to see what kind of guy made that kind of leap?"

She shook her head. "I was already interested in you."

"How come?"

"I can't explain it, not in any way that makes sense. I was drawn to you before I knew your name. Or what you looked like, or anything about you."

"That's very mysterious."

"I know, and I don't mean to be mysterious. I'm trying to think how to say this, but what difference does it make? I'll just say it. I knew Marilyn Fairchild."

"Oh."

"Not well, we weren't friends, we were barely acquaintances. She found me my apartment. We were friendly enough, but I never saw her after that. And then I heard she'd been killed, and there are murders every day, it's a fact of life, but somehow . . ."

"It got to you."

"I wondered who it could be, how it could have happened. And then they announced your arrest, and it turned out you were a writer, you lived in the Village. It wasn't some degenerate who crawled out of the sewer, some drooling psychopath who spent his childhood wetting the bed and torturing animals. She met some guy in a bar and took him home and he killed her."

Before he could say anything she put a hand on his wrist. "I know you didn't do it," she said. "But I didn't know then."

"How could you? How could anyone?"

"When I learned that was you at Stelli's, I had to go over there, I had to meet you, to introduce myself. I didn't know that was your agent, she could have been a wife or a girlfriend, but I had to do what I did. Of course I heard about your good news, the place was buzzing with it, and maybe that gave you more of an aura, I don't know, but I think I'd have done the same thing anyway."

A lot to take in, he thought. He leaned forward, touched his finger to the underside of her breast. "When did you get the piercing done?"

"A couple of months ago. Do you like them?"

"Yes, but it must have hurt."

"It's an interesting story," she said, "and one I've never told. It's a long story, though."

"It's not as though I've got a train to catch."

"It may show me in an unflattering light." She sat up on the bed, gathered her legs under her. "But maybe that's important. You have to know who I am."

"YOU NEVER WENT BACK."

"No," she said, and touched her nipples. "I decided these were enough."

"And once with Medea was enough?"

"Well, that was her decision. If I went a second time, it would be a simple business transaction."

"You think she'd have stuck to her guns?"

"Maybe I could have changed her mind. But maybe not. She's a strong woman, she seems to know what she wants and what she doesn't want. And maybe once was enough. One piercing was enough."

"Two."

"One session of piercing, then. One visit to the piercer. Did you like the story?"

"Well, take a look," he said. "Consider the physical evidence."

She reached out, took hold of his hardened penis, held it gently in her cool hand. "I knew your cock would like it," she said. "What about your mind? Do you like me as much as before you heard the story?"

"More."

"Because now you know I'm hot?"

"I already knew that. No, because I know you better."

"And the better you know me, the more you like me? I wonder if that will be true when you hear the rest."

"I thought you only saw her once."

"There are other people. I have a lot of stories, and you might not like them all."

"Try me."

"Not tonight. It's late, and you have a book to finish. And I've already cost you a day's work."

"I got some work done before Maury called."

"And you'll work tomorrow, but when will you stop working? And would you like me to come over?"

"Come around dinnertime. Say six-thirty? We'll have an early dinner in the neighborhood, then come back here. And Scheherazade can tell me another story."

twenty-seven

AT TWILIGHT, A trim gentleman in his later years walked at a brisk pace in Riverside Park, approaching the Seventy-ninth Street Boat Basin. He wore a navy blazer with brass buttons, a pair of white canvas trousers, and a black-billed white cap in the style of a Greek fisherman. He stepped confidently onto the floating dock and walked to his boat, the *Nancy Dee.* A couple of other boaters saw him and greeted him with a word or a wave, and he acknowledged them with a sort of half-salute, raising his right hand, index finger extended, to shoulder height.

He climbed aboard the ship, and in due course piloted the small vessel away from the pier and out onto the Hudson River.

IT WOULD HAVE BEEN simpler, the Carpenter thought, if Peter Shevlin hadn't gone straight to his boat. If he'd gone home to change first into his idea of what a proper yachtsman ought to wear. But no, he'd gone from the subway to the restaurant and then directly to the *Nancy Dee,* almost as if he knew this would be his last night at the helm and wanted to maximize his time on the water.

So he'd been wearing business clothes, quite useless to the Carpenter. On the other hand, perhaps it was as well that the man had been bareheaded. A cap might have cushioned the blow.

It had been easy enough to find a blazer. All the thrift shops had them, and he'd been patient enough to search until he found one that was a perfect fit. It was missing one of its cuff buttons, and frayed the least bit at the collar, but that just made it look like a treasured old garment, the veteran of years of faithful service.

The white duck trousers were new, purchased at the bargain store in Greenpoint, along with a fresh supply of socks and underwear. The Greek fisherman's cap had been harder to find, and he'd decided that any white cap would do, then happened on a store on Eighth Street that sold nothing but caps and had every imaginable kind, including just the one he was looking for. It was a perfect fit, too, which would probably not have been the case with Shevlin's. The man had had a small head.

Which, minus its teeth, now rested somewhere on the bottom of this very river, wrapped up tightly in plastic along with the tire iron that had served so well to dent Shevlin's skull and, in due course, to knock the teeth from his jaw. It had done good service, the Carpenter thought, and deserved burial at sea, as did Shevlin, or what was left of him.

The teeth, too, were in the river. No need to wrap them up or weigh them down; they sank like the anonymous pebbles they would soon become. And Shevlin's hands, rendered unidentifiable, had also been consigned to the depths.

It was, he thought, as if the original Peter Shevlin had ceased to exist, and had been reborn in the person of the Carpenter.

HE GUIDED THE SHIP southward, past the piers where several cruise ships lay at anchor, past the floating museum that was the USS *Intrepid,* past Battery Park City and, beyond it, the site where the twin towers had stood. And on, around the tip of Manhattan Island, and under the three great bridges in turn, Brooklyn and Manhattan and Williamsburg.

Once there had been a prominent jazz musician who had a spell when he stopped playing with other musicians, stopped performing in clubs and concert halls, stopped recording. Instead he would walk out to the middle of the Williamsburg Bridge and play for hours.

Anywhere else in the world, the Carpenter thought, they'd have done one of two things. Either they'd have told him he couldn't do that, or they'd have all come out to hear him, until the man gave up and went home.

New York had left him alone.

HE RATHER REGRETTED THE loss of the tire iron, now resting on the river bottom with the head of Peter Shevlin. It had served him well, like the saw and boning knife, also consigned to a watery grave. And the hammers, and the chisel. A workman, he thought, was as good as his tools.

But it was in the nature of Providence to provide. Why, it was right there in the word itself! And, even as he lost the tire iron, he'd gained something even more useful.

It was a handgun, and Peter Shevlin had kept it on the top of the brassbound captain's chest in the little cabin. A pair of clips held the gun in place, so that it wouldn't come crashing to the deck when the boat pitched and rolled in high seas. The Carpenter wondered what high seas Shevlin had expected to encounter, and decided they were no less a likelihood than the need to repel pirates, which would seem the gun's logical purpose.

A war souvenir? Shevlin was too young for World War II, too old for Vietnam, but he supposed he could have served in Korea.

The Carpenter considered the gun. He'd never owned one, wasn't sure he'd ever held one aside from a BB gun at a carnival shooting gallery and the cap pistols he'd played with as a child. Handguns, he knew, were of two sorts. Revolvers had cylinders, which revolved; hence their name. The others were pistols, and had clips.

This one lacked a cylinder, so it was a pistol. And, yes, moving that little lever released the clip, which contained nine little bullets. Or did you call them cartridges? He rather thought you did.

A drawer in the captain's chest held a box that contained more cartridges. The label proclaimed them to be .22 caliber, and they were identical to the ones in the clip. Surely military sidearms were of a higher caliber, weren't they? And the gun looked too new, too modern in design, to be half a century old.

Shevlin, alone in the world, had bought the gun as a ticket out of the world. Then he'd bought the boat, and decided to live. But kept the gun on the boat, just in case he changed his mind.

He was pleased with his analysis of the gun's history, pleased to have the weapon on the boat with him. He liked the way it fit his hand, noted how natural it felt to point it here and there, taking aim, his finger resting lightly on the trigger.

It might be a useful tool. And, if he needed it, it might serve for the final sacrifice.

THE CARPENTER HAD ALWAYS assumed he would take to sailing like, well, a duck to water. He didn't see how it could be terribly difficult. Oh, it might be tricky in an actual sailboat, where you had to know how to use the wind, but a boat powered by a gas engine couldn't be all that difficult, could it? It wasn't like flying a plane, where you had a third dimension to contend with. You just stayed on the water's surface, and steered to the left or the right.

It was, he had learned, a little more complicated than that, but not prohibitively so. And it was his good fortune that boating was evidently a pursuit the late Peter Shevlin had come to in recent years. Perhaps he'd bought it for consolation after he'd been widowed, naming it the *Nancy Dee* for his late wife. The *Dee* might stand for either her middle name or her maiden name, he thought. Or for *Darling,* or even *Deceased,* if Shevlin had had an unhappy marriage and a savage sense of humor.

Or perhaps a previous owner had named the boat, and Shevlin hadn't gotten around to changing it.

In any event, the man had equipped himself with several manuals on the art of handling small boats on open water, and one in particular the Carpenter found to be remarkably straightforward and easy to understand. He didn't know that he emerged from it capable of passing a licensing exam, but he found he could take the boat out and make it do more or less what he wanted it to do. This gave him a sense of accomplishment, and was a source of real pleasure.

And there were charts, too. The Carpenter couldn't read them, but he didn't have to; someone, Shevlin or someone assisting him, had marked routes on the charts, letting one know just where to steer the vessel.

Shevlin was neat, probably a core requirement for the owner of a small boat, and kept the place shipshape. There was far less space than the Carpenter had enjoyed in Evelyn Crispin's flat in Boerum Hill, but what space there was suited the Carpenter just fine. And, best of all, there was no goddamned cat to feed.

DURING THE HOURS OF darkness, the *Nancy Dee* sailed counterclockwise around the entire island of Manhattan.

This was the first time the Carpenter had circumnavigated the island. On each of his previous outings he'd ventured a little farther from home, then turned the boat around and gone back. But he knew it was possible to make the full trip. The Circle Line did so every day of the year.

And it went smoothly enough. He sailed up the East River, passed beneath the bridge built to carry the number 7 subway, the line that ran out to Flushing Meadows and Shea Stadium. He took the West Channel past Roosevelt Island. He went on past Gracie Mansion, the mayor's residence, then navigated the channel separating Manhattan from Ward and Randall's Islands. Then he was in the narrow Harlem River, passing under one bridge after another, and eventually he turned sharply left, heading west now, heading back toward the Hudson.

And he knew (although he doubted they told you as much on the Circle Line) that, while he was circling all of the island of Manhattan, he was not encompassing the entire borough. Because on his right at this very moment was a geopolitical quirk, a little chunk of land that by all rights ought to have been part of the Kingsbridge section of the Bronx, but that was in fact a part of Manhattan. There was an historic reason for this anomaly, and he had known it once, but he couldn't recall it now. If he had his books . . .

The Henry Hudson Bridge, and now the Hudson River. He headed the boat south, with the spectacular two-tiered span of the George Washington Bridge in front of him. What a view, thought the Carpenter. What a voyage. What a magnificent city.

IT WAS STILL DARK when the Carpenter pulled into his slip and tied up his boat. He was tired. It was extremely relaxing to be out on the water, but it was also exhausting. He undressed, hung up his clothes, and got into bed. The boat rocked him quickly to sleep.

When he awoke, he dressed in the same clothes he had been wearing. His backpack held a pair of dark trousers, and after he left the Boat Basin he'd stop at Barnes & Noble and change in the men's room. He'd stow the white pants and the cap in his backpack. The blazer could go there as well, if the day was a hot one. Otherwise he'd wear it, as the garment was no less suitable ashore.

Shevlin had hung a calendar on the wall alongside the bunk bed. It was from Goddard-Riverside, a social service effort, and each page bore the amateurish art of a different senior citizen, with the artist's name and age listed. Children noted their age on their letters and drawings, the Carpenter had noticed, and so did the elderly. *I know this is rubbish,* they seemed to be saying, *but consider how old I am. Isn't it remarkable that I can even hold a brush?*

The calendar was hung to display the current month, August. Soon it would be time to turn the page, and the Carpenter did so now, to have a look at September's masterpiece. It was the work of Sarah Handler, who was eighty-three, and it showed a bowl of round objects, which the Carpenter took to be apples.

He picked up a red marker and circled a date. Then he turned the calendar back to August.

twenty-eight

HE HAD A surprisingly good day at the keyboard. He'd anticipated trouble, having so utterly rearranged the furniture in his life. For months—since whatever happened with Marilyn Fairchild, incredibly enough—he hadn't had sex. Aside from various cops, Maury Winters, and that rummy of a PI, he hadn't had anyone in his apartment in longer than he could remember.

Add in the fact that he'd just quit smoking and it seemed likely that the words would slow to a trickle, or dry up altogether. Instead, they poured down in buckets.

He'd finished for the day, showered and changed, and was sitting at the window when she showed up right on time. They went to Mitali's for Indian food and he told her the patch was helping.

"But it was tricky getting it. You need a prescription for the thing, can you believe that? Every newsstand or deli will sell you all the cigarettes you want, but if you want to quit you've got to see a doctor. I went to this little drugstore on Bleecker, I don't know how they stay in business, and I slipped the guy a hundred dollars."

"You had to schmear him to sell you a patch?"

"I told him he'd be saving me time and money, and doing me a big favor. He looked around, like somebody might be watching us. I wonder if any of the guys in the hip-hop outfits are selling patches in Union Square. If not, they're missing a good thing."

Walking back to Bank Street, she slipped her hand into his.

THE JAZZ STATION ON the radio, with the volume turned low. She said the same thing she'd said yesterday. *I'll do anything you want. You can do whatever you want with me.*

For answer, he drew her close for a kiss, put a hand on her bottom and pulled her loins tight against him. He was hard, but that was nothing new. He'd been that way in the restaurant.

She said, "Anything you want. And whenever you want, except for Tuesdays and Fridays."

"Shrink appointments? Personal trainer?"

"Sex," she said. She raised her eyes to his. Her gaze was open, un-guarded. "I'm going to tell you about Tuesdays and Fridays," she said, "but I want you inside of me while I tell you. Can we do that? No, from behind. See how wet I am. I've been like this all day, I had to masturbate, I couldn't help myself. Now you're nice and wet, you're wet with my wetness. Now take it out and put it in the other place. Yes, yes. I want you in my ass. Oh, yes. God, you're big, it feels wonderful. Now don't move, don't thrust. Can you do that, John? Can you just stay like that?"

"I can try."

"Oh, God, don't move. Oh, I can't hold back, I'm going to come. Oh. *Oh.* Don't move, please don't move. Is that all right? Are you okay?"

"Yes."

"Jesus, I love you. I do, you know. Don't say anything. Can you just stay in me and not move and not say anything? Yes, you can. Oh, you're an angel. Now I have to think where to begin. Maury Winters, your lawyer. The last time I saw Maury he took me to a fancy French restau-rant. We had just ordered dessert when he went to the bathroom, and while he was gone I got under the table, and when he came back I sucked him off.

"It was very exciting. I always love doing that, but I especially liked two things, surprising him like that and doing it in public. No one could see us but it was entirely possible someone saw me get under the table, and I know there were people who saw me get out.

"At least one, and that brings us to the man I see every Friday night. I won't tell you his name, but I'm going to tell you everything else. I love you, John. I love your cock in my ass. I'm going to tell you everything."

SHE TALKED FOR A long time. She didn't censor her speech, didn't check it in her mind but let it flow out unimpeded, as if she were an open faucet and the words were water. Sometimes she would feel disembodied, lost in space, and then the hard bulk of him inside her would bring her back, and she would tighten around him and go on.

She told him about Franny, although she didn't use his name or iden-tify him beyond saying he had been a public official, a man used to exer-cising authority. She told him about the boys, Lowell and Jay. She told him about the man from Connecticut and the man from Detroit. She told him about Reginald Barron. She told him about Chloe.

She told him about her toys. She told him about the times she spent by herself, and what she did, and what fantasies she used.

She told him she felt alive, as she had never felt before. She told him she worried sometimes that she was crazy, that she was out of control.

When she had run out of things to tell him she lay still and felt him still hard inside her, felt his hand resting lightly on her hip, felt his mind touching hers. She felt that she could almost talk to him without words, that her mind could speak silently to his. Almost.

Aloud she said, "Do you hate me, John?"

"Of course not."

"Am I disgusting?"

"You're beautiful."

"But does it disgust you, what I do? You could make me stop. I don't want to stop, but I would do it for you."

He was silent for a moment, but she wasn't afraid of what he would say. She could feel his mind, so gentle against hers, and she knew what he said would be all right.

He said, "It's what you do, Susan. It's who you are. It's your art."

Something broke within her and she felt tears stream down her cheeks. "Oh, my darling," she said. "Oh, lie still, lie perfectly still. Don't move. I want to do this for you."

And she tightened around him, tightened and relaxed, tightened and relaxed, milking him, milking him, until at last he let out a great cry and emptied himself into her.

"IF I'D HAD ANY idea what it would do for my sex life," he said, "I'd have quit smoking years ago."

"It must be the patch."

"Jesus, no wonder you need a prescription."

Showers, cups of tea. She was holding one of his books, *Nothing but Blue Skies,* studying the dust jacket photo. She asked when he'd shaved the beard.

"The night we met."

"Seriously?"

"I was trimming it," he said, "and that's hard to do when you're in a hurry. And I thought, oh, the hell with it, and the next thing I knew it was gone. I didn't intend it to be symbolic, not consciously, anyway. But I must have, because I'd had it for years, and out of nowhere I'd just landed this ridiculously huge contract, and zip, no beard. If you want I'll grow it back."

"It's a handsome beard," she said, "but don't grow it back. I like being able to see your face. What you said before, that sex was my art. That may be the most beautiful thing anybody ever said to me. It made me cry."

"It's true, isn't it?"

"It's entirely true, and I never knew it until I heard you say it. It's the craziness that keeps me from going insane. Isn't there a song like that?"

"Sort of, but I don't think it's about art. A country song."

"Then it must be true, if it's in a country song. You know the one thing New York doesn't have?"

"Anybody better-looking than you."

"A country-music station. Or if there is then I can't find it."

"There's one," he said, "but it's no good. Chirpy disc jockeys and nothing but Top Forty shit. You like country music? Hang on a minute."

He got out his Bobby Bare album, the one where Shel Silverstein wrote all the songs. It was vinyl, so he put the A side on the turntable and adjusted the volume. After the third cut played he said, "You've got to hear this one," which was unnecessary, as they'd listened to the first three in respectful silence.

The song was "Rosalie's Good Eats Café," a story song about the habitués of an all-night restaurant, and it ran over eight minutes, and when it ended he took the record off and put it away. "I just wanted you to hear that," he said. "We'll listen to the rest another time."

"I can see why you like that song. I mean, besides the fact that it's terrific. It's a novel, isn't it?"

"That's exactly what it is. There was a DJ who played that cut all the time. He got in trouble, because he wasn't getting enough commercials in, but he played it anyway. You're too young to remember."

"The other day your lawyer told me I was too young to remember *To Have and Have Not*. The movie, not the novel. I remember it just fine."

"Because they show it on television. That album was released in 1973. Were you listening to much country music in 1973?"

"I was eight, so what would I have been listening to? Supertramp. God, do you remember that group? No, of course not, you're too old to remember Supertramp."

"Touché. I remember the Bobby Bare album because I was a college freshman, and that one song made me realize I wanted to be a writer."

"Really?"

"Well, I already half knew, but that closed the sale. I realized I wanted to tell stories. Can I ask you something? And what's so funny?"

"Can you ask me something? Duh, no, I don't want to reveal any-thing of myself to you. Ask away."

"You started off thinking I killed her. Marilyn Fairchild."

"Well, it's more like I assumed it."

"What changed your mind? Reading my books?"

"That's how I got to know you."

"And you sensed that the person who wrote those books couldn't commit murder."

She was silent for a moment. "No," she said. "Not exactly."

"Oh?"

"One thing I got from the books," she said, "is that anybody could commit murder. Not that there's a lot of killing in your work, but you get the sense, well, that anybody is pretty much capable of anything."

"I guess I believe that. I didn't realize it was a message I was send-ing."

"It's one I got. There was one story, 'A Nice Place to Visit,' except that's not right. This young couple, they're in a motel—"

" 'A Nice Place to Stop.' God, you're amazing."

"What, because I remember a story?"

"It's the book I'm writing," he said, and explained. She said she couldn't wait to read it, and he said it was almost done, he'd reached that point where it was all clear in his mind and it was just a matter of getting it down right. And then he asked her again how she knew he was innocent.

"You said you didn't do it," she said simply.

"The prisons are full of people who'll tell you they never did a bad thing in their lives."

"But I don't believe them. I believe you."

He looked at her, thinking what a treasure she was, thinking how brave she'd been, willing to risk it all in order to let him see her real self. Did he dare to be any less daring himself?

"Come here a moment," he said, leading her to the bookcase. "I don't know if you happened to notice this."

"The rabbit? Yes, I was looking at it before. It's southwestern, isn't it? Zuni, although they're not the only ones carving them nowadays. May I?" He nodded, and she picked it up. "I think it's very good. The stone's beautiful, and the carving's perfectly realistic, and not decadent the way some of them are. Not Roman Empire decadent, but when you know the artist is just going through the motions. Is it the only fetish you have?"

"Unless you want to count an enthusiasm for women with shaved twats and nipple rings."

"Well, it's a nice one, and I'm glad to see you're taking good care of it. Cornmeal?"

"Stone ground."

"Where did you get it?"

"Gristedes."

"Idiot. Where did you get the rabbit? Were you in that part of the country, or did you buy it locally?"

"Neither," he said. "I brought it home from Marilyn Fairchild's apartment."

AS HE SPOKE, A line ran through her head. A catchphrase, it had turned up everywhere for a while, until people got tired of it.

I could tell you, but then I'd have to kill you.

Listening, she could feel his hands on her throat.

Her heart was beating faster, but the cause could as easily have been excitement as fear. Maybe the two weren't so different, maybe that explained the appeal of roller coasters and scary movies.

When he'd finished she said, "But you don't remember killing her."

"No, but I can imagine it vividly enough. Maybe that's a form of memory."

"Do you always imagine it the same way?"

He shook his head. "Different versions."

"That sounds like genuine imagination, not a memory slipping out the back door because your conscience has the front one blocked. John, I don't think it proves anything. You know you were in her apartment, you know you were with her. You already knew that."

"I didn't know there were holes in my memory. I thought I was a little vague about leaving her place and getting back to mine, but if I was so far gone I picked this little critter up and brought him home without remembering any of it, I must have had a hole in my memory big enough to drive a truck through."

Or stick your hands through, she thought, and fit them around a woman's throat.

"If you'd found the rabbit the morning after . . ."

"And I could have, when I put my socks on. What would I have done? I'd have picked it up and stared at it and wondered where the hell it came from."

"And when the cops came the first time?"

"They weren't looking for the rabbit. Oh, would I have made the connection? I don't know. I might have thought, oh, that's where the damn thing came from. But I might just as easily have thought someone gave it to me years ago and I'd managed to forget the gift and the giver."

"When they came back a second time—"

"The rabbit was listed on the search warrant. So what would I have done? Either pulled it out right away and showed it to them or prayed they wouldn't find it. But all this is hypothetical. They didn't find it, and I didn't find it myself until long after they'd come and gone."

"And now it's eating up all your stone-ground cornmeal."

"That's why it stayed hidden until I got the big contract."

"Why? Oh, then it knew you could afford to feed it."

"You got it."

She said, "John, everybody knows the Carpenter killed her. Maury told me they offered to let you walk. That was very brave, turning them down."

"It shows moral strength if I didn't do it. I'm not sure what it shows if I did."

"If they had one more piece of evidence, one more link—"

"But they don't."

"The cleaning person, I forget his name . . ."

"Jerry Pankow. That looks like a link, but is it? The Carpenter reads the papers, he learns how this poor guy cleaned up the crime scene and then discovered the body. Let's give him a few more to find, he says to himself. Let's see what other potential crime scenes he cleans. That might appeal to his sense of humor."

"You think he has one?"

"The nail in that woman's forehead in Brooklyn? Call me the Carpenter and I'll sign my work for you. Yes, I think he has a sense of humor. He's not the Joker, laughing at Batman while he terrorizes Gotham City, but he's got a sense of humor."

"Couldn't the same sense of humor lead him to take something from her apartment and put it here?"

"Toward what end? So the cops'll think I did it? They think that already. Besides, I'm a light sleeper. And he'd have had to break in while I was sleeping, because the rest of the time I was holed up here."

"You left a few times."

"Only a very few, and only briefly. How would he get in the door? He's the Carpenter, not the Locksmith."

"Do you always double-lock your door?"

"Except when I forget. Okay, I could have forgotten, or not bothered if I was only going to be gone for a minute, and yes, it locks when you pull it shut, but if you know what you're doing you can open it with a credit card. I used to do it myself when I forgot and locked myself out."

"So he could have done that. You used to do it? But then you stopped locking yourself out?"

He laughed. "Well, no, once in a while I'm lost in thought and go out for cigarettes with my keys still on the dresser. Another thing I don't have to worry about now that I'm an ex-smoker."

"But when you did lock yourself out, then what?"

"There's a key under the mat."

"Which the Carpenter could have used."

"If he thought to look there. Susan, come on. Remember Occam's razor?"

"From college, but I forget what it is."

"A philosophical principle. When you hear hoofbeats, don't look around for zebras. Because it's probably horses. That's my example, not that of the bishop of Occham, but you get the idea. When there's a simple and obvious explanation, it's generally on the money."

She nodded slowly, looked at the rabbit in the palm of her hand. She asked if anyone else had seen it. No one, he said. She alone had been in his apartment since the rabbit turned up.

"And you're the only person I've said a word to. You notice I checked first to make sure you weren't wearing a wire."

"Checked very thoroughly, too."

"Well, you can't be too careful."

I could tell you, but then I'd have to kill you . . .

She said, "John? Thank you."

"For letting you know you might be sleeping with a murderer?"

"I already knew that."

She closed her fingers around the rabbit, reached out with her other hand to touch him. She had to have her hand on him while she said this.

She said, "I told you everything about myself, all the fucking, all the weird shit in my mind. But I held one thing back."

"You don't have to—"

"Yes I do. John, maybe you killed her and maybe you didn't, but what you have to know is I don't care. I honest to God don't care."

"You don't care if—"

"—If you killed her or not. No, I don't. I care about you. I want them to drop the charges, I want you to be out from under this cloud. I want everyone in the world to know you never killed anybody. But I don't have to know it because it doesn't matter to me. You think maybe you killed her? So fucking what? I love you just as much if you did. Maybe more, for all I know." She raised her eyes to him. There were tears in her eyes and she blinked them away. She said, "Can you take me to bed? I need to come. Can you make me come?"

WHEN IT WAS TIME for her to go he went downstairs with her, walked her to Eighth Avenue. An empty cab sailed by, not even slowing down.

"Didn't see us," he said. "Too busy talking on his cell phone."

"Listening to bad music," she offered.

"And munching on raw garlic. I don't think it was the right cab for you. Tomorrow's Friday, so I guess you'll be busy, won't you?"

"Does it bother you?"

"No, I think I like it. I've got work to do, but I think I'd like it even if I didn't. Friday's the one you're turning into a girl, right?"

"That's the one, but what I'm really doing is teaching him that he's kinkier than he thought he was."

"Well, so am I, evidently, because I'm already looking forward to hearing about it. I expect a full report."

"And while I'm doing him, I'll be thinking how I'm going to get to tell you about it."

"And I'll be imagining it, writing scripts for you in my mind. Here's your cab. I'll see you Saturday, okay?"

She nodded, kissed him.

He said, "I'm glad we found each other."

"Oh, baby," she said. "How could we help it?"

twenty-nine

THE EYE-OPENER, JIM Galvin had to acknowledge, was probably a mistake. If you waited awhile, if you had a decent breakfast in your belly, eggs and rashers and a link or two of sausage, and here it was getting on for lunchtime, surely no one would begrudge a man a drop of the hard stuff. If you held out until midafternoon, that was even better. But when that first one went down the hatch before breakfast, or instead of breakfast, well, that didn't look so good. There it was, John Jameson's finest, in your belly and on your breath, and no one who smelled it was going to mistake it for altar wine.

On the other hand, nothing else really got you going after a bad night. He knew men who swore by Valium, said it straightened you out without knocking you out, and left your breath discreetly unscented. But he also knew a man who'd developed a Valium habit and almost died trying to get off it. Poor bastard wound up in Beth Israel hospital, where they told him Valium detox could be tougher than heroin. *Thanks all the same, but I'll stay with the whiskey. It'll kill me, too, in its own good time, but at least it'll taste good going down.*

Last night had been a bad one, though it had seemed good enough while it was taking place. A few bars, a few old friends, a few new ones, and a couple of laughs. A feeling of abiding love for the old friends, for the new friends, for the whole human race. A sense that it wasn't such a bad old world after all.

Grand thoughts, grand feelings, and there were only two ways he knew of that a man could get to have them. Have a fucking jelly doughnut for a brain, or have a couple of drinks.

He'd had the latter, and now he felt as though he had the former, and that the jelly was oozing out of the doughnut. So he took down the bottle and filled a six-ounce jelly glass halfway full. And picked it up and looked at it, like you'd look at—what? An old friend? An old enemy?

He drank it down. Just the one, just to take the edge off, just to lighten the load the least bit.

He had breakfast around the corner on Avenue B, in a Ukrainian place where they didn't worry any more about cholesterol than he did. He had salami and eggs and crisp hash browns and three cups of lousy coffee, and by God he felt fine by the time he walked out of there.

Now he had to figure out something to do with the day.

HE WAS OFF THE clock. Maury Winters had given him a lot of hours, first rooting around for the writer, Creighton, and then doing some background checking on a couple of prosecution witnesses in a robbery case. The robbery case pleaded out, with a better deal resulting in part from a lead he'd developed, so he had to feel good about that, and Maury was probably feeling good about him.

But he hadn't been able to turn the trick for Creighton.

He'd figured there was probably a limit to what he could accomplish, given that you didn't need psychic powers to know the writer was guilty. Lady walks into a bar, walks out with a guy, and wakes up dead, you don't reach for the tea leaves and the crystal ball. You pick up the guy, and he goes away for it.

So he'd gone through the motions, but he'd been a good cop and he was making an effort to be just as good at this racket. Before he'd been busting his ass to put bad guys in prison and now he was working almost as hard to keep them out, which seemed weird now and then, but the work itself wasn't all that different. It was a similar mix of headwork and footwork, and he had the head for it. And the feet, although they were starting to go on him.

He'd done what he could for Creighton, coming up with a couple of witnesses who could at least blow a little smoke up the prosecution's ass, and then the fucking Carpenter came along and opened up a whole new world of possibilities. All you had to do was link him to Fairchild and you could get Creighton off the hook.

A couple of ways it could have happened. Harbinger had been sighted in the neighborhood, he'd been confirmed buying gasoline at Thirteenth and Eighth, so he could have staked out Fairchild same as he did the one in Brooklyn, staked her out and followed her home.

Say he watched her apartment, and let himself in when she let herself out. He waited for her to come home, but when she did she had Creighton with her, two of them and one of him, and Creighton was a big guy, so the Carpenter'd be in the closet while they did a little mattress testing. Then

Creighton went on home, and out pops the Carpenter, just in time for sloppy seconds. And, just to make sure nobody else comes along for thirds, he strangles her and takes off.

Or, even better, he gets his first look at her when she walks into the Kettle of Fish, and tails her when she walks out with Creighton. He gets into her brownstone—how hard is that, he times it right and Creighton holds the door for him on his own way out. Knocks on her door, says he's back, he forgot something. *Yeah, what did you forget, I'll get it for you? You won't be able to find it. Lemme in.* And she opens the door and he says *I forgot to kill you, you stupid bitch,* and he does.

Maury liked that, he could sell it to a jury, hey, coulda happened, reasonable doubt, yadda yadda yadda. Put him in the Kettle, Maury said. Put him in the brownstone. Put him on the stoop of the house across the street, sharpening his dick with a whetstone. Anything, just put him in the picture, and it's frosting on the cupcake.

Couldn't do it. Couldn't fucking do it, and all he was doing was following the cops around, because they'd showed the Carpenter's picture all over the neighborhood, as if everybody hadn't seen it enough times in the papers and on TV. Both bartenders at the Kettle, the day guy and the night guy, looked at the picture and said sure they recognized it, it was the Carpenter, and what else was new? Had they seen him before? Yeah, in the *Post,* in the *News,* on CNN, on New York One, on *America's Most Wanted,* on every fucking thing but *Seinfeld* reruns. But up close and in person, in the bar? Nope, sorry, can't help you out.

Great.

HE WENT BACK TO his apartment, thinking it hadn't been that long ago that cops wouldn't walk here except in pairs, and not even then if there was a way to avoid it. Now he'd had to call in favors to find a place here he could afford, and it was four flights up and not a whole lot nicer inside than when they were thrilled to get fifty-five dollars a month for it. The good part, by the time a broad climbed up four flights of stairs, she wasn't going to change her mind. She had too much invested in the whole business.

The stairs were either keeping him in shape or killing him, and he was never sure which. He got to the top thinking he deserved a drink for that, but decided he'd collect later. Because, off the clock or not, he wondered if there wasn't something he could do for Creighton. Had to be something nobody thought of.

He went over his notes, made a couple of calls. And sure enough, there it was. It might not go anywhere, if there was one thing he'd learned on the job it was that anything you tried had a chance of going nowhere at all. But if you tried enough things, and if you used your head and your feet, now and then something paid off.

He could have had a small one on the strength of that, too, but decided he'd wait. He locked up and went down the stairs, which was always a lot easier than going up them. Funny how it worked.

HE WALKED ACROSS TOWN, taking his time, and it was early afternoon when he got to Sheridan Square and walked into the Kettle of Fish. The day guy was behind the bar, which figured. Eddie Ragan was his name, same as the last president Galvin had thought much of, though twenty years later he didn't look as good as he did back then. Bartender spelled it different, though, left the *e* out. With the *e* it was Irish, and without it who the hell knew what it was. Probably Polish, probably cut down from something with thirty *z*s and *w*s in it.

"Hey, Eddie," he said.

"Hey, how ya doin'?" A nice easy smile, you had to say that for him. "You gonna show me that picture again?"

"You remember, huh?"

"I may not remember every last person who showed me that picture, as many as there've been. You I remember. Bushmill's, right?"

"Actually it's Jamesons."

"Hey, close enough. Rocks or water back?"

He took it with water back, and while he sipped the water he nodded for a refill. Part of the job, on or off the clock. You go to bars, you want to get information from bartenders, you can't sit there sipping a Coke.

And, watching Ragan do it again, he remembered that, by God, he had been drinking Bushmill's the last time he'd come in. He'd stopped someplace else first and that was the only Irish they had, and it went down well enough, so he stayed with it at the Kettle. He thought of telling Eddie he was right after all, but why bother? What difference did it make?

"What I wanted to ask," he said. "Forget the picture I showed you."

"You and everybody else, but fine, I'll be happy to forget it."

"What I was wondering," he said, "was if you happened to recall a fellow, probably came in here by himself . . ."

"I get lots of those."

Fucking moron. "Didn't say much," he went on patiently. "Maybe didn't speak at all, but he ordered a drink and then never touched it. Stood there or sat there for a while and then—"

"Walked out and left it there," Ragan said. "Tuborg!"

"Tuborg?"

"That's what he drank, except he didn't. Just like you said, the sono-fabitch sat there with the bottle and the glass in front of him, and next

thing I knew he was gone, and he never took so much as a sip of that beer.
I thought he stepped out for a minute, I thought he went to the john, I
even wondered if he did a Lenny Bruce and died there. Gone, no for-
warding. I never saw him again."

"Did you ever see him before?"

"I don't think so. I know I never saw him pull that shit before, because that I would have remembered."

"What did he look like, Eddie?"

"I dunno. Older guy, wore a cap. You see an older guy in a cap, that's
all you see, you know what I mean? Anyway, I got a lousy memory for
names and faces. Drinks, that's something different. I'll swear on a stack
of Bibles it was a Tuborg he ordered. Shit, if you're not gonna drink it,
why go for the imported stuff? Rolling Rock's good enough if all you're
gonna do is look at it."

"You remember his voice?"

Eddie was leaning on the bar, propped up on his elbows. He screwed
up his face and scratched his head, and Galvin decided he looked like a
fucking monkey, found himself checking for an opposable thumb.

"You know," he said, "I don't know that I ever *heard* his voice. You
see the Tuborg sign? I think he pointed to it, and I said *Tuborg?* and he
nodded. Or we got Tuborg coasters. Maybe he pointed to one of them.
What's sure is what kind of beer it is, that part I wouldn't forget. You
know, I could of sworn you had Bushmill's last time you were here."

Jesus, he thought, would there ever be a time he let something slide
without having it come back to bite him in the ass? Evidently not. He
said, "You know, I've been thinking, and it was. I never order Bushmill's,
but that particular day . . ." And there he was, delivering the whole fucking explanation, and this moron was nodding along happily, thrilled to
have gotten something right for a change.

And now he could drag out the picture. "Eddie," he said, "could this
have been him?"

"That's the same picture? Holy shit, are you telling me the Carpenter
was here watching a Tuborg go flat in front of him?"

"Does it look like him?"

"Jesus, is it? Like I said, I never really looked at him. I have to say it
could be."

A definite maybe, he thought.

"When was this, Eddie?"

"There's a good question. I'm thinking. Been a few months, that's as
close as I can come."

He wasn't a lawyer, wasn't in court. Where did it say he couldn't lead
a witness?

He said, "Eddie, you figure it was around the time Marilyn Fairchild got killed?"

The monkey face, indicating Deep Thought. "You know, that's right when it was."

"Oh?"

"Like maybe one, two, three days later. You want to know how come I know? Because I was thinking, suppose I get asked about this. And it was that murder put me in that frame of mind."

"And this would have been in the afternoon?"

"Just about this time of day. Nice and quiet, the way it is now."

"Who else was here, do you happen to recall?"

"Well, Max was here. Max the Poet, he's always here. Hey, Max!"

The wine drinker looked up, turned. Long face, wispy beard, long fingers wrapped around a glass of the house red. I get like that, Galvin thought, somebody please shoot me.

"Max," Ragan said, "you remember that guy, couple of months ago, ordered a Tuborg and didn't drink it?"

Max thought it over. "I drink wine," he said, and turned away.

Did that mean he wanted a drink bought for him before he remembered anything? Galvin asked what the hell that was supposed to mean, and Ragan shrugged and said that was Max, that's how he was, and he didn't remember shit.

Who else was here, Galvin asked him, and it wasn't just like pulling teeth, it was like pulling teeth with your fingers. "Draft Guinness," he said, finally, snapping his fingers and grinning like he'd pulled off a miracle. "Two guys, they're in couple times a week, sometimes together, sometimes not. Actors."

"Actors?"

"Or maybe writers. Last I heard, it was something about a screenplay, but I don't know if he was reading it or writing it. Way they pay for their Guinness, they're movers."

He didn't know which company they worked for, or their names, or where they lived. Just that one was taller than the other.

"Or maybe it was the other way around," Galvin said, and Ragan looked blank for a moment, then got it and grinned.

"They moved this woman from her boyfriend's place, and one of them was saying she liked him, and maybe he should have hit on her. Whoever she was, she stiffed them on the tip, or the next thing to it."

He went over it, found more questions to ask, but that was about all he got. He wrote it out in Eddie's own words, or what his words would have been if the mope spoke English, and went over it with him and got him to sign it.

Which the bartender did, without hesitation. "You know," he said, "I had a feeling. That's another reason I know it was right after the woman got killed, because when I picked up the glass and the bottle it came to me that this could be a clue."

"To the murder?"

"Not to *that* murder, but if all of this was, you know, like a movie. A TV show. Whatever. I mean, say something like that happens, and you have a shot of the bartender, and he's holding up the glass, holding up the bottle, thinking these could have prints on them. I remember I had the thought, I should keep this glass. You know, just in case."

Jesus, was it possible?

"Did you?"

"Did I what?"

Mother of God. "Did you keep the glass?"

A slow smile. "Yeah, matter of fact I did." And he pointed to a whole shelf of glassware above the back bar. "It's one of those," he said, grinning like a fucking chimpanzee. "But don't ask me which one. It's hard to tell them apart."

IT TOOK THE REST of that day and half of the next, but he found the moving men. There were half a dozen moving firms based in the Village and Chelsea, plus no end of Man-With-Truck operations. If it was just a guy with a van and a helper he was shit out of luck, but this sounded like guys who picked up day work when they weren't going to auditions, which meant they worked for a company.

He didn't have much to go on. A choice of three dates, draft Guinness (because the one thing he trusted Eddie on was who drank what), and a moving job for a woman. And Eddie'd come up with one more item, a colleague of the two named Big Arnie, with a droopy eyelid.

Big Arnie turned out to be the straw that stirred the drink, even though his name wasn't Arnie at all. *I know a guy like that,* the desk man at one place told him, *got an eye goes like this, and more so at the end of the day than early on. And he's big, but his name ain't Arnie. It's Paul.*

Big Paul had worked for him, but not lately. He'd had some complaints, no need to go into that now, but the last he heard Paul was working for Gentle Touch, on West Eleventh.

Which was his next stop, where he learned that Big Paul didn't work there anymore, hadn't for a while, but yeah, he was working for them around the time Galvin was asking about. And yeah, the books showed they had a local move on such and such a date when the client was a woman, a two-person job, and I guess I can let you have their names.

And he found them, and questioned them separately, and they both remembered the incident. They didn't remember the guy, they never even saw the guy, but they remembered what Eddie went through, pouring another bottle of Tuborg into two glasses and making them taste it, to make sure the case wasn't skunky or something. Fucking scene Eddie turned it into, when all it was was a guy didn't finish his beer.

Sign a statement to that effect? Yeah, I suppose so. Why the hell not?

thirty

NO WAY HE was gay. No fucking way.

Jay McGann paused at the threshold, then let himself be drawn into the wet warmth of Susan's pussy. He lay on top of her, felt her smooth female flesh under him, tasted her mouth.

Would a gay man be doing this?

Earlier, he'd feasted between her legs, and Jesus, wasn't that a treat, hair pie without the hair. No gay man would be caught dead doing that, not if his life depended on it, not if his own mother came to him in a dream and told him he had to. Pussy was what Wheaties claimed to be, the true breakfast of champions, not teatime with lavender napkins.

Not that there was anything wrong with being gay . . .

But he wasn't. A gay man wouldn't be thrusting gently but firmly with his hips, moving his rock-hard cock in and out of that sweet channel, that velvet vulva, that pathway to paradise.

And only a man who was genuinely confident about his sexuality would welcome the touch of a pair of hands on his buttocks, male hands, Lowell's hand, taking hold of him firmly, pressing the cheeks together, coaxing them apart. He drew in his breath sharply at the touch, and again at the touch of Lowell's cock at his own opening, his own portal, his very own entryway.

Oh Christ it'll never fit he's gonna tear me apart . . .

But he knew better. It had fit before and it would fit now, and he held himself in check, stopped his thrusting into the woman beneath him, and opened himself up to the man behind him. His sphincter tightened of its own accord—*That's why they call it an asshole*—but then it relaxed, and now the head was in, and that was the difficult part, and now it was all in

there, he'd taken it all, had almost sucked it in, greeting the insistent guest
with open arms, making him welcome.

Oh, God, this was good. Fucking and being fucked, giving and getting. Heaven. He didn't even have to do anything, could let Lowell supply
the power that moved him within Susan. Sheer heaven.

All right, maybe he was bi. You could argue that everybody was,
though not everybody was honest enough to admit it and act on it. Most
straight men were too frightened of that capacity to let themselves feel it,
let alone do something about it. And most gay guys, well, they were
warped one way or another, had it hooked up so that they couldn't fuck
women without thinking they were fucking their mothers.

But if you got past your hang-ups, you could do anything with anybody and feel good about it.

And it was part of being a writer, wasn't it? Tasting all of life, not just
the blue plate special. Drinking deep at the well. What was it Flaubert
said? *Madame Bovary, c'est moi.* Not, oh, yeah, I knew a girl like Emma
once.

Nothing human is foreign to me. He couldn't remember who said
that, but it was some writer, it had to be, and he got it right. You couldn't
write it unless you could first find it somewhere in your self, and how
could you do that if you were paralyzed with fear over who you might
turn out to be?

Oh, Jesus, it felt good . . .

So many people didn't get it. Same as one drop of African blood
made you black in the old segregated South, same as one grandparent
made you Jewish in Nazi Germany, in some equally objective eyes one
interlude with another guy made you a screaming queen. Like that old
joke about Pierre:

*Ah, monsieur, do you see that bridge? I, Pierre, built that bridge. I
built over twenty bridges. But do they call me Pierre the Bridge Builder?
They do not.*

*Monsieur, do you see that lion? I, Pierre, tamed that lion, and all the
other animals in the circus. But do they call me Pierre the Lion Tamer?
Alas, you know they do not.*

But suck one cock . . .

What was he when he heard that joke, twelve? Thirteen? About the
age he was when he got his first blow job, at good old Camp Tamaqua,
from good old Henrietta. Henry Blankenship his name was, but everybody called him Henrietta, which would have been cruel except the kid
honestly didn't seem to mind. And he surely did like to suck cock.

It felt great. I mean, a blow job generally does, and at that age, with no experience, Jesus. But he remembered how he'd sat there with old Henrietta's head bobbing in his lap and thinking how great it would be if he could get a girl to do this to him. I mean, that's not exactly gay, is it? To be getting head from a guy and wishing it was from a girl?

And it was just curiosity that made him imagine what it would be like to do what Henrietta was doing. I mean, everybody did that, didn't they? Imagined it? And if he imagined it sometimes late at night when he was lying on his camp cot and spanking the monkey, well, that was natural enough, wasn't it?

Here, as far as he was concerned, was the acid test: On this night and other Tuesdays, he had blown Lowell and been blown by him, had fucked him and been fucked by him. Had he enjoyed it? Yes, damn right he had, even as he was enjoying it now.

But had he ever done it without Susan present? Had he ever had the slightest interest in getting together with Lowell, or any other man, on some day or night other than this one, with no woman to share the fun?

Absolutely not. Never happen.

While, on the other hand, he'd do Susan all by himself any day of the week. And he'd make love to his wife, as he did several nights a week, though not on Tuesday, not after a night of excess like this, and Wednesday was a stretch sometimes, he had to admit. But he did it, and enjoyed it as much as ever. More, really, because he was a more sexual being as a result of everything he was doing on Tuesdays.

Oh, Jesus, that felt great. Oh, here we go, all three of us at once. Oh, wow . . .

So his primary orientation was heterosexual, no question about it. Gay? Him?

You gotta be kidding.

"JAY? TELL SUSAN ABOUT your mystery."

"Are you writing a mystery, Jay?"

"No, of course not," he said. "I mean, Raymond Chandler pretty much did it, didn't he?"

"Your real-life mystery," Lowell said. "The little man who was or wasn't there. You know, that your aunt told you about."

"Oh, Mr. Shevlin."

"Who's Mr. Shevlin?"

He yawned, stretched, felt entirely at peace with the world. He was lying between them, and he put one hand on each of them, slipped a finger into Susan, curled fingers around Lowell. "If I could change one thing," he said, "I'd make this big old thing just the tiniest bit smaller."

"Just wait," Susan said. "Pretty soon you'll be wishing it was bigger. Tell me about Mr. Devlin."

"Shevlin. He lives in the same building as my Aunt Kate, who's my father's kid sister. Twice married, twice divorced, and she's the one they thought was going to be a nun, so go figure. Anyway, Shevlin's an older man, and a couple of years ago his wife died and he bought a boat."

"And it turns out he murdered her?"

"Jesus, no. Woman died of cancer, by the time she died everybody said it was a mercy. The mystery is that Shevlin disappeared."

"When he bought the boat? I'm sorry, I'll shut up."

"Not when he bought the boat. I don't know when exactly. A few weeks ago. My aunt's friend, I forget her name, she knows Shevlin better than Kate does, and I think she's got a special interest in him. What's the expression? I think she set her cap for him."

"I haven't heard that in years."

"And her name's Helen, I just remembered. Anyway, Helen told Kate that Peter—that's his name, Peter Shevlin—that he hadn't been around lately. It's a big building, there must be a hundred, hundred and fifty apartments in it, so Shevlin was just somebody Kate would nod to in the elevator, and not seeing him for a few weeks wouldn't set off any alarms for her. But Helen had an interest, so she noticed."

"Maybe he went to the Catskills."

"The Jewish Alps? Peter Aloysius Shevlin?"

"He's making up the Aloysius," Lowell said.

"I get the point," Susan said, "but isn't there an Irish Alps? Or don't you people get any farther away than Rockaway?"

"As soon as the fucking stops," he said, "the ethnic slurs begin."

"Or the Inland Waterway," she said. "Maybe he took his boat all the way down the coast."

"Except it's still at the Seventy-ninth Street Boat Basin. Most of the time, anyway."

"Most of the time?"

"Helen called him on the phone," he said, "and she got the doorman to open the door and see if he was lying in a heap somewhere, but he wasn't. And then she called his office, and all they would tell her was that Shevlin was away and they weren't sure when he'd be back."

"If Mr. Shevlin was off for a dirty weekend," she said, "with the cute little widow from 12-J, I could see where Helen could be a real pain in the ass."

"I gather she's persistent. Next thing she did was walk over to the Boat Basin, because maybe she got the same idea about the Inland Waterway."

"And there it was."

"No, it was gone."

"So where's the mystery?"

"She went over the next day, or whenever it was, just to make sure. And it was back again."

"So he came home."

"Except he didn't. Never showed up at the apartment building."

Lowell said, "I say he's living on the boat."

"And not telling his office where he is? And sleeping there, when he's got a big two-bedroom apartment half a mile away? And wearing the same clothes every day?"

"Well?" she said. "What's the explanation?"

"Damned if I know," he said. "That's what makes it a mystery."

thirty-one

SHE WAS AT the gallery, going over some numbers, when she became subliminally aware of a familiar voice. And looked up, and there he was, standing with Chloe in front of one of Jeffcoate Walker's more alarming visions and encouraging her to tell him what the painting meant to her. He had his back to her but she recognized the jeans and the deep green polo shirt, recognized the V-shaped body, tapering from broad shoulders to a tight little butt.

She felt a tingle, and a less welcome tremor of anxiety. She was supposed to go to his place tonight, and here it was two in the afternoon, and here *he* was, in her space. It wasn't as though he didn't have a right, and she'd been planning on inviting him to see her workspace and examine her stock-in-trade, but this was unexpected, and the least bit unsettling.

She got to her feet, glided over there, planning her opening line, but he sensed her approach and turned. "Chloe was showing me around," he said. "You looked completely engrossed in what you were doing. I didn't have the heart to disturb you."

"I think I'll wait and let my bookkeeper work it out," she said. "I keep adding it up and getting different totals every time." She turned to Chloe and smiled, and Chloe got the message and found something else to do.

She showed him a couple of paintings, then took him to the back office. "That's Chloe," she said.

"I figured that out for myself," he said. "And I don't blame you a bit."

"Even if she works for me?"

"Even if she works for the FBI."

"She's yummy, isn't she? Would you like to fuck her?"

"It never entered my mind."

"Because you probably could. The three of us together, or I could just wrap her up with a bow and send her to you for your birthday."

"The gift that keeps on giving."

"She's got rings in her nipples, too. And big soft titties like bowls of cream."

"You trying to get me hot?"

"Uh-huh. What brings you here, anyway? I'm supposed to come over tonight and tell you a story."

"My turn first."

"Your turn for what? Oh, to tell *me* a story? Did little Johnny get into mischief last night?"

"Never left the house. Worked all day, ordered a pizza, and worked some more."

"Is there any leftover pizza?"

"Ate it for breakfast."

"Greedy pig."

"We can order more tonight."

"No," she said, "pizza's like revenge, it's better cold. What's the story you're going to tell me?"

"I'm not going to tell you anything. You have to read it yourself."

"I don't . . . you finished the book?"

"The first draft. I'll have a couple of weeks of tinkering to do before I'm ready to show it to Roz. But you could read it now, if you wanted."

"You're sure you wouldn't mind?"

"I'd like it," he said. "In fact I couldn't wait to find out if you wanted to, and that's why I'm here. I don't know if you'd want to close early—"

"Come on," she said. "I'll tell Chloe to lock up when she's ready to go home. You and I are out of here."

HE SET HER UP at the table with the manuscript and a cup of coffee. He'd run spell-check, but that didn't work if the mistake was a word in its own right, and at first she circled typos in red pencil so he'd find them more easily. But that slowed her down, and she decided she'd catch them when she read it through a second time. For now she didn't want anything to get in the way of the story.

And it was a good story, the protagonist richly human, like John but unlike him, the other characters sharply drawn, the prose and dialogue deceptively simple, transparent as glass. Early on she was overly conscious of who had written it, aware that she'd have to offer an opinion, and that kept her from getting as completely drawn into the story as she would have. But that changed, and everything else fell away, and there was nothing but the perfectly real world of Harry Brubaker.

She read for a couple of hours, until the letters started moving around on the page. She looked up, and he was on the couch with a magazine. She was a third of the way through, she told him, and she didn't want to stop, but she thought she probably had to.

"It took months to write," he said. "I shouldn't expect you to read it at one sitting."

"I want to, though. But I don't want to skim. I want to read all the words. It's wonderful, honey."

"You really think so?"

"Oh, yes." And she told him some of the things she liked, and his aura seemed to expand with each thing she said to him. At length he told her she'd better stop, that she wouldn't be able to find enough good things to say about the rest of it.

"Anyway," he said, "it's your turn."

"To what? To tell you a story? Gee, I don't know. I'd feel self-conscious, little old me presuming to tell a story to a big old super story-teller like you."

"Force yourself."

"Well," she said. "Okay, then."

And she recounted the events of the previous evening. The first time she'd done this, telling him last Saturday what she'd done with Franny the night before, her excitement had been held somewhat in check by the fear that he'd turn jealous or spiteful. He'd liked her stories before, but now she was relating current history, and maybe he'd find that threatening.

But he hadn't, and now she felt at ease, enjoying her own story and his interest in it. Then the phone rang, and he let the machine answer it, then moved quickly to take the call when he heard Maury Winters's voice.

He picked up and said, "Hello, Maury?" Then he listened for a long moment and said, "No kidding." And he mostly listened, interjecting other uninformative one- and two-word responses. It seemed like a good time to go to the bathroom, and when she got back he was off the phone and on his feet, standing at the bookcase with the little turquoise rabbit in his hand.

Suddenly she knew, but she waited for him to tell her.

"They dropped the charges," he said. "Fabrizzio called a press conference and made an announcement. That way she gets to talk about new evidence and the commitment of the district attorney's office not only to prosecute the guilty but to safeguard the rights of the innocent. Maury says when you beat them it never hurts to let them look good."

"But how did—"

"That detective, the drunk I couldn't say enough bad things about. Maury let him go, but the guy did some extra work on his own. He thought of a question to ask the bartender at the Kettle, something nobody asked him before, because why should they when they had a picture to show him? It's complicated, but Maury says his final bill's going to include a big bonus for the guy, and I said we should include a case of his favorite poison while we're at it, because I owe him a big one."

"You're off the hook."

"Completely." He kissed the rabbit, put it back in front of its dish of cornmeal. "When I turned down that last plea offer," he said, "I had the thought that I was setting myself up for disaster. That I was pushing it that extra inch, and now they'd find new evidence, and it would be the kind of evidence that would kill me in court. Because that's the way you'd do it in fiction. The guy has damn near everything, a Get Out of Jail Free card, and that's not enough, and the next thing he knows he's screwed, and it's his own fault. I told myself come on, you're not writing this, it's not fiction, but I was still a little worried."

"And now you can stop worrying."

"I really can, can't I? I'm glad I finished the book before I heard. So that there was still that underlying little bit of tension."

"Quite a day for you," she said. "You finished the book and the state dropped charges. The only thing I can think of to follow that is a blow job."

AFTERWARD SHE SAID, "I was in the middle of a story, but somehow I get the feeling I should save the rest of it for another day."

"It would give new meaning to the word *anticlimactic*."

"But there's something else I could tell you. It's a story one of them told, and it hasn't got anything to do with sex. Or maybe it does. It's hard to tell."

"Oh?"

"What it really is," she said, "is a mystery. Maybe I should ask your detective friend about it."

"Now you've got me interested."

So she told him the story Jay McGann had told, about his Aunt Kate's friend Helen and the missing Mr. Shevlin.

"He's living on the boat," he said. "Except why would he? Scratch that, it doesn't make sense. I know. He took off, went out of town for the summer, and one of his friends is taking his boat out for him."

"They're not like dogs," she said. "You don't have to walk them twice a day. And he was funny about his boat. He wouldn't even let Helen onto it."

"A busybody like Helen? I can't say I blame him. You're right, it's a mystery."

"I wonder if I should tell somebody."

"You could tell this guy Galvin, but not unless you wanted to hire him to investigate. Which would make you more of a busybody than Helen."

"It would, wouldn't it? Maybe I should just let it go."

"You could tell a cop," he said, "if you knew one. I know a couple, but I'd just as soon not see them again. Besides, this is up on the Upper West Side, right? If he lives near the Boat Basin."

"West Eighty-sixth Street is where he lives."

"Or lived."

"You don't think . . ."

"I'm just being dramatic. He's miles away from the Sixth Precinct, where Slaughter and Reade are stationed, and no closer to the pair who wanted to tie me to the whorehouse murders."

"I know a cop," she said. "Well, a former cop."

"Is he a private eye? Because then you've got the same problem you've got with Galvin."

She shook her head. "He's sort of retired for the time being. He used to be the police commissioner."

"And he's a friend of yours? Perfect. He's probably not in a position to do anything, but he can tell you where to go, or just pass the information on for you. You have his number handy? You want to call him?"

"I'll be seeing him the day after tomorrow."

"Today's Wednesday, so that means . . . Friday? He's the guy you see Friday nights?"

"Shit," she said.

"A former police commissioner. The only one I can think of is Ben Ward, and he just died the end of June." His eyes widened. "Buckram? Francis X. Buckram—"

"Francis J."

"I stand corrected. Francis J. Buckram is Franny? He's the guy who likes for you to wax his private parts and fuck him in the ass?"

"You're not supposed to know that."

"You mean he doesn't feature it in his press releases? Damn, that's hard to believe. Look, don't worry. I won't say a thing. I'll giggle a little, but that's all I'll do, swear to God. Yeah, tell him. Seriously, I mean it. He'll know what to do."

thirty-two

HE COULD FEEL him out there.

William Boyce Harbinger, alias the Carpenter. Born December 18, 1939. Height five feet ten inches, weight 155 pounds. Color of hair, gray. Color of eyes, blue. Complexion, fair.

Out there, somewhere in the city.

Waiting.

It was getting to Buckram. He couldn't think about anything else. The way he was these days, he damn well needed those Friday nights, and he no longer cared what she did to him. She could draw blood, she could tap a vein and drink from it. Anything, just so she got him out of his self for a couple of hours.

Phone calls piled up. He hadn't returned any in weeks, and now he'd changed the outgoing message on his machine: *Hi, I'm away, and not able to retrieve messages or return calls. Try me again sometime in the fall.* That struck him as abrupt, and he'd thought of adding something along the lines of *Have a nice day* or *Enjoy the summer,* but decided it would be hypocritical. He didn't care what kind of a day any of them had, didn't see why anyone should enjoy the summer.

Or any other season.

The Carpenter was enjoying the summer. Cooling his heels, biding his time. Getting ready for something that would make his Chelsea fire-bombing spree look like a Boy Scout campfire.

What was he waiting for?

IT WOULD BE ON a Wednesday. Last year the date had fallen on a Tuesday, he remembered that much, everybody in the city remembered that much. There was a line in a Gershwin song about Tuesday maybe being a good news day. Well, that Tuesday had been a bad news day, the ultimate bad news day.

This year, September 11 would fall on a Wednesday.

There was no way to know that was what the Carpenter was waiting for, and yet he knew it with an unyielding certainty, knew it without knowing how he knew it. That was the day that changed his life, wasn't it? Well, his and everybody else's, but the Carpenter took it personally, and it wasn't hard to see why. Lost his whole family, lost every piece of furniture in the room of life. And turned overnight from a harmless old coot with a penchant for New York City history into a maniac who seemed set on finishing what the fucking terrorists had started.

God damn them anyway, the sons of bitches.

If he could just do something about them . . .

But he couldn't, of course, and neither could anyone else. They were safely dead, gone to spend eternity with seventy virgins, and maybe that was punishment enough. He tried to imagine a Catholic equivalent, where St. Peter handed good little boys the keys to a Carmelite nunnery. Here you are, sonny boy. Enjoy yourself. Just be careful they don't smack you with a ruler.

ON THE MORNING OF Wednesday, September 11, there would perhaps inevitably be a ceremony at Ground Zero. The new mayor would be there, along with the old one, and the governor, and every local politician who could shoehorn his way in. And, the White House had just announced, the president of the United States would be there as well. He'd speak at Ground Zero in the morning, and during the afternoon he would address a session of the General Assembly of the United Nations.

Somewhere in the city, Buckram was certain, the Carpenter was thinking about September 11, last year's and this year's. So, he suspected, were half the terrorists and bona fide nut jobs on the planet. If there was a more obvious target, a stronger magnet for terror, he couldn't think what it might be. The Prez himself, standing right where it all happened, on the anniversary of the day it happened.

And what could he do about it?

Nothing, he thought. He couldn't do zip, but then again, neither in all likelihood could the Carpenter. There'd be security up the wazoo, cops and Secret Service agents a mile deep. No question the Air Force would resume overflights, and God help any pilot who wandered off course that morning. Nobody was going to get anywhere near either site, Ground Zero or the UN.

But the Carpenter might try, and he might get lucky. The damnedest rank amateurs managed to turn up at the right place at the right time, and

before you could say Squeaky Fromm or Sirhan Sirhan or John Hinckley or
Leon Czolgosz or Charles Guiteau, well, there was the shit and there was
the fan, and who'd have thought they'd have wound up so close together?

Or just possibly (because, after all, you didn't want to lose sight of
the fact that he was nuttier than a whole pecan orchard) the Carpenter
wasn't all that interested in Ground Zero or the United Nations. Maybe
he'd figured out a way to squirt nerve gas into the ventilation system at
the Chrysler Building, or bring down a bridge, or float a barge full of
plastique onto Liberty Island. Or maybe he'd find some other place to go
crazy with Molotov cocktails. Yankee Stadium, say, or a rock concert, or,
hell, anyplace full of people.

He wanted to do something. But he couldn't even go tell anybody. He
had access, he could call anybody in the NYPD or the city government
and he'd be put right through. To say what? That he thought the Carpenter might try something on September 11? *Gee, thanks for sharing that,
Fran. That's very helpful. Sharon, if this clown calls again, I'm not here.*

Maybe he should go search Central Park for a willow tree. Cut himself a forked stick like the dowsers used to witch for water. Peel the bark
off, stand in Times Square with the thing, spin around a few times and
walk in the direction the stick pointed. Let it lead him straight to the Carpenter.

If he thought there was a chance in a million it would work, he'd
fucking try it.

FRIDAY MORNING HE WOKE up with a headache and a sour taste in
his mouth. He showered and shaved and brushed his teeth and took a couple of aspirin, and while he waited for them to kick in he wondered if
maybe he shouldn't skip his weekly trip to London Towers.

At eight o'clock he was there, getting a big smile from her smartass
doorman. He got on the elevator, and by the time he got off it he had an
erection. He felt like one of Pavlov's dogs.

And she saw it the minute she opened the door, motioned him inside,
felt it through his clothing, told him she wanted to see it.

"The hair's starting to grow back, Franny. We're going to have to wax
you."

The cuffs, the rawhide thongs, the leather hood. Her hands, her
mouth. The cock ring. The toys. The smell of hot wax.

God help him, he loved it.

"FRANNY, SOMEBODY TOLD ME something a few days ago and it
seems to me I ought to pass it along. I'm not sure if it's a police matter,
but I figured you would know who should be told about it."

He was dressed, all but his shoes. She was dressed, too, and had shifted gears smoothly, no longer the sexual taskmaster, suddenly a woman friend seeking advice. It was harder for him to make the adjustment, but he sat down to hear what she had to say.

And learned about a man who'd disappeared, an older man, a widower, who'd failed to turn up at his office and was not lying dead in his apartment. Nothing remarkable there, he thought, but she went on to tell how the man, one Peter Shevlin, kept a boat at Seventy-ninth Street, and the boat came and went, apparently of its own accord.

The Flying Dutchman, he thought.

"I'm sorry," she was saying. "Now that I hear myself telling you this I'm struck by how ridiculous it sounds. He's probably turned up by now, he was probably never gone in the first place, just trying to avoid the old battle-ax who's trying to lead him to the altar."

"Probably," he said, but drew out his notebook just the same. "Better give me the names again," he said. "It'll give me something to do."

thirty-three

IN THE EARLY morning hours, when the sky was just beginning to lighten, the Carpenter's wife paid him a visit.

He noticed her perfume first. It was a scent he hadn't smelled in years, in decades. She'd worn the same perfume as long as he'd known her. Woodhue, that was the name of it, by Fabergé. He bought her some every year on their anniversary, and at Christmas, and on her birthday. And then one day he'd noticed that she was wearing something else, and wondered why, and she explained that there'd been a change in her body chemistry, evidently, because her old perfume no longer smelled very nice on her or to her.

And so she'd changed scents, to something a little spicier, a little heavier, and that became the perfume he bought for her three times a year, and you would think he could remember its name now, but he couldn't. He remembered Fabergé Woodhue, however, and recognized it the instant he smelled it.

And then he just felt her presence, there in the little cabin of the *Nancy Dee.* Next he heard her voice, speaking his name. *Billy?* She alone had called him Billy. His parents, contemptuous of nicknames, never called him anything but William. Friends in school had called him Bill. At work he was William, or Mr. Harbinger, and Carole called him William, too, in front of other people.

When they were alone she called him Billy.

Billy? Can't you see me?

And then of course he could. She was young, she looked as she had looked in the early years of their marriage. Not the girl that he met and fell in love with, but the young woman with whom he had set about making a life. She was wearing the blue dress he'd always liked. He'd wondered whatever happened to that dress.

"Carole," he said, "I thought you were dead."

I am, Billy.

"But you're here."

I can't stay long.

"You're so beautiful," he said. Had he ever told her that when she was alive? He must have, he'd thought it often enough. Yes, surely he'd told her.

You used to tell me that all the time, Billy. I never believed you.

"Do you believe me now?"

Oh, yes. Billy, I miss you.

"I miss you, too, my darling."

I wish you could come home with me.

"Soon," he said. He looked at her, took in her gentle smile, breathed in her scent. "You're wearing Woodhue," he said.

She smiled, delighted. *Yes, do you remember? I always wore it. It seems to agree with me again. Isn't that funny?*

"I'll buy you some for your birthday."

Oh, Billy. That would be very nice.

"Carole," he said, "do you see the children?"

Oh, yes. They miss you, too.

"And you're all right? All of you?"

We're all fine, Billy. Everybody's fine.

He had a million questions to ask her and couldn't think of a single one.

I wish you could come with me, Billy.

"I have something I have to do, my darling."

Oh, I know. Men always have their work, and it's important that they do it.

He'd done his work for years, and had it been so important? Any of it?

"I'll be done soon," he said. "A matter of days."

I have to go now, Billy.

"Don't go," he said. "Not quite yet. Stay a few more minutes, Carole."

But she was fading, disappearing even as he looked at her. He watched her fade away to nothing, and felt her energy dissipate. The scent of her perfume lingered in the cabin for a time, after every other trace of her was gone.

thirty-four

THE DOORMAN'S NAME was Viktor, and his English pronunciation was careful and deliberate. Yes, Peter Shevlin lived in the building, and it had been a while since he'd seen him. But he understood one of the other men checked his apartment, and everything was all right.

"I think maybe he goes away for vacation," Viktor said.

"That's possible," Buckram allowed. "I understand one of the tenants was asking about him. A woman, I believe her name is McGann."

"I don't know this name," Viktor said, and asked him to spell it. He looked at the list of tenants, moved his forefinger down the page as he scanned the names, looked up, shook his head.

Buckram took the list from him, checking for first names. No Kates, but one Katherine, a Mrs. Mabee. If Kate McGann had kept her husband's name after the divorce, and if it had been Mabee, well, then there she was. A definite Mabee, he thought, and grinned.

"Mrs. Mabee," he said. "Was she asking about Mr. Shevlin?"

"She does not ask me. This woman asks." And he pointed to Mazarin, Mrs. Helen. "Every day she asks. You want I call her?"

"Let me start with Mrs. Mabee," he said.

KATE MABEE, NÉE MCGANN, was a small woman, barely over five feet tall. The first thing she did, even before she asked to see some identification, was tell him she used to be taller. "I'm shrinking," she said indignantly. "I'm down three or four inches already, and it's not like I've got them to spare. I swear it's not fair. I got a sister-in-law, I should say an ex-sister-in-law, but I stayed friends with her after I threw him out. You would say she's statuesque. Three years older than me, and she hasn't lost an inch. She can still pick apples off the trees."

"While all you can do," he said, "is charm the birds out of them."

"Oh, Jesus, an Irishman," she said. "Now that I've let you in the door, why don't you show me something that says you're you?" He showed her some membership cards—the Detectives' Endowment Association, the International Narcotics Enforcement Officers Association, the National Association of Police Chiefs. And his driver's license, with his picture on it.

"I know who you are," she said. "You were the commissioner."

"For a few years, yes."

"And now you want to ask me about Peter Shevlin? Jesus, what has he done? If he took money and ran, I hope it was at least a million. Less than that and it's not worth it, is what my father used to say."

"My father said the same thing."

"I suppose it's too early to offer you a drink?"

He said it was, but she should feel free to have one herself. Oh, but it was hours too early for her, she said with a laugh. A small drink before dinner, she said, was her limit, and she'd give that up soon if she kept on shrinking. Not that the two were related, it was calcium fleeing from her bones that caused her to shrink, but the shorter she got the quicker the drink seemed to go to her head, and she was beginning to suspect she'd do better without it.

She was good company, but she didn't have much to tell him about Peter Shevlin, just that he seemed to have gone missing and that her friend, Helen Mazarin, was up in arms about it. She'd been to the police, and once they'd established that she was no kin of Shevlin's, that she was not even his lady friend ("though that's not to say she wouldn't like to be"), that a search of the apartment had shown no signs of foul play, or of Shevlin himself, and that he was not suffering from Alzheimer's disease or any other form of senile dementia, they told her there was nothing they could do. It was a free country, they told her, and a man could pick up and go away for a while if he got the urge.

She went back a second time, explaining about his boat, the *Nancy Dee,* how sometimes it was there and sometimes it was not. It was a different policeman she talked to the second time, and he agreed to take a statement and file a missing persons report, but she had the feeling he just did it to get rid of her.

"You know about the boat? How it's there one minute and gone the next?"

Like so many things, he thought, but he said yes, he'd heard about the boat.

"You should talk to her yourself. Helen Mazarin, she's got a good heart, but I'm afraid she's a bit more interested in Peter than he is in her, though I'd not be the one to tell her as much. She's right here in the building, you know, and just two flights up, so you can take the stairs if you don't feel like waiting for the elevator. Would you like me to call her and tell her you're coming?"

HELEN MAZARIN WAS A strawberry blonde, though he had the feeling she hadn't started out that way. Time had thickened her at the waist and widened her hips, but she remained an attractive woman for her years, and the way she sized him up confirmed that she had not lost interest in the game.

I'm too young for you, he thought. At the very least, you need a man old enough to grow pubic hair.

She took him into her kitchen, sat him down at a table with an enameled tin top not unlike the one in his own mother's kitchen, and poured him a cup of coffee. "I'm glad they're taking this seriously," she said. "I got the impression the officer I spoke with was going to throw my report in the trash the minute I walked out of there, but here you are."

He explained that he was a retired policeman, that this was an unofficial inquiry. "A friend of Mrs. Mabee's thought I could help," he said, and she nodded, impatient to begin, not really caring whose ear she had as long as she could pour her story into it.

There wasn't much he hadn't already heard. Peter Shevlin had disappeared, or perhaps more accurately he had ceased to appear. And it wasn't like him to go off like that without a word to anyone, not that he was a man given to a great deal of conversation, but to walk off and not come back? It had been a couple of weeks now since she had seen him last, and she ordinarily saw him every few days.

And the boat, that was the great mystery. How he loved that boat! The *Nancy Dee,* that was its name, named for his wife, a lovely woman, Nancy Delia Shevlin, and what a cruel lingering death she'd had. She'd gone to the Boat Basin, thinking he might be there, and the boat was gone. And she'd gone another time, and it was back in its slip, and yes, she was quite certain it was his boat, for didn't it have the name painted on it for anyone to see? The *Nancy Dee,* and it came and went, yet she never saw it actually coming in or going out. In fact the last several times she'd gone it had been there, with no signs of activity aboard, but she swore it had been gone on at least two occasions that she'd seen with her own eyes.

Maybe he'd left on an unannounced vacation, he suggested, and gave the use of the boat to a friend. But no, she was sure this wasn't the case, and he'd realize as much if he knew Peter at all, because the man was very possessive about that boat. She'd hinted a time or two that she wouldn't mind keeping him company on a cruise of the harbor, and one time she'd more than hinted, she'd outright asked, and he'd merely smiled and changed the subject. He'd made it quite clear that the *Nancy Dee* was for himself and himself alone, and if he wouldn't even allow a friend aboard for an hour, how likely was it that he'd turn the boat over to a stranger to use in his absence?

He said, "The policeman you talked to, the one who took your state-ment and filed a report. Do you happen to remember his name?"

She'd written it down, she said, and went off to look for it. He was beginning to wonder why this had seemed like a good idea when he woke up this morning. Because it didn't seem that remarkable to him that Shevlin (or anyone else) would just as soon not welcome Helen Mazarin at the dock and pipe her aboard. Nor did it seem out of the ordinary that the man, probably driven half mad by Mazarin on a daily basis, had slipped out of town without letting her know about it.

For this he'd gotten up early, put on a suit and tie and, for the first time in longer than he could recall, included a shoulder holster in which his service revolver, a .38-caliber five-shot Smith & Wesson, had long re-posed. The cops all carried more powerful guns, .45 and 9-mm autos, a necessary response to the heavier weaponry that the bad guys had. He'd signed the order allowing the change but had never upgraded himself, be-cause what did the commissioner really need with a gun in the first place? So why not stick with the one he was used to?

He'd felt silly donning the holster, sufficiently so that he took it off and returned it to the drawer where he kept it. He locked the drawer, put the key in another drawer, put his jacket back on, and was out the door before he changed his mind once again and went back for the gun after all. He hadn't been able to shake the odd feeling that he was going to need it.

While he was at it, he grabbed his cell phone. He never bothered to carry it, never got calls on it because he'd never given out the number. But it would be handy if he needed to make a call. It saved you the trouble of finding a pay phone that worked.

It made more sense than the gun, anyway. Weighed a lot less, and he was more likely to use it.

He had a Kevlar vest, too, and had made a big thing about that, as part of a campaign to get cops to wear them all the time, not only when they expected to be shot at. Because how often did a cop expect to be the tar-get of hostile gunfire? If you actually expected it, you'd stay home and call in sick. But it was a funny thing, the bullets were just as deadly whether or not you saw them coming, so he insisted his cops wear their vests while on duty. Not all of them did, of course, but he made a point of setting a good example, at least if there was likely to be an opportunity to display it to the news cameras.

It actually occurred to him to wear the vest today, but it was summer, for God's sake, and you could sweat to death inside the damn thing, and it weighed a ton, too. And he was just going to talk to people, and so he did not expect to get shot at. And if by some incredible fluke, if by some crazy quirk of fate, if his wild-ass wholly irrational hunch paid off and the Carpenter was somewhere in all of this, well, there was no reason to believe that William Boyce Harbinger had ever owned a gun, or had one in his possession, or even knew for sure which end the bullet came out of. A Kevlar vest wouldn't do you any good if somebody came at you with a hammer and a chisel, and only slowed you down if you were trying to outrun a Molotov cocktail.

So it was home in his closet, and that was fine, because he felt silly enough carrying the gun.

She came back with two names written on a slip of paper, and was reaching to pour him another cup of coffee. He stopped her, took the slip from her. The top name had an asterisk next to it, and she explained that was the man who'd taken her statement for the missing persons report. The other man was the one she'd talked to the first time, just in case he needed to talk with him as well.

And he'd let her know as soon as he found out something? He told her she could count on it.

SHEVLIN'S APARTMENT BUILDING WAS on the north side of Eighty-sixth Street, between Columbus and Amsterdam. That put it in the Twenty-fourth Precinct, Eighty-sixth Street being the dividing line, but Helen Mazarin had not gone to the Two-Four station house, three-quarters of a mile away on West One Hundredth. Instead she'd reasonably enough walked four blocks to the Two-Oh on West Eighty-second, and Buckram did the same.

The desk sergeant, Bert Herdig, had a big round red face and not much hair, and what he had left was cropped close to his skull. He recognized Buckram right away, called him Commissioner before he could introduce himself, said it was an honor to have him there, and what could he do for him? Did some fool of a patrol officer hang a ticket on the commissioner's windshield? If so just hand it over, and it would go no further.

"A woman came in a few days ago, filled out a missing persons report," he said. "Her name's Mazarin, and the missing man's Peter Shevlin."

"Of Eighty-sixth Street," Herdig said, and stroked his chin. "Don't tell me something's happened to the poor man."

"Well, that's the question. He hasn't turned up yet."

"He might not, if he's playing golf in the Poconos."

"Is that where you think he went?"

"It's where I'd go," Herdig said, "if I had the time and the money. Could I ask the nature of your interest, Commissioner?"

"A favor for a friend."

"Ah, right," Herdig said. "Everybody has friends and sooner or later they all want favors. Mrs. Mazarin's the friend?"

He shook his head. "The friend of a friend."

"Ah. You've met the lady?"

"Just this morning."

"She'd come in once before I saw her," Herdig said. "Did she mention that?"

"She did."

"Tony Dundalk talked to her then, and more or less sent her on her way. Because it didn't sound like any cause for alarm."

"And she came back."

"She did. I thought, let's put the lady's mind at ease, so I took her statement and filled out a report."

"But you didn't send it in."

He shook his head. "Sending it in doesn't accomplish anything. Nobody's gonna be running around knocking on doors, looking for an old man who's minding his own business. All that happens is somebody wants to know why I'm sending in an MP report on a case that doesn't meet the standards. I made her happy, but I stuck the report in a file."

"And let it go at that."

"No," Herdig said, "I called his place of employment, spoke to the head of the department. No, Shevlin hadn't been in for whatever it was, a week or so, something like that. And yes, they'd had a call, said he wouldn't be in. They didn't seem concerned, and after I talked to them neither was I."

"Did she tell you about Shevlin's boat?"

"To tell you the truth," Herdig said, "I had a little trouble following her on that subject. Did I miss something important?"

"Probably not. Did you take notes when you talked to his employer?"

"His department head. Yes, I took notes."

"And filed them? I wonder if I could see the file."

Herdig looked troubled. "Uh, well," he said. "You know, I'd do anything to help here, Commissioner, but there's a question of official standing. My understanding, you're no longer officially connected with the department."

"Not for a few years now."

"So you've got no official interest in this particular matter."

"None," he agreed, "which is convenient all around, isn't it? It means I don't have to file a report, and neither do you. It also means nobody's going to ask you where the regulations say you're supposed to take down a statement and fill out a missing persons report and then conveniently lose it in a file drawer somewhere." He smiled pleasantly. "Of course," he said, "if I pick up that phone and call around, you're likely to get a call back from someone with so much brass on his uniform you won't be able to spot the blue underneath it. And I guarantee you he'll have enough official standing to mobilize the National Guard."

"I take your point," Herdig said. "Just give me a minute, okay?"

PETER SHEVLIN WAS EMPLOYED by a firm called Fitzmaurice & Liebold, with an address on Sixth Avenue that would put it in or near Rockefeller Center. His supervisor, and the man who'd put Herdig's mind to rest, not that it was all that troubled to begin with, was one Wallace Weingartner.

Buckram bought a couple of sandwiches at a deli, got a can of Heineken to go with them, and had lunch on a bench in Central Park. The beer made the enterprise technically illegal, in that he was consuming an alcoholic beverage in the park. Striking a blow for freedom, he told himself, and enjoyed his meal.

He was eating al fresco so he could make a phone call, and he'd always felt the use of cell phones in restaurants was an infinitely greater evil than, say, drinking a beer in public. After he'd bagged his trash and dropped it in a litter basket, he returned to his bench and managed to get the number at Fitzmaurice & Liebold, whose offices he was reasonably certain would be closed today, the Saturday of Labor Day weekend. But you never knew what sort of workaholic Wally Winegardner might be, so it seemed worth a try.

The offices were closed, of course, but the voice that answered gave him options; if he knew his party's extension he could press it, and, if not, he could find it by entering the first three digits of the party's last name. He pressed 9-4-6, the numeric equivalent of W-I-N, and that gave him a choice of two parties, neither of them Winegardner. He tried to get back to the previous prompt but couldn't navigate through the system, so he gave up and broke the connection and went through the whole thing again. This time, on a hunch, he pressed 9-3-4, for W-E-I, and learned in short order that Wallace Weingartner's extension was 161. He pressed that, and after four rings got a voice mail pickup, with a woman's voice— Weingartner's secretary, he supposed, or the firm's official telephone voice—inviting him to leave his message at the tone.

He rang off and put the cell phone away. He could let it go, he thought, but that meant letting it go until Tuesday, because the office would be closed tomorrow and Monday. And Tuesday was the third, and a week from Wednesday was the eleventh.

And he couldn't help thinking the Carpenter was out there. Well, hell, everybody damn well knew he was out there, but he also felt he was somehow connected to the disappearance of Peter Shevlin.

Made no sense. If he really thought so, he should stop trying to figure out how to track down Weingartner (and wouldn't you think a cop with a name like Herdig would jot down the German spelling?) and call someone who could hook him up with whoever was heading the Carpenter task force. But he couldn't do that, because if he had the guy on the phone right this minute he wouldn't have anything substantive to tell him. He didn't even have a hunch, for God's sake. Just a feeling, and one that made increasingly less sense the more he examined it.

He got out the phone again, called 1-212-555-1212, and actually got to talk to a human being, who came back and told him that Wallace Weingartner didn't have a listed phone in the borough of Manhattan. Not in the 212 listings, anyway. He tried 917, the code for local cell phones, figuring old Wally might have his phone along even if he was up in the mountains or down on the Jersey shore. He could call the poor bastard without even knowing where he was.

No listing.

He put the phone in his pocket and gave up.

VIKTOR WAS STILL ON duty, and not happy at the thought of letting him into the Shevlin apartment. When pressed, he explained that he was a Russian Jew from Odessa, in the Ukraine, and that the building's super and all the other doormen and maintenance personnel were Hispanic. If anything turned up missing from the apartment, who would they say took it?

"My shift is up at four. Then is Marcos. You tell him what you want, he lets you in. No problem."

"If I have to come back," he said, "it won't be at four o'clock, it'll be twenty minutes from now, and you'll still be on duty. And I'll have a couple of uniformed cops with me, and I'll pick the ones with the loudest voices."

Viktor turned away, looking unhappy, and found a key in the desk drawer. "Here," he said. "You go. Anybody asks, you can tell them I never set foot in that apartment."

No, he thought, instead you gave a total stranger the unattended run of the place. For that they ought to give you a medal.

He went upstairs, let himself in, sniffed the air, and was grateful for what he didn't smell. Because it was entirely possible Shevlin could have been lying dead somewhere in the apartment, in a closet or under a bed or in the tub with the shower curtain screening him from view. If his death had been close enough in time to the earlier visit, and if the doorman who'd made the last check had just taken a quick look around . . . well, the poor bastard would be pretty ripe by now.

But in fact the poor bastard wasn't there at all. Buckram spent the better part of an hour trying to learn something useful, and invading Shevlin's privacy rather thoroughly in the process. You learned that in police work, learned to search drawers and closets without blinking, to go through papers and correspondence with the enthusiasm of a voyeur and the ardor of a spy.

What he didn't find was anything to establish Shevlin's presence in the apartment since Helen Mazarin had decided he was missing. His checkbook didn't have an entry after that date. There were newspapers stacked beside a chair in the living room, magazines arranged on the coffee table, none of them more recent than the date of his presumed disappearance.

There were pictures, mostly of a woman whom Buckram took to be Mrs. Shevlin. In one she appeared as a bride barely out of her teens, standing beside a slim young man with dark hair and a shy smile, who looked to be wearing a tuxedo for the first time in his life. No pictures of kids, nor did he recall Mazarin mentioning any children. A childless couple, married young, lived for decades until the wife died and left the husband stranded.

Like the Harbingers, he thought, in a West Side apartment building just two blocks from here. Not so grand—the Shevlins were in one of the great Art Deco buildings on Eighty-sixth, with high ceilings and an impressive lobby, the Harbingers in a more modest building on a less desirable street. But then the Harbingers had had children to support.

Both men wound up childless, though.

He picked up the wedding picture, wishing it would tell him something. She dies and you buy a boat, he told the young Shevlin in the picture. You're seventy-two years old, you could certainly afford to retire, but how much time can you spend putt-putting around New York Harbor? So you go to work every day, and you come home, and on nice evenings you go out on your boat.

Where the hell are you?

He wished he could find a more recent photo of Shevlin. The wedding portrait was useless, you couldn't show it to people and tell them to add fifty years to the kid in the picture. He'd thought Mazarin might have a snapshot of the man, most likely taken against his wishes, but she'd said she didn't. She wasn't much of a photographer, she'd said.

When he first entered the apartment he'd wished he'd thought to bring a pair of Pliofilm gloves. He was careful not to touch anything until he'd established with his eyes as well as his nose that there wasn't a dead body in the place, or any signs of a struggle. In their absence, there was no reason anyone should presume the place to be a crime scene, so he didn't worry unduly about breaching its integrity with his fingerprints. He kept them to a minimum, though, and put the things he touched back where he found them.

When he couldn't think of anything else to do he went over to the phone, looked at it for a few minutes, then picked it up and dialed. If there was ever an investigation, and if they ever pulled the LUDS, there'd be a record of the calls he made, calls placed from Shevlin's apartment after the man had disappeared. But it probably wouldn't come to that, and yes, he could have used his cell phone, but the fact was he hated the damn thing.

He started calling the Information number for different regional area codes, asking for Wallace Weingartner. 718 for Brooklyn and Queens, 516 and 631 for Long Island, 914 for Westchester County. There was a W. Weingartner in Manhasset and a W. B. Weingartner in Bedford Hills, and he called those numbers, and the first turned out to be Wanda and the second answered to Bill. Both claimed to know quite a few Weingartners— he didn't ask if they knew each other—but neither knew a Wallace.

The 202 operator found a W. Weingartner right across the river in Hoboken, so he tried that. And got a computer-generated voice mail response inviting him to leave a message. No indication what the W stood for, and no reason he could think of to leave a message.

He locked up and went downstairs. Four o'clock had come and gone, and Viktor had gone with it. A younger man, presumably Hispanic, presumably Marcos, was on the door. He couldn't think how to give him the key without confusing him, or getting Viktor in trouble, or both. And why should anybody else need to get into the apartment? If he remembered, he'd return the key to Viktor in the morning. Or find it on top of his dresser in six months and have no idea what it was or where it had come from.

HE WAS HALF A block away when he remembered he'd promised Helen Mazarin a report. He had taken down her number, and he called her now on his cell phone. He reported essentially that there was nothing to report, but that he didn't see any real cause for alarm. He'd look into it a little further, though.

The boat, she said. Had he seen the boat? He told her he'd have a
look at it on his way home. Would he like her to come with him? It would
be no problem, she could be out the door in half a minute.

He said he didn't think he'd have any trouble finding it. The Boat
Basin wasn't that large, and how many boats was he likely to encounter
named the *Nancy Dee*? It was nice of her to offer, but he figured he'd
know Shevlin's boat when he saw it.

But if it wasn't there?

Well, he said patiently, then there'd be nothing to see, would there?
She was still thinking about that one when he rang off.

THE BOAT WAS THERE, and he didn't have any trouble finding it.

There were three ramps leading across the water to the floating docks
where the boats were moored, and each had a locked gate restricting access to boaters. The locks looked easy to get through, and even easier to
get around. All you had to do was step over the thigh-high railing to the
side of the gate, take a few careful steps along the concrete ledge and one
big step over the water to the ramp, and you'd finessed the whole business. If you did this furtively, anyone watching would spot you for an intruder. If you acted with the casual nonchalance that was the birthright of
every policeman, an observer would figure you'd left your key home.

He walked down the ramp, made his way through the maze of floating docks, found the *Nancy Dee,* and climbed aboard. It struck him as
comfortable enough, and probably seaworthy. Nothing you'd want to
cross the ocean in, or sail around the Horn, but it looked as though you
could take it on the water if you had to, which was more than you could
say about a lot of the moldering old wrecks tied up at the piers.

The entrance to the cabin—he didn't suppose you called it a door—
was locked. He squinted through the glass—he didn't suppose you called
it a window—and couldn't see any signs of life. He knocked, listened,
knocked again.

Behind him, and not all that far behind him, a man asked him what he
wanted.

He turned, saw a heavyset man about forty, with untrimmed dark hair
and an untrimmed full beard. He could have played heavies in pirate
movies. The man's question was reasonable enough, but for the first time
Buckram was just as glad he'd brought the gun along.

"I'm trying to find Peter Shevlin," he said. "You know him?"

"I know there's nobody home on that boat."

"So do I, now that I knocked. Do you know Shevlin?"

"Don't pay much mind to names," the man said. "So I won't even ask
you yours."

And don't ask me mine, seemed implicit in the statement.

"You know the man who owns this boat?"

"You some kind of a cop?"

"I'm trying to get in touch with Mr. Shevlin," he said.

"You didn't exactly answer the question, did you?"

"Why should I? You haven't answered any of mine."

"People around here mostly got better things to do than answer questions, especially when they don't know who's asking 'em. One thing we do know, we know you don't go on a man's boat without an invitation. You're standing on his deck."

The son of a bitch had a point. He got back onto the pier, and the man yawned, showing Buckram what he'd obviously not shown a dentist in ages.

He said, "Answer a question, and save us both some trouble. Have you seen Shevlin in the past two weeks?"

"I don't keep much track of time. Or of who I seen and when I seen 'em."

"Has anybody taken the boat out recently?"

"What's it matter?"

What he wanted to do was kick the big son of a bitch in the knee. Knock his leg out from under him, then shove him off the pier and into the water. The water was no pure mountain stream, but he'd come out of it cleaner than when he went in.

But then, grudgingly, the dipshit answered the question. Sometimes the old man boarded the boat at night. Took it out for a couple of hours, then brought it in.

That was all he was going to get, and as much as he'd expected. Nor did he figure to get much more from anybody else. He'd do better going into some dark holler in the Ozarks and asking if there were any illegal stills operating nearby. He understood those folks really knew how to make you feel welcome.

thirty-five

THE CARPENTER, WEARING his yachting clothes, the cap perched jauntily on his head, sat on a shaded bench in Riverside Park. He waited while the shadows deepened and the last of the sunset's glow faded from the darkening sky. He didn't see anyone coming or going from the Boat Basin, and judged it safe to board the *Nancy Dee*.

He was doing just that when a voice said, "Hey, Shevlin."

The gun was in the cabin, clipped to the top of the little chest of drawers. He had the key to the cabin in his hand. If he could just ignore the voice long enough to get into the cabin and get to the pistol . . .

"Isn't that your name? That's who he was askin' for."

So this person didn't know Peter Shevlin, wouldn't unmask him as an imposter. And his information might be important.

The Carpenter turned, smiled at a black-bearded mountain of a man, a Hell's Angel costumed as a wharf rat. "We never met, but I seen you around," the man said. "Don't want to stick my nose in, it's not my nature, but you had a visitor, and I figured you'd want to know about it." And he told of a man who'd come aboard the *Nancy Dee* late that afternoon, a well-dressed middle-aged man who sounded like a cop.

"But he didn't flash any tin, and he didn't push it like a cop would. And he got off your boat when I called him on it."

"There's a lawsuit," the Carpenter said. "They want me to appear as a witness, and it's all very tiresome."

"Figured it was something like that. Just thought you'd like to know about it."

"That was thoughtful of you. I appreciate it."

"Hey," the man said, "we got to stick together, you know?" He grinned. "We're all in the same boat."

. . .

ONE LOOK AT THE river told you it was a holiday weekend. Even at this hour there were still plenty of boats out. He loved the way they looked, small private craft enjoying the city's great harbor. The little sailboats were especially attractive, and it looked like fun, sailing around as they did, pushed by the wind. It would be silent on a sailboat, too. You wouldn't have the noise of the boat's engine.

But you'd have to know what you were doing. He supposed it was the sort of thing a person could learn, and felt a momentary pang of regret that he never had. It was something one ought to have done earlier in life, and for a few minutes he allowed himself a fantasy of what might have been, pictured himself at the helm of a small sailboat, accompanied by his wife and children. He'd bark out orders—*Mind the boom! Hoist the jib!*—and they'd hasten to carry them out. He didn't know what the words meant, but he'd have learned that whole vocabulary, and they'd sail away the hours, sail away the days.

Someone had put his feet on the deck of the *Nancy Dee*. Someone had come around snooping, asking questions, looking for Peter Shevlin.

This was not good at all.

He looked out over the water, considering the implications. It was possible, of course, that the intrusion had been as trivial as he'd explained it to the bearded man. Someone with business with Shevlin might have gone looking for him; failing to find him at his apartment, he could then have tried him at the Boat Basin. In that case he wouldn't know that Shevlin had gone missing, and would either keep looking in a tentative way or drop the matter.

But it was more likely that someone realized that Peter Shevlin was missing, and that was why he'd had a visitor. Perhaps it would be best, for the next few days, if he came to the boat later and left it earlier. Should he avoid sailing altogether? That might not be necessary, if he took the proper precautions.

He owed a debt of gratitude to the man with the black beard, and wondered if a bullet might not be the best way to pay it. Because, for all that his warning was useful, his knowledge was dangerous. He had looked the Carpenter right in the face, and the Carpenter's face had been made familiar to the entire city, and indeed to the world beyond.

On the plus side, whenever the man looked at him in the future he'd recognize him as Peter Shevlin. That was all to the good, until the moment the fellow spotted a newspaper photo or watched *America's Most Wanted* and experienced the shock of recognition. *Why, that's Shevlin,* he'd say. *No wonder he looked familiar.*

Invite him on board, sail out onto the middle of the river, far enough so that a shot from a small-caliber gun in a closed cabin wouldn't reach another human ear. Wait until the man was distracted, because he was huge, he might be harder to kill than Rasputin. Then put a bullet into the back of his skull, into the base of his brain.

And then what? He didn't have the boning saw, it was down there in Davy Jones's locker, and it would be hell dismembering a man that size in the close quarters of the boat's cabin. No, just get him overboard, but even that could not be done without difficulty.

All in all, he decided, killing him presented more and greater risks than letting him live.

Besides, the Carpenter thought, the man would die soon enough. They all would.

THE MARINA WAS ON the Jersey side of the river, a ways upstream from the Boat Basin. The boats moored there were several cuts above the ramshackle lot that were his neighbors, and the *Nancy Dee* looked like a poor relative in their company.

But that didn't make the rawboned man with the bandage on his cheek disinclined to take his money and sell him a five-gallon can of gasoline.

"Oh, and a case of beer," the Carpenter said as an afterthought. "In bottles, and make it whatever's the cheapest."

The man said he had Old Milwaukee at a real good price, but that'd be cans. Did it have to be bottles? The Carpenter said it had to be bottles. There was something about drinking out of a can, he said, and the raw-boned man said he knew exactly what he meant.

He wound up with two cases of Bud Light. ("You know what? Make it two cases, I don't want to run out in the middle of a holiday weekend.") The bottles had twist-off caps, and he twisted them off one by one, pouring their contents overboard. He filled the two cases with the empty bottles and carried them into the cabin.

That made five cases, or sixty bottles. And ten gallons of gasoline, which was far more than he'd need. Sixty twelve-ounce bottles would hold 720 ounces, or a little more than twenty-two quarts, which was not much more than five gallons. Of course you had to allow for some spillage, the Carpenter thought. And anything left over would just add to the final sacrifice.

He wouldn't fill the bottles yet. He had to store them in the cabin, where they wouldn't be readily seen, and he knew his cloth wicks would not be airtight. In a closed space, the fumes could reach dangerous levels. He wouldn't want that.

But he had his bottles empty and ready, his strips of cloth already torn, the gas on hand waiting to be poured. He was prepared.

He was back at his slip by three in the morning. He waited long enough for anyone who'd been disturbed by his engine to go back to sleep. Then, quietly, he changed his clothes, loaded the white pants and the cap into his backpack, and went ashore.

thirty-six

CREIGHTON SAT ON the couch and thought of a cigarette. He didn't necessarily want one, but the thought came to him, as it often did. With the day's first cup of coffee, at the end of a good meal, after lovemaking, or when a conversation seemed to require a pause, that little break you got when you shook a Camel out of the pack and put a flame to it. He told himself, not for the first time, that a mind was a terrible thing to have, and turned his attention back to the television set.

America's Most Wanted was on. They'd just dramatized the story of a West Virginia man who'd violated an order of protection his girlfriend had taken out against him, and in the process had violated his girlfriend and the girlfriend's eleven-year-old daughter. The actor chosen to play the serial violator seemed an odd choice for the role, slim and blond and nerdy, until they showed a photo of the real miscreant and he looked as though he ought to be running Microsoft.

And now it was Carpenter time. John Walsh told how tips had led law enforcement officers to kick in a door at a motel in Waycross, Georgia, while others surrounded an RV parked at a KOA campground in Kalispell, Montana. In each case, an elderly gentleman who on close examination proved to look nothing like the photo of William Boyce Harbinger was arrested and released with apologies.

"But we're getting closer," Walsh assured his viewers, and went on to announce that another New York City murder, that of real estate agent Marilyn Fairchild, had been definitely credited to the Carpenter.

"He makes it sound as though the program's responsible," Susan said. "Not a word about James Galvin, PI, or the public-spirited author who hired him."

"I talked about him this afternoon. Gave him credit."

"By name?"

He nodded. "If they don't cut it," he said, "it's a nice plug for him."

He'd spent the afternoon at NBC's Rockefeller Center studios, taping a show segment with Matt Lauer. They'd watch it tomorrow morning on CNBC, and it would air later throughout the week on both of the network's cable channels. It was not the first national TV he'd done since Leona Fabrizzio's press conference, nor would it be the last; Tracy had booked him on Dominick Dunne's new show on Court TV, and was working on Larry King. He was, she'd told him, a dream to book. He was a writer, bright and articulate, and he'd been accused of a horrible crime with yummy sexual overtones, and not only was he as innocent as a newborn lamb, but through his efforts the crime had been added to the Carpenter's lengthening list. It was early for publicity, but the opportunity was too good to pass up.

"Call me crazy," she said, "but when the book comes out, I'm not ruling out *Oprah*. She's done with the book club, but that doesn't mean she's not booking authors."

The publicity was so hot, and making everyone at Crown so happy, that you could easily lose sight of the fact that there was a book in there, too. But there was, and Esther Blinkoff was reading it over the weekend. He had the feeling she'd love it whether she liked it or not, but he also expected her enthusiasm to be genuine.

Because he'd felt right about this one from the first day, and the three readings the book had had so far confirmed his feeling. He'd read it himself, of course, catching typos and overused words and redundancies and the occasional awkward phrase, and his was hardly an objective reading, but it was a relief to discover that he liked what he read. Susan was his ideal reader, the one he'd been writing *Darker Than Water* for before he knew she existed, the one for whom he'd been writing all his life. He'd expected her to love it, as indeed she had, and for all the right reasons; her reaction was reward enough for writing it.

But not the only reward he could expect, according to Roz, who could be counted on for an honest appraisal. Artistically, she assured him, it was at least as good as anything he'd written, and probably his best work. From a commercial standpoint, it was even more impressive. "The crime angle got you the contract," she told him, "and the numbers plus the publicity angle had this book headed for the list before you wrote it. But *Darker Than Water* would be a candidate even if, God forbid, those cops had never come knocking at your door. What's so funny?"

" 'God forbid'?"

"Well, face it, the way it turned out it was a blessing. But without all that, if you just walked in and laid this on my desk, I'd do the same thing,

I'd run half a dozen copies and have an auction. And I wouldn't get three million dollars, but I'd get something in the high six figures, I guarantee you that. You're already rich and famous, sonny boy, and you're gonna be richer and famouser. What do you think of that?"

SUSAN HEARD HIM SINGING in the shower. She loved that, it was such a guy thing. Like karaoke, but without making a public spectacle of yourself.

She'd joined him in the shower the other day, effectively ending the concert but starting something even better. She loved soaping him, loved that he had all that hair on his body. It contrasted so nicely with her own.

Should she go in there now? No, she decided, it wasn't the sort of thing you wanted to do too often. She'd think of something else, something special.

She picked up the little rabbit, touched the smooth stone to her cheek. Was she losing her mind or was the cornmeal disappearing from its bowl? There did seem to be less of it than the last time she'd looked.

She kissed the creature, informed it that it was a little pig, and put it back in front of its dish.

He'd bought a bunch of bananas the other day, and they looked ripe enough to eat. She peeled one, and it was just right, ripe but firm. She closed her lips over the end of it and savored the feel of it in her mouth, then got an idea. She ate that banana and peeled another one.

When he got out of the shower she was waiting for him in the bed. "I've got something for you," she said.

"I'll bet you do."

"It's a banana," she said, "and I hid it."

"My goodness," he said. "Now where could you possibly hide something like that?"

"I think you should look for it," she said, "and if you find it you get to eat it. But there's a catch."

"I was afraid of that. What is it?"

"You're not allowed to use your hands."

And what an inspiration that turned out to be. He didn't stop when the banana was gone, didn't stop after her first or second or third orgasm, and how could you count when one sort of rolled over into the next, and finally he was lying on top of her, his cock buried inside her, bigger than the banana, firmer than the banana, oh God sweeter than the banana, and he was kissing her, and his mouth tasted of pussy and banana, and if they could synthesize that combination everyone would want to pour it over ice cream, and he was fucking her with a lazy rhythmic roll of his hips, taking his time, taking his time, and she looked into his eyes and they were looking back into hers, and she couldn't help herself, she couldn't help herself, and she took his big hands and put them at the sides of her throat.

"Oh, yes," she said softly, and pressed his hands tighter against her throat. "Oh, please, yes."

HE AWAKENED TO THE smell of coffee brewing.

It was the perfect aroma to wake up to, and in fact you could use the coffeemaker as an olfactory alarm clock if you wanted, loading it up with coffee grounds and water, and setting it to start its brewing cycle when you wanted to get up. That had always struck him as too much trouble, but here was the perfect solution: have someone sleep over, and let her wake up before you.

And bring you coffee in bed, which she did a moment later.

She was dressed, and looked beautiful. "I went out for the *Times*," she said. "It's a holiday weekend, so it's smaller than usual. It only weighs ten pounds."

She'd been about to wake him, she said, if the smell of the coffee hadn't done the job. His interview with Matt Lauer was due to air in ten minutes. Meanwhile here was the Book Review section.

They sat on the couch with separate sections of the newspaper. The TV was on and tuned to the right channel, with the sound muted until the show came on. He tried to read a review of the latest offering by a South American magic realist, then tried to read Marilyn Stasio's crime fiction column. But his mind kept wandering away, imagining the reviews *Darker Than Water* might get. Would they like it? Would they hate it? Did it matter?

And there was Matt Lauer, wearing the same jacket he'd worn the day before. He put the sound on, set the paper aside. His interview would probably be later on in the show, but he wanted to watch the whole program.

Beside him, Susan leaned gently against him, and he put an arm around her, drew her close. Jesus, a new game, Hide the Banana. How'd he get so lucky?

And then he remembered how she'd taken his hands and put them on her throat, how she'd kept them there, pressing them to her. *Please,* she'd said, as if begging.

He sensed something unpleasant, some unthinkable thought, hovering just out of sight, just out of reach. He took a breath and willed it away and made himself pay attention to what Matt Lauer was saying.

thirty-seven

CHANNEL-SURFING, BUCKRAM happened on Matt Lauer, interviewing a terrorism expert on parallels between the Carpenter and the demento with the mail-order anthrax. The most striking point of similarity, he thought, was that so far nobody had managed to catch either one of them. It had been almost a year since Mr. Anthrax started spreading his powdered cheer, long enough for him to have slipped everybody's mind, including, apparently, the fucking Bureau.

He stayed with the show, though, muting it during the commercial, and the next segment paired Lauer with John Blair Creighton, the writer, whom Buckram had seen last at Stelli's. The guy had been on top of the world that night, and he looked even happier now, happier than anyone had a right to look on a Sunday morning.

Right off the bat, he found out the reason. Somehow he'd missed hearing that the DA's office had thrown in the sponge and dropped charges. Nice for Creighton, he thought. Had to feel good if he was really innocent, and had to feel even better if he wasn't.

And then Creighton was giving credit to Jim Galvin, mentioning him by name, saying he'd worked the case on his own time.

He watched the show through to the end, then found Galvin's number and called. It was busy, but he got through five minutes later when he tried again.

"I know two things about you now," Galvin said, before he could say more than hello. "You've got cable and you skipped church this morning."

"Everybody's got cable," he said, "and I've skipped church every morning for the past twenty years. Longer than that, if you don't count weddings and christenings. That was some nice pat on the back he just gave you, and some nice piece of work you did."

"Phone's been ringing off the hook," Galvin said. "Of course I never saw it myself. I was watching female bodybuilders on ESPN Two."

"If I'd known about that," he said, "I wouldn't have wasted my time on Matt Lauer. Seriously, congratulations. It's gonna bring you some business. Plus some offers to be on some shows yourself, which'll bring in more business."

"Yeah, but don't worry. I'll fuck up a few cases and be right back where I am now. But thanks, Fran. I got lucky, but it's luck I made for myself, so I don't mind taking a bow for it. And I got the guy out from under, and that's something."

"You think he really didn't do it?"

"No, the DA gave him a walk because he's got such a nice smile."

"He was using it a lot this morning," Buckram said. "That's one happy fella. Seriously, what's your best guess?"

"The man paid me," he said, "which he legally didn't have to do, although in another sense he did have to. But he also gave me a nice bonus, which he definitely didn't have to do, plus he sent over a case of booze."

"Your brand?"

"Better. I drink Jameson, and that's what he sent, but he made it the twelve-year-old."

"Only an innocent man could do a thing like that."

"My reasoning exactly," Galvin said.

HE WALKED UP TO Seventy-ninth Street, took a bus, got off at West End Avenue, and walked the rest of the way to the Boat Basin. The *Nancy Dee* was right where it had been when he'd been warned off it by the very guy who always used to beat the shit out of Popeye until he downed the can of spinach. That's who he looked like, the surly son of a bitch.

No point in moving in for a closer look. No point in coming here at all today. He had a damn good explanation for Helen Mazarin, although he wasn't going to bother delivering it. Shevlin had taken a trip somewhere, and yes, his boat left its slip occasionally, and not because some friend of Shevlin's had been given permission to take it for a spin. That tub of shit with the beard had borrowed it without permission, he or one of the other lovelies who lived there. Knew the owner was out of town, and their own waterlogged wrecks weren't going anywhere, so why not sail away on the *Nancy Dee*? He couldn't imagine anybody who knew boats would have a hard time gaining entry or starting the engine, and if they brought it back Shevlin would never know it had been gone.

Obvious, once you thought of it.

He just missed his bus back across town. Typical, he thought. A wasted trip gets a little longer. And this was Sunday, so God knew when there'd be another.

He caught a cab and went home.

HE WAS GOING THROUGH his notebook, tearing out pages with obsolete and often meaningless notes on them, and came to a phone number. WW, and ten numbers starting with 202.

It took him a minute, but then he cracked the code. W. Weingartner, and the *W* would be Walter or Winifred or Wilma, or maybe Why Bother.

He picked up the phone, dialed the number, and a woman answered. He asked for Wallace Weingartner, and she said, "Yes."

When she left it at that, he said, "Uh, is Mr. Weingartner at home?"

"I'm sorry," she said, "but I never respond to telephone solicitation. In fact this number is on a national Don't Call list, and you're in violation of a federal regulation. I suggest you act accordingly."

And she hung up.

The day, he thought, was just getting better and better. He hung up himself, and went into the kitchen to see if there was a cup of coffee left in the pot. He was pouring it when he realized the voice had sounded familiar, though he couldn't place it. Maybe all irritated women sounded alike. God knows there were enough of them around.

He picked up the phone, pressed Redial. When she answered he said, "I'm not a telemarketer. I'm trying to reach the Wallace Weingartner who's a department head at Fitzmaurice & Liebold."

"That would be me."

"Yeah, that was you on your office voice mail. I knew I'd heard it somewhere. I'm sorry, because of the name I assumed—"

"Of course you did," she said. "Everybody does. It's W-*a-l-l-i-s*, my mother was absolutely starry-eyed nuts about the Duchess of Windsor, and I've spent my whole life trying to figure out why. I don't think I got your name."

"Francis Buckram," he said. "That's Francis with an *i*."

She had a good laugh, rich and generous. "I thought it might be," she said. "How can I help you?"

He explained that he was calling on behalf of neighbors of Peter Shevlin, trying to find out what had become of the man.

"I believe he's ill," she said. "He failed to come in one day and didn't call, which is very unlike Peter, and later that same day I had a call from either a cousin or brother of his, I don't remember which."

"Saying that he was ill."

"Yes, and I got the impression that it was serious, the sort of thing one doesn't recover quickly from." She paused, then said, "If at all."

"I see."

"I was shocked," she said, "because Peter had been perfectly fine the day before, though he's not a young man, and I guess things can happen suddenly. But the brother rang off before I could ask him how we could reach Peter. We'd have sent flowers, of course, and called to find out more about his condition."

"And you never heard anything further."

"Not yet, no. I've been hoping the brother would call back, but so far he hasn't."

He told her he'd let her know if he learned anything, and gave her his own number in case she found out more before he did. After he'd rung off he still realized he had no idea what sort of business Fitzmaurice & Liebold carried on, or what Peter Shevlin did there.

Whatever it was, he had a feeling he wouldn't be doing it anymore.

FIRST, THOUGH, HE SPENT the better part of an hour on the phone, doing what he should have thought to do yesterday. He called area hospitals, trying to find one that had Peter Shevlin for a patient. He didn't think Shevlin was in a hospital, didn't think he was alive, but he had to make the calls to rule out the possibility.

Hadn't the Carpenter done this before? In Brooklyn, in Boerum Hill. Hadn't he called Evelyn Crispin's office, said she'd been called out of town?

So that no one would come looking for her.

So that he could live in her apartment, water her plants, feed her goddamn cat. Live there in perfect comfort, at least until the smell got too bad and drove him out.

He might have moved on by now. Might have holed up on Shevlin's houseboat for a few days or a week. But he'd have killed Shevlin somewhere else, not on the boat, so he wouldn't have the same problem he'd had with Crispin.

Unless his visit yesterday had spooked him somehow, in which case he was in the wind. So long, see you later.

But he didn't think so. He'd had a feeling about this one right from the start, from the minute Susan started telling him an apparently pointless story about someone neither of them knew. Right away he'd thought of the Carpenter. That was the only thing he thought of, the only thing that could have made him take even a cursory interest in the business, let alone get off his ass and get involved.

Something occurred to him, and he went looking for the photocopies

Herdig had made for him at the Two-Oh. He read Shevlin's description—
height, weight, age, complexion, color of hair, color of eyes.

At seventy-two, Peter Shevlin was ten years older than the Carpenter,
but everything else was pretty much on target. If you put the two men in a
lineup they probably looked entirely different, but that was the point; you
could put them in a lineup, because they were close enough in physical
type.

Close enough to fool the big galoot with the black beard? Popeye's
worst nightmare?

Yeah, maybe.

If he'd been working the case with a partner they'd toss ideas back
and forth, batting them around, throwing verbal spaghetti on the wall to
see what stuck. He was running a solitaire version of the same game,
tossing his own ideas in the air and taking a swing at them.

Maybe he needed a partner. Maybe he should call Galvin, let him try
for another brass ring.

Maybe he should call whoever was heading up the Carpenter task
force. Odds were good it was someone he knew, and a hundred percent
certain it was someone who knew him.

And if the Carpenter was hanging out, keeping an eye on things?

No way they could infiltrate an area like the Boat Basin in force without making their presence obvious. If he was on the boat, well, fine,
they'd have him sewn up tight. But if he wasn't?

And if he had never been there in the first place, if Peter Shevlin was
having a hot time with somebody else's wife and didn't want the world to
know about it, then what? And wouldn't the word get around that a certain former police commissioner was just a little bit past it?

You couldn't go in without backup, he thought. Not unless you were
out of your mind. Not *even* if you were out of your mind.

But you could take a look first. You could do that much. Hang out,
sneak a peek, make sure the wild goose was there for the chasing. You
could do that, couldn't you?

He took his cell phone, his holstered .38. Found a set of handcuffs,
dropped them in a jacket pocket. And, feeling a little foolish, and wishing
the day were cooler, he stripped to the waist and dressed again, this time
with the Kevlar vest underneath his shirt.

thirty-eight

T HE *NANCY DEE* was still in its slip.

Buckram had figured it would be. The Carpenter would use darkness. He was, from all accounts, a man who shrank from the limelight and sought out the shadows. He'd almost certainly board the ship after the sun had set, when there was less light to be seen by and fewer eyes to see him. If he was going to take the boat out, he'd do so then. Or he'd keep his hands off the tiller and catch a few hours of sleep, leaving well before daybreak.

What was the best way to do this?

He could board the boat now. He'd had a glance at the lock on the cabin door earlier, and it hadn't looked terribly challenging. And why should it be? Out on the water you worried about pirates, not burglars. He'd added a handcuff key to his key ring before he left the apartment, and while he was at it he included the flat strip of flexible steel that had opened more than a few doors for him over the years. He'd be inside the *Nancy Dee*'s cabin almost as quickly as if he had the key.

And then he'd be waiting there when the Carpenter showed up. He'd hear the man coming, feel the boat shift when he came on board, and have a gun in his hand when the man came through the cabin door. With the advantage of surprise, he'd have the son of a bitch collared and cuffed before he knew what was happening.

And if it was Shevlin?

Well, hell. He'd tell him he was under arrest for making everybody crazy, and then he'd relent and send him home to Helen Mazarin, which would be punishment enough.

But it wouldn't be Shevlin. Shevlin was dead, he was sure of it, and the man who came into the cabin would be the man who'd killed him.

There were other approaches he could make. He could stake out the
Boat Basin and grab the Carpenter as soon as he showed up. He might be
hard to spot in a crowd, but he wouldn't be in a crowd, he'd be by himself, heading for the pier.

Mr. Harbinger? No, don't move, and keep your hands in plain sight.
Down on the ground, hands behind your back . . .

Easier with two people, easier still with three or four. Hard to corner
a man when you were by yourself. You could run at him full speed, tackle
him without warning, but you ran the risk of bystanders misreading the
situation and interfering—plus a whole lot of egg on your face if you
tackled some visiting fireman from Waukegan.

And if the tackle wasn't perfect, and if the Carpenter made a break
for it, then where were you? Even if you were willing to shoot at him,
against regulations for cops, flat-out illegal for a private citizen, you
risked missing him and hitting somebody else.

No, the best thing was to lay in wait and take him by surprise.

Now?

Now the sun was still high in the sky, and hot enough to make him
question the wisdom of the Kevlar vest. Riverside Park was a human bee-
hive, swarming with joggers and skaters and parents pushing strollers and
people walking dogs. Everybody on the Upper West Side who hadn't escaped for the holiday weekend had apparently decided to come to the
park for a breath of fresh air. There wasn't any, not at the moment, but if
some happened to blow down from Ontario, they were ready to grab their
share of it.

Hard to spot anybody in that sea of people. He looked for a place to
sit, passed up a bench he could have shared with a woman who was feeding pigeons, shared another with an Asian man who was reading a copy
of *El Diario*.

He sat back, relaxed. But kept his eyes open.

THE MOVIES WERE BETTER during the week.

The films, of course, were essentially the same, irrespective of the
day or time they were shown. But the theaters served better as refuge and
dormitory on weekday afternoons, when even the most popular films
drew tiny audiences. Saturdays and Sundays attendance increased dramatically, which was good for the theater owners and the film studios, but
not as good for the Carpenter.

Still, he'd learned how to manage. You showed up when the box office opened, bought a ticket for a film. If there was a foreign-language
feature with subtitles, you chose that, knowing that it would remain relatively deserted no matter what day it was. Failing that, you avoided any

picture designed to appeal to the young. Anything animated, anything with children or animals on the poster.

If the featured performers were ones he recognized, the audience was likely to be sparse. Because that meant the actors were older than average, and so were the people who came to see them. Such films were among the more popular on weekday afternoons, when the elderly made up the greater portion of the audience. On weekends, however, when senior rates were not available, the old folks stayed home, and the young watched Brad Pitt or Scooby-Doo.

There were other useful maneuvers. The best seats, from the Carpenter's point of view, were on either side against the wall, and at the rear of the theater. This did not put you all that far from the screen. In the old days, when screens were much larger and movie houses cavernous, it was a different matter. But you were as far away as you could get, and unless the showing was a sellout (and it wouldn't be, unless you'd made a gross error in your film selection) there'd be no one sitting near you, neither to the side or immediately in front.

Because screens had gotten smaller along with the theaters, you might not be able to see too well from where you were, and if you'd been lucky enough to find a foreign film, well, you could forget about trying to read the subtitles. But entertainment wasn't the point. A secure and restful environment, that was your prime consideration.

The tricky part came when the picture ended. You couldn't just stay in your seat and wait for the next showing, because they'd clear the house and walk through the length of each row, picking up at least some of the popcorn tubs and candy wrappers left behind by the departing moviegoers. You could try saying you'd come in halfway through the picture, he supposed, but he wasn't at all sure that would work; worse yet, it invited attention, and that was what you most wanted to avoid.

What you had to do was plan. By the time you bought your ticket, you already knew what film you'd go to after you left the first theater. Today, for example, the Carpenter had been one of the first at the box office, one of the first to take a seat—in the rear, of course, and against the right-hand wall—for a showing of a film starring Clint Eastwood. He dozed through the commercials, dozed through the coming attractions, and dozed on and off through the picture, opening his eyes each time gunfire roused him and checking his watch before drifting off again.

When one such check showed only fifteen minutes before the film was scheduled to end, the Carpenter left the theater, having to disturb only one person, a tiny little woman perched on the aisle seat. Anyone who noticed him leave at that point in the film would take him for a man who had to go to the bathroom, and the Carpenter did precisely that. Nor was the visit undertaken purely for purposes of deception; the Carpenter could have held out until the end of the film, but welcomed the opportunity to relieve himself.

Having done so, he went to the refreshment stand and bought popcorn, then headed for the theater that was next on his list, where a film based on a Henry James novel was scheduled to begin in twenty minutes. The timing was right, and he couldn't imagine that any film based on anything by Henry James could draw a young audience. Carrying his popcorn, mingling with other people with the same destination, the Carpenter did not look like someone sneaking into a second film that he hadn't paid for. He didn't see how it could occur to anyone to stop him and demand a look at his ticket stub, and of course no one did.

The commercials and coming attractions were the same ones he'd seen before the first picture, and indeed ones he'd seen repeatedly in recent days. He found them comfortingly familiar. And the feature film, once it started, was wonderfully soothing, with no gunfire to rouse him, or even voices raised in anger. The interruptions had played a useful role during the Eastwood movie, but now the Carpenter was perfectly willing to doze right through to the end. Two films would provide him with all the sleep he needed.

He closed his eyes and settled in to enjoy the show.

YOUR TWO WORST ENEMIES on a stakeout were your bladder and your brain.

The first was obvious. Sit around for hours on end, and sooner or later you had to take a leak. Even if you were a camel, the time came when you had to go. If you were in a parked car, you brought a jar along, hoping when you used it that nothing happened in midstream, that you didn't get caught in a firefight with the jar in one hand and your dick in the other. And, since things rarely happened that abruptly, and often didn't happen at all, you were generally okay.

If you didn't have a car to sit in, if you were in fact out in public view on a park bench, a jar wouldn't help. You'd be better off getting on all fours and lifting a leg against a tree, hoping they'd take you for a funny-looking German shepherd. So what you had to do was desert your post, and that was acceptable when you had a partner who could watch twice as hard in your absence. When you were alone, well, it meant that for a while there was no one minding the store.

Your bladder was a problem once every hour or so, or more frequently if you'd been spending too much time at Starbucks. Your brain was dangerous every minute you were out there. Because it could get bored, and it could wander, and the thing you were waiting for could happen right in front of your eyes and you'd miss it because your mind was somewhere else.

It was a funny thing, but detectives weren't the best choice for a stakeout. Patrolmen tended to be better, especially veterans who had never got a gold shield and never would. It wasn't that they were stupid, or lacked ambition. What they lacked was imagination.

And imagination was the common denominator of detectives. It wasn't enough by itself to get you a promotion, good luck and good connections played a bigger role than anyone cared to admit, but still it seemed to be part of the makeup of virtually every detective he'd known.

On stakeout, it was a curse. A sufficiently unimaginative man could stare out a car window at a front door, or crouch in a closed van listening to a wiretap, for hours on end, thinking of nothing but the job he was doing. A man with an imagination would try to do just that, but his mind would jump from one thing to another, going off on tangents, and he'd lose track of what put him there in the first place.

Again, a partner helped. The two of you could talk, and one could bring the other back to the here and now.

Alone, well, it was a problem.

Right now, for instance, he was working hard to stay on top of things. He'd peed not twenty minutes ago, at the men's room of the café, and had resisted the urge to pick up a small bottle of Evian water at the bar on the way back. And now he was watching the crowd, keeping an eye on the approach to the Boat Basin gates. He looked at another pigeon feeder and wondered why people fed the birds, what it was they got out of it. And he started thinking about pigeons, and how you never saw a young one and rarely saw a dead one, and why was that, anyway? And was it true that kids from the Asian subcontinent, or from Central America, or from Vietnam, trapped pigeons off the street for their parents to cook in their restaurants? And hadn't they said the same thing a generation or two ago about the Chinese? And wouldn't they have said much the same about the Irish, but for the fact that no Irish immigrant had ever opened a restaurant, and who would have gone there if he did? And . . .

He caught himself, forced his mind back to business. It was going to be a long day, he thought. It felt like it had been a long day already.

THE CARPENTER WAS WATCHING a newsreel.

They had newsreels all the time when he was a boy. Coming attractions, and then cartoons, and a short, either a travelogue or something funny, and then the feature. Followed, more often than not, by the second feature, itself preceded by more cartoons and coming attractions.

Now you got commercials, and animated exhortations to put your trash in the basket and be quiet during the movie.

Once, he remembered, there had been a newsreel theater near Times Square that showed nothing but newsreels from morning to night, a sort of theatrical version of CNN. Television had put paid to that enterprise, as it had meant the end of newsreels altogether. So the Carpenter couldn't be watching a newsreel. It had to be a dream.

He was awake enough to reason that out, while sufficiently asleep to remain in the dream and go on watching the dream newsreel. It was in black and white, of course, as newsreels were meant to be, and it included moments the Carpenter had seen in newsreels, or might have seen—the mushroom cloud of an atomic explosion, German soldiers goose-stepping, Allied troops liberating a concentration camp. Then, still in black and white, a plane sailed into the World Trade Center tower, and flame billowed, and the building fell in on itself.

There is an announcer throughout, and the Carpenter can hear the words he speaks but can't make them out. And then one word leaps out, the word *Carpenter,* with nothing intelligible before or after it. And there he is on the screen, dressed not as he is today, in dark trousers and a dark nylon sport shirt from the store in Greenpoint, nor in the clothes he has in his backpack, his yachting costume. No, on the screen he is wearing a dark suit, like one of the ones he used to buy at Brooks Brothers, and a striped tie, and he's surrounded by a crowd, and they're cheering, they're all there to honor him.

Savior of the city, he hears the announcer say, and President Eisenhower is there, smiling that huge smile of his, and Mayor Wagner, and John Wayne, and they're giving him some sort of reward. And now the noise dies down, and he's supposed to say something.

And can't think of a thing to say.

That's unsettling enough to wake him, or seems to be, and he opens his eyes, or thinks he does, and now the screen fills with the image of a stunningly beautiful woman. He thinks at first that she looks familiar, and then that he knows her, and of course it's Carole, his wife, and she's looking right at him.

Carole . . .

I'm right here, Billy.

Why did you leave me, Carole?

I told you I could only stay for a minute. Didn't I tell you that?

The first time, Carole. When you took the pills. Why did you do that?

Oh, Billy.

You should have told me.

You would have made me stay.

*No, I'd have come with you. I tried to follow you, but then I woke up.
It wasn't my time.*

No, Billy.

I had things I had to do.

I know you did.

But I'll be along soon, Carole. I can't do much more. I get so tired.

I know you do.

Are you going again, Carole? Don't go.

I have to, my darling.

Carole? I'll be with you soon, Carole.

His eyes were open. Had they been open all along? And his cheeks
were wet. Did anyone notice him weeping? No, there was no one near.
No one noticed a thing.

And the movie was back, the Henry James movie, with women in
gowns and everyone looking sensitive and aristocratic. And an audience,
even on the Sunday of Labor Day weekend, that filled fewer than half the
seats.

There were two people between him and the aisle. They rose to let
him past, sat down once he was by them. Their eyes never left the screen.

The men's room, the stairs, the sidewalk outside. He'd walk home,
get something to eat along the way. He knew he ought to eat, although he
wasn't very hungry. He hadn't touched his popcorn.

ONE TRICK, FRAN BUCKRAM thought, was to move around a little. If
you sat in the same spot forever, your eyes on the same scene, it got
harder and harder to pay attention to what was in front of your eyes.
If you got up and walked around you got the blood moving, and when
you sat down again on a different bench you saw things from a different
angle.

It helped, but what would help even more was to have something to do.

A book or a newspaper would be handy. And what could look more
natural than a man reading? Always the chance, though, that he'd get
caught up in his reading and miss the man he was waiting for. Of course
that wouldn't happen if he had something he couldn't read, and he found
himself wondering about that Asian man he'd seen earlier with his Spanish newspaper. Was he on a stakeout of his own?

He got out his cell phone, tried to think of somebody to call. Arlene?
No, he really didn't have anything to say to her. Susan? Yeah, right. She'd
tell him to take off all his clothes and handcuff himself to the bench. Then
take two enemas and call her in the morning.

He called his own number, thinking he'd check his messages, then
heard his own outgoing message, the one that told people not to leave

messages, and saw the futility of that. And what an arrogant message he'd recorded—*I'm too busy for you, so don't leave me a message, but try me again later when I might have time for you.* Nice, very nice.

Even if he had a paper it was getting too dark to read. Good, he thought. Pretty soon it would be dark enough and the human traffic sparse enough to think about boarding the *Nancy Dee*. First, though, he'd better get something to eat. He'd pee while he was at it, but peeing wouldn't be that much of a problem once he was on the boat. There was bound to be a toilet, which you were probably supposed to call something else. The head? That sounded right. So he could go to the head, or pee in a waste-basket (and God knew what they'd call that) or a bottle. Or in the corner, because it wasn't his boat, and the man whose boat it was would never know the difference.

THE CARPENTER HAD WALKED all the way back from the theater, a distance of about two miles. He'd taken his time, stopping to buy a sand-wich, eating it as he walked, stopping again for a can of soda. The sun was down by the time he reached Riverside Park, but the day was still bright, and the sky over Jersey was stained red and purple.

It was a wonderful city for sunsets. You couldn't see them from his old apartment, and that was the one thing he would have changed about the place. It did something for a person to see a beautiful sunset.

He walked through the park, walked a hundred yards or so past the Boat Basin, sat for a few minutes, then walked back the way he'd come. Looking at the people, paying attention to what he saw.

Something felt wrong.

He'd felt glimmerings of it on the way back from the movie house. He thought about the date he'd circled on his calendar. Well, he'd made the circle on paper with a felt-tipped pen. He hadn't carved it in stone. Who was to say he couldn't move it up?

A year, of course, was the conventional period of mourning. Making the final sacrifice a year to the day after their magnificent sacrifice had a certain poetic value, not to mention a mathematical precision. But how trivial such considerations seemed to him now.

The sooner he carried out his mission, the sooner he could rest. And he was tired, so tired, in a way far beyond what sleep could cure. His spirit ached with the tiredness he felt.

He could rest. And he could see Carole again, and his children. And all the other poor sweet innocent sacrificed angels. That gentle fellow with the shaved head. Buddha, he was called. And that poor woman in Brooklyn, and the prostitute, Clara.

Oh, so many of them.

Yes, he'd made up his mind. He'd decided. He wouldn't wait any longer.

But first there was the sensation he felt, the awareness that centered at the back of his neck, that atavistic animal sense of being sought, of being hunted. And hadn't he been told just yesterday that someone had come to his boat, someone had been looking for him?

He studied the people in the area. There were two men who seemed to him to be without apparent purpose, but who nevertheless had a purposeful air about them. As if they might be watching and waiting for someone.

One got up and left, and the Carpenter watched until he was sure he hadn't merely changed seats. Then he turned his attention to the other, not looking directly at him but observing him out of the corner of his eye. The Carpenter was in shadows, where he couldn't be seen easily, and he had the knack of disappearing, of attracting no attention. This man did not have that knack. He was, in fact, quite the opposite. There was something magnetic about him. He drew the eye.

The Carpenter let his eye be drawn, kept it on the man. He looked familiar, the Carpenter thought. His face was one he'd seen before, perhaps in the newspapers or on television.

Not in a newsreel, though. He wasn't old enough to have been in a newsreel.

And now he was on his feet, headed south on the bike path, walking by the water's edge. And he paused at the very gate that led to the *Nancy Dee,* but no, he wasn't entering, he was just taking a good look.

The Carpenter smiled.

The man turned, and the Carpenter watched him make his way to the path that would take him to the Boat Basin Café. The Carpenter smiled again, and made his own way carefully and unobtrusively to the slip where the *Nancy Dee* lay waiting for him.

He'd have liked to paint out the name. Call it the *Carole.*

Inside the cabin, he left the light unlit. When his eyes accustomed themselves to the darkness he went over to the chest of drawers and took the gun from its clip, slipped it into his pocket. Then he sought out the cabin's darkest corner and wedged himself into it, standing there like a statue in a niche. If no one came, he'd remain still and motionless for two, three, four hours, waiting in patient silence until it was time for his sacrifice.

If anyone showed up before then, well, he was ready.

TEN-THIRTY, AND STILL NO sign of the son of a bitch.

Which was fine, actually. This way he could be on board when the

Carpenter showed up. It was late enough now for him to make his move. If Blackbeard gave him any grief, he'd drag him around the corner and cuff him to a lamppost.

No point sneaking or skulking. That would draw attention quicker than anything else. No, the thing to do was walk right out on the pier and hop on board that boat as if you owned it, and that's just what he did. He had the urge to go over to the helm, grab ahold of the wheel, and gaze off into the distance like an old sea dog.

But he'd be wasting time. He walked over to the locked hatchway, drew out his key ring, went to work.

THE CARPENTER'S MIND WAS adrift, bobbing in a sea of thought. But he came to suddenly, sensing a presence. Moments later he heard footsteps on the pier, and then felt the boat tilt as someone came aboard.

He hadn't moved since he took his position in the corner of the cabin, not even when his mind was all drifty. Nor did he move now.

He heard someone trying a key in the lock. But who would have a key? He wondered if he should have left the hatch ajar. He'd thought of it, decided it might look suspicious. But if the fellow couldn't get in—

If he couldn't get in, well, he'd just go away. Which would actually simplify things.

Even so, the Carpenter hoped he'd be able to open the door. And he listened as whatever the man was using scraped the metal, scraped it again, then caught and forced it free. The hatch came open, letting a little light into the cabin, but none that reached the corner where the Carpenter was waiting.

He didn't move, didn't breathe. Until the man came in, and found the stacked cases of empty beer bottles, the cans of gasoline, the heaped strips of cloth. The man stiffened, and the Carpenter sensed he could tell what he was looking at. The man lifted one of the bottles from the top case, then put it back where he'd found it.

The Carpenter drew his pistol, took one step forward, pointed the gun at the back of the intruder's neck. And squeezed the trigger.

Instead of a *bang!* he heard a dry *click!* The gun was broken, or improperly loaded. But not entirely useless. Even as the man started to spin around, the Carpenter drew the gun back and used it like a hammer, like a tire iron, swung it with all his strength against the back of the man's head.

He fell to his knees, tried to brace himself, tried to rise, tried to turn.

The Carpenter hit him again, and this time he fell all the way and lay still.

thirty-nine

SUSAN HAD LEFT around noon, telling him she had a million things to do, letters to answer, bills to pay, clothes to wash. And no, he didn't have to go downstairs with her, there would be no end of cabs, or she could just hop on a bus up Eighth Avenue, or even walk, it wasn't that hot out, it might be pleasant to walk. And she kissed him, and he got up from the couch and let her out, and she kissed him again, and he stood at the door until he heard her leave the building, then went to the window and watched her walk off down the street and disappear around the corner.

He liked her walk. A good no-nonsense athletic stride, but no less feminine for it. And her ass looked great in slacks.

He'd been glad she was going yet reluctant to see her go. This was the first time she'd stayed the night, and in fact he hadn't had many women stay over since he'd moved back into the Bank Street apartment after the divorce. There'd been ladies he'd spent the night with, and one a couple of years ago he'd spent a whole lot of nights with, and had given some thought to spending all his days and nights with, until she'd announced out of the blue one day that this just wasn't working out, and anyway she was moving back to Santa Cruz.

But with Jessica—that was her name, Jessica Duncan, and thank God she'd moved back to Santa Cruz—with her and the other less frequent overnight companions, he'd almost invariably gone to their apartments. They generally preferred it that way, given that he lived in one room and everything stank of cigarette smoke. (And what, incidentally, was he going to do about that? He seemed to have quit smoking, he was almost ready to start cutting the patches in half, and one symptom of his new status as a former smoker was that he was beginning to notice the way his

place smelled. Not while he was in it, but when he came back from out-
doors, the way you'd notice some cat lover's litter box. Jesus, was he going to turn into one of those obnoxious ex-smokers who wrinkled their
noses when someone two blocks away lit a Marlboro? Yeah, he thought,
he probably was.)

It wouldn't hurt to have the place painted. And he could get rid of the
upholstered furniture, the couch and the comfortable chair, both of which
should probably be replaced anyway. That wouldn't eliminate odors entirely, but it was a start, and time would do the rest.

So many things to think about, just to keep from thinking about what
he didn't want to think about:

His hands on her throat.

HE ALMOST CALLED HER after he heard from Esther Blinkoff. She'd
begun with an effusive apology for interrupting his holiday weekend,
then told him it was only fair since he'd completely monopolized hers.
She and her husband were at their house on the Jersey shore, spending
their last long weekend there prior to closing it down for the season, and
what had she done ever since they got there Friday? She'd ignored everybody and locked herself away with *Darker Than Water,* and it was all his
fault that she'd been unable to stop reading.

Usually, she confessed, she'd wait until she got some other in-house
readings before announcing her own reaction to a manuscript. But why
wait? She knew everyone was going to love the book, knew Sales would
go out of their minds for it, and all she had to do now was figure out just
which month to publish. The sooner the better, of course, but not so soon
that the book didn't have all the groundwork laid for it.

And so on.

It was what Roz had told him to expect. Esther had three million reasons to love the book, so how could she not? But her enthusiasm moved
him all the same, and he reached for the phone to share it with Susan,
then decided it could wait.

Why the hell had she put his hands on her throat? Pressed them there,
when he moved to take them away?

Please, she'd urged.

Please *what?*

HE HAD DINNER ALONE, came back and picked up a collection of
O'Hara's short stories. He skipped through it, reading a couple of old favorites, wishing he could write like that.

On his way back from the bathroom, he checked the rabbit's dish.
Susan had said the cornmeal was disappearing, and he looked for himself

and decided she was seeing things. Or, more accurately, not seeing them. He picked up the dish and sniffed it, and it seemed to him that it smelled of tobacco smoke.

Now you're really being nuts, he told himself. And dumped the dish in the garbage, wiped it out, and added fresh meal from the sack in the refrigerator.

Live a little, he told the rabbit. We're going to be rich, you can have fresh cornmeal every day for years.

But how'd you get here, anyway?

He looked for his copy of Blake's poems, found "The Tyger." There was one line he wanted to check, to make sure he remembered it correctly. Yes, there it was:

Did he who made the Lamb make thee?

He put the book back, picked up the rabbit, looked into his little eyes. They were some dark stone, maybe obsidian, and they gave the animal an expression of great alertness, which was all to the good; if you were going to talk to a little turquoise rabbit, you wanted to feel it was paying attention to you.

Why did I pick you up, and why don't I remember it? And what did I do just before I picked you up, or just after?

And why did she put my hands on her throat?

forty

ONE PURCHASE THE Carpenter had made was a small plastic funnel, and it was proving a handy tool indeed. He had used wide-mouthed fruit juice jars for his first Molotov cocktails, and they'd been easy to fill, though less easy to fit with stoppers. Nor were they readily available by the case in a riverside marina. Thus the beer bottles, and the funnel, which speeded up the task while keeping spillage to a minimum.

The Carpenter filled twelve bottles at a time, stoppered them with the cloth wicks, and carried each full case out of the cabin and onto the open deck, where any fumes would dissipate quickly in the open air. He paused periodically to have a look at the intruder, who had not yet regained consciousness, and who might indeed be dead by now. He'd had a pulse when the Carpenter first checked, but he hadn't stirred, and it seemed possible that he might have died of a burst blood vessel in the brain, or some other effect of the two blows he'd taken to the head.

His pockets had yielded some treasures, most notably a pair of handcuffs, which encouraged the Carpenter to look further. He'd found a gun, a fully loaded revolver, and maybe this one actually worked. He seemed to recall that pistols had a tendency to jam, as his had evidently done, and he didn't think that was the case with revolvers. He'd put the pistol back on top of the chest of drawers, held there by the clips, and transferred the intruder's pistol to his pocket.

Stripping the man, he'd found what he at once recognized as a bulletproof vest. Well, it wouldn't have kept the Carpenter from putting a bullet into the back of the intruder's neck, had the gun worked. The Carpenter tried it on and liked the feel of it, the comfort it somehow provided. He'd put his clothes on over it, liking the bulk and weight of it. Then he added the shoulder holster, and transferred the gun from his pocket to the holster. He practiced with it, drawing it, then returning it to the leather holster. He felt as though he were now secretly protected, as if by a guardian angel.

The intruder, in marked contrast, was naked, and entirely vulnerable. He had no body hair, the Carpenter noted, although he had a full head of hair and the beard of a man who'd last shaved in the morning. The Carpenter ran a hand over the smooth skin and wondered at its cause. Some disease? Or had the intruder deliberately removed the hair, perhaps for some religious reason?

Francis Buckram, that was the intruder's name, according to the cards in his wallet. And he was some sort of policeman, which explained the gun and the handcuffs. It was while he was using those handcuffs to anchor the intruder to the chest of drawers that he remembered where he'd heard that name before, and realized why the man had looked familiar. He'd been the police commissioner once.

And how had he found his way to the *Nancy Dee*? That was something he might ask the man, if he ever came to. And if it wasn't necessary to kill him right away.

When the fifth case of bottles had been filled and transferred to the open deck, the Carpenter cast off the lines securing the boat to the pier and maneuvered the *Nancy Dee* out of the Boat Basin. When he was perhaps twenty yards from the nearest of the moored vessels, he cut the engine and let the boat drift. Then, with a match, he lit the little kerosene lantern.

It was a handy thing, a black sphere eight inches in diameter, flattened on the bottom so it would stay upright, with an adjustable wick at the top. The Carpenter had taken it home from a construction site, where it burned at night to keep trespassers from stumbling into a pit. Now, lit and properly positioned, it greatly simplified the process of lighting the wicks of his firebombs.

He checked his watch. The hour was right, getting on to three in the morning. The Boat Basin was dark and silent. The party had ended in the large houseboat at the southern end of the basin, and the celebrants, like the other houseboaters, were tucked into their bunks. The owners of the other vessels, who lived elsewhere, were either awake or asleep, but in any event they were not here, and thus were of no concern to the Carpenter.

Who picked up a gasoline-filled beer bottle, lit its fuse, and lobbed it high in the air, aimed at a ramshackle houseboat some thirty yards distant.

Before it landed, he had a second bottle in hand.

HE WAS ON THE verge of consciousness when the first explosion roused him. He opened his eyes, blinked, registered that he was naked, with his right hand cuffed, the other bracelet hooked to the brass pull of the bottommost drawer in a brassbound chest of drawers.

He pulled, but the drawer wouldn't move, and he saw why. The vertical sides of the chest had extensions that were locked in place to keep the drawers from rolling free in uneven seas. By the time he figured this out there had already been a second explosion, and now there was a third.

And something was burning. He could smell it, and the cabin was unevenly illuminated by the flames.

What the hell was going on?

Molotov cocktails, of course. He'd seen the makings earlier, the bottles and rags and cans of gas. He didn't see them now, but he heard them, exploding one after the other.

He had to do something. He swung around, braced his feet against the chest of drawers, tried to pull hard enough to break the drawer loose, or yank the handle from the drawer. All he got for his troubles was a sore wrist.

Where were his clothes?

He saw them, on the deck at the far end of the cabin. He stretched out full length, levering himself along the deck with his left hand, reaching out with his feet. He caught hold of a piece of clothing, pinning it between his two bare feet, and drew his legs back, trying to reel in the garment. He lost his purchase on it but then regained it and brought it close enough to grab with his free hand, and it was his jacket, and he went through the pockets and didn't find a thing. His cell phone had been in one of those pockets, and it would have been useful now, but it was gone.

He stretched out again as far as he could, hurting his right wrist in the process, reaching with his feet, wishing he could see more clearly what he was doing. He caught hold of more cloth, brought it closer, grabbed it with his left hand. His pants, and one pocket held some coins, and what the hell was he supposed to do with them? But another pocket contained his key ring, and he was almost certain he had a handcuff key with him. He held the key ring in front of his face, dropped it, picked it up again, and yes, there was the key, and—

And the explosions had stopped, he realized that, even as the hatch opened. Scrambling, he tucked the key ring under his backside, kicked the trousers away.

And lay there, naked and unable to move, as the Carpenter came into the cabin.

"YOU'RE AWAKE," THE CARPENTER said. "I thought you might be dead."

"What were the explosions?"

"You know what they were."

"I saw the bottles, the gasoline. But what was the target?"

"Oh," said the Carpenter, surprised at the question. But you couldn't really see much from where the man was lying. You could see that something was on fire, but wouldn't know what it was.

"The boats," he said.

"At the Boat Basin? Why would you want to burn them?"

The answer was too complicated, and the Carpenter decided not to waste time on it. The man's trousers lay by his feet, not where he'd left them. He asked the man what he was looking for.

"My cell phone."

The Carpenter pointed to the dresser top. "Right next to the pistol. Mr. Shevlin's pistol, I was going to shoot you, but there must be something wrong with it." He drew the revolver from the holster. "I hope there's nothing wrong with yours," he said, and pointed it at the man, interested in seeing what his reaction would be.

But there was no reaction. He might as well have been pointing a flower at him. Instead he asked another question. "Why are you doing this? Not just the boats. Everything. Why?"

Now that was an interesting question. Maybe he wouldn't shoot the man, not yet. Maybe it would be interesting to have a conversation with him. He was, after all, an important man. Or had been important, running the police department of the world's greatest city. He might have interesting things to say. And then he could play a role in the last sacrifice.

But all of that would have to wait. "I have to move the boat," he told the man, and, holstering the gun, he made his way back on deck.

AS SOON AS THE hatch closed behind the Carpenter, Buckram retrieved the ring of keys from under his buttock. He rolled over on his side, reaching with his left hand for his imprisoned right wrist, wishing that at least it could have been the other way around, with his less agile left hand immobilized and his right hand free.

Jesus, he told himself, you can always find something to complain about, can't you?

He heard the boat's engine turn over, heard sirens in the distance as fire engines sped toward the burning Boat Basin. The boat was moving now, away from the raging fire, and toward what?

The man had set a trap for him and he'd stumbled right into it. And he'd be dead right now if the pistol hadn't misfired. Peter Shevlin's pistol, according to the Carpenter, and it was supposed to be on top of the chest

of drawers, and so was his cell phone, and if only he could get the little
key into the little hole, which he couldn't quite see but it had to be right
about there, and—

The catch released and the cuff fell away from his wrist. He flexed his
fingers, willed feeling and circulation back into the hand. The Carpenter
had cuffed him too tight, an easy mistake to make, and safer from the
Carpenter's point of view than too loose. What he hadn't done, and Buckram was glad of that, was cuff him correctly, with a cuff on each wrist and
his hands behind his back.

The way Susan had cuffed him, for example.

But he didn't have time to think about Susan. Didn't have time to
think. His hand was cramped, as if he'd slept on it, but he'd be able to use
it. He got his feet under him, found a handhold, and managed to hoist
himself into a standing position. Then his head spun, and he sagged
against the chest of drawers. It was all he could do to stay on his feet.

There was the gun. A .22, from the looks of it, with a three-inch bar-
rel and crosshatched black rubber grips. He went to pick it up but it
stayed where it was, resisting him.

What was holding it, magnets? No, some sort of gripping devices,
and if you pulled a little harder it came loose. His right hand had trouble
getting a grip on it so he transferred it to his left hand.

Great. He was armed with a gun that wouldn't fire, and that his oppo-
nent knew wouldn't fire. And the boat had stopped moving, and the hatch
was opening.

His mobility was his one asset, his foe's ignorance of it the closest
thing he had to an edge. He couldn't lose it.

So he got back down onto the floor and slipped his hand into the cold
steel cuff. With his left hand he closed the cuff, but just a little way, fastening it loosely enough that he could slip his whole hand right out of it.

At least he hoped he could.

THE CARPENTER HEADED THE *Nancy Dee* south, just as he'd done
when he circled the island. Manhattan was on his left, his port side, and
he stayed as close to shore as he conveniently could, past the old railroad
yards. The first pier he came to was that of the Sanitation Department, at
Fifty-ninth Street, and he stepped away from the tiller and lobbed two of
his firebombs onto it. They exploded with a satisfying roar, and he kept
heading south, not waiting to see what effect they had.

More piers, and he had the tiller locked so he didn't have to tend it, he
could go on lighting and hurling his bombs whenever he drew abreast of
a likely target. Once he missed, and a bottle, its wick aflame, fell harm-

lessly into the water, neither breaking nor exploding. No matter—he had plenty of bombs left.

Ah, and now he'd come to where the cruise ships docked. There was only one berthed there tonight, and it was enormous, rising as high as an apartment house, holding as many people as a small village. He sailed as close to it as he dared, saw an opening on one of the lower decks, and scored a direct hit with one of his firebombs. The explosion echoed, the flames leaped. Oh, they'd probably put it out, they'd probably keep it from spreading, but they'd have their work cut out for them.

And then Pier Eighty-three, where the Circle Line vessels were berthed.

And this ship was not so tall, not so forbidding, and there was a vast amount of open deck space. The Carpenter rained bombs on the ship, setting fires everywhere. There'd be no human sacrifice, not unless they had a night watchman aboard, but the ship itself was sacrifice enough. Such a powerful symbol . . .

Enough for now. The Carpenter headed for open water, set the *Nancy Dee* on a course to cruise south at a leisurely pace in the middle of the river. And went to check on his passenger.

THE CARPENTER SEEMED IN an exalted state, as if the flames he'd created had borne him aloft. He didn't seem to notice that the handcuff was loose on Buckram's wrist, and so far he hadn't noticed the gun.

Would the gun fire? According to the Carpenter, it had jammed. That was possible, automatics were notoriously subject to jamming, but it wasn't the Carpenter's gun and the Carpenter didn't know a lot about guns. It was at least as possible that the gun had been loaded with a cartridge clip but, for safety's sake, didn't have a round in the chamber. The Carpenter, squeezing the trigger a single time, would have succeeded in chambering a round. If he'd pulled it a second time, he'd have put a bullet in Buckram.

Well, it was possible. And, unless he could come up with something better, any minute now he'd get to bet his life on it.

He had his right thigh over it, screening it as much as possible, but it was impossible to be sure it wasn't partially visible. And what was unquestionably visible was its absence from its place on top of the chest of drawers. So far the Carpenter hadn't glanced over there, and might not notice anything if he did, as transported as he appeared to be by the night's events.

"The ship's burning," he announced.

"This one?"

"Of course not. And this is a boat, not a ship. Though it, too, will be
burning soon enough." He smiled, and it changed his mien curiously from
exaltation to resigned sadness. "Soon it will all be over."

"You said the ship was burning. What ship?"

"The Circle Line," the Carpenter said. "They have different ships
with different names. I didn't notice the name of this one. Have you ever
taken their cruise around Manhattan?"

He had, years ago. Someone had booked the ship on a weekday evening for a private party to which he'd been invited. He hadn't had a
chance to see much, had been stuck in one conversation after another,
barely got out on deck.

He didn't say any of this, though, because the Carpenter hadn't
waited for an answer. Instead he'd gone on to recount something of the
history of the Circle Line, and some of the more impressive sights to be
seen on that voyage. If the Carpenter had seemed sad a moment ago, now
he spoke with the enthusiasm of a teacher lecturing on a favorite topic.

Buckram said, "You don't hate the city, do you?"

"Hate it?"

"That's what everyone thinks. That you blamed New York for the loss
of your family, that everything you're doing is an act of revenge. But
when you talk about New York you sound like a lover."

"Of course," the Carpenter said. "I love New York."

"There were all these books in your storage locker . . ."

"My library. I've missed my books."

"You know a great deal about the city."

"One always wants to know more."

"Then why the hell are you trying to destroy it?"

"To destroy it?"

"With killing and burnings and explosions and . . ."

He stopped. The Carpenter was shaking his head. "Sacrifice," he said.

"Sacrifice?"

"Trying to destroy the city. As if I would want to do that. Don't you
understand? I'm trying to save it."

And he began to explain, spinning a complicated story full of local
history, with the Draft Riots and the Police Riots and gang warfare and a
maritime disaster, all the horrible things that had happened in the last
couple of centuries, wrapped up in a theory of death and rebirth, suffering
and renewal. Sacrifice.

"I wanted to die," he was saying now. "I wanted to share in their sacrifice, to be a part of it. My wife took pills. I found her dead in our bed.
Do you know what I did?"

Again the question was rhetorical, and the Carpenter didn't wait for an answer. "I took pills," he said, "and lay down beside her, intending to go where she had gone. And do you know what happened? I woke up, with nothing worse than a bad headache, and the deepest sorrow I have ever known. I thought of Cain, making an offering to God and having the smoke go off to the side. And then I came to realize that my sacrifice had not been rejected. It had been postponed, because I had work to do. I had to sacrifice others to the greater glory of the city."

There was more, and Buckram listened, took it all in. The Carpenter was insane, which was hardly news, but insane in a surprising way. He'd killed all those people—and God only knew how many he'd added to the total tonight, at the Boat Basin and wherever else his bombs had landed. All those deaths, and he didn't have anything against any of them, didn't have the slightest wish to do them harm. Didn't think he was harming them, thought he was ennobling them.

And what was he doing now? Walking over to the can of gas, twisting the top off . . .

"Chelsea Piers," the Carpenter was saying. "It's this great project at the water's edge, with restaurants and sports facilities, even a driving range. Can you imagine that? A driving range in Manhattan?" He shook his head, awed by the wonder of it all. "We'll be there soon. And this little boat of ours will be a bomb, filled with combustible fumes, and I'll run it into the pier, and that will be the last sacrifice." He beamed at Buckram. "And you'll be a part of it."

Buckram couldn't wait any longer. Once the lunatic started sloshing the gas around, the cabin *would* be a bomb, and a gunshot would set it off. He said, "I don't think so," and wrenched his right hand free of the cuff, grabbing up the gun, hurling his body to the side and firing the gun as he moved.

The recoil wasn't that massive, not from a .22, but it was enough to dislodge the grip of Buckram's weakened right hand. But the shot was right on target. It took the Carpenter squarely in the center of the chest. His jaw dropped and he stared and took a step back, but he didn't clutch his chest and his knees didn't buckle and he didn't fall down, the way a person generally does when you shoot him in the heart.

Oh, Jesus. The fucking Kevlar vest. It saved a life, but not the one it was supposed to.

And the Carpenter had his own gun drawn now, Buckram's .38, and he pulled the trigger, and the sound was much louder in the little cabin. The bullet missed, and Buckram groped for the .22, grabbed it finally with his left hand. He raised it, and the Carpenter, his hand trembling, fired a second shot, and this one didn't miss. Pain seared Buckram's belly, pain almost too much to bear, and he remembered something Susan had said, something about pain being nothing but a sensation you make wrong, and he dismissed the pain and brought the gun to bear and made the Carpenter wrong instead, made him wrong forever, squeezing the trigger three times and hitting him three times in the face and throat.

And watched him fall, and lie still.

WHEN THE FIRST BULLET struck, smack in the center of his chest, the Carpenter felt a rush of joy. He was going to die. His sacrifice was complete, he could let go now, and in a moment he would be with Carole.

But he hadn't died, he wasn't even hurt. He'd felt the impact of the bullet but it didn't seem to have injured him. So he'd been right after all, he thought sadly. He had to kill this man, and then he had to complete the sacrifice.

He fired and missed, fired again and hit the man. Not in the chest, where he'd aimed, but much lower. But he'd hit him, and now the man would die, and then—

Then three shots, and in a mere instant the Carpenter was hovering above the scene, looking down, seeing two bodies on the cabin deck. One was Buckram, the man whom he'd shot and by whom he'd been shot in return. And the other, of course, was his own.

And, seeing himself lying there, the Carpenter felt a veil lift, and knew for the first time, knew with perfect certainty, that everything he'd done in the past months had been completely and overwhelmingly wrong. The realization was crushing, blinding, devastating.

And then, just as quickly, it ceased to matter. Because he was drawn into the vortex now, whirled into the long tunnel, and Carole would be waiting for him at the end of it.

He let go, and sailed away.

OH, JESUS. A RED-hot poker in your bowels, and you could tell yourself it was just a sensation, but it was more than that. It was bad news, because you'd been gutshot and you were going to die.

The cell phone. That was his only hope, and of course the fucking thing was on top of the chest of drawers and he was on the fucking floor, pardon me, the fucking *deck*, and what he needed was Medic Alert, because he'd fallen and he couldn't get up.

Had to.

Couldn't.

Fuck that. He *had* to.

He got to his feet, grabbed the cell phone, then fell down again and felt it spill out of his hand. Groped around, got hold of it. 9-1-1, he thought. Easy to remember, same as 9/11, the day it all started.

And, talking to the 911 operator, telling her who he was and where he thought he was and what had happened, a thought came to him. He pushed it away until he'd gotten the message across to her, then let go of the phone and sprawled on his back.

And the thought was there again. His mother, telling him how he had to wear clean underwear every morning, in case he got hit by a bus. Because what would they think in the hospital?

And what would they think, he wondered, when they found Francis J. Buckram, the former commissioner of the NYPD, stark fucking naked and not a single hair on his balls?

The worst part, he thought, as his consciousness began to fade, the worst part was that he wasn't going to be around to see the expressions on their faces.

forty-one

THE FIRST THING she thought was that he didn't look so bad, not as bad as she'd feared. And her second thought was that he didn't look so good, either. His face was so pale, so drawn, and there was gray in his hair that hadn't been there before. He had tubes coming out of him, monitors hooked up to him.

His eyes were closed, and she drew a chair up next to the bed and just sat there for a while, watching him. Then she said, "Franny?"

His eyes opened, focused on her. Light came into his eyes, and his lips showed the slightest suggestion of a smile.

"I'm sorry," she said. "I shouldn't call you that here."

"That's okay."

His voice was weak, but it was his voice, with the force of his personality behind it. He brought his hand out from under the covers and she laid her hand on top of it.

"I hate to tell you this," she said, "but I can't give you a blow job. I had to tell them I was your sister. Oh, shit, did I do something wrong?"

His face was twisted in pain. He got hold of himself, said, "Jesus, don't make me laugh," and set himself off again. And she struggled not to laugh herself, and of course that was hopeless, like trying not to laugh at a funeral. She slapped herself in an effort to make herself stop, and evidently that struck him as the funniest thing he'd ever seen.

And she thought, isn't that a fine thing, I spent all that money on handcuffs and dildos, when all it takes to torture you is a funny line.

Somehow she managed to keep the thought to herself.

"YOU'RE A HERO," SHE told him, when they'd both got hold of themselves. "You went out single-handed and caught the Carpenter."

"If I'd gone in with backup," he said, "the Boat Basin would still exist, the Circle Line wouldn't have lost a ship, and a lot of people would still be alive."

"Possibly. Or he may have gotten away. As far as the city's concerned, you're a hero. There's a lot of speculation that you'll run for mayor in 2005."

"I'd rather shoot myself," he said.

"Really?"

He nodded. "But not in the belly. Once is enough. A doctor came in the other day and told me there was no reason I wouldn't be able to perform sexually. I said I'd just as soon wait a while, if it was all the same to him."

"So you wouldn't have wanted the blow job anyway, is that what you're saying?"

"I'll take a rain check. You didn't really tell them you were my sister, did you?"

"It was the only way I could get them to let me in. You're tired, I've stayed longer than I should have. Franny?" She leaned over, kissed him. "Feel better," she said. "What's so funny?"

"I figured we'd get around to kissing," he said. "I didn't realize what it would take."

SHE TOOK A CAB from the hospital, showered at her apartment, changed into jeans and a blouse and flats, and walked down to the Village in time to meet John at the Waverly Inn, just down the street from his apartment. They ate in the garden, then sat over coffee and watched the sky darken. They took the long way home, walking all the way down to Bleecker and returning via Perry Street and Greenwich Avenue.

"I think he'll be all right," she said, "but I don't think he'll be the same."

"None of us will."

She thought about that, nodded. No one was ever the same, she thought. Every day changed you. Some days changed you a little, some days changed you a lot, but each increment of change was essentially irreversible.

A little later he said, "I don't suppose the Carpenter told him anything about a woman he ran into on Charles Street."

"I didn't ask."

"I somehow doubt it came up while they were blasting away at each other and waiting for the boat to blow up. And now we'll never know."

"One thing we know is that you're innocent."

"We know there are no charges against me, and won't be. So we know I'm not guilty. But we don't know I didn't do it."

"How much does it bother you?"

"I'm not sure it does. I know I think about it. I sort of wish I knew."

"Sort of?"

"Well, I tell myself I wish I knew one way or the other. But what I wish I knew is that I didn't kill the woman. If I killed her, then I'd just as soon not know. And don't tell me that doesn't make sense, because I'm well aware of that."

"It makes sense to me."

"And that," he said, drawing her into his arms, "is why you're the girl for me."

And a little later she said, "Am I?"

"Huh?"

"The girl for you."

"Damn right."

"Good," she said.

AND IN BED, AFTER they had made love, slowly, lazily, and with a sweet urgency at the end, after he'd smiled at the reflexive urge for a cigarette, less frequent now, less intense, but still there, after all of that he said, "There's something I've been wanting to ask you."

"I know."

"You know?"

"That night, whenever it was. You've wanted ever since to ask why I put your hands on my throat."

"You've known."

"Yes."

"And just went on waiting for me to say something."

"And wished you would and hoped you wouldn't," she said. "John, I love you."

"But?"

"No, it doesn't come with a *but*. When I first became obsessed with you—and yes, that's the right word, it was an obsession—"

"If you say so."

"You spoke to me right away, through your books. But I was ready for your books to speak to me. From the very beginning, I wanted something from you. I didn't know it, not consciously. John, do you know what I wanted?"

"I think so."

"But you don't want to say it. Well, in that case you know. I wanted you to kill me."

"You didn't know it consciously. When did you find out?"

"When it stopped being true."

"And when was that?"

"When I put your hands on my throat. When I asked you to do it."

" 'Please.' "

"Yes. That's what I was asking for. And you wouldn't, of course, and I suddenly realized that was what I was begging for, and realized, too, that it was no longer something I wanted. That I had probably stopped wanting it our first night together. Or even earlier, when I went to Medea."

"The piercing lady."

"Yes."

"Shave and a haircut, two tits."

"When I started expressing myself sexually," she said, "and making art out of my madness. When I started to discover that I could be me and still be alive. But there was a part of me that never woke up and caught on, and that part didn't stop wanting you to kill me."

"Until I didn't."

"Until you didn't."

"Maybe it really doesn't matter what happened on Charles Street."

"Duh," she said. "Haven't I been saying that all along?"

"YOU KNOW," HE SAID, "all things considered, there's really only one thing that makes me think I might have done it."

"The rabbit."

"The rabbit. It's not like me to take something. I must have been in a bad way to do it, and if I was that far gone . . ."

She got up, brought the little rabbit back to the bed with her. "It's adorable," she said, "but I can't believe you took it intentionally. I think it was inadvertent. I think you were looking at it, holding it in your hand, and then she called for you to come into the bedroom, or whatever, and halfway there you noticed you still had the rabbit in your hand. And you didn't want to go all the way back to where you found it, and you didn't know where else to put it, so you stuck it in your pocket for the time being."

"Intending to put it back later."

"And then you went to bed with that poor crazy lady, and when you were done all you wanted to do was get out of there. So you forgot all about the rabbit, and when you came home you thought, oh, hell, I'll have to give it back, which means I'll have to see her again."

"I could have put it in the mail."

"And would have," she said, "if you'd seen it first thing the next morning, but you didn't and by the time you did . . ."

He thought about it. "You know," he said, "that's perfectly plausible."

"I know, and it's a lot more plausible than your taking it on purpose, no matter who killed the woman." She looked at the rabbit she was holding, then at him. "I mean, it's not as though a rabbit's a likely totem animal for you. I see you more as a bear."

"Yeah, I guess I'm sort of bearish."

"Ursine," she said. "And if anyone's a rabbit, it would probably be me."

"Well, you sure do fuck like one."

"It's settled, then," she said. "You be the bear. I'll be the rabbit."

forty-two

ON SEPTEMBER 11, 2002, sunrise came at 6:31 A.M. The forecast called for partly cloudy skies, with a forty percent chance of showers in the late afternoon.

JERRY PANKOW, WHO WORKED for a catering service and didn't have to report until nine, had not broken the habit of early rising. He was up before dawn, took a long hot shower, and thought about the cute guy he'd picked up over the weekend. Really sweet, in and out of bed, but he could have been a guest on *I've Got a Secret*, because he sure did. Wasn't wearing a wedding ring, but was wearing the mark the ring had left, and kept touching the spot nervously. Married, clearly, and new to the sin that dared not speak its name, which in recent years had become the sin that would not shut up. Lou, he'd said his name was, but he'd stuttered a little getting it out, and Jerry's guess was that his name did in fact start with an *L,* but that it was anything but Lou. Dressing, he wondered if he'd ever see him again.

AT 7:24, A YOUNG woman in a white uniform attached a fresh bottle to one of Fran Buckram's IV lines. "Oh, good," he said. "Breakfast." She giggled as if she'd never heard the line before, which struck him as unlikely.

He closed his eyes but couldn't get back to sleep. He hoped they'd let him out of here soon, and wondered what he would do when they did. Mend, of course, and eat real food again, and do a lot of physical therapy, but what would he do after that?

Not run around the country making speeches. Not run for office. Not hang out a shingle as a private investigator. None of the above, but what?

He'd think of something.

. . .

AT 7:40, JAY MCGANN came back from his morning run and went straight to the shower. He was dressed by eight, and by the time his wife got to the table he had their breakfast ready. He'd be at his desk by nine, as he was every morning. Writing was a business, after all, and if you wanted to get anywhere with it you had to approach it in a businesslike fashion.

He asked his wife how her omelet was, and she said it was fine, and then she asked him if anything was wrong. No, he said, nothing was wrong. Why? Because you seem different, she said.

"Well, now that you mention it," he said, and he told her he'd been thinking that he ought to get an office. Someplace just for writing, so that he could go there every day and do his work and then come home. John Cheever, he told her, had had an office early in his career in the basement of his apartment building, and every morning he put on a suit and tie and stuck a hat on his head, and he rode the elevator to the basement and went into a room and took off the jacket and the tie and the hat and went to work. And put them on again at five o'clock, and went home.

She said, Just for work, right? And he said, Sure, what else?

AT 8:12, JIM GALVIN woke up on the couch of his Alphabet City apartment. He'd taken off his shirt and shoes but was still wearing his pants and socks. There was a bad taste in his mouth, and a pounding in the back of his head.

He drank a glass of water, threw it up, and drank another. When that one stayed down he drank one more glass of water with a couple of aspirin. He showered, and when he went to shave his hand was trembling. He put the safety razor down and went into the other room, and there was still plenty of booze left in the open bottle, and most of the bottles left in the case. He poured himself a drink, just a short one, and when he resumed shaving his hand was rock steady.

MAURY WINTERS GOT UP four times during the night. Around seven he decided that was as much sleep as he was going to get, and got busy taking the fistful of herbs he took every morning. He wondered if they were doing any good. One was supposed to shrink his prostate, which would be a blessing, but so far he couldn't see the difference.

He checked to see if they'd delivered the *Times* yet. They had, and he brought it in and read it. At eight-thirty his wife told him breakfast was ready, and he told her she was an angel. While he was drinking his second cup of coffee, his wife asked him if he'd had a good night.

"Every night above ground's a good night," he told her. "Every day being married to you is heaven." And he got up from the table and went over and gave her a kiss.

EDDIE RAGAN DIDN'T OPEN his eyes until 9:20. He wasn't in his own apartment, and it took him a moment to remember where he was, and even then he couldn't pin it down geographically. He could ask the woman who'd brought him home with her, but a check of the apartment's other rooms didn't turn her up. Off to work, he thought.

He'd hung out at the Kettle for a while after he finished his shift, and then he and a couple of people went next door to the Fifty-Five, and then where? It got a little hazy at that point, but he wound up at Googie's, late, and that's where he pulled the dame, and she'd brought him back here.

What the hell was her name, anyway? He couldn't remember. They had a good time, he remembered that. Nice rack, and she gave head like she could teach school in the subject, he remembered that. He couldn't quite picture her face, but was sure he'd recognize her if he saw her. Well, fairly sure.

She drank Sambuca, straight up in a little cordial glass, with three coffee beans in it. That he remembered.

LOWELL COOKE WAS AT his desk by nine-thirty. He went right to work returning phone calls and answering mail. He had a lunch date scheduled with an agent making her fall trip to New York, and one of his writers was coming by during the afternoon. And, of course, he had a stack of manuscripts to read if he ever found the time.

At breakfast his wife had asked him if everything was okay, and he said of course it was.

I'm gay, he wanted to say, but he hadn't been able to say it, any more than he'd been able to say his name to the fellow he'd been with Monday night. I'm Lou, he'd said, and his companion for the evening had been polite enough to pretend to believe him, and to call him Lou throughout.

God, what was he going to do?

STELLI SAFRAN RARELY GOT to bed before three, and rarely got up before noon. Today, though, a muscle cramp woke her around ten. She went to the kitchen and ate a banana, on the chance that it might be a potassium deficiency. Or maybe it was calcium, so she drank a glass of milk.

Then again, she thought, maybe it was butter and sugar and flour, and wouldn't it be terrible to suffer cramps because of a deficiency of any of those essential elements?

She got out a mixing bowl and made pancakes.

. . .

AT A QUARTER TO eleven, Esther Blinkoff returned a call from Roz Albright. They told each other, not for the first time, how excited they were about *Darker Than Water,* and eventually Roz said that she had a new writer she was also very enthusiastic about, a woman, she'd published some short stories but this was her first novel.

Think Bridget Jones meets *The Lovely Bones*, she said.

Esther said she'd love to see it.

CHLOE SIGURDSON OPENED UP the Susan Pomerance Gallery at eleven. She'd been coming in earlier lately, a change Susan had made in order to give her own schedule more flexibility. This day Chloe didn't have much to do other than listen to the radio and talk to friends on the phone. Susan came in at eleven-forty-five, changed the station to WQXR, took a moment to brush her hand over Chloe's breasts, then across the top of her head.

"I'm leaving early," Susan told her. She was going to her boyfriend's apartment, she'd brought him a present.

Chloe knew who she meant. The writer, Mr. Big Shoulders.

He's cute, she'd told Susan, and Susan had said, Would you like to do him? Maybe I'll give you to him for his birthday.

She wondered if Susan was kidding. Maybe, maybe not. Sometimes it was hard to tell with Susan.

But she knew one thing. When she grew up, she wanted to be like Susan.

JOHN BLAIR CREIGHTON ROSE early and went to the gym. It was a new one, right around the corner at Greenwich and West Twelfth, where the Greenwich Theater used to be. Years ago, not long after he'd moved to Bank Street, he joined the Attic Gym, which then occupied the floor above the movie theater. The gym went out of business when the theater expanded and became a duplex, and now the theater was gone, and a new building had gone up to house this new gym, and a few days ago he'd joined it.

He had a workout and a sauna and a shower, ate across the street at the Village Den, but waited until he got home to have coffee. He got halfway through his second cup before he wondered what he was going to do next.

Writing was great, he thought. You suffered and you agonized and you were beset by doubts and fears, and then you finished a book and felt absolutely ecstatic, convinced that you were great and your book was great and your future was coming up roses.

That lasted for about a week, and then you realized that you were washed up, that you'd never do anything decent again, and look at you, you indolent slug, why were you just sitting around doing nothing? Why weren't you writing something?

So he sat there, trying to think of something to write.

And then the bell rang, and it wasn't cops, it wasn't Jehovah's Witnesses, it wasn't the kid from Two Boots. It was Susan, and she'd brought him a present.

And shortly thereafter they were in bed, and she was telling him a story. And, on the bookshelf, a magnificent white bear with turquoise eyes shared the dish of stone-ground yellow cornmeal with the little turquoise rabbit.

It looked as though they were going to get along just fine.

AND ALL OF THEM, like everyone else in the great city, waited to see what was going to happen next.

a word of clarification

This is a work of fiction, issuing entirely from the imagination of the author. The names of some prominent persons, and the situational and circumstantial elements of other New Yorkers, are used only for verisimilitude.

The perceptive reader will have noted the conspicuous absence of the author's publisher, HarperCollins, from the list of bidders at the book auction. This was done to maintain suspense; as everyone knows, had Jane Friedman had her heart set on acquiring *Darker Than Water*, no power on earth could have gotten it away from her.